Praise for Michael Frost Beckner
&
SPY GAME

"Pass the popcorn!"
—*Amazon Editors' Pick*, Vanessa Cronin, Sr. Editor

"Brilliantly executed... Full of twists and turns, these are first-class spy novels with a smart, gritty atmosphere."
—Charles Cumming, *New York Times & Sunday Times Best-selling Author of KENNEDY 35* and *BOX 88*

"A thinking man's thriller... A real adrenaline blast... I loved it!"
—Robert Redford

"Beckner is an utterly distinctive voice in spy fiction. Nobody captures the halls of mirrors, the complexity of personal relationships, and betrayals of espionage, quite like him. Cerebral and unvarnished, with dialogue so sharp it's like dancing on hot coals. You'll swallow this book whole."
—I.S. Berry, *Edgar winning Author of THE PEACOCK AND THE SPARROW*

"Michael Frost Beckner serves up a judicious blend of showy action, political intrigue, ticking-clock suspense, and CIA one-upmanship for mainstream entertainment."
—*Variety*

"There is nothing like *The Aiken Trilogy*... Laced with absurdity & stylistically daring ... Beckner [is] a razzle-dazzle showman at the top of the thriller heap."
—Editor's Pick, *Publishers Weekly*

"Beckner is one of the most unabashedly duplicitous writers I've ever encountered ... Brilliant work."
—Stephen England, *Best-selling Author of the SHADOW WARRIOR Series*

"Michael Frost Beckner is the rarest of spy novelists, a beautiful and compelling writer who also has a mastery of tradecraft and a deep understanding of how espionage really works."
—Joe Weisberg, *former CIA Officer and EMMY Award-winning creator of The Americans*

Kaleidoscope

A Spy Game Serial
Part 6:

New Year's Day

Michael Frost Beckner

MONTROSE STATION PRESS

Las Vegas
2025

Copyright © 2025 by Michael Frost Beckner

Published in the United States Montrose Station Press LLC, Los Angeles.

ISBN 9798992993257 (paperback)
ISBN 9798992993240 (eBook)

Quotations from T.H. White's The Once and Future King (1958) are used under fair use for literary commentary and transformative fictional analysis.

Excerpts from the following works are quoted under fair use for literary and artistic purposes. All are in the public domain in the United States:

Gerontion by T.S. Eliot

Four Quartets, Little Gidding, V by T.S. Eliot

Four Quartets: East Coker by T.S. Eliot

The Waste Land by T.S. Eliot

"Hark! The Herald Angels Sing"(Public Domain)

"Silent Night" (Public Domain)

"Cossack Lullaby" (Public Domain)

"O God, Our Help in Ages Past" (Public Domain)

Printed in the United States of America

Jacket design by Andrew Frost Beckner

Alyona

KALEIDOSCOPE:

NEW YEAR'S DAY

"The only thing which mattered was that you should try your hardest to do what you thought was right."

—T. H. White, *The Once and Future King*

Prologue

A HANDFUL OF HOURS?
  One final sunset?
Tomorrow's dawn?
 Perhaps she would leave tonight, folding herself into the envelope of near silence they shared, few and precious minutes each night these last three years.
 When darkness falls on Stalingrad.
 When the high-pitched/relentless tat-tat tat-tat-tat *of the pneumatic jackhammers attacking foundation remnants; when the deep diesel churn, thick chugging, the backfires of the Stalinets-80s, the S-65 tractors dragging girders/clearing rubble, stills; when the irregular rhythm of axes, mauls, the clunk of cold chisels cracking timber and hewing stone—strongarmed by the shout of Russian orders—becomes for Nikoláj and Sofiya, too much the stuttering burp of PPSh-41s, too much the angry rumble of T-34s, the crack of rifle butts breaking doors, of sappers clearing trenches, then beyond bearing becomes the metal screech, clacking gears, clang of hoist chains on rail-mounted portal cranes: rotating turrets and elevation gears raising artillery tubes; the crackle/hiss/buzz of the arc welders forever indistinguishable from the short-circuits of damaged ar-*

mor; from the whoosh-sizzle of flamethrowers across the bunkers and pillboxes—a plague of concrete warts that even now in 1955 their city cannot exsect from its back, from its extremities, its face. Darkness a blanket. That still after-moment when all of it—present met with past—takes pause, takes rest, enshrouds; when voices still, lungs breathe. Ever only fifteen minutes: those quiet shared minutes when electricity is diverted from the civilian grid to power the floodlights that keep the city's reconstruction ablaze throughout the night.

Maybe tucked inside that peaceful pocket, Sofiya would release the world and go. Not vanish. Dissolve. Vapor into vapor, heat into heat, her breath joining the steam, mingling/rising off the hammers and the scars. Dissolve the precariousness of individual will.

"Bud' ostorozhen, Yasnoglazyy." Be careful, Bright Eyes. *Sofiya's voice ragged. Face pale. Glistens sweat. "Bitoye steklo—"* Broken glass—

Fit of coughing.

Rag.

Blood sputum.

Maybe she will use the syringe as soon as he and Daria descend the grated metal stairs. Cross the dark and littered floor of their squat inside Zavod Tekhnosteklo No. 3, the half-collapsed Technical Glassworks Factory Number 3, and, snaking between rusting trolleys, bins of glass cullet, duck through the hole in the chained-but-leaning doors onto ulitsa Burdenko to join the Radiant Future of Communism.

Sofiya won't tell him when.

Won't allow him to know.

It is sin enough Nikoláj has acquired her the morphine. He does not believe in God, how could he when his all-and-only memories are war and death?

But Sofiya remembers. Before the war. Remembers when families knew peace as His greatest gift of love.

Knew love sacred.

If she doesn't tell him when or even if, she will shield her precious Kolya, and he their precious Daria from her mortal sin of suicide.

Four-year-old Daria. Triangle of red glass pinched between thumb and forefinger. Turns it in the smoke-dimmed flicker of wax stubs she and her mother scrounge from churches.

Paints her vision red.

"Ya vsyo ischu krasnye, no ikh pochti net." I keep looking for the red ones, but there's almost never any.

"Bud' ostorozhen. Bitoye steklo rezhyet khuzhe vsego." Be careful. Broken glass cuts worst of all.

A shard from the ruby glass Tekhnosteklo No. 3 produced/cut for military rangefinders. For signaling equipment. Before the gold chloride ran out.

"Polozhi v banochku. Budet krasivo, kogda ty sdelaesh' svoyo okoshko." Put it in your little tin. It will look beautiful when you make your window.

Dented aluminum: a mess kit saucepan. Daria's little tin. Filled with a kaleidoscope's worth of colored glass fragments. Green and brown, blue, yellow and honey amber and orange.

"You'll help me when I make it, Mama?"

On her cot. Eyes shut. Head nestled in smoky/ashy mattress stuffing as a pillow. Sofiya manages a stretch of her lips. Smiles thin.

"It will be about you, Papa, but dressed as Dobrynya Nikitich. The clever knight who fought the dragons and protected the princess and the princes with his golden spear."

Kolya didn't cry once in the war. Not once since Sofiya found him—as she'd tell the story—perfectly still, standing fist-clenched and quiet, no more than five years old, watching her, willowy and eleven, struggle from the rubble of Children's Home No. 2, where after two direct hits by Luftwaffe bombers, the pair of them were the only two who survived.

Her tiny mouse.

Her crafty Kolya.

Her partner-in-crime. Her protector. Lover now her spouse. A father-soon-widower of eighteen. As easily going-on-thirty. Or sixteen. Or forty. Depending on what you seek, what you want to see, he makes himself that.

The paperboy.

The typist.

Black-market snake. Nomenklatura bull. Pathetic prole.

(Some call him, "Wraith.")

Dull or bright, healthy or hungry. Crushed or bold, greed or need, fear or succor: Kolya goes on that which makes it go.

If Kolya turns from the empty window, turns and looks at them, Kolya Yurenev will weep and by that fail them both. He smokes. He watches the southern freight spur rail yard.

His ears ring—

they've never stopped; never will

—smoke and dust billow from his world collapsed and somehow he's standing apart from it and watching, not thinking, no more ideation than a sponge engorging fire and destruction as water and life and to him comes a "bigger girl"—the one who teaches letters and words; bleeding, every inch of her (his her) coated in gray powder (even the blood); she thinks nothing but him and charges (he doesn't so much as twitch) and she envelopes him in her bony arms and repeats his name over and over again in his ear and pets him (rubbing their lives into each other) and squeezes everything out of him but her.

They burrow beneath the war. They hide. They steal. They live.

Sofiya.

"He'll wear red for his cape." Daria's small grubby finger sorts her treasure. Imagines a window. "Brown for his armor, orange for the knight's wings on his back, and he'll be riding. He'll have a blue horse and wings on his back like the firebird."

His wife's eyes open once more. His little girl smiles. A little nod at the mass pile of books: scrounged, traded, borrowed, stolen—some burnt-edged and incomplete (no matter, Sofiya says, and reads and reads and reads to them)—lugged-everywhere-books, children's books (she taught him/teaches Daria now; "A faster learner than you, Kolya")*, books piled beside Sofiya's cot: a tabletop tower of words on which the syringe lies beside the blue vial.*

"When you're finished with the medicine Papa brought, we could break the glass. I'd be careful, Mama. It's the blue I've always wanted. For his horse."

The cerulean blue. Daria's eyes. His.

Kolya spreads a tarp over his two typewriters, his pens, his inks and stamps and piles of blank letterheads. Goodbye to all of that; they've done their necessary work.

Daria places a comforting hand on Sofiya's moist and fevered brow. "You'll feel better tomorrow."

"I know I will, Bright Eyes." To him: "What did it cost you?"

Ink-stained fingers flick his butt into the night. "Paper necessary to Golosov."

"A forged letter for morphine? Kolya: what did it cost you?"

♛ ♛ ♛

WHEN GOLOSOV ASKED what's your wife sick with, Kolya said what he always said. "The war. She got sick from breathing it."

A dark corridor. Wood-framed, empty factory office stalls. Milky pebbled glass in those frames: cracked, holed, or jagged-edged gone. Wire-dangled, a bulb flickered inside the last of them. Beneath it: Kolya Yurenev. Blackout cloth still hung where windows once sparkled sunlight. Ash and grit coated the floor. Cardboard folder between his hands, he waited on Leonid Golosov, a mid-level housing bureaucrat with Party credentials, assigned to reconcile overlapping reconstruction claims in the Kalininsky District. Seated behind a desk. Large. Nervous. Heavy air spouting through turgid lips. Two letters stamped *HOUSING COMMITTEE — URGENT* on the flat, empty desk before him. One page is signed *Chairman Belugin*. Another, *Chairman Lagunov*. One reads *Reallocation of Assets*. Another *Immediate Suspension*.

"You convinced them to write me contradictory orders! *Convinced* them? How does this possibly help me?!"

"They're all the same. They write what they fear. Then they write what they think their superiors fear. Then they fear what they've written."

"Who do they think you are?"

"Whomever they want me to be. They're the ones particular. Not I." Eyes alive with quiet predation, Kolya withdrew a third document. "I just give them what they already believe they desperately need."

Golosov snorted. Kolya placed a new page on the desk. Perfect letterhead. Perfect phrasing. Perfect forgery.

Golosov read. "*Per directive 38-B of the District Housing Allocation Committee, all provisional usage waivers are subject to review and reclassification by qualified Liaison authority...* Yes, yes-good... *In accordance with Section IV, Paragraph 12, facilities deemed non-operational may be reassigned without further requisition, provided intent to occupy is submitted in duplicate...* Mmm-my: *Effective June first... authority granted to Senior Housing Liaison...*" Eyes flitted to Kolya. "This references a vote that never took place. And this seal—it's the old quartermaster's, retired last fall."

Kolya shrugged. Reached to reclaim his work.

Golosov held it back. Narrowed eyes; anxious to be convinced. "There is no Liaison."

"Who might suspect this most—? You'll choose him."

Golosov stared. Chewed his lower lip. Nodded agreement with himself. Unzipped a worn leather case. "You are very, very good at what you do."

Kolya caught his wrist as Golosov attempted to slide the documents inside. "Where's what you owe me?"

A reedy voice met Kolya from the doorway behind. "I have what you came for. Paperboy." Unsurprised, Kolya didn't turn. "You've been hard to locate, Kolya Yurenev. But you've been writing our mail for two years. Before that, issuing fake ration books."

A guillotine blade of guilt fell across Golosov's face. Kolya twitched a smile at him. Released his wrist with a pat.

"They aren't fake."

"They aren't yours to issue. You know the penalty you face, Nikoláj Yuryevich. Yes, your father's name was Yuri."

Kolya pretends a father's name doesn't matter to him at all. "If I thought you would arrest me or shoot me, I'd not have let you follow me this past month."

The man behind him chuckled. "You let us?"

Kolya didn't raise his voice. Didn't move. But he seemed taller, as if the space around him had to adjust, and the blue of his eyes became the blue that is the hottest part of fire. His street-rat raincoat seemed to lose its dinge; hung in menacing match to the leather worn by the man in the doorway.

"You fit my plans." Kolya.

The man smirked because he didn't want to know how nervous this man—a teenage boy an instant before—made him. But he had what the wraith wanted. He opened a black-gloved fist.

A vial of morphine in glass cerulean blue.

♛ ♛ ♛

"THERE'S DARKNESS in those people." Sofiya.

"Only the darkest of us survived. The rest—pffffpt."

"They're animals. They can mimic, but they cannot love."

Kolya knows.

"Promise me: she'll never be alone in the dark."

He's promised her a dozen times over the last three days. For all the adult conversation Daria has missed, Daria has picked up on this. Watches her father for his answer. Kolya gives Sofiya a solid nod.

"Papa?" Daria needs to hear him say it again.

Their eyes meet. The color is exquisitely matched, and deeper within their eyes: the light-reflection of life/projection of perception perfectly duplicated. A mirror to time lost unattainable because it is the past in one of them, the future in the other. Too far to reach back and grasp; too distant to ever run down and capture. Daria trusts her mother. Trusts the purity of faith in promises. She only releases Papa's gaze after he says:

"Ya tebe obeshchayu." I promise you.

Sofiya lets her eyelids shut. Draws five, six, seven breaths through her nose. Deep. Patient. To inhale Kolya's words as living air. Draws Daria's air toward her too and into her dying lungs to take with her. To float her away when she goes. She chokes back another coughing fit. Wants to open her eyes. Eyelids twitch. Weakness drags her soul with hands too strong to fight. Feeble: "Wrap Daria in my scarf."

Kolya wraps Daria. He thumbs the three chipped plastic buttons. Blue, red, green; the shape of toy balloons. Seals the girl's coat. Tells their daughter, "Kiss your mother goodnight."

Daria doesn't need Papa to instruct her. Kolya moves to the door. Stairs wait. She leans. Kisses Mama's cheek. Sofiya straightens her daughter's face between her hands. Hard clarity. "In this family, from now on, like this:" she kisses Daria goodbye on the lips.

The scamper of following feet. Grated metal; death knells every downward step. Her mother whispers-mutters through the door—

halfway down, Daria stills

—mutters-murmurs-calls: "Daria—your glass."

Daria is four. She doesn't comprehend finality. Her father nods her back. When she reappears clutching her tin, he adds, "You might find some new pieces on your walk."

Daria doesn't comprehend finality, but her heart knows it and is bursting to tell:

Your walk/our walk? Our walk: *your* walk.

She tries to smile, to pretend. Like Papa does so well. She nods. Too obedient, Daria follows, and her shoes explode tiny clouds of lead oxide dust.

Insidiously fine gray powder, it will haunt her until it ends her life.

When they are gone, Sofiya lifts the syringe from her stack of books. Clutches the syringe in one hand, the vial in the other, and asks forgiveness from the darkness;

waits for the echo of battle destruction-transformed-re-formation to fall silent and allow her to give herself to Love even though love's judgment is harsh.

❦ ❦ ❦

THEY WALKED THE NIGHT. Slowly out of Burdenko, out of the Tsentralny District south of the city center. Cautious to avoid the police patrols that guarded the stacks of construction material for someday-recapture of the heavily shelled industrial zone. Careful to remain invisible to the military patrols who hunt squatters and scavengers. Some would say like cats hunt rats, but Kolya knows these men. Knows the soldiers hunt rats like dogs. Where cats hunt rats as prey and there is a kind of justice in that, dogs hunt rats for sport. Kolya placed each step with care. He had not rewritten their lives this far to let the story end tonight unfinished. Unread. And he would not let Daria become a forgotten footnote in the Rodina's grand illusion, a soft corpse in hard rubble with her dribs of colored glass—flyspecks—soon bulldozed, buried in the margins. A truth no one would read.

Obeshchay mne: ona nikogda ne budet odna vo t'me. Promise me: she'll never be alone in the dark.

"I miss Mama. Where's Mama?"

"Shh. Shhhh. You know where she is. She's resting."

Past dark rail sidings. Past shattered sheds and abandoned rolling stock. Zigzagging between oily puddles past dormant kilns, coal bins, remnants of oil depots, they crossed the lower factory belt.

"When can we rest?"

Daria onto his shoulders. One hand gripped his hair. Her tin of glass rattled gently in the other.

They threaded north into the Krasnoznamensky District. A transitional zone; refurbished industrial buildings shared space then gave it up entirely to monotonous housing blocks.

Darkest part of night past, the battle sound of construction equipment swelled, increasing the closer they got to the flood-lit city center.

Bombs. Artillery. Skyline burns to night-light our rathole.

Kolya rested against the wall of a condemned structure. The date on the notice, a year before. Somehow missed the wrecking ball.

And Sofiya. That's that.

"Why are there window frames without windows?"

They leaned between two blank wooden fixtures. Kolya recognized them as empty icon cases. The wall, part of a roofless Orthodox chapel.

Sentimentality only serves the man who carves gravestones.

"I don't know, Daria. Let's go around the other side. We can get some rest there. No one will bother us."

"Why couldn't we just-rested with Mama?"

"You know she's sick. She wants you to stay well."

Kolya carried her into the open-air chapel. He made a nest with his jacket. He covered her with Sofiya's scarf.

"I won't get sick. I want to rest with Mama."

"You don't want to miss the first lilacs, do you?"

He employed a smile to coax one from his child. Everything about him ached. He pretended it was only physical. He stroked her hair and watched sleep steal upon his daughter.

"We can bring her back some?" Mutter/whisper/murmur.

"Just rest. Rest."

"Why's everything always have to be so far?"

Daria's eyes closed. Her hands moved. Cupped the tin of colored glass in the center of her little chest. He waited. Watched. Her chest rose, it fell, she slept. Kolya tested the tin—to move it aside. Daria's grip tightened. Sleeping lips moved.

"No."

❧ ❧ ❧

BEFORE DAWN, workers emerged. Kolya and Daria followed ulitsa Kommunisticheskaya, angling northeast.

Posters of Stalin.

Posters of Khrushchev.

Narrow sidewalks: growing hustle.

They passed the ruins of a school. Passed a bakery. The smell of yeast, smell of coal smoke.

Worker ranks grew around them, bootfalls synced, shoulders hunched in parallel rhythm. No one spoke. The air had the hush of a rule: *Everything not forbidden is compulsory.* When Daria, later, found that phrase—her first/her favorite book in America—she'd already known it and named it Soviet.

"Will we come back tomorrow? To Mama?"

Kolya didn't answer.

Around 4:30 a.m., past Prospekt Lenina where rails curved toward the Volga, they hurried across the tramlines.

Hurried past the Pavlov House ruins.

Hurried past the scorched shell of the central Museum of Defense.

"You're going too fast!"

They stood in the Ploshchad Lenina. Lenin Square. The dark bronze statue of its namesake revolutionary caught the first rays of sunlight on the tip of his upraised finger. Spark/blaze/fire. Stalingrad Station-1 loomed. Two clocks: one frozen, one ticked. The five-o'clock hour arrived. Sentries smoking cigarettes. Disinterested in the approach of father and child.

Daria's eyes searched. Young linden trees, poplars—sapling trunks in short iron cages—hinted springtime buds. Tulips in border planters poised to lift their necks and open flowered eyes.

Daria's eyes roved past military cadre cars idling beneath smoke-fouled streetlamps.

"There: the lilac bushes, Papa!"

She pulled his hand. Arm extended, he let her lead as it brought him to the Black ZIM-12 where the man with the leather jacket, reedy voice, climbed from the backseat with his orders.

"Good morning, Nikoláj Yuryevich."

Daria pretended she didn't notice. Stared at the lilacs. Desperate for first blooms.

Kolya said, "As promised, Major Voinov."

Major Arkady Voinov, on assignment from Department K of the 2nd Chief Directorate, attached for internal review to the First Chief Directorate's Active Measures group, signaled a KGB matron waiting beside the next car beyond.

Pleasant, not frightening at all, the woman walked to Daria's scarf-wrapped back. Daria stared at the lilac bush; she didn't want to turn. The matron tapped her shoulder. "Daria Yureneva?"

Something wrong. With the lilac bushes.

"Daria, you've been addressed." Father/daughter eyes meet. Cerulean blue. Perfectly matched: it should mean more: it should mean everything.

"The buds. Look, Papa. They're all brown. They're all dead. Look at them."

"Frost. I guess."

"Look at them!"

In her eyes: all the future he wishes her to see; all the past he saw—that won't come to her by his decision. The same eyes: hers forever to chase his when she looks in a mirror. When he knows not to look. And no matter what they do, how hard they try—how much harder they fight, forgive, they condemn, hunt mercy, hollow in pain—the perfection of that fit is an allusion.

A mockery.

A lesson for others to learn but denied any-thing/everything for them.

"You said I'd go with you."He straightens Sofiya's scarf. Daria is breathing fast but doesn't cry.

"We made your mother a promise. This is how we keep it.""*Your* promise. You keep it by breaking it?"He brushes back her hair. "One day, when you're safe, you'll understand."

Kisses her forehead.

Desperate, she kisses his mouth.

Kolya gets into the Major's car.

The matron gently turns Daria. "If you're as special as we think, you'll become a hero of the people."

"My Mama's dead."

"What's that? This in your hand?"

"Nothing." Daria dropped her tin of colored glass in a public trash receptacle. She went into the dark car without being told.

Christmas

1.

T HE BUILDING APPEARED TO boil the earth around it.
Superheated steam coursed from the windows
of Haus Eichelberg, the Middle Cycle girls' dormitory at Lyceum Marrow. A scorching exhalation from
the wide-flung doors, windows, vents, chimneys, hair-
line cracks. The night recoiled. The hot, moist air
surged outward and upward, creating temporary thermal columns that roiled chaotic patterns. Created a
steam scoured radius, curdling the ground fog that
recoiled at its edges. Herr Tollenreider, the school's
groundskeeper, noticed gentle snowflakes snatched,
blistered, thrown when they met the billowing cloud.
Some melted midfall. Others caught the turbulent
updraft and refroze; scattered sideways as ice-glit-
ter against dormitory walls. Tollenreider bounced in
steel-toed fire boots, agitated by the flow of scalding
water pouring around and between them down the front
stone steps. Out across the sidewalk. Onto the turnabout
road, the parking lot where it slushed and melted snow,
pushing it outward to a point where the steam's heat
vaporized and the water left a thin, icy crust refrozen in
chaotic swirls.

Framed in silhouette by the Mercedes Sprinter head-lights, Michael Kingston materialized wraith-like from the nubilous swirl. A large, worn-leather tool bag hung from a strap over one shoulder; he carried a pair of heavy-duty PVC plumber's chest waders draped across his other and down his back like a lifeless/headless corpse.

The crust crunched beneath his heavy feet.

Michael stopped before Herr Tollenreider, shook the snow-splats from his hair and shot a breath—once, twice, each side of his mouth—blowing his surfer locks away from his eyes. He greeted the groundskeeper in German. Agreed: This was a fucking disaster.

Contract out for an accident, what do I expect I'm gonna find when I get here?

Good thing I'm not here to fix it.

"Sure. Fixed plenty of boilers before. From the amount of steam and overflow, I'd say all your water heaters have blown."

"It's flooding from upstairs. All the bathrooms, show-ers—every floor." Tollenreider showed his hands. Both palms blistered. Fixtures too hot to touch.

Michael nodded, sympathetic. "Industrial sys-tem—school like this, people paying a fortune to make sure their kids never get a cold shower, what happens in the rare instance—not so rare tonight, eh?—when the boilers go catastrophic, the valves au-tomatically open. Otherwise—be more than your hands burned." His hands pantomimed an explosion with the puffed-cheeked blast of a sound effect.

He flipped the waders off his back. Tugged into them.

The sabotage he'd paid for: activated remotely. Contract set up by Lulu's Chechen. Let the fire department and the real plumbers—emergency lines blocked for now—sort it out.

"Your HVAC plant is the below-ground floor?"

"Sir, the water is scalding. It's up to your knees down there."

Michael snapped suspender clasps. "And the building's evacuated?"

"Yes, sir."

"Alright. Listen. You stay out here. Right here. Don't let anyone back inside."

"I don't understand. The system is supposed to automatically call the fire department."

"They're probably on their way. You have a system schematic?"

Tollenreider fumbled through jacket pockets until he found it. Handed it over.

Michael didn't need it but shook it out, gave it a look like it was the most important thing in the world. His confidence eased Tollenreider's mind; like everything Michael said so far, he pushed the old fellow toward mental surrender. Tucked the schematic into his chest pocket. Said: "I don't think it will take more than fifteen minutes. Keys?"

Tollenreider fumbled with a large ring, trying to find the right one. The groundskeeper's burnt fingers made this difficult.

The moment Michael's every action, every word played to: "Just give me the master."

"*Ach...Natürlich.*" Of course. Tollenreider let the ring hang from the tip of the master key and placed it in Michael's hand.

👑👑👑

DIDN'T NEED THE MASTER KEY to access the Haus Eichelberg physical plant, but he removed it and a second key from the heavy ring. Dropped the rest. Stifling heat blasted as he pushed through the heavy metal door. Michael pulled on fireproof gloves. Rushed down the stairs with the scalding water draining from the ground floor hallway.

Concrete walls slicked with condensation. Steam tangled in metal latticework. Emergency lights glowed red in churning vapor clouds. A short and heavy exhale. Like a blowgun aimed at the elephantine task confronting him. He descended the last step into superheated water, calf-high and rising. Reminded himself his blowgun dart was poisoned. Didn't need a map. Had studied the architectural plan plenty. Good thing: he couldn't see much more than a foot or two in front of his face. Sweat ran rivulets. Air tasted wrong; his lungs stung. His skin. Reminded himself superheated steam melted insulation; fumes/faint whiff of scorched wire sheathing: air turning toxic. Plowed forward, made the second turn, pressed on.

Michael recruited/ran agents. Surveillance, dead-drops, secret writing stuffed into concealment devices. He hadn't trained for this. Not at the Farm. Not in the field. Nobody runs a boiler room op. They got people for that. Specialists like Hal. But ops come how ops come. In the field, even the crowned-best ops officer is always tested.

"Michael has a Kingston way of doing things." Mutterers at headquarters. Muttered at every station I posted. By friends. Colleagues. Muttered by rivals. But even a Kingston is bound to meet that day—Christmas Eve? C'mon—where they fail to retain their crown.

What Michael hadn't rehearsed, he'd fake like muscle memory. Found what he was looking for—five industrial-grade water heaters—time to fake it now.

Viessmann storage tanks. Electric. Tall. Cylindrical. A row of monoliths sweating heat. Steam battered the walls like lungs forced to hold a breath, failing/blasting, sucking air again. Console: lights cycling. Four down—red. One green.

Blink. Green to red.

Then the loop: units waking, dropping, waking again. No flipped switches. No cut wires. No fingerprints. Just a recursion trap. Code fed from a safe distance. Clean. Elegant. Hacked.

Four red again; the room sighs.

Then four green; water shoves. Gusts of scald. Steam hammers.

Michael squatted. Unzipped the leather tool bag in the water. No tools inside. A fire blanket folded around an insulated breaker pole, a battery-jumped override handset. Wedged the pole between conduit clamps. Reached the panel. Held the override. Waited.

Green. Red. Red. Red. Red.

On the next pass he jabbed the handset into the control socket. Overrode the automation.

Steady. Three heaters stayed down. Two continued to pump. Enough pressure to keep the valves open and bleed the upper floors. Flow dropped, heat eased: encouragement to Tollenreider he was hard at work. Boots and waders gumming, intense heat bleeding through, he splashed to the opposite wall.

A red metal plate: *FEUERWEHRSIGNAL AKTIV.* Fire Department Signal Active.

It wasn't.

Michael hummed, searching a melody.

Above the sign: a Siemens 195-B relay box. Dead. No clicks. No pulses. No uplink.

Michael wiped fog from the box cover. These systems weren't wireless. The call line severed digitally. He popped open the relay with the edge of Tollenreider's master key.

Pressed the reset. Nothing.

Pressed again.

Held.

Hummed the tune to Lulu's song.

Click. Hard reboot. Analog override. Michael waited. Sang in Russian...

"Silently the crystal moon shines / On your cradle blue..."

Another click. Green LED. Then faint: the metallic squawk of a handshake ping. Outbound signal reestablished; Stein am Rhein fire brigade en route. Sang louder:

"Fairy tales I'll start to tell you..."

Michael waded to the far end of the Middle Cycle girls' dormitory HVAC plant. Steam curled/water seeped beneath a heavy locked door. Here Tollenreider's key became necessary. And louder:

"Songs I'll sing you too—"

From somewhere above, a voice quavered. A girl's voice, tentative but true: "Eyes are closing, drift to sleep now." Their song joined in confirmation: *"Bayush-ki-bayu."*

👑👑👑

IN THE MIDDLE CYCLE GYMNASIUM, the stay-behind students huddled in blankets. Frau Kohler paused in checking names against a printed roster to answer her cell phone. A call from the fire brigade. The signal just through. She'd checked with Tollenreider. The technician from the Schaffhausen plumbers satellite office had reduced the water flow already more than half; must have gotten the word out to the fire department. They were on their way. Frau Kohler shushed three goof-off boys who, in fact, had the situation better in hand than she.

"It's a terrorist attack."

"It's a kidnapping."

"Somebody's bodyguard is going to be getting a big shit banana in their stocking if it is."

Frau Kohler went back to her list. "Alina?"

No answer.

"Alina Voronina...? *Wo ist Alina?*"

Wide-eyed, the "kidnapping" boy elbowed his pals. They lost their puckish grins. Frau Kohler thrust the roster into Herr Asendorf's knuckle-popped hands. "Continue."

"Where are you going?"

"Um das Gör zu finden." To find the brat.

Exhausted. Embarrassed. She zipped her jacket and, collar-clutching, scurried out the door.

♕ ♕ ♕

AS THE FIREMEN MOUNTED their three trucks and EMT vehicle, the watchman made a second call. He dialed Herr Biedermann at the Stadthaus, the Lyceum's official liaison to municipal emergency services and donor relations. Not a secret; if he hadn't called, one of the others would have. The firehouse took "donations" to ensure such contingency.

Lights flashing. Sirens blaring. The four vehicles roared from their station house in clouds of diesel and raced for the border and the Lyceum Marrow while throughout the town luxury sedans, SUVs, and sports cars lit up/coughed to life as Herr Beidermann spread the word through the contingent of bodyguards left behind with holiday holdover charges.

♕ ♕ ♕

A SUNG CALL and answer brought Michael to Alina. Lulu's living heart. Stairway alcove, steaming water brooking round the corner and tumbling down the stairs. It waked against the melting toes of Michael's boots. He found her huddled on a student-style desk chair dragged from her room. Her athletic shoes, knotted together, dry/draped around her neck. Double pairs of thick wool, handmade socks—kind babas knit in Siberia—swollen with water, dripped and steamed on her feet. She gave Michael a pensive look.

"Mne strashno ikh snimat'. Voda ochen' goryachaya. Kazhetsya, u menya voldyri. Ya ne khochu smotret'." I'm afraid to take them off. This water's way hot. I think I have blisters. I don't want to look.

Michael said, "Let's look anyway."

From the ground floor below, other end of the dorm, Frau Kohler's voice echoed. "Alina! ALINA!"

"Peel out of them. Dry off. Put these on."

Michael handed her a towel from his tool bag. Tore open a package of tube socks. They examined her bright red feet.

"Maybe a couple. On your heel. Here's one on your big toe. It'll be fine."

She pulled on the fresh socks. Michael readied her shoes. Gave them back, one at a time.

"I'm just going to ruin the shoes and burn my feet again!"

"Alina Voronina!" Frau Kohler's shouts: the far end of their floor. Closing on them.

Whispered: "Nope." He hoisted her onto his back. Headed back down.

Alina lips near his ear. "My Dobrynya Nikitich."

Back onto the ground floor. A *No Admittance* door. Out with the master key. Quickly inside. Locked behind. "And who's a one-a-those?"

"A fairy tale knight. Like your American Lancelot."

"It's British. Lancelot."

"See? You know who I mean."

They moved through a utility room. Less water here; the cement floor centered to a drain. A window-paned door. Another turn of the key. Onto the loading dock.

Michael scanned the wall. Alina saw it first. Pointed. He put her on her feet. Engaged the automatic door. As it rose, Michael pulled the other key from his pocket. A "VW" on the bow. Matched Herr Tollenreider's T5 Transporter flatbed. Tollenreider's rusted workhorse.

He yanked the passenger door. "Get in. When I pull out, you'll duck below the dash."

Peeled off his waders. Eased behind the wheel. Engaged engine/checked girl. Lanky, teen-awkward, normal pigment. But unmistakably hers; another Lulu in the works.

"What are you waiting for?" As if she were the boss.

As if she were Lynn.

"Commotion."

"You're not at all how mother described you. I pictured you differently."

"How?"

Lulu-esque sneer. "Not like this."

"Boring—? That's what my ex-wife saw in me."

"Tonight is boring?"

"Let's hope so." Michael could feign insouciant like the best teenager.

Alina gave a single laugh that said he couldn't. "Mother said you look like Uncle Kolya."

"I've been told."

"He's so old. I don't see it so much."

My birth. Kolya Yurenev: "My love. He's beautiful." And my mother says, "He has your eyes."

"He and I have the same eyes."

"*Ehhhnn!* Wrong." She grinned. "His are blue. Like the *most* sky-blue. Yours are gray. Rain clouds." She peered at him, twinkled. "No—wait. I'm wrong. Smoke."

Michael grunted.

"May I call you Michael? Or is it 'Mister' or 'Sir?'"

"Sir Michael's good."

He felt peculiar. Like his blood held too much oxygen. He was suddenly conscious of every detail in the dirty gray truck. The sparkle of Alina's blond hair. The vibrant glow of her skin. Smell of earth and diesel and old coffee. Felt his eyes against his eyelids. Every blink. He focused on the night. Christmas snowfall into ground-clinging fog. All of it sparkled. Dazzled in the high campus lights.

Doris presses my cheeks between her hands. "Mine are blue. Dad's are brown. When you mix them, you get gray."

In the distance: sirens. Michael shifted the T5 into gear. Foot held the brake. They would be here soon.

"She's in love with you, you know."

"Did she tell you that?"

"Didn't have to. She gave you her song."

Firetrucks blasted horns. They were coming to the gates. Michael eased the maintenance truck forward. Down the ramp. Nosed outside. Craned his neck.

"I thought that was your song." No one in sight. "Head down, Alina." He pulled into the falling snow.

Ducked below the dash. "She's sung it since I was a baby." She peered up at him. He flashed an encouraging smile. His every sense tingled alert. Alina: "You're not *so* boring to look at."

"You should see me in tin-can armor." He winked. He drove.

♛♛♛

LEV RAKHLIN beat the firetrucks to Lyceum Marrow. Pulled in next to a white Mercedes Sprinter. Logo'd with HVAC Service and Repair company he knew enough to know was bullshit. The decals were crisp. The bolts on the rear plate, a little too new. He filed the license number by reflex. Later, someone would run it. Not now.

He had planned to lie down early. Was about to change out of his "uniform": old gray blazer he'd worn throughout his Ministry of Internal Affairs career, the Alexander Julian knock-off black "wrinkle-free" slacks. Had a dozen pairs. With Lulu cancelled, he'd planned to surprise Alina—who tolerated him, barely—with a Christmas brunch. That was before old Biedermann called. Some kind of flood at the Lyceum. An accident nothing would convince him was accidental. Hadn't yet unclipped his holster; his Czech CZ 70 still on his belt, he grabbed the fob for his BMW E63 M6. The V10 "Competition" model—of which he had none. Not in this town. Lights churning, sirens blaring, the emergency vehicles pulled in around him. Other bodyguards crowded cars behind. Saw Frau Kohler distressed, gesturing. A little tipsy on her feet.

Lev Rakhlin hadn't been Ministry since the FSB internal review. The one the FSB hadn't asked for. The one that floated up from some internecine pit and sank three men before it touched the surface. One fired. One vanished. One poisoned in the hospital by tea. Rakhlin saw the tide coming. Stepped sideways. Into security. Into silence. Into the payroll of those whose protection was a kind of witness relocation—except he never had to disappear. They made sure of that.

"Alina. I can't find her, Herr Rakhlin."

Herr Asendorf—holdover students in holiday tow, agitating, making him anxious—made his way over. Most of the hotheads from town swarmed him, searching for their principals. Rakhlin assured Frau Kohler: Alina would be fine.

Stepped back. Out with his phone.

He dialed Kravtsov, the banker in Skhodnya. Asked if his watchers still had Lulu and Michael Kingston—caged at the dacha—in sight. (Rakhlin had already made Kingston: ex-CIA, rogue, written-off.) Kravtsov said yes. Rakhlin said no. Not Lulu. Not Kingston. A problem; he'd handle it from here. Punched off.

Noticed the Volkswagen T5 rolling out the gates. Didn't blink. Time would tell how hard he needed to chase it. For now, he needed leverage.

Back to his car. Swore under his breath. The EMT truck blocked him in. He called for someone to move. Voice always polite. Always calm. Always heard. Made another call while he waited. Herr Biedermann at the Stadthaus. Terse with no more asking.

"Lock it down."

He watched the flatbed vanish into snowfall and fog.

♔♔♔

ALINA KNEW ONLY THAT she and her mother were going away. Somewhere the oligarchs who murdered her father, who kept her and Lulu imprisoned in luxury's shell could not find them, somewhere the darker forces of the Federation—the Kremlin— whose long, swift sword her grandfather had served with his life, which her 'Uncle' Kolya now used to protect them—enslaved by the very blade he wielded—would not know how to discover, and that was good enough for the girl who loved and trusted her mother as a Christian nails faith to their cross.

Michael, only looking for a "yes" or "no" to his conversational, "So do you know where Lulu's taking you?" dropped the subject. He knew where he was taking Alina. Knew he wasn't going with them. Knew that not knowing—strike that—*never* knowing was saddest but safest for everyone involved.

Alina mused. "I hope it's an island with a big, white beach." But Michael's thoughts travelled to a secret place inside her earlier words. Kolya's eyes.

"His are blue. Like the most sky-blue. Yours are gray. Rain clouds. No—wait. I'm wrong. Smoke."

Just as hidden, Michael's future waited with his past in Baku. The father he would discover. The father he feared to name. And the memory of Doris—their walks along the Kingston sand, her voice, her hands, her eyes.

The color of the beach glass I place in the center of Lynn's sun-lit, lifted palm.

A mother's hands pressed on him, as though she'd known this moment would come and left him no protection but silence. And no grace for the girl beside him.

A raising *whoop-whoop* penetrated the cab. Off Route 13, onto the Rhine bridge. Snow clung in windless flakes. Fog hugged the river, low and dirty, as if exhaled by something ancient and drowning. Bridge iron slick with frozen vapor. Steam curled from the grates like breath through teeth.

A voice: flat, metallic over a PA. *"Fahrzeug auf der Rheinbrücke! Sofort anhalten und Motor abschalten!"* Vehicle on the Rhine bridge! Pull over immediately and kill the engine!

The Lyceum Marrow VW maintenance truck the only vehicle on the bridge. A police car, all lights off, blocked the exit.

"Unbuckle your seatbelt." Michael let up on the gas.

"You can't stop. They all take money."

"Alina: do it."

She did.

Another siren whoop. Silence. Again, the PA's metallic bark: *"Sofort anhalten und Motor abschalten!"*

Michael answered with high beams. Only one cop. On the hand mic. On the bridge behind the driver's door.

"Your mom trusts me. You have to trust me. Climb on my lap."

Panicked eyes. "Don't you want me to duck?!"

"His partner will shoot me if you duck. Quick."

Their brights caught the officer's partner. Along the center divider. Crouched behind a concrete bollard. Pistol ready.

Michael tugged her across his chest, struggled a downshift, floored the accelerator. "Put your head across mine! Ear to ear!"

Struggled with the wheel against her back. Felt her trembles. Felt her heartbeat. Felt Alina's cheek, her panting breath across his.

Closing fast. First officer drew his sidearm. His partner—no shot through Michael's window—almost stepped into the lane, thought better. The VW roared past. More resolute, the man at the car braced his sidearm over his door.

Michael took the door, took him, wrenched his wheel into the police vehicle, swerved off the bridge—

Side mirror: cop car spinning, rear quarter bite/metal scream, smashed the divider. Rearview: bridge partner sprinting to the downed driver; hand on chest radio, shouting—

The VW bounced, groaning into the medieval town.

"We're fucked," Alina panted.

Michael shoved her off, fighting for control. "Eh—un-expected...but expected. Buckle up but be ready to jump out."

Cranked hard into the first street. Faster—then clutch/brake/downshift: whip-turned. An alley. Back to speed. Sirens. A cross-street: repeat. Dog-legged another alley. Midway down, wrenched into an open garage.

"Out! Out! Out!" He leaped from the cab. Alina behind him. Wrenched down the garage door. Pitch black. Michael spun into her. Grabbed her wrists. Harsh whisper. "Grab my belt, other hand on my shoulder, lean into my back. Trust my steps."

Sound of a door. Cold inside, just as dark. Stairs and up. Alina matched Michael step by step. They reached the top. Faint light bled through blanketed windows. The place was empty. Immaculate but for a duffel waiting at the end. Michael yanked it open. Pulled out two black snowsuits.

And Lulu's pistol.

"Goes over your clothes."

Alina changed. Michael listened. More sirens all directions—one loud ripping past below. Longest minute in Alina's life, then: zipped. Then: "Okay."

"Hand on my back. Keep tight behind me. You'll see better this next part."

She saw he didn't pocket the pistol. Another door then swiftly through a cluttered gallery over the street. Long corridor—building across the street—to more stairs. Down. More doors. Another garage. Rustic. Empty but for a waiting Ducati. Fob on the motorcycle seat.

"Put this on." Handed her a helmet. Strapped it for her. "Been on a motorcycle before?"

Pale face peering out. Shook her head. "Shouldn't we just hide here?"

"They'll door-to-door to find you." He snapped her visor. Hit the fob. Engine whuffled like a blowing horse ready to run. Michael threw a leg over the motorcycle saddle. "Up behind me. We got fifteen minutes. You hold those two grips back of your bottom." He rolled them forward. A wicket door. "Don't change your mind. Don't think you're better off holding me. You're not. When we got to go fast, it's going to surprise you and this thing's a rocket—"

Front tire pushed open the door: a foot alley, centuries-old artery, the kind built before engines. Empty. Wet. Not made for noise.

"You let go: you'll fly right off the back."

They eased into the narrow alleyway and rode out. Soft, even and slow like a horse, snorting at forced trot.

Fifty yards. One hundred. Bolted, blast-loud, through a cross street. Sirens increased in din/faded into distance. Bolted another street. Back into the alley, slow trot, abruptly a turn. Into a park—

"Hang on."

They hit the stairs fast, rubber to stone. Onto the quay. Dawn on the water. Snowfall: ash on black glass. More throttle. More speed. They ripped the silence.

👑 👑 👑

"THE COP." Michael.

"Will live. Probably."

After Lulu's Chechen hustled Alina into the cabin out of sight, after the Italian motorcycle sank in the river, it was just the two of them, shoulder to shoulder in the open pilothouse of the single outboard, 7-meter Jeanneau Merry Fisher.

"You have what I need?"

The Chechen watched the water. "I have Lulu. Waiting for you."

"We weren't supposed to meet again."

The river was clear. "I answered your question." The old bear increased speed. Wide arc and a double-back to Switzerland.

A Bell 429 helicopter waited in the gravel lot of the Marina Wangen am Untersee. Small. Private. A single boathouse. The Merry Fisher slid against the foam-padded berth. A break in the snow, a break in the clouds, sunrise lit frostbitten gravel.

Lit Lulu.

The Chechen cut the engine. Michael watched Alina rush her mother. A fierce embrace. Whispered instructions. Answering nods. Alina ran for the bright red helicopter. The pilot helped her in. She paused in the hatch. Waved once to Michael.

He held up his hand and she was gone.

"Thank you." Lulu's cheeks glistened.

"I've never seen you cry."

"Maybe that's because you're not good at seeing."

Michael. Faint smile. Only love passed between them.

"I'm leaving," he said.

Lulu nodded.

The Chechen handed Michael a Swiss-tagged Škoda key fob. "It's full." He clapped Michael's back. Shook a fist in the air between them. "The Skvoznyak."

"Grítsa."

For a moment the Chechen looked like he would say something. Shook his head. Turned his heel.

Michael and Lulu stood alone. Her cheeks brighter, wetter. She laughed at that and brushed them. "Not another word from you."

I step to her. I don't speak. I take her hand. Our footsteps crunch gravel and ice and we climb into the helicopter. We put on our headsets. We nestle together. Rise over the marina—rotors lyo-lyok, lyo-lyok, lyo-lyok *the air—over the river, over the countryside.*

Smaller, smaller, the world below gives up its aggression: truth/lies, hate/love, blood and borders, history and legacy; every human-drawn line—less than air.

"There's a briefcase on the passenger seat. All the identity you need. Oh, and take this. It's most important."

She whipped around, a practiced move that caused the twin ropes of her snow-hair braids to brush his chest, flip up his face. Not hard. Not this time. She smiled over her shoulder and joined her family.

The helicopter lifted into the air. Floated a moment.

A red balloon.

A tilt of rotors. A rush. Away.

The balloon man kisses my mother. Kisses her forehead.

Silas. Hurt. Shrunken.

Yurenev kisses Doris's forehead.

She grabs his face. Kisses his mouth. Eyes wide. Hard. Matched.

Blue and blue and a red balloon.

Michael found he was sitting on the dock. Arms round his knees, clenching his fist.

He opened his hand imagining he still felt the linger of her fingertips when she pressed the thing into his palm.

GPS coordinates? A map?

A future?

"An island with a big, white beach."

A miniature icon. The *Znamenie*. Our Lady of the Sign.

This moment. This now. This Lulu.

He sat on the ice-cold dock. Icon in his fist.

Gone.

Humbled. Emptied. Ashamed of the weight of it.

Sat long enough to know he should not rise, that this thing was not meant for him, that it had come to him, yes, but would not remain with him, moving on as it had through other unworthy hands, blessing and curse at once.

But why?

Lulu at her paneled mirror. "And that is surrender. Nothing is hidden."

Why for him/why shouldn't it be him? He opened his palm, blue enamel fire stared back. Knew himself seen. Judged.

"Her gesture says, 'I have no weapon. No deceit. Look and see me as I am.'"

He clenched it closed, knowing himself both weapon and deceit. He rose, moving forward with it, not to keep as a talisman, a charm, but an apology.

An apology carried. An apology never enough.

2.

HAL KINGSTON, NOT MUCH of a spy, never having wanted to be one, growing up among them—getting the need for but not the attraction to—was a damn good Recon Marine. As a clandestine paramilitary seconded to the Agency: even better. Better than most—he'd hasten to say "all"—knew how to stalk and how to kill and, because he was expert, how not to fight at all before he decided permanent outcome. But, put into Camp Abu Omar as a spy and "caught"—

Didn't feel like a capture; felt like getting busted.

Thrown into the oversized shipping container/interrogation cell they called the Goat Shed, he admitted to himself: he'd been right to stay out of the trench-coat business.

In the desert scorch super-cooking him, sweating out every bit of water and salt—blood, too, from Vale's and Bors's fist-kisses getting him into the chair, from the extra yank to the flex-cuffs—he knew that even after dozens of desert missions, he'd only known its heat as a persistent unshakeable companion: it grabbed at you the minute you arrived and held on night and day until you were 30,000-plus feet above it and bugging out. You remembered, prepared to meet it next time, and felt gladness leaving its grip. This time, if he got out, the mark this steel oven—*this* heat—left on his soul would be permanent. This heat wasn't merely aggressive, persistent wretchedness; it burned transformative. Intimate and defiling. After this—if he made it out—it wouldn't be a memory like you remember a stolen kiss or first sex, but spiritual rape or his first experience killing a man. If Hal didn't soon get a visitor banging the hatch, it wouldn't matter. Death was a worse desecration; and as his vision narrowed, edges burning out to white, Hal knew: Death had joined him in this solitude.

There's an irony in that: I'd already invited Death to this place; planned to say goodbye to this hell camp and its two ghosts right here on my own terms. Some Christmas this is turning out.

In the Goat Shed they used a steel chain like dog fighters use for a pit bull. A detainee-rated restraining system. Bors, Vale—Hal, too—belted "recruits" into the deck-bolted chair. Locked to a floor-mounted ratcheted spool, they could work their magic touch all night without any slouching; if they wanted them standing, on knees, or laid-out: throw the clamp, release the slack. But no one off the leash.

Darkness itself having taken refuge from the heat, when dehydration took Hal, it came a white dry flash.

Then the water.

Who knows how long later?

Half a PET bottle on his face. The other half, his mouth until he gagged and retched and his tongue split with his swallow, then a palm on his forehead pushing back his skull. Another slapping his cheeks. Didn't need to open his eyes to know it wasn't Bors or Vale: they weren't pussy slappers.

Hal opened gritty lids from dry eyes. Vision washed out. Starred. Grainy. Asian guy in his face. The pussy doing the slapping. Another doing "mean looks" just behind. Dress-up BDUs—like they'd come from gift boxes with extra/personal measurements. Like sand was new to them. Didn't mean these two weren't military, just their home team outfits sported a different flag.

Speaking Mandarin. Chinese flag.

Hal returned to life, and they switched to English. May as well have kept with the Chinese; all Hal knew about KALEIDOSCOPE was jackshit nothing. They knew more about CINDER CROWN, more about the Caspian Oil Conference starting the next day in Baku—

Least I haven't been out that long...

—then he did. Or wanted to. Hinted they knew a great deal more about his father than Hal ever would. Or cared. A pair of gloaters. Maybe trophy hunters. The slapper wore eyeglasses. Gold. Up close, in his face, not gold colored but plated. A subtle Montblanc arrow on the temple; they'd changed out of suits for their visit. Spooks like this kept their hands clean.

Hal's op plan for his last trip to the Goat Shed hadn't included him in the chair. Now, he'd need their help.

A new flurry of questions. Hal lolled his head. Slapper grabbed his chin, and Hal gave him his all with his forehead. Aimed at the bridge of the man's nose; hit air. But his foot did better. Swiped the guy's legs out from under him. Hammered his heel into Slapper's ankle.

A nice shriek for his trouble. A mouthful of Chinese from the other one. As Slapper came to his feet, his partner lunged for the rachet clamp.

They pulled Hal from the chair. He put up just enough shoulder struggle and lunge to get a real toss-around. Wall bounce beat down.

Hal gave them a message for their mothers. Extra-special for their daughters. Hammered to the floor for that—that's where they left him.

※☆☆☆

COLONEL CHENG, director of Wànhuātŏng, China's answer to KALEIDOSCOPE/Kalaydoskop, should have limped. Needed to if he didn't want to exacerbate the ankle sprain. He wouldn't let the American stooge, Houton, see his pain. His weakness at having been bested by a chained Kingston dog. His ego had gotten the better of him, but this little diversion into the desert—once Houton told him the infiltrator was a son of Silas Kingston—was worth the pain; being handed the honor of ordering the execution would be something to share when he finally confronted the old man. Cheng would wrap his ankle once back on the jet to Baku.

Houton held the rear door of his armored Mercedes G-Class for the trip to the airfield. He'd drive. Take his money at the plane. Bors and Vale to follow.

"As you suspected." Cheng flung a lazy finger at the Goat Shed. "Nothing to say."

The two Chinese in the back. Houton slid behind the wheel.

Cheng leaned back. Relaxed into the throb. Shut eyes as though bored. "Finish him."

He didn't mind the pain. Pain clarified. He'd lost something in that shed—but he'd recover it from the father. At Baku. At scale.

Houton nodded. Radioed Bors. As he turned the SUV around, aimed for the gates of the empty camp, the three of them watched Bors walk to the Goat Shed. Charge his handgun. Unlatch the door and step inside. The Goat Shed was an oversized steel shipping container; his single shot rang loud in their wake.

👑👑👑

THE HEAT. The solitude. Obscene pain and that charge of electricity inside him that had kept him going since before his birth. Since Doris's breast and life. Hal lay there, bloody face in the sand-caked grit of the Goat Shed deck. His will, his soul drew breath and blew a spark inside him. He rolled. Back to chair, shouldered around its legs. It didn't matter the time you had left, just that you used it. Shouldered his way into a seated position his face pressed into the metal where the chair's back legs connected with its back panel. Turned his back to the rachet clamp Slapper'd left open. The jagged metal teeth of the spool gear. Looped his arms backwards over the handle. Hands under the clamp. Middle of his restraints.

Just so you don't take off a hand. Though that'd work.

Hal clamped his teeth. Slammed his back on the rachet clamp handle.

Crack! Snap!

He plunged forward. Knocked into the waterboard bench. Hands into the bucket beneath it and what waited there. Outside: latch thrown. In a sense he'd wanted this since Fourth of July. He'd waited for it since Halloween. Committed to it, sitting out the fall at the top of the Foxtail Farm beach stairs smoking his father's Dunhill. Planned it since he worked-over his first recruits the first night in the Shed. This was the kill box for the two men who would have seen his brother and his sister dead at Dulles.

Bors came through the door, gun aimed. Hal felt all his life rush out of him. Like fire shooting out a line direct from his heart: the electricity connecting his body to action. That moment life leaps out beyond you, outside of you; outside your opponent too, your prey: it's the same electric charge blasts from both of you—you both call it life—but it's become it's own thing. One thing. Meeting between you. And only one of you gains it back. A quarter second, half, maybe one second (if you're good you control seconds/divide them into forever) then it's done and a body falls and that electricity becomes all of you again and none of them.

Bors's eyes: the empty chair.

Hal's: Bors forehead.

Bors probably had similar training and experience to Hal; the empty chair didn't throw him. Peripheral vision already warned, and the chain on the floor did instant math for aim. But the eye naturally follows the weapon and that's that quarter-second of forever. Bors and Hal fired simultaneously. Bors missed. His last thought went with his training/experience: an HK P7K3 .22/custom-integrated suppressor. Fuck.

Hal grabbed the leash-key from body. Took Bors's Beretta M9. Checked the rounds. Checked the action. Checked the camp for Vale. Found him loading comms equipment into an MRAP vehicle. Put three rounds in his chest. One in his skull.

Salt burned at his eyes. Went to find water. Clean up. Get gone.

3.

A QUARTER-HOUR INTO ELEVEN o'clock, minutes to count before the moment of another Christmas, Boone Kelso rolled Calvin Kirby, Richmond DA, into the tarp he'd stolen and reserved for old Silas Kingston. The fog thick among the pines, brown and soupy, he walked ever-widening circles kicking the snow till his toe hit stone and, for the rocks near enough bowling ball-sized and not too deeply buried, he dug those up with cold wet hands. He brought them back and dropped them onto Kirby, soft and dead and foolish—how he'd ended in this situation. Boone figured five would be enough to sink him straight with no mess from the current.

He didn't mind the body being found one day, so long as it was a day after winter passed and spring with its life-renewing thaw. Summer would be just fine as Boone Kelso's ascendance would be complete and purified, the man he'd been in gathered deeds and bitter patience would by then have broken through the crust of his own accepted indignities to the hardness of love distilled to universal purity.

He brought the last two stones, their granite faces glopped with slush and loamy twigs. Dropped one on Kirby's chest and it settled into his flesh below a dead-still rib cage and Boone paid it an extra second's attention knowing, were their places reversed, any rock dropped on him would roll right off because a man who's hard doesn't go peering into a trap in the woods he knows first-step-toward-it is set to kill him.

Soft men lose their heads. Soft men die.

He didn't like the way Kirby's club-mud-dled/mixed-up face baby-pouted at him like they were somehow partners in Kirby's mortal stupidity. Like in being killed and killing they shared a bond. He threw the last rock onto it and broke its nose which somehow fit Kirby's dead portrait better anyway. The rock slid off. Off Kirby. Off the canvas.

Boone Kelso nudged it back with his boot. Crouched and tucked an edge of the drop cloth all the way over the body and three of the stones—two on the right side, the one on the chest—tucked it all in, wedging it tight, before heaving the corpse over the last two stones, over one more time again, then it was wrapped well and ready to seal. He ripped long lengths of cloth-backed duct tape. Wound the dead man like a mummy.

He gripped the tarp at Kirby's shoulders and dragged it through fog, thick as dirty cotton batting, to the sound of the water. His mind went back to the purity—grown and hardened inside him; earned and sought as payment long and unreasonably owed him tonight. Universal/universe justice. Purity/pure love nurtured, fed, born in a post-embryonic, post-puberty, post-man metamorphosis of his physical, and metaphysical substances in a chrysalis dug from a hard-row Alabama prison cotton field. Christmas Eve was the night the enveloping

wings of his imagination-made-manifest in seizure of
art-as-life should have spread brilliant glimmering black
and resplendent between the heavens and the sins of
Foxtail Farm: that place of death delivered one night
of holy birth, but this asshole he hauled up the river embankment had to push his snoot into a business
transaction suspended and waiting eighteen years that
he had no power to prevent. Border ice uneven raw and
slippery, he hauled Kirby's body roughly to the edge.
Scanned the bank—both sides—St. Leonard Creek. Fat
and deep and rolling heavy. Rolling sluggish.

The only love worth a damn on this earth was pure
love. Pure love transcendent of the body/place/time and
the moment-mental. Pure love expressed itself soul to
soul on a plane unnecessary of the bondage of the physical realm; soul-love/soul-connection existed beyond
the temporal trap. Boone Kelso captured that love the
only way pure love can ever be caught: on canvas in
art's interpretation. His last and perfect portrait; free of
the common, petty-minded ego of men, he'd removed
himself in everything but spirit to allow Doris Kingston's
soul a path to that pure love expression whole/univer-
sal through the tenderness of his hand, the gentle, the
tempestuous, the ageless wisdom/childish wonder/sex-
ual magnificence of that woman in the fire strokes of his
brushes. The silver ice-flash of his knife.

This was on his mind as he got around the body,
slipped away from it down the embankment, feet catching in the snowdrift and muck at the bottom and pulled
himself up again, noticing as he did the sky half clear,
snowfall stopped but no less swirling, as wind raced
from the Patuxent River and blew the loose fall from the

pine boughs overhead and swirled it up from the boil of fog clawing over the wide creek bank. He grabbed Kirby at the foot end and tilted him, bundling the legs over one shoulder like hauling a sodden sack of cement and, careful not to fall a second time, forced the dead man upside down.

Boone Kelso had freed Doris to pure love's perfection, to witness and receive its call, beauty enfigured timeless face-to-face with beauty corrupting as time's prisoner bonded in the chains of Silas Kingston, the corrupter's power. Doris had died that beast's slave—earthly love raw and human—the physical and false destructible in life, but pure love, her pure love, Boone Kelso painted. Preserved. Sexed and saved. For pure love is atomic matter: it can be glimpsed and named through great art but cannot be created nor can it be destroyed. Pure love can only be transformed.

He summoned a mental picture of Doris as, transformed, she awaited him: warm, sweet-breathed with candy cane Christmas. It gave him that extra burst of strength to dig his soles into the ice, and shoulder Kirby's loose hips over his shoulder, get his hands down around Kirby's arms, his knee into Kirby's back and teetering him on his collar—his broken neck-bent head—upright.

Sweet Candy Charlotte.

Shoved the canvas wrapped body over the edge. Watched it plunge head-down into the froth of black water. Watched it spin. Watched it bob horizontal and watched it roll; Boone dogged it down the shore. Five steps, ten—

Sweet Christmas Doris—

Eager eyes, Christmas candle flicker in her eyes-drowning-mine—

"Call me my name; call me Doris; and carry me; and hold me—"

—until water, filling the open seams and saturating the sack, the body tilted. The current abandoned it to the stone's slow claim of canvas, clothing, and cold flesh until Calvin Kirby was seen no more.

⚜ ⚜ ⚜

IT WAS HOW SILAS would have it every year: the serving of Communion coincident with the stroke of midnight; from Christmas Eve to Christmas morning: the Host and the Precious Blood served at the altar rail of the Foxtail Farm chapel, and Melody must have received it for she was now back in the front pew, last at the far end, the others, standing, singing. From the aisle inward: Paige, then Leigh; Charlotte, Little Silas, Jack, then Clive; beside him Silas—the two preciously close since Clive retrieved the Hennesy Timeless, as though they now had some strange secret—and she beside Silas. This, the best they could do for immediate family.

"Yea, Lord, we greet Thee, born this happy morning;Jesus, to Thee be all glory giv'n!Word of the Father, now in flesh appearing!"

Michael, Lynn, Hal—if Silas knew where, he'd not offered it and Reverend Vivi who had prayed for the three of them, for their safety and their blessing this night of the Savior's birth had only said "in distant lands" among the other appeals offered, and Melody hadn't registered any of it over Boone's curse looping in her mind.

Lawyer's out. Just you n me n them now. Give young Doris a smooch. Merry Christmas, girl.

The smoke of the candles, the heavy and lingering fragrance of frankincense and myrrh Vivi had swung in the censer processing to the altar, bit at Melody's eyes and dizzied Melody and Silas caught her elbow.

"We're sitting, Angel. You okay?"

Melody gave him a weak smile. Staggered/dropped into her seat. Hal's pistol in her coat pocket softly thunked. And, as Reverend Vivi continued the service with the post-communion prayer, Silas added—"And now...kneeling...?"

The gun made a muffled scrape. If Silas noticed he didn't remark. Whispered without meeting her eye. "A little late to tell you, but maybe you should have removed your jacket? Hot in here."

She didn't hear.

Just you n me n them now. Give young Doris a smooch.

Her eyes flashed Charlotte. Unselfconscious about her braces, the girl smiled back. They prayed. Melody moved lips. Muttered by rote. Her eyes found Doris's stained-glass window half-hidden in its dormer behind the altar.

Nika.

Cupid "Scrapefoot" Williams: a toddler holding her hand.

The Kingston beach along the Patuxent.

Melody's hands fumbled with the lit taper Silas handed her. The others sang *Silent Night.* She stared at glass-Nika; beach glass for her dress, green. And she noticed something she hadn't before. The dress wasn't abstract; the beach glass had been purposefully/specifically cut. Square neckline. A side-hem vent where a triangle of glass gleamed tobacco brown.

Jolting. Melody must have been singing because now she caught her breath and held it.

The top of her foot is the color of my eyes—

Boone: "Get her new-made dresses, her patterns, and her portable machine you're learning on."

—except for the blood. Mama's blood, spilled from the cup of life and by my hand.

"Silent night, holy night, Son of God, love's pure light..."

The light, golden from their candles, golden and flickered from the chandelier above the aisle and from the altar: all gold but nothing pure. It threw shadows, dark and evil across the window, and in that flicker the chandelier's arc tied itself into a noose.

Give young Doris a smooch. Merry Christmas, girl.

And Melody saw the shadow-noose above the Scrapefoot child:

The rope hauled, Colonel Claypoole and two unnamed militiamen hanged by the neck the bloodthirsty malefactor from the iron bell frame under Jesuit Authority, his body left as an example until the Twelfth Day of Christmas.

Melody saw it. All of it. And her family sang:

"Radiant beams from Thy holy face, With the dawn of redeeming grace..."

And her mind flooded with another image she'd seen and denied many times inside their home, inside the mirrors:

Doris Kingston impossibly framed in each looking glass.

"Jesus, Lord, at Thy birth, / Jesus, Lord, at Thy birth."

Doris hangs by her neck from a silken rope. Flames consume her with horrid, flashing/laughing/lapping tongues of fire.

For a moment, her burning corpse spins against the window glass. Her family's voice grows louder:

"Silent night, holy night,Wondrous star, lend the light..."

Melody silently prayed. Not words but deeper: the depth of all her emotions. From behind the glass where the clouds were parting, a star burned through. Pinpoint through the pane above Nika's free hand. Melody hadn't noticed the free hand before; Nika's open palm held up like a blessing. Glass answering starlight as a blessing.

"With the angels let us sing / Alleluia to our King..."

But with the golden candlelight flicker, with the blaze of white, the blue/green/amber stained-glass pattern of the Patuxent—behind the figures—changed to brown.

Albany, Georgia. The week after their house/her mother's body went up in flames.

The fresh car. Fresher blood.

And the river. The Flint. Harkened on by thunder and lightning and running backward.

"Christ the Savior is born..."

Silas called after her as, chased by waves of memory, the surge of Boone Kelso, Melody ran from the Foxtail Farm chapel.

"...Christ the Savior is born."

✲✲✲

ST. LEONARD CREEK. Underwater. The bundle, those last remains of Calvin Kirby, sunk at an angle. Head down. Head angled with the current. The canvas-bound head hit a sloped rock face. The rest of the body slid after it, seeking a riverbed resting place with that rock face its headstone. Half a trunk and the twist of barren limbs of a sweetgum had beaten him to it. Wind and water had worked it to a cradle; moss bearded at the crooks. The old tree had stood in the water many seasons, its dead limbs braided with long green hair of moss, like drowned mermaids' fingers clutching whatever the river gave. As the bundle dropped into the arms of the dead and broken tree, gripping branches turned Kirby horizontal, perpendicular to the current. A mere four feet from the surface. He balanced between the rock face and the snagging branches. Almost buoyed. But still heavy.

For a breath it seemed the current might lift him free, teetering between the weight that pulled him down and the drift that would not let him go. A plain thing, really, a waterway current: the past keeps step; it lays its hand on the present. It pushes. It jars. It will not stop because it is a force beyond life and choice and any human decision. It makes itself known equally, without choosing, among the living. Amid the dead.

Battered, the body bundle bouncing now, hard, the stones inside the tarp pushed against the tape. A light mist of bubbles escaped the seam. One rock popped, sank as Kirby lifted. A hollow sucking rose from the tarp as the water rushed in, the creek taking back its breath. The bundle tore loose—the sucking again—air from a bottle with its stopper torn, or a hole in a throat—and the bundle rolled back up the rock face on the current and swept off in a rush of foam, spinning down the St. Leonard Creek's course.

♛ ♛ ♛

DAMN BALLOONS. Balloons belong to New Year's—not Christmas. Harker sat in the Georgian armchair that had once graced their perfect 18th century (replica) parlor. This very same house. Back the first time he and the Missus lived here. Back before Silas Kingston end-ran him out of the Agency the first time. Past midnight, real Christmas now—he'd never been a greedy Christmas-Eve'r—one day: Christmas Day: American way. He'd deliberately pulled the chair onto the maple-flex dance floor. His dance floor. His love and joy—the chair didn't belong there—four legs planted hard into his pride. But that's how he felt.

Damn 'em all. Me too, if I can't get this right.

He swirled his Galliano around the ice in his glass. Watched the balloons fail at different heights. Buoyancy like rank. Up one day, down the next.

Guests had made a swell time of it. The usual courtiers to his hospitality—his and the Missus's that is. The IC intriguers, the military-industrial easy money overlords, fawning arms-laundering foreigners, neo-con fantasists.

And me, their jingle-hatted jester. They knew.

He knew.

And they knew he knew. *Pennsylvania Avenue wants a general running the shop.*

All party, all night. The smiles the kind men wear when the promotion's not yours. He thought he'd noticed Clapper drop in and drop quickly out; shortly afterward, he'd heard the whisper like a leaky balloon—

Barry O's looking for my signed adios on the old Resolute. First of the year.

The heater cycled. Forced air directed its breath at Harker, and balloons of red and green and white drifted his way across the dance floor. His pride and joy; marring it purposely with his (replica) Georgian chair. He kicked them away. They drifted back. When he'd given in to the Missus on her "They'll make it oh-so-festive on your dance floor" idea, he'd given his wife clear instructions the balloons be Advent gold and pine green; he'd gotten Langley Food Court on Columbus Day Sbarro.

Green. White. Red. Place looks like a fucking Italian bachelorette party.

When they'd sold this place (after Silas Kingston drove the knife in his back for saving the world from an al-Qaeda nuke—thank-you-very-much), the house had been perfect. A 1930s Colonial Revival in Langley Forest; with his return to Langley, his long-awaited/hard-fought ascendancy to the Director's desk, the Missus made an unplanned/unapproved visit to the aerospace airheads they'd sold this house to in 2001. Offer made/offer accepted, they'd moved back.

Mistake.

Harker knew it now. Glared at the place where the pocket door once delicately divided the two traditional and gentle parlors: torn out, the period crown/mantel, aerospace-cadet remodeled: low-arched and bricked like a Spanish dungeon. This glass "pavilion" obscenity—their grotesque add-on.

Harker and the Missus had taken out most of the techno-LED, and dumpster'd the disco mirror ball (even the airheads knew *that* was too much and left it behind), and Mrs. Harker said: "Think of it as an English solarium, Jeremy. Climate-controlled. And the views: Tysons' glow, the parkway, your Headquarters—*almost* like you can touch it. Jeremy: think of the entertaining we'll do. Think of the maple-flex floor your heart's been set on."

He batted at a pair of half-deflated floaters. Today, Christmas. Tomorrow: his planned triumph over Silas Kingston. Had that bullet-headed Angletonian conspiracist really believed a document dump would have prevented his KALEIDOSCOPE review prior to dismantling?

Can one man be so vain he believes he can stop the tide?

Bible, I'm sure, tells the story of King Canute and the trouble of that.

"Hmmm." He drank. He scowled. He bounced his chair legs into the flex. Pride before the fall. Maybe that's not in the Bible.

Not on my watch—watching me.

He detested Silas Kingston. Hated him—if you got right down to it. The arrogance. The cold, self-serving single-mindedness. The man was permanent winter. Put his allegiance into something he pretended—Silas

Kingston *deluded* himself—was bigger than the national interest.

If you don't serve the nation, you have no business in government.

(End up serving cranberry, creamy cheese and crunchy nut endive vessels. Party to the rest of the backstabbers who serve you *up.)*

Silas Kingston and his mystical, magical KALEIDOSCOPE saving the world...without a thought to national security.

That flood of KALEIDOSCOPE effluvium designed to sink his review. Silas tried to stall him, but Harker would have him apart—if not by the thirty-first, before January was out. That. Was. Certain.

And where will I be for that?

He stared into his oily vanilla liqueur: he wasn't facing Silas's dismantling. He faced his own.

What did Silas say, over trout bones, his eyes like wet river stones? What is it we argued...?

"CIA acts as firefighters."

"We put out fires." What I told him. "In most cases, before they happen."

"Here's the thing." Smug and bastard. "Whether you're working from immediate intelligence or an intelligence profile many years in the collection, you're acting or reacting on immediate situations—firefighters—and let's both admit, sometimes arsonists."

Harker laughed. Then. Right in his smug face. But twenty-three November kept replaying: al-Omar gone; DDO Gravin— "gone to al-Nusra"—and his offhand nail hammered after it: "Not like we don't have Special Forces there already." Since that noon, the ground moved. A little every day. He saw it clearly now. Aleppo worse with every sitrep. Patriot batteries to the Turkey border pushed "in their lane"—CENTCOM running the brief. "For deconfliction" now meant his desk was read-only. Calls taken two floors down. He got the slide after the decision—DCIA read-only.

Then the annex came after wheels-up: signature block pre-typed, "effective on receipt"; vetting shaved one click to match a pallet already in the air to the border strips. He initialed because the cargo was airborne. No debate. No choice. No principles: just countdown to "go."

Me: pissed off at Silas/at KALEIDOSCOPE wasting time up the street with Baku while my own house burned me down—?

And suddenly the balloons faded from his vision and Harker saw it:

Baku is the valve. Turn it, and the Syria fire loses pressure. Silas isn't skipping the fight. He's fighting us—and them—at the hose.

Baku, not Aleppo; valves, not brigades. Not guns and ordnance to last year's enemy to fight this year's—

What's the crime in profit?

KALEIDOSCOPE: starve the proxy and the proxy shrivels.

(The Resolute. New Year's. My resignation.)

The hub already south—the vocabulary now targets/effects—verbs that come with runways. He sat at the head; the head felt unseated. And the thought he didn't like: if the building goes to barracks, maybe the only men left who know a match from a torch are the two who can't stand each other.

He'd scorched Kingston in his head for an hour. It guttered. What stayed was the thing he didn't want.

Silas right?

Not about the sermons he sells or the nonsense name. About us. Firefighters is the cover; arson is the practice. If the building goes to barracks and the republic to procurement, the snow buries both in the ash.

Different winters. Same ground. Never friends. Not partners. But extinction is a language men understand. A drowning man doesn't ask the lifeline its philosophy. Its politics. He grabs the rope.

Don't gut him this week. Stall. Listen. Keep Kingston breathing to keep myself alive. To keep my Agency from becoming a barracks with a seal scuffed by Army boots.

Not to convert. To hear what survives the match. Hold the scissors. Hold the memo. Leave the window a crack. See if the room still breathes.

Something in him shifted. Small. Unwelcome. But current took it. Harker didn't like the feeling. But he didn't deny it. Upstairs: tap run, tap stop; a drawer.

The Missus steps into her closet.

He thought back an hour ago. Foxtrotting through the wrong-color balloons—"Isn't it fun, Jeremy?"—rubber squeaking under her heels, the little pop, her laugh, her "Feels like dancing through snow."

He set the glass on the piano they hired in to get it played.

A balloon scudded the baseboard.

Don't strike another match.

His spirit plunged.

Dammit: I need him.

👑👑👑

Sᴛ. Lᴇᴏɴᴀʀᴅ Cʀᴇᴇᴋ filling/strengthening: past Broomes
Island, past Mills Creek, Island Creek, Solomons. Deep
in the run. The tarp bundle of Calvin Kirby's corpse
spun like a rifled round, the channel shouldering it
toward the Patuxent. As the body spun, the bundle Boone Kelso so carefully, tightly, so meticulous-
ly wrapped in heavy tape kept working loose. Most
harm is inherited; it rides down from upriver—family,
secrets, money—until someone stands in the channel.
The stone on Kirby's chest worried the opening with
every turn—gravity pulling, its rough edges widening the
gap—until, on the next revolution, it punched through,
peeling canvas lips and, like a thing born, plummeted in
a stream of black silt afterbirth to the grasses and muck
of the bed. The water rushed in. The canvas bellied.
The weight shifted to the three remaining rocks: by
his knees, his calves, his feet. Bottom-heavy now, the
bundle rose toward the skin of the river. Canted as if
riding the wash. The canvas flared like wings and the
Richmond DA's crushed head, his ruined face haloed in
a mist of crimson.

👑👑👑

Fᴀɪɴᴛ ᴛɪɴɢᴇ, light blue in morning darkness: the digital dash clock illuminated eight minutes past the
one o'clock hour in Calvin Kirby's Captiva Sport as
Boone Kelso slowed onto the Governor Thomas John-

son Memorial Bridge, northbound from the MD-4 at Solomons. The Richmond DA's wool fedora low and tight on his head. Brims bent down, front/back, conceal- ing. His hands covered now by Kirby's lamb's wool-lined cold weather gloves dug up from the small suitcase he found/searched in the backseat. They rested, ginger on the dead man's rental car steering wheel. Fingertips light at seven and five. Careful not to disturb Kirby's pristine (he hoped) fingerprints on the rest of the wheel. Two cars of southbound traffic blazed at him. Passed. And halfway across, he prepared to pull over, up alongside the riverside rail, but light flashed in his rearview mir- ror—another vehicle up behind—and he kept going, easy pace, but by the time the vehicle went around, taillights dimming out of sight, Boone Kelso was already over the opposite shore.

Kept pace. Slow/careful. Just continued continuing. Didn't worry a whit about his crack neighbor's Subaru. That burned-paint faded bitch-ride tucked deep in the trees, back of the St. Leonard Creek bridge where even come daylight, hidden between the foot abutment and a thicket of swamp elderberry, it would remain hidden from sight: highway, bridge span, water and far shore. Only problem he could see with that would be getting the bitch out. He'd wedged it back there after dump- ing the not-so-"busy"-anymore body in the wide, deep run. Took the lawyer's long coat, before he'd wrapped him, glad to find the man's wallet inside-pocket; found the fedora going back up, where it had rolled when he knocked the fool down. Only things that said he *wasn't* Calvin Kirby when he took the waiting car: the Ziploc'd gun and the gift for his new-Doris shimmery red just like he'd paint her. Buttoned into Kirby's coat and close to his heart.

Kirby's cell phone lay dull and black on the passenger seat beside him, his text to Melody deleted—first thing he'd done before engaging the engine. He glanced at it now and then, half-hoping the girl might call. He'd answer. Maybe even chat. Just to keep the illusion alive—whoever ended up searching it—that her not-so-shining-armor lawyer was still with the world and active.

Crossed Hunting Creek twice—shallow/iced—and another bridge at Sewell Branch and got out. But swamp and shallow and iced again: it just wasn't good enough. Kept driving. Mind back to Georgia. Back to that first July right after he brought the hellhouse down. After he lost his truck and he and Melody were caught with too much water and not enough bridges and he looked at her different, thinking—

Took me more than thirty years to join the life-taking club she's already president of since bratty ten.

South River Bridge at Edgewater was impossible to pull over; Severn River Bridge above Annapolis would've been perfect were it not for the police SUV parked right on it—a do-gooder in a stupid furry hat waving a flashlight like a Salvation Army Santa swinging a bell and Ho-ho-ho'ing a bridge ice warning.

Past two ayem. Onward. Hit his turp-absinthe and blazed always on Christmas fire and the thought of his new little Doris in the *1920s Slut. Size: Small* that he would caressingly dress her in; how she would respond to artist-fingers—pure-love—like her virtual-namesake yearned so many years when Silas Kingston had kept them apart, stupid and unknowing of their constant con‑tact so many years after.

Doris's secret/unsatisfied lust for Boone keeping him alive with her letters. Encouragements. Cash money.

Off the US-50 onto the I-695. The Patapsco River. Middle of the Francis Scott Key—

Silent night. Holy night.

Not a stitch of traffic. Snow sugar-shaking down again. Middle of the middle. Out and around and right up to the railing.

"Fore!"

He sailed the brain-bloody 9-iron out over, down, and into river—

Just like that Georgia rebar shaft, into that bloody flood

—where it would never be seen again.

IT BEGINS. It ends. It both is and is not the every-night un‑winding. The play and repeat of Oscar Mayers blister‑ing, the Pringles, the sticky root beer jug. The glug-glug turpentine, the snores, the gun in my too-small hand. None seen/all felt. The helpless horror. Bullet pain I both inflict and now share with Mama. Her pain gone forever burns my heart ever more.

My face wet.

Sleeping hands, Melody shifted her pillow.

Why can't I dream "Christmas"?

And the burn of the campfire, the burn of the bullet in my ten-year-old heart reflects as candle fire on Doris's window.

My window. The shadow noose forms. Jesuit rope.

Keep my mind. Stay thinking!

First presents: the common room: books for the girls: dragon—dinosaur(?)—squirt guns for the twins. Think that. Dream that. Funny—Silas let them fill water and shoot the Yule log.

Silas: "What're you worried? Nothing'll put it out. It'll burn thirteen days no matter what we do. Clive here gave it a real Kingston light."

Fire. Water. Steam, smoke, ash.

(Who's Clive? Who's he really, *Mel. Think.)*

Fire in the glass. Fire fingers running up the noose. Boone Kelso face—leering behind it. Multi-colored flicker. His serpent tongue licking the panes.

Licking Nika.

Licking her dress. A neat side slit at the hem catches firelight—

Mine.

Mama's patterns. My dress.

The hardest pattern. Not for him. Not to sell. Just for me.

Clean, wide straps; sharp corners; no trim; a simple bias. A side-hem vent like Prada.

"My green dress doesn't look right for this place."

Al's Luau Restaurant/Bar. Smyrna, Georgia. Hawaiian shirts, big colorful skirts, and dudes in baggy shorts.

(Base Marines. [Who's Clive?])

"I'd say you finally grew into the thing."

Knee-length at fourteen. Upper-thigh at seventeen. Too tight across my chest.

"I'm not your hooker!"

"Be somebody's, girlie. We got plans and things to do."

Like me sending you to prison, you sonuvabitch!

Nika pulls open the door—

Not me/me (why is Nika in my dress?)

— a double-paned safety-glass door with a hibiscus cut into it.

Hal unknown/unmet inside.

Why is she in my dress?!

(Clive and Silas: those looks between them.)

Dragon squirt guns shooting water-fire. The thunder of the river. I push the door and Nika tugs, and I feel the water: heavy behind the glass, the hibiscus spins, colors drop, refract—

"Don't go in there!"

—and the sound of a stopper torn from a bottle: I'm through the glass.

Inside is outside. Dawn is night.

The rain comes down in ropes and I am alone, ten years old and frightened—the bullet burns inside me where it never goes away; the smell of smoke in my hair—left sitting on a—"Don't you move from there!"—an Albany, Georgia, mailbox, the water over its legs and over the shoes in the window of the Pine Avenue Florsheim store. Streetlamp globes: fuzzed moons.

Reflected in store window glass: otherworldly light, a living light of its own; the Flint River boils and hisses—yellow-brown and flooding and laughing and undoing itself.

I'm facing it, breathless at it flung and churning out beyond its base and taking everything with it unstoppable. Elemental. Natural/engulfing as God.

"I'll get us a car. That truck was bad news anyhow with those plates." *Boone piles my lap: Mama's portable machine. So wet I don't feel it anymore. Smoke smell and the earth smell and the ozone of electricity sparking from the poles of the Oglethorpe Bridge. Boone stuffs the dress patterns, ragged/soggy envelopes, and Mama's hand-drawn jobs in dirty plastic grocery bags greasy wet against my small tight chest.* "Unless you want to go to jail for what you've done, you don't move! Hear me? You don't talk to no one!"

Boone gone.

The river laughs and gibbers, metal scraping the sides of the bridge in wrenching screams—hardly any room left under it—cars bobbing, scraping, smashing.

Hal, face without the lines of desert sun and gun sights, dry as a saltine, leans against my mailbox as it was at the Luau bar the moment we met.

"You a bit young for this place?"

"It says restaurant. I'm old enough. 'Less you'd like me to leave?"

"Not at all! I want you to tell me your name."

"How do you spell Nika?" *(Did I say that?)*

"Melody fits you. That iced tea? I can get you more."

"Big spender."

He sucks his umbrella drink straw. Takes out the pink tissue paper umbrella. Twirls it in fingers.

I forget my bullet burn. I forget Boone Kelso and his desire to sell my soul I'd give this man anyway, this smile, these kind eyes for free.

How'd Boone know Hal'd be there?

Heartbeat.

Rain hammer.

Heartbeat.

"If you even try to put that umbrella behind my ear, I'll punch your—"

Hal tucks it behind his ear. And smiles. And smiles, and sucks his straw, and smiles—and I marry it right there, that smile—and the sound increases.

The sucking sound. An absinthe bottle: stopper popped. A sucking sound: the wound in my Mama's chest (and me holding the gun).

Lynn's throat whistling.

The river sucks the loudest, drawing everything just past me, back into its own mouth.

A backwash wave—muddy/foamy giant hands swelling and clawing their way back for the Oglethorpe. Half-a-house—its rooftop splitting/spitting shingles. Livestock. Dead cows, mad eyes. Staring. A picnic table pops up. Tries to walk on its legs and the river eats it because all rivers come back devouring.

A Jeep Wagoneer, throwing water like a boat. The sucking lengthens, a throat under the bridge learning to breathe in reverse. "Get down from there, Mel! Get in!"

Hot eyes through open window. Rain shoveling inside. On Boone's head a holly crown.

One woman's light, one man's dark | Bound beneath the holly bark.

Blood in his fingernails, hands blood-washed-pink, grip the wheel.

The Dark King: green leaves for enduring life. Red berries for virgins' fertility.

*An offered hand. "I'm Hal. You here with your folks,
Melody?"*

"Get real."

"Real as nothing you can fake."

*"I'm on my own." Just truth. And never spoken, not
then: "I came in here—forced—to meet you. Just so's you
know."*

*He puzzles over me sorting the pieces into a jigsaw
kind of kindness-pattern on his face.*

*Boone Kelso throws the body of the black stranger in
gold wire glasses off the Oglethorpe.*

*"Hal: I'm still ten and I've already met Cupid Williams
when my daddy killed him for his car. I'm so alone."*

*A rebar rod—bloody too—over the edge into the loud
long suck.*

"Why don't you cry?"

"My tears all spent with the rain."

♔ ♔ ♔

THE TARP UNVEILED. Two more stones slipped and sank to
the mud where St. Leonard Creek opens into the Patuxent, and Kirby's body, upright, helicoptered around the
pivot of his feet. A pocket in the ragged canvas held the
last hunk of granite against his shoes. The bed shoaled,
mud and silt hilling and rising to meet Calvin Kirby. Like
an anchor dragging, he churned it black and a cloud rose
around him. Up he floated until the top of his ruined
head, hunched shoulders, bent back, broke the snowy
surface. Breached, he glided forward.

BWI Airport. 3:42 a.m. Rental car return. This wasn't the Christmas Boone Kelso wanted, but it was the one given him, and he'd always known he'd have to take care of the Richmond lawyer who'd dogged him since before he'd gone into Fountain Correctional to pick cotton for the State of Alabama.

A snow-blown lot. Triple line of cars. Lights-on in the concrete company bunker, but not a damn jack-off in any mood to come out and offer him help he didn't want anyway. Pulled Kirby's Captiva into the middle lane. Pulled the key from the ignition by its little ring, confident he hadn't touched the black plastic where Kirby last thumbed it, last time he switched the motor on. Rifled the glove box. Contract found. That and the key—through it—went into the steel box without his breaking stride as he dragged the dead lawyer's roll-away—

Inside: Ziploc with Melody's revolver.

Inside: Doris's portrait dress—*1920s Slut. Size: Small.*

—through the belching gray exhaust, around the shuttle bus, boarded in darkness.

Southwest Departures. Hat brim down. Jacket collar high. The carry-on roller scratching wet and ice behind him: Calvin Kirby for the cameras. Inside, immediate right to the escalator. Down to Arrivals. Out to the curb. Walked across the traffic lane. Into short-term parking. Out the back. And out to the service road. Head down.

Collar high/tight. Hat tight/brim low. Snow blew wet and sticky and the air stunk like diesel and sewage.

Didn't take long. A beat-up and white-rusty '90s Econoline. Some crap written in Spanish on the side—*Arriba y Lejos*—with a dumb cartoon of a swooping jet. A Dominican leaned out: "Ride, mister?"

Nod.

"Cash, only."

Another nod. Boone Kelso made Kirby pay, then both of them disappeared: *Arriba y Lejos:* Up and Away.

♔♔♔

HAL'S PISTOL inside the pocket of her down robe, Melody descended the gray-lit staircase, getting a jump on Christmas morning to boil cocoa before anyone awoke. She glanced at Doris in the landing portrait—dream-distrust between them—and Silas waiting at the foot, Beaumont leashed.

"Why don't we all three take a little walk before the toy bomb goes off?"

Melody met his gaze. Longed for relief.

"Still carrying?" Silas.

He knew in the church. Her shoulders slumped. She patted her pocket once.

"Good. Makes two of us." He gestured her to lead. "Tell me how bad you think things are."

"And?"

"I'll bring glad tidings of great joy: you're probably wrong."

Melody shook her head back and forth and more than once until they were out the creaky porch screen door.

Her breath clouded as she shared with Silas her confession to Calvin Kirby; they stopped at the woods where she showed him her phone. Showed him Boone Kelso's text.

Lawyer's out. Just you n me n them now. Give young Doris a smooch. Merry Christmas, girl.

She led him through the thicket to Charlotte's holly tree.

Silas read Boone's carved message: "'One woman's light, one man's dark / Bound beneath the holly bark. / Berries red, Beaumont dead, / If a single word is said.'" Scrunched his forehead. Side-eyed her. "Better painter than a poet."

"I think I better call the police."

Silas ran his fingers over the words. Studied like a blind man. "If Charlotte hadn't come, he'd still have carved the first part." Circled a finger in the frigid air. "Something here that's been hamster-wheeling in his mind." Tapped the first couplet. "Written but unseen. Around and around and around."

"Did you hear me? I need to call the police."

Her phone in her mitted hand. Silas closed his hand gently over hers. "He sent that message from Kirby's phone, right?"

"It's what I showed you—yes." She pulled her hand, her phone, free.

"Sweet angel, if we call this in, and Kirby's missing—dead, most likely—you're not just a witness. You're the last known contact. They'll take your phone. Your messages. Plural—how long'd that go on? Hm? Then there's that gun in that Ziploc Boone Kelso thinks as much his vengeance as his insurance—you going to tell them about that? That whole long-ago history: who's going to believe you didn't protect him all these years?"

"With the children—? His weird Charlotte-Doris obsession? We can't let him come here."

"If he was still coming for Christmas, he'd already be here."

She stared into the white woods. Her eyes caught a flock of cardinals, red flashes diving into the hedgerow. "He is coming."

Silas nodded. "But he's giving us time to get ready."

Time to fix those stairs.

He laid a hand on her shoulder. Drew her focus to his face. Held her gaze. "No police. This is yours to finish. And I'll go one step further."

She lifted an inquisitive brow.

"Your poor friend Kirby agrees with me."

♛ ♛ ♛

THE SHOAL FELL, the Patuxent current took him, dropping him and shooting him supine, feet-first, toward Peterson Point where the mixing currents tugged and drew him deep. The canvas pocket his shoes shared with the final stone snagged in a broken tangle of fallen loblolly and dead branches—hungry hands—dragging Calvin Kirby down. Down, down to where his journey ended. Law, if it earns the name, is two acts at once: hands on the swinging chain, a weir in the tide—not to drown a man, but to break the force so a family can breathe. Twelve feet below the surface. Upside down. Arms flung wide and pinned by weed-slick pine: an inverted crucifix. Satanic? Saintly? Say the thing and tie it off; keep it nameless and the current finds you again at the bend. Here he would remain unclaimed, worried by silver flashes schooling in green mermaid hair. The sucking holds.

"MERRY CHRISTMAS!" Jack and Little Silas, led the charge, thundering down the stairs, painted Doris appearing as if counting them off—the twins, Charlotte and Leigh, Clive and Paige—as they rushed into the common room where the Yule log glowed and snapped and cocoa cups and coffee steamed beside hot, buttered fruit cake.

"What ho! Look at my lambs!" Silas roared. "And a Merry Christmas indeed." He flashed devilish eyes to Melody. "Fire at will!"

Her grin quickly became a giggle; Melody showered the children with both barrels from the dragon-headed squirt guns, and everyone laughed and Christmas Day passed in pleasure at Foxtail Farm.

4.

C OMPUTER-FIRED, THE HOLY TRINITY church bells rang bright, the sound rising against low and threatening clouds; unable to puncture, penetrate, to ascend and soar, their carol tumbled ragged to the earth—the echo faintly heard inside the Lincoln Town Car Signature L idling at the curb. 36th Street, Georgetown. Senator Theresa Ossani waited. Watched her private chauffeur emerge between columns better suited for a Greek temple than a Jesuit church. He jogged down eight stone steps. Opened her rear door. Two bulletins passed inside. "The choir's only just begun, Senator. The side door is unlocked, aisle empty, and an usher has blocked your holiday seats."

"Thank you." One graceful, black stockinged leg out; her Casadei blade heel glimmered sharper than the wet pavement. She looked back.

Gary Gravin. Dutiful husband/CIA DDO, non-dutifully not moving. Eyes shut. Fiddling with his beads.

"Gary. Come all ye oh-so-faithful ..."

She tapped his knuckles with the bulletins.

He looked. Took one. "Resa. Please."

"Inside is where we pray today." She cocked her head toward the steps. "Do me a favor and leave your

Kingston drunk girlfriend outside the doors where she belongs."

"*That* is why I'm praying for her here. Before I join your Christmas pageant. She's my officer. She's in an impossible box. Just give me a minute."

Theresa pulled her leg back inside. Power couple parishioners, power-coupled to Christmas-colored children who passed on the sidewalk damp and snuffly. A pair of white-haired widows with flurry-dusted shoulders greeted, linked arms, went up the steps. Theresa's driver closed the door. Stepped to the bumper. Folded hands.

Sealed inside in the heater's blow, Theresa and Gary regarded one another. He said, "Merry Christmas. I do love you."

"I know that. So, you won't mind I add my own prayer to yours?"

"She has zero chance without me. I made my bones rescuing people. It's who I am."

The vow came and stayed. Ineluctable. Bright.

The Sarajevo/Banja Luka exfil corridor. Families out two at a time; a hand signal at the corner, a knock that meant go now.

"Yes, you like your myth tidy: Providence, Merit. Secret medals for clandestine triumphs, one after another—the one's that brought you into my arms."

He didn't argue. Couldn't. Just waited for the velvet stroke of her iron threat.

"But your marquee—got you to the Seventh Floor?"

"Don't."

"Wasn't Providence that arrived you. That was me—PRC sovereign sleeve tucked in a Luxembourg shell; the Doha cutout; courier lifts we let run until the Delaware seats lit up."

"Point made. Stop it."

"You never want to say out loud what I buried at Treasury—CFIUS, the donor letter. I killed it. That's the only reason the building calls FIR STRIDE your success." She held his hands over the rosary. "And you're welcome."

"I let Lynn die?"

"Silas Kingston must bleed, and your building learn: there are no saints in energy."

The heater did something to her perfume. Car smelled Christmas-only-better. Her eyes, flecked gold, mesmerized. She caressed his cheek. He shut his eyes and hated how much he liked it.

A rain of rockets: back into the apartment block.

He muttered. "And this is the price."

His conscience gently crumbled.

Back into the fire when I didn't have to.

A Muslim infant given into a mother's arms.

Distant, distant; I've done my part. Plentiful 'nough. Times change; life goes on.

Gary nodded. Pocketed his rosary.

Lynn. God: somehow do what I can't anymore.

He indicated the door. He was ready. Theresa tapped glass. Her driver responded. Gary slid dutifully after his wife. "Just for the record: nothing ever happened between us."

This time one leg followed the other. "Good. You won't miss her touch when she's gone."

They made their way down the side of the church. A walkway past the original St. Ignatius Chapel, built by the Jesuits in 1794; an announcement board behind glass displayed a colorful flyer for the first historical lecture of the approaching New Year: *Maryland Jesuits and Slavery*. The words made a short bridge to river country; Kingston country; Gary Gravin didn't cross it. He escorted his wife—both of Theresa's hands serpentine around his biceps—into the church for Christmas morning Mass. The side door where no one might find offense in mistaking her, nibbling now his ear, for his mother.

♛ ♛ ♛

SHE'D SLEPT through Christmas Eve. Slept through Christmas morning and the day. Neither the dim light of the fluorescent tube under its thick plastic shield nor the spiritual light of the Nativity could awaken Lynn Kingston, who crashed into a death-like slumber, once returned to her secure supply room imprisonment.

After her sham murder trial.

After her genuine death sentence.

Fetal, tucked against the block wall shared with the code room once meant for her betrayed: Roman Sayadov. Watched over by the black dome, the red-light eye of her camera companion.

Somewhere, middle of Christmas night, the pang of her empty belly roused her. The bolted chair and interrogation table—removed before the trial—left an empty space in the center of the room. Wrapped in her blanket, Lynn crept onto the floor. Sat. Bunched her legs, embraced them. Air through her nose. Down her scar-thick throat. Lynn fed her lungs and exhaled fully.

Made sure fear and hope expelled in equal measure. Did this until only love—cold/hard, pure/true—remained. Until the internal infinity of it attached to her soul, a soul she'd learned too late in life she'd never cared for. Centered in present stillness: body/room, breath/body, love/soul—she stared into infinity's external representation. Comfort guard-gifted mistakenly to her: the two facing mirrors of her prison.

Acrylic mirror on the back wall.

Acrylic mirror on the wall beside the handleless door.

Her image duplicated. Repeated into darkening depths. Gone were the mocking/twisted hallucinations of her detox. The projections: Silas, Michael, Doris; the Enchanted Forest Lady in the Lake; the Layla she aspired to, killed alongside Roman.

Even Leigh.

Especially Leigh.

Lynn saw only Lynn.

To count past each of her. To count past herself and arrive, and maybe see the thing she missed that made her—

made myself: the essence of my mistakes I must release into that blackness beyond my reflection before I go.

Lynn looked beyond. To that time/place/thing waiting deadly, jagged, neck/throat black-toothed and dried blood hungry for more—

"I'm not scared! It didn't scare me: you *did. Dickhead."*

"Lynn. Don't say that. He came right away."

Gone for what felt like hours. Sobs. Pathetic time-stopped-hours-and-hours. Bite it back. Swallow whole down my throat. "Why's this stupid room here anyway?"

Lynn focused far enough into the mirrors, far enough past herself and remembered in black infinity the vanishing point willed away—too large, too fatal, too doomed.

"It's just a wall. One boost and over. Don't you want to try those oranges? No one lives there, no one eats them."

"Michael: they're not ours. I'm not going over that wall and stealing things."

"It's fruit." He's sixteen. "Don't be like such a kid."

"Shut up." I'm eleven.

"Come ooooon, Lynn. You're the one who wanted to 'go exploring'. I'm just following your idea."

Cicadas sawed the silence in trees above them. "I know a place." My eyes bold. "Foxtail Farm. A door you *don't know."*

Michael's whip-sharp laugh. "I know every door."

"Not this one."

North Vista Outhouse. Wine cellar/basement descent. Stair creak complaint also a summoning. Their feet move lightly, Lynn leading. Sure.

Before the wine racks—before full concealment—but you must look closely to see the door's outline matched to the natural meeting-lines of cut and hammered planks. No bigger than the door on a child's playhouse.

She crooks a finger in a knothole. A hard jerk. Scratch of old wood.

"When'd you find it?"

"I spied on Dad one day."

"He see you?"

Head shake. Flip my hair.

"You go in?"

Head shake. She drags it wide. A place of blackness pure.

Michael pushes past. Inside. "I can't see anything."

Lynn beside him. "Leave the door open. Our eyes will adjust."

And when they did...Michael... "Ho-ly shit."

Wander. Touch. No way to comprehend.

Then the dare.

Lynn's feet on the wooden platform.

"Put your head in."

"No, Michael."

"Chicken. Do it."

Head forward. Into the collar. Arms out along the yoke. The loudness of her breath. The weakness of her nervous laugh.

Be-brave, be-brave, be-brave—

Screech of a hinge. "Oops—fuck." *The click of iron.* "Uh-oh."

"Michael?!"

"Oh, shit. I was kidding. Oh-shit, ohshiiiit... "

"It's on my neck!"

His fingers spider. In front of her face. Out of sight. "Oh, shit!"

"It's tightening! Don't touch anything else!"

"Lynn—I'm sorry! I'm sorry!"

"Shut-up-shut-up-shut-up."

Nose to nose. His eyes welling. "I didn't mean to."

His backing to the door. "I'm sorry."

"Shut up!"

Staggers. "I don't want to get in trouble."

"God damn it! Get Mom!"

His feet hammer up. Hammer out.

Breath shakes.

Hands shake.

Neck/throat sting and ache.

Dark rust/darkest red: down the black wood iron-bound: old dried blood. She presses her chest, beats her heart against T-stocks.

Knees shake, and if she falls—if she loses her legs—Lynn knows the teeth will snap her throat.

Sobs now. Black teeth bite harder. Time clamps harder. Slows. Time slows.

He's left me. Abandoned me.

Hours. Hours. Hours.

All alone to die in pain. A place/a thing where time has stopped.

Time-stop-surrender.

"Oh, Linny, honey." A warm hand upon her temple. Silk sleeve against her wet cheek. "Don't be scared. And don't move." Click!

A key without apology. We never asked how. Did we?

"I'm not scared! It didn't scare me: you did. Dickhead."

"Lynn. Don't say that. Michael came right away."

But he didn't.

"I'm just sorry. Lynn. It was too dark." Mumbles: "We're not going to tell Dad, are we?"

Packed dirt under the device. Doris holds Lynn. Her mother strokes her face, strokes her forehead (Lynn swallows sobs down her bruised, unpunctured throat), strokes her face and Doris says, plainly and to the air—to all the ghosts of this Place of Blackness—but especially to Lynn Kingston as her own mother once said to her: "You'll never be alone in the dark."

Her eyes shift to Michael. The cerulean blue fills the void between them with life. Michael's eyes are smoke.
"Promise, Michael: I want your vow."
"Okay. What?"
"What I just said and on your sacred honor."
Bigger than the collar that took her at the throat and wrists to claim her bones; bigger than the world. "Lynn: I swear, I pledge, I vow—my whole life, for all of it—I will never leave you alone in—" His eyes drift from his sister's to his mother's and back to Lynn; changes a word: "to the dark."

They never mentioned that place of blackness. The infernal machines, the secret door that concealed it and soon afterward Silas concealed further with a wine rack. Never once—like it never happened. Ever. Erased between Lynn and Michael.

Lynn never forgot, of course, the horror of that time-dilated afternoon, the death she faced and yielded her soul to—its inexorable/inevitable pressure—making it so, so it must be. Stamped the memory on her soul and hid from that. Did not tell; did not forget, just piled fresh horrors upon that soul like dirt over a grave impossible to fill and let it hold the memories as she willfully averted her inward gaze and refused to acknowledge she had a soul. Not anymore.

Took up alcohol at thirteen.

Lying as adult career. Stealing—secrets.

And the room closed behind her, her soul left safely/forgotten inside. The simplest torture chamber of all: memory.

Lynn drew her focus back from the vanishing. From where, light lost, her first image—small and gray and blurred like ash—grew larger as she withdrew from the mirror, the scrying, her vision toward herself along her repeated and coalescing image, out and seated in her blanket on her cell-room floor. Rose, suddenly, at the sound of her door unlocked.

The black dome, red-light watched; a guard delivered a sandwich tray. On it, a section of folded newspaper.

Lynn had given up asking for the news, for anything to read. Weeks ago. "What's this?"

Her guard handed her the tray without comment. Locked her back inside. Lynn put the tray on her cot. Took up the *Post's* Metro section for the following morning.

Embassy says 'criminal incident' under review; U.S. aid not requested

Ex-CIA official alleges deadly incident and detention of U.S. operative; agencies won't confirm

By Staff Writer
December 26, 2012 | Washington

The Embassy of Azerbaijan notified the State Department that a "criminal incident involving an invited American guest" occurred on its diplomatic grounds at 11:48 p.m. on Thanksgiving night (Nov. 22) and is "under review by internal embassy security," according to diplomatic correspondence reviewed by this newspaper. The embassy told State that no U.S. assistance was "requested or required."

A former senior CIA general counsel official, speaking on the condition of anonymity to discuss sensitive matters, alleged that the person detained is a U.S. intelligence officer and that a fatal shooting occurred inside the compound. The claims could not be independently corroborated, and the Embassy of Azerbaijan did not respond to requests for comment.

A State Department spokesperson said the department is "aware of reports," and—citing ongoing processes and the sensitive nature of incidents on foreign sovereign grounds—declined to provide further details, including whether U.S. consular officials had been granted access. The CIA declined to comment.

District officials said the Metropolitan Police Department was not called to the scene. The Diplomatic Security Service referred questions to the State Department.

No arrests have been announced, and no names have been released. This newspaper generally withholds the names of individuals in alleged incidents unless charges are filed or identities are confirmed by authorities.

B3. Beneath the fold. Hunger gone, Lynn felt nothing. *At least you tried, Rusty.*

Dropped the newspaper over the sandwich. Lowered the tray to the floor and scooted it with her bare heel beneath her cot. Cocooned inside her blanket. Would show the red light nothing. Would sleep again on this:

This is how darkness keeps its promises. Clear-eyed and unassailable.

♛ ♛ ♛

A sweaty mound of eroticized disgust, Morton Drexler listened to the glorious hush only Christmas delivered to the busy streets just beyond his Sleepy Hollow neighborhood where, worsening for years, the subwoofer thump from sound systems jacked from nightclubs and jammed into automobiles stealing shortcuts off Route 7—chanting raps pounding chest-cavity contusions; the horns; the screams of rubber at the light; sometimes kids' fireworks for no holiday Drexler saw on a calendar, while more often, as time stumbled belligerent to the dashed hopes for gentrification of his little neighborhood, the pop-pop-pop of all-too-adult/too-deadly—child-like only in their stupidity—gun fights for no reason at all: made this one night the only silent night of the year. The one calendared night of the year where the incandescent crown of Skyline—the 1970s high-rise development at Bailey's Crossroads—was imaginable in its orange sodium-vapor glow a fireplace crackle through the shifting branches and leathery leaves of the old Southern magnolia he could see over Deleta's seal-slick shoulder through the paint-stuck bedroom windows over the sagging porte-cochère, where the tree had already knocked down the decorative doweling of its balustrade rail.

Better than staring at the grinning Buddha fondling—or being fondled by (Drexler couldn't tell)—a Disneyfied koi-fish blue and black and purple that centerpieced the back of her full-body collage.

Or a calendar girl in tennis togs. Teenage Lynn up for the shuttlecock. Lighter than air, simple, pure, colorful-clean as a balloon.

The radiator burnt the air still around him. The laughing Buddha twice as healthy as Drexler.

He'd bought the place in 2004—height of the gentrification that siren-songed most of his generation into the bust that followed the housing boom in 2008—bought it for that tree that reminded him of his Southeast Texas boyhood and a swing so big, so strong he could set and pump it now. Instead of pump this lady/escort/whore in his bed with his bitter dreams and regrets, and kissing her lips when he didn't want to—

"My lips is my courtesy for you, Morty. You always been there for me since the start. And you still treat me gentle and nice even when yo no more 'llowed on top or behind, and you're not one a'them muthafuckas pretendin' a crappy fuck-pad-apartment or motel is some way to treat a lady. Abusive fucks. An' you 'vitin' me into yo' mansion. Right here. No head down in the car, or park my ride somewhere else... Kissin' my mouth, Morty, is my extra thank you 'cause you's a gen'leman and that's a fact. You can kiss me again right now if you want."

You taste like that coke I let you cook in the sterling spoon I fetched from my meemaw's flatware chest and let you smoke sickly sweat and topless/tits-hanging in my kitchen. And I bury your face in mine, clutching and desperate, and I breathe your breath.

"Deleta, you know as well as I, this place is a dump."

"C'mon, Morty, no long faces—not the night of our Lord—"

"Honey, this place is a dump. Whole neighborhood."

A 1920s Tudor/Colonial Revival he once envisioned he would lift from disrepair when loyalty paid Silas Kingston lifted him to KALEIDOSCOPE. The front walk upheaved by magnolia roots; iron spear fence with one bay bent; concrete lions at the steps, one ear sheared off, toothless silent growls between fluted columns furred with lichen.

The radiator hissed. Deleta snored. Wasted-beautiful: her once unblemished body she'd danced the silver pole in smoky red spots, then laps—his—and G-string tucked dollars, and he'd worshipped her compelling flesh and who he pretended it made her but wasn't; excited over fantasy prospects after a whispered "Help me outta here, Morty, start my own service? Lots more I'd do for you—grateful I'd be t'ya." And the sexy tattoos, like a fighter pilot's fuselage kill-decals as her business increased, and she was always, at least for a time— "Yeah, I'm still thinkin' 'bout nursing school—" but wasn't. He knew it from the first time she'd said it and he coldly snickered to himself mocking her. And then the comic book drawing board she let her glorious body become; the crack she let become herself.

I never helped her because I only pretended I was looking at her/out for her while pretending Deleta's name began on an "L" and ended at Foxtail Farm.

Disgusting. Degraded this woman as I've degraded myself.

Evil—probably. Mine.

Not hers. Mine. Not the woman in my bed; the wrong one on my conscience: the club calendar with its pretty lies.

The radiator popped. A shutter click. The room held still the way a photo lies when you don't look at the hands, and he was shaking her awake before the echo died. "Deleta."

"Wha'? Morty—cut it out!"

"Deleta. You gotta get up. You get outta here."

"Bullshit I'm going anywhere 'cept back to sleep. You leave me alone—you fat fuck."

Drexler heaved a breath. She thought it was over—heaved her own. "I'll give you some sugar in the morning."

He felt the deep-ache of his psychic insignificance center in his mass. Except for his ponderous breath, the rise and fall of his chest, Morton Drexler was motionless.

"No. It's no good. I'll double last night. Call it a Christmas bonus. But you have to leave—" He pounded the floorboards with his feet. Heaved himself off his side of the bed. Looming and massive. "We're done. This is wrong. It's over. For the love of God, it must end now. This minute. Get-the-fuck-out-of-here!"

He lumbered to his dresser. Dug all his cash from his wallet. She gave him a skeptical laugh. But Deleta got out of bed. She sauntered to the chair where she'd strewn her candy cane-striped lingerie and her dress. Opened her purse. Smeared on lipstick and smacked her lips at him, kissing the air. Naked. One leg cocked, foot balanced on the points of her toes. Rotated a hand open-palmed between them like a *Hey, Big Spender*.

He paid her. She folded the wad and pushed it into her purse. He watched her dress. Listened to the house creak, the front door groan, and she was gone.

Drexler envisioned the club calendar again—Roman's holiday freebie. Month: April. Post-Rock Creek Tennis Club Women's Tournament/Spring Mixer: the group shot that wasn't. The Lynn—back row, racquet in hand—who wasn't.

Her face: too young, too innocent. Too much hope.

Strange how memory can gather itself into a close-up. What had bothered Drexler from the moment he'd seen the photo now came clear. Not the age discrepancy—Lynn's young face pleasing to the ache. No.

The racquet head.

That was the thing that loomed large in his mind's eye.

Wrong head.

Wrong grip.

Badminton dressed as tennis, down to the shuttle scuff on the strings.

Badminton: a yard game played at home. And now Lynn Kingston sat in a cell for it. The Agency didn't lift a finger.

Drexler sat in the hush. Let the lie resolve.

Whoever wanted to blow Lynn's cover to Azerbaijan, take apart her operation, knew her face and the name underneath would do the job. The Russians? They'd have a hundred ways to get a better photo—make a better job of it.

What am I thinking? If they'd clocked Layla as Lynn, they'd have just picked up the phone.

Only two sources presented themselves for the photograph in the calendar built to burn her: Lynn's own albums or Foxtail Farm.

But Silas—all bad things to all people—would he burn his own daughter? His blood? His flesh?

A strange new light burned inside Morton Drexler, fat and naked in the dark and morning cold. A star that pointed, not comforted. The pattern felt like Silas: break, pretend to mend, then let the pieces scatter.

A crooked fence don't straighten with time.

Just leans harder.

Wednesday, December Twenty-sixth

1.

H OW FAR MUST TIME play back?

Photographs fall on a bedspread. Michael Kingston had come to settle a debt and he carried it hot.

Backwards in fresh repetitions; turn the glass until the pattern locks: this it is, this it was, this will be again.

Prints in black and white.

Michael... Father Cevik... Their Trabzon dead drop.

Compromised by Kalaydoskop long before the Turks rolled us up.

The crumbling Byzantine towers of the Vazelon Monastery—now, more than a year later—give way to Baku's Flame Towers. That they weren't yet publicly opened made no difference to Nikoláj "Kolya" Yurenev. The photos on the bed. The bed inside a private suite of rooms. Kalaydoskop secure on his own exclusive floor, thirty-three floors above the sea.

THE KALEIDOSCOPE TWISTS backwards. Briefcase on the Škoda passenger seat. The Pinwheel dead-man's promise: ready-made Kalaydoskop cover. Red-cover foreign passport—*Mikhail Nikolaevich Morozov*— *Michael son of Nikolai. Kolya petty flex.*

Mikhail's internal passport. Green SNILS slip. INN printout. His Moscow registration sheet—*registratsiya po mestu prebyvaniya*, the all-important *propiska*—Moscow address, dates, stamp and seal, and like that: Mikhail Morozov backstopped as a real person in Russia.

Underneath. Backstop the backstop; employer letter with the blue round seal: *OOO Vektor-Servis* (Vector-Servis LLC); plastic employee ID, faded/scuffed—his own face: workaday workaholic.

Underneath. Expo registration print-out with barcode. Sberbank card. Thin stack of small USD. Clean phone and a spare. Two SIMs—MTS Moscow, Azercell Baku.

And fancy that, a pen that writes in the cold and upside down. Probably zero-g as well.

Michael whipped the Škoda off the lake road. Shot into long-term parking, Zürich airport. Black glass. Rain combs the windshield. Gutters run. Halogen wash. His face staring back—already someone else.

Ticket. Gate. Gangway. Wet ramp, spray off the tug.

♛♛♛

MORE PHOTOGRAPHS fall onto the coverlet.

Frankfurt: Michael paying his cutout to die at Dulles. Giving him the *Arthur Danford*—forgery of his forged passport. Giving him the black leather jacket—bona fide his last Christmas/last gift from Lynn.

Glossy color stock: Rue de la Survette, Geneva. Michael with Helene Favre. Seamstress in a mirror; impish smile reflected at him.

Living color: Michael beside Kolya/Kalaydoskop as if the most natural thing in the world: the two of them right here, right now. The legacy of the blood they share. A casual intimacy on the edge of Kolya's bed.

Last time we were in a room together there was a white table, you had Dr. Kiselyov waiting on your order: the scalpel for my newborn throat before my first breath. A lethal injection for my mother. Doc said you didn't even blink.

Photos between them. Whole images of a life turned to shards. Michael seated with Pinwheel, dinner at Der Seespiegel.

"Try to expose me—blow my cover? My career's over. Try harder."

More pictures scatter. He'd lived them.

Michael on the run: Lyon, France. Vienna. Prague. Next—collapsed; arms of the teenage addict in the Kursk alley. Abed in the Russian security services mental hospital outside of Tula. Breakdown of summer; insanity of fall.

Back where I began.

Fingers in scissor rings. Hands in surgical gloves.

A black-and-white mosaic falling onto a bedspread.

✼✼✼

HE'D FLOWN the Zürich straight-shot to Istanbul. Turkish Airlines, cabin dim. A seat in back. Heads snoring all the way to the bulkhead.

Trabzon hotel room— "This kaleidoscope needs controlling. Kingston hands on it."

Lynn bites through the phone: "Enough with the kiddie toys!"

"I am going to get my agent. You are going to help me."

"Forget it! This isn't climbing the neighbor's wall stealing oranges."

"You never climbed."

Until I dared you onto the stocks. Into the collar. Abandoned you alone in the dark.

Atatürk past midnight. Low lid on the field. Windows filmed with damp. Half-lit fluorescent hush.

My Picasso'd Kalaydoskop into the padded envelope—

Cleaning solvent burned the air. Airport coffee burned his throat.

Funny, how random events preload our future. Sea glass robin's-egg blue, scraped from wet Trabzon sand. Smooth. Rounded. Centered in my palm: opaque from beach friction. Into the envelope.

Dawn push back from the gate. Turkish Airlines' morning run. Atatürk to Heydar Aliyev. Cabin: ghost-blue.

"It's pretty. This'll be the official first piece. Okay? I'll save all the best ones from now on. You and Mom and Hal can help me find them."

Taxi onto the runway. Velocity. Nose up. Windows crystallized with ice.

Mom: "What makes the best ones best?"

Marmara a hammered plate; the Bosphorus a dark cut.

Lynn: "Magic. Magic memories."

Black Sea milk-pale. The Caucasus: sawteeth of snow.

This is for us, Lynn. Erase the memories that killed your magic.

Caspian like tin.

I won't fail you again.

A plastic cup of tea shivers on the fold-down tray. Bleak rings ripple from its center. A flight attendant collects it and the tray goes up, and—

Flaps. Landing gear. Bounce—wheel shriek—

—Heydar Aliyev International Airport. Baku, Azerbaijan.

A taxi and three turns later, Michael pushed through the outer doors of the Baku Expo Center and into the check-in hall. The Caspian Sea Oil Conference. Registration counters populated by young Azeris—smart uniforms, bright greetings. A video wall behind them: the Caspian Oil & Gas sponsor reel running end-to-end. In HD, the circular clarifier at the Heydar Aliyev Oil Refinery's wastewater unit: a rotating bridge scraper; skimmer arm; scum trough; peripheral drive. Something about it—the shape, the turn, the ever-changing rainbow of petroleum waste—catches his eye.

Holds it. A twenty-first-century water wheel laid on its side and turning in perpetual revolution.

The rest of the wall: a veritable vision board of backlit blow-ups—movie posters, or better, travel-agency ads for the next most magical place. All gloss, all promise; fossil fuels as beauty. Sangachal Terminal, spectacular dusk flare—pipe racks, slug catcher, separator trains, manifolds. The Azeri–Chirag–Gunashli PDQ sparkling like an offshore paradise. Tengiz on the golden Kazakhstan steppe—walking-beam pumpjacks beneath blue flame at the gas-sweetening stacks. A tank farm in a snowfield. The artificial islands of Kashagan behind their ice berms. Pipelines through fields of sunflowers, and across cut canyons. Pretty spigots and interdependencies on offer and two men locked in subterfuge to leverage the sale.

Beyond that, Silas/KALEIDOSCOPE, Kolya/Kalaydoskop, none of it meant a thing to Michael Kingston. He knew no more about exploration, recovery, processing, transport, and the deal-making/geo-politics behind it than what, briefly and infrequently, he picked from headlines and skimmed clips while hunting something else. Oil and gas—? Once Michael decided he'd end up here, he'd made a point of not learning a damn thing more about it.

Kolya can't use me to compromise anything I don't know. I'll prove it soon as I open my mouth.

👑 👑 👑

THE MAN WHO WOULD BE his father delivered the next photograph. A long-distance zoom, black-and-white/magazine-clean: Michael—vicuna Kiton tuxedo, Lulu—Cristallini mermaid-cut gown, glittering champagne; her balcony twenty-five stories above Presnensky on the Third Ring Road, the night of their first dinner.

"You love her—? Loved her?"

Michael didn't answer.

"More than Gwen?"

Life, like a kaleidoscope: the turn that makes the same shards into something else, and somehow the same. Kolya lit by the penance suddenly owed—Michael to his enemy—for the sins of false honor and excessive pride Michael suddenly felt, as though he'd felt it forever, a wheel he couldn't escape. The wall's steel clarifier was the modern wheel; the one turning in him was older, crueler. The groaning wood of an undershot wheel in a mill race; a river that delivers the past in perpetual motion. Troughs scoop what's already lived, rise wobbling, brim at apex—momentarily singular, briefly apart from the dumb, merciless flow—then tip. Memories spill. Drive the shaft and gear, crush seed-life to powder.

Kolya slapped the last three photos down with a careless viciousness that carried them onto the floor.

Back of Der Seespiegel; Michael over the man Hal killed—taking his gun.

Helene Favre dead in Michael's arms.

France, the switchback road from the monastery-castle, the Château de Ripaille: the murder weapon Kolya-recovered in pieces.

The memories fold back into the river.

"I killed two muggers in a Paris railyard. Got a picture of that, too?"

"I do."

Michael lurched to his feet. Grabbed the pics—every last one of them, bed and floor.

"I'm not afraid to face my crimes—so save the Silas trap. I'm not my father." Dropped them, two-handed and just as viciously, flat into Kolya's lap. "And neither are you, old man."

Kolya met Michael's gaze with a derisive grimace. Hardly would call it a smile, though Michael couldn't name another word you could call it.

"Mikhail." He drew out Michael's Russian name; a kind of relish of a long-held wish to speak it aloud to him. Eyes cerulean blue and cold. "Had I offered you the truth; the depth of what that means—to all of you, except Silas—you wouldn't have had the courage to meet me."

Annoyed, he threw the photographs into Michael. They fell between them. Michael glared. Kolya reached into his breast pocket. The one over his heart. He withdrew a large, thin leather wallet and held it between them.

"The only one that matters." He put it in Michael's hands.

Michael opened it.

FRACTURE PRESENT.

Fracture past.

Lock the image to forecast meaning from abstract pattern. Michael let his mind slip—present/past the turning lens. Not the madness of summer, not the insanity of fall, but a stepping apart in idea/ideal; a weighing of time differently: the unremitting pull of time isolated and removed.

Back to the hall, back to his arrival. Back to the frigid rain-wash pouring down the glass outer wall. Queue ropes in braided burgundy zigs-chutes-zags. The registration counters with their smart young Azeris. Badge printers coughing out ID/all-access cards in little fits. Deft hands fitting cards into plastic sleeves, sleeves strung on black lanyards and formally adorned—lanyards over soft bent necks—like knightings. The metal gates and waist-high scanners spit attendees past the glass-hung eye-candy of the sponsor wall. And the main hall spread past that—country banners/booths—out of reach until you were ordered and badged.

Sound carried. Shoes squeaking on the polished concrete slab floor, greetings hailed; boots counterpointing cellphone jingle, elevator dings; heels clicking into the murmurs of first meetings—into the tournament atmosphere of the exposition hall: open, wide, ablaze beneath a high truss roof, rainy-day light dimly trapped in its ribs.

Michael's eyes, made blank, walked to a small U.S. Commercial Service table. Just like America: asserted first position past security. To the right. A draped rectangle. Neat stack of brochures. Clocked a roundish woman clocking him. Round head—neat round curl riding her brow; sunny eyes without warmth. While she punched his timecard in a mental slot—knew him, no doubt—Michael had never seen this roundish woman before. Her eyes disengaged. Clicked her tongue to herself and balanced a placard on the tablecloth as if it were a tea party place card. Made a small *mmm-huhn* complimenting herself, followed by a birdlike whir. Too far to read the name off her badge, it wouldn't surprise him when he did. *MS. WREN.*

Fit Meryl Hofmyer to a tee.

Michael's turn at the counter. Offered his red Russian passport. Slid his email-printed registration barcode to the toothsome clerk. She compared his face against the government photo, Russian already in her mouth.

"*Kakoy kontingent, gospodin?*" Which contingent, sir?

"*Moskva. Administrativnyy.*" Moscow office. Administrative.

She frowned at a drop-down her world didn't fit. Continued Russian. "*Gde imenno? Ministerstvo? Goskompanii? Chastnyy sektor?*" Where exactly? Ministry? State company? Private sector?"

A hand set down on the counter between Michael's page and the clerk's fuchsia nails.

"*On moy referent; komandirovan cherez Vektor-Servis.*" He's my assistant; seconded via Vektor-Servis.

Kolya's voice was low, perfectly balanced between kind and irrefutable. He tapped the round blue seal on the secondment letter. The printer woke. Coughed again. A lanyard looped toward Michael in the young woman's delicate hands.

Kolya intercepted and bestowed it. "*Dobro pozhalovat', Mikhail.*" Welcome, Mikhail.

Away from registration, Kolya didn't bother with the security gates. Hand on Michael's elbow, friendly/controlling, he cut them left.

Michael didn't care—had nowhere else to be.

A side door. Wet, cold air off the airport road. A rain-splashed black S-Class idled at the curb.

Kolya. "Let's go."

He grabbed the door for Michael who slid in, Kolya family-close thighed-up beside. Neither spoke. Kolya watched Michael's face. Waiting. Expectant. Michael didn't care—watched a set of towers grow large between the swish of wipers: three curved glass blades rising silver and gleaming above the Bayıl hillside; ringed by cranes—construction only recently completed—the Flame Towers appeared a crown above Baku Bay breathing light into the gray and the Mercedes swept beneath the middle building's empty portico and stopped.

Not until Kolya's driver opened Michael's door did the total control Kolya had over him hit Michael with flash flood force. The psychotic motorcyclist—Lulu's younger bodyguard—grinned.

"Old boss vanish—new job for me, *Amerikanski.*"

Kolya chuckled. Gestured Michael into the middle tower.

Private lift. Hush of carpet. Suite door. Key.

The antiseptic note rose in primal memory; this room the first room: waiting all these years.

HER FACE alive. A child unmistakably Doris.
When did I last see you smile?
Hardly once during your cancer.

In my heart, I declared you dead while you lay, still breathing, in your bed.

Her eyes—a darker blue than he remembered, highlighted with diamond cerulean crypts—

Kaleidoscope-patterned. Unblinking. Vivid. Confident. Perfectly matched to her father.

Her lips: straight and tight with just the slightest—maybe Michael-hoped/wished/maybe nothing—sly smile.

Like the familiar smile that arrived without invitation and tightened a corner of his own mouth. Michael stood at the floor-to-ceiling window, draperies pulled, faint light illuminating the inside of a cloud the color of his eyes that swirled the penthouse floor of the second Flame Tower. Made mirrors of the fat and rolling raindrops, their squiggled trails. Cast the gloss of the old photograph, pulled from Kolya's wallet, in a greenish sheen. The edges, slightly serrated, preciously brittle, quivered—but only barely—as Michael pincered the upper and lower corners between the tips of the forefinger and thumb of both his hands. An artifact. An answer.

Depicts a classroom. Language studies. Latin letters beside the Cyrillic, slang phrases on the chalkboard: *Don't flip your lid. Cruisin' for a bruisin'. Made in the shade.* Pronunciation guides below. A map of the United States. Training, not childhood. The fact of it enough.

"Her mother—Sofiya, my wife—named her Daria. As Doris, she named you Michael... Lynn... Hal..."

Michael shushed him.

His mother: just a girl. Dressed in parade uniform—brown dress, wool tights, white apron, red scarf—Daria sits in the front and is the focus of the photographer; snapped the moment she knows this, the moment she looked. Hopeful. And something else where hope has sprung from.

Les Dikiy. The Forest Wild. With the Chechen inside the snow cat.

"I only know one story of Kolya ever feeling love. A daughter. He was very young, the mother died. He turned her over to the State when he entered the KGB. And when he returned from the Higher Intelligence School in Moscow, she was gone."

"Adopted?"

"He claimed she'd gotten sick and had died. But Pinwheel told me, once, that was a lie Kolya spread because the true manner of death was unspeakable."

She married my father and loved him.

Both her hands are folded on her English reader; her pencil is set straight. And Lenin gazes proudly upon her from a small brass profile, his face against a background of a red star afire garlanded by a red banner with the Pioneer motto: *Всегда готов!* Always ready!

His wound. His weak spot. Michael's point of attack. And yet, having lost her, gotten her back in Moscow to witness the flesh of his flesh delivering life—he'd have taken it? Destroyed us?

The unspeakable death was his own weakness allowing us to live. Allowing Silas—his enemy—love.

He wiggled the photograph. "May I have this?"

Kolya nodded. Moved to a cabinet. "A drink?"

"Water's fine."

Michael tucked his mother's childhood into his sports jacket pocket. Remained beside the window. Kolya tossed him a plastic bottle.

"My mother came in as a sleeper—Indiana tornado, a cover—and you ran her against Silas Kingston? Why? He was a nobody. A raw recruit. Might easily have amounted to nothing. A total waste of all her training."

"They ran her against James Angleton. Only, he didn't take the bait. Like you say—a waste. KGB Directorate S let me have her for Kalaydoskop."

"And Doris ran him for you?"

Kolya rubbed his forehead. Like something hurt deep inside. Deeply. Gave his head a bitter shake. "She refused us both."

Michael offered nothing.

"Pell and Glatisant—that was hers. KALEIDOSCOPE money. A vast fortune, I'm told. What I could do with that... Silas gave it all to her." Shrugged. Poured himself a brandy. "No idea what she planned for it and Silas told me he didn't care."

"Makes two of us. Is he still working for you?"

"He and Angleton never *thought* he was." Kolya chuckled to himself. "Yet his KALEIDOSCOPE has been in check ever since they believed him *tripled*. We're opponents. And while the system each of us would like to see for the world is in total opposition, that system stands apart from both our services. Each which has its own kind of evil neither of us supports."

"Your system's worse."

"Mikhail: the alternative to both is worse. That's for another conversation. But for that, it seems if things were only blood between us, we could grow fond of each other."

He nodded Michael after him. Through double interior doors—a dining room. Nowhere else to go, no place he had to be except where he had chosen to come—

Clear-eyed and unassailable—right, Lynn?

Kolya opened his hand. Gestured at a folder on the table. Official writing—classification, warning and a name, ПЕПЕЛЬНЫЙ ВЕНЕЦ, "Ash" or "Cinder" Crown—painstakingly created by hand, splendid in artistry, disturbingly devotional. Beautiful, the way a trap is. Waxed thread. Brass prongs. No halftone rosettes, no drum ghosting. Dry, archival, paste and paper; vaguely monastery medieval but for one detail. Slashed in red grease pencil, simple, angry graffiti defacement: three bold crowns.

"Hope you got an 'A.'"

Annoyed/ignored. "This is CINDER CROWN. Silas's operational intent to remove my piece from this board. Look."

Like the first page in an ancient history or fantastical novel, a painstakingly drawn battle map of the Iraq-Iran borderlands. Ink incursion arrows. Pencil hatch unit designations. Force tallies. Thin watercolor wash for rivers. Calligraphied mountains.

The paperboy.

The typist.

The obsessionist.

Pages lifting and settling under Kolya's hand, each sheet making a different picture from the same parts. Corner-mounted photographs of highways, towns, defenses, oil infrastructure. Ignition points.

And the little crowns in red.

"A KALEIDOSCOPE backed and trained insurgency. To take place in twelve to twenty-four hours. Your father trains the actors. Chooses Iranian ground. He scripts insurrection—little burns at Ahvaz, Abadan, Bushehr—so the harm reads indigenous. In Tehran another unit, infiltrated in over months, quietly bridging with students naïve and hopeless ready to flood the streets in protests. The ignition point flashes. The ayatollahs shout. Moscow—good ally that we are—rages, denounces, supports, and we are tugged off this floor and into the quarrel."

Michael chugged from his water bottle. "It's bound to fail. An exercise in mass suicide."

"Not something your father's KALEIDOSCOPE cares about. He refers to it as sacrificial ignition."

"Plain English?"

"If CINDER CROWN reads as uprising, Kalaydoskop leaves Baku. If it reads as Langley, we stay. That is the point."

He rolled the next page. Abadan–Kharg flow sketched like veins; Ahvaz ringed once; Bushehr underlined. A compressor block pared to bone. A penciled timing ladder, simple and exact. Handwork on the table; control in the words. The ink had already passed sentence; the page, set and quiet, knew the verdict before any man opened his mouth.

Michael swigged the last of his water. Spun the plastic bottle on the table. It wobbled to quiet. No bargains with the man who would have cut him and dosed her. "Bravo. And don't think that I care—because I don't."

"You should. This is the reason why I brought you here. You will denounce CINDER CROWN and Silas

Kingston, publicly, as former officer of the CIA and as his son."

"No chance, old man."

Grins that hardly-a-grin of his. Mocked. "But Mikhail, be reasonable. I've already booked one of the Conference's media rooms."

"Put on a puppet show for all I care. I won't do it. I told you right through the door, I'm finished. The uniform doesn't fit and the name Kingston isn't for sale."

Hands gathering his work. "Then why did you come?"

Michael watched Kolya, his grandfather, the progenitor betrayer of their blood, watching him. The way the lion watches the waterhole. Lazy tail twitching at flies and hitting them. Michael knew there was a better lesson—how to spare instead of smite—but this was not the hour for it.

"Unlike my father, I'm willing to pay in person for the privilege of rejecting you. With my life."

Halfway through that, about at the word *privilege*, Kolya pulled his cell phone. Attended to it, tapping away, and now he spoke without even a glance at his grandson.

"That's not how the irrevocable trust works."

Found what he wanted on his phone. Smiled, like an old man proud of himself for mastering a mysterious technology. Caromed the device off the empty water bottle across the table to Michael. He let the circle run.

When it stopped spinning, Michael understood what Kolya meant. The display showed live video.

A view from the black dome, the red-light eye:

Lynn Kingston, huddled in a blanket. A light directed into her face shrouded the rest of her makeshift cell in darkness. Her female minder held the sides of Lynn's head between her two palms, forcing her face to camera.

2.

THE MIDNIGHT AFTER CHRISTMAS, "Smith"—whose given name was James "Jamie" Dowse—the Foreign and Commonwealth mid-level (and static at that) political officer at the British Embassy in D.C., that bitter fellow who'd collected the grubby Pret-a-Manger sack from Fergus Lott at the Washington, D.C. Ellipse—day-and-a-half earlier—peeled the cling film from his wife's heirloom Johnson Christmas china. Somewhere beneath the congealed gravy and cold turkey, the parsnips gone squooshy, "Genuine Hand Engraving" candles glowed bright on a mantlepiece above a crackling fire, big-bowed presents forever waited their unwrapping, and the stout little Christmas tree smiled with garlands and cartoon angels. All Dowse could muster was a sour, "A fine Christmas," and reflected upon why it most certainly was anything but.

Yesterday, seated for the traditional Ambassador's Christmas Luncheon, having gone through the patriotic, sentimental, and the comic toasts over smoked salmon with small frisée salad, a subtle aide materialized like a Christmas spirit—*poof*—at the far end of the formal table. Whispered into the Secret Intelligence Service Head of Station's hair-fuzzed ear. He nodded...nodded—nodded her away. Retrieved his cellular device and tapped out a message. Dowse's attention went with everyone else to the gleaming silver trolley rolled in by the head chef in immaculate whites and *toque blanche*, the Ambassador doing first slice of the beef Wellington, when Dowse's phone vibrated in his breast pocket. Read the text. Lifted a look of surprise to the HOS. Received a broadly mouthed, "Right. Now."

Before his beef arrived, Dowse was in overcoat and grumbling, climbing inside a taxi that, through the snow and slush, brought him to a cold, wet wooden bench at the Ellipse.

"I'm Smith. You have something for me?"

Smith envelops Fergus's Pret-a-Manger bag with his coat. Recoils at the whiskey reek. "Better be bloody worth it."

"Queen'll bloody think it is."

A grubby old book of King Arthur fairy tales and a thumb drive. No doubt *just* what Her Majesty's waiting for under her tree.

Where they dig up these damn drunks...?

Traffic a bloody nightmare, by the time Dowse returned to the embassy only a skeleton staff remained.

"I'm a diplomat," Dowse told his empty section. "Not an SIS errand boy." Dealt with the log. The busy all-knowing/utter-lifeless computer acknowledged him.

FK/EMB/2012-12-24/FR-01
Ellipse, Washington D.C. / 1310L
Political officer James "Jamie" Dowse ("Smith") received

package from field contact.
Logged to Political Section pending verification.[FELL KING]

Spirits dim, stomach hollow, Dowse trudged, damp of shoes, shoulders, spirit to the kitchen. A plate under foil waited for him in the staff meal room. Beef deader than Wellington in his armchair at Walmer Castle. That and a pitcher of ice water.

"A fine Christmas," he said to the cold beef. Choked it down. Clambered the stairs to the HOS's suite. The "Night Manager" sorrier for himself than Dowse, didn't have specific instructions for the sandwich-bagged Lott material; it was to go out in the diplomatic pouch to Vauxhall. Dowse knew the rumors about "Old Sot Lott." More Don Quixote than King Arthur—year-after-every-so-often showing up to chase Cold War phantoms somewhere down in the Maryland swampland. SIS hadn't had the time for its useless man today and Dowse wasn't about to let Fergus Lott waste any more of his holiday.

Rode the lift to the basement. Soft footfalls along corridors, hollow and silent; chemist emporium tinsel already slipping from its strips of tape. Dowse ID'd into the safe-room for the diplomatic pouch. The courier for the evening had been released home "on-call." Dowse spun the combination, stuffed the Pret bag in the safe like leftovers into the fridge. He wrote to the ledger half-heartedly.

FK/EMB/2012-12-25/SAFE-01
Item secured in Embassy diplomatic safe. (Political Section
Control).

Status: Held pending courier consolidation (holiday staffing). Officer: James "Jamie" Dowse (Political). Next: Bag 25 Dec / night dispatch.

Clicked the door shut.

👑👑👑

THE KIDS AND MARY—literally a bride who'd been late to her own wedding (not cold feet, not his Mary, but a busted zipper no one was allowed to mention. Ever)—had spent Christmas Eve day last-minute shopping at Tysons Corner Center; ate their supper early at Seasons 52. He'd have liked not missing that. Home, the one night of the year the little ones anxioused to bed early, Mary, as was her tradition, viewed reruns of the Queen's Christmas Broadcast on YouTube through the telly, sipped port and ate tinned butter biscuits, Dowse trudged into their walk-in closet—folding card table, shears, paper, ribbon, and tape—and did his "fair share" (unfair because it was every last gift including his own) of the wrapping. Yet, by the time he went to bed, knuckles scissors-sore, he'd practically forgotten the wretchedness of his day. Snow drifted the windows, icicles formed, he drifted to sleep.

Eyes popped wide— "Daddy! Come quick: it's Christmas!"

Midday. Paper crowns askew; the children ignoring new toys and building a fort out of cardboard and ribbon and asking if they could throw it in the fire when they were finished. He said "yes" because on Christmas it was Mary's job—always—to say "no," and Dowse drowsed in his fat chair moving only enough to keep his holly-etched port sipper filled with fortified wine. The turkey smelled like London in his mother's kitchen and all was right with the world. BBC played *Call the Midwife* and *Wallace & Gromit* specials and the stereo competed with the shrill voices of boys now men long-gone in Christmas choirs cut into vinyl forever and treasured by Mary as if she'd known and hugged them all.

Dowse's phone thrummed.

Mary found it face-down under a napkin among strewn cake crumbs and the colored foil and little cardboard strips from their morning crackers faintly smelling of matchheads. Mary read the screen: *Counsellor (Political)*. Mouthed a "sorry," handing it over.

Dowse frowned. Clicked the line active. "Dowse."

The Head of Station was not one to yell. He ground words in his teeth like peanut shells before spitting them out. "Where? Is? It?!"

"In the safe."

"*Why* is it in the safe." Not interrog- but accusatory.

"Because it's Christmas Day and the courier's off rota. If you had special handling instructions, I did pop in at your office—"

"London wants it out. Today. Next available uplift. You will carry it to the handover and you will confirm. Understood?"

The line went dead. Dowse set down the phone. He did not rise. Poured another measure of port. The children squealed; bombarded their box castle with wrapping paper wads like trebuchet stones. His boy, David, "missed" landing one in the fireplace. He and little Petra cheered. Dowse stared at the flames consuming the wrapping paper. "I am a diplomat." He sipped. Wadded and threw his own paper catapult ball into the fire. Watched it burn black to gray to ash. "Not an errand boy."

Let the clock run while, in the magical digital ether never programmed for Christmas, a log entry was born.

FK/EMB/2012-12-25/TASK-HOS-01
Directive: HOS WASHINGTON to Political Officer (Dowse) —
prepare item for 25 Dec dispatch.
Priority: EXEC (FELL KING). Confirm courier handover. Report manifest number.
Planned uplift: BA 15:30L (diplomatic secure rotation), subject to officer handover timing.

♛ ♛ ♛

PAST TWO O'CLOCK, he finally went in. The corridor smelled of burnt cinnamon rolls. Or Christmas scented mop-water. Dowse couldn't pin it. He signed the ledger. Removed the Pret bag. Swapped it to a MOD-sealed pouch. The stamp landed with a wet thump.

FK/EMB/2012-12-25/PREP-DB01
Political Officer (Dowse) transferred contents to MOD diplomatic pouch.
Seal: MOD/1225/2138 applied; contents inventoried.
Status: Ready for courier dispatch (IAD). (FELL KING)

Cinnamon *pretzels* (he'd seen a Wetzel's wrapper).

Too rushed, too-dull a razor, the courier was all red-dotted cheek and jaw, a blue blazer jacket, cat-shed white and in need of a sticky roller, and a lanyard with his various cards and photos and pass-through barcodes—a royal flush to getting him through Dulles and into the *To Fly. To Serve*. British Airways skies.

Seal verified; manifest signed.

Dowse watched the young man lock it to his sleeve cable. Said, "I'll drive."

"Kind of you, sir. But I've got this." A wink. "Be a'nice surprise from my mum."

"Delightful." Key fetched from his pocket. "Orders say I watch you board."

"I'm sorry, sir. Christmas an' all. We hurry, there's a three-thirty flight I'll just make. Get yourself home before flaming pudding."

Dowse looked at the clock and did not move. He watched the minute hand like a water wheel catching and letting go, the grind of it steady, indifferent. "A fine Christmas," he said again, but did not go. There was some business fetching his overcoat. Warming his car.

Dulles. And a missed flight. The 15:30 uplift slipped because a diplomat *isn't* an errand boy and Dowse stood in the bright terminal hush and watched the paperwork decide the hour.

FK/EMB/2012-12-25/ATT-1530

Attempted uplift: BA 15:30L — **DECLINED (officer unavailable / delayed arrival).**

Action: Hold pouch for next secure rotation.

Neither of the next two BA flights equipped with a certified diplomatic safe, Dowse watched his courier board the overnight. Stopped back at the embassy and logged it with a "So there!"

FK/EMB/2012-12-25/HAND-01
Embassy Political Officer (Dowse) → Diplomatic Courier
Time: 2259L. Seal verified; manifest EB/DC-1225-N issued.
Flight: BA 23:45L (diplomatic secure). (FELL KING)

After midnight, Boxing Day already, FCO Political Officer assigned British Embassy, Washington, D.C. ate his cold turkey and squooshy parsnips. "Bloody bugger of a Christmas this turned out to be." The empty air took the words in stillness; and if he wasn't an errand boy then the river wasn't a river, because it took what he'd left to the clock, fetched it round the bend and let the river do the rest; Foxtail Farm downstream, time's wheel already taking his delay between its teeth, and all of them lashed to it, turning, ground to the pattern already set—and being reset—his one small hour making ash of the children's Christmas wrapping box fort a shard among shards, awaiting the Lord's light that makes of pieces a single memorial window.

♕ ♕ ♕ ♕

No matter how many times he took this ride, the razor-nicked, blue-blazered (still kitty-furred) courier—silent passenger in the unmarked MOD Mercedes Vito—felt a tightness in his chest. A small dislocation of time, almost time travel: Whitehall's grand façades given way to London's ancient back. The soot-dark walls of the last narrow lane pressed in as the van threaded the service alleys behind ministries that have managed affairs of state since... well, since England. A final jolt. Slushed grit under salt-rimed tires. Flaking gates. Corrugated roofing. Yellow floodlights burning at noon.

A corporal, beret and parka, checked the pouch against the manifest. Indifferent as the carousel man taking tickets; his Tweedle Dum bent over a thick ledger. Biro scratched D-23 into permanence.

The courier's breath fogged ahead of his steps along the cold corridor between tight walls; a chain swung, clinked as the MOD seal came down, wet red wax already darkening.

FK/MOD/2012-12-26/EXH-01
Embassy Diplomatic Courier → MOD Diplomatic Bag Service
Whitehall Service Yard / 1330Z
MOD seal re-affixed; chain entry D-23 ledger. (FELL KING)

The embassy courier logged next.

FK/MOD/2012-12-26/LOG-OUT-01
Embassy Diplomatic Courier (Dowse handoff, Dulles 25 Dec)
delivered pouch to MOD Exchange.
Seal verified, chain of custody closed at Whitehall Service Yard
1332Z.
Courier released from duty. (Note: personal leave — Boxing
Day tea, family residence, Surrey.)

Went off the clock and out of the stream. Unclipped the security cable beneath his shirt. Snaked it out his sleeve. Rubbed the mark it left and left the cable on the counter. "Off to Mum's," he went to find the driver assigned him.

   Another corporal—beret/parka combo—applied the fresh MOD seal.

♛♛♛

THE POUCH, arguably safer now then it yet had been, security amped up. Two officers in stab vests and sidearms under their coats, entered and took receipt of the pouch. Returned outside. Walked it with one of the corporals, to their up-armored/grimed-up unmarked van. The officer with a clipboard climbed in beside the Thames House driver. His partner, cradling a folding stock Heckler & Koch neat under a blanket, hopped into the open back. *Torero*'d the blanket onto the cold metal seat of the cage. Lapped his HK. Received the diplomatic pouch from the corporal. Signed. Locked inside.

FK/MOD/2012-12-26/LOG-IN-02
Custody transferred to MOD/MI5 Secure Escort Team (2 officers, armed).
Escort ID: MOD/SEC-TH-12
Vehicle: unmarked Vauxhill Vivaro (secure compartment).
Route: Whitehall Service Yard → Thames House, Millbank.
Departure: 1345Z

The van passed through the Millbank gates, past tourists who didn't notice/didn't care. Three barriers. Two code checks: palm and passphrase. Down into the basement. White walls. Whiter lights. Stainproof gray carpet. Black cameras/red eyes. Intake Room. The Thames House officers placed the pouch on the steel table, empty and waiting; two more officers stood witness. Robots speak more than this crew.

Wax cracked.

Book and the thumb drive flat in the glow of controlled light. Individually acknowledged. Clipboard signatures. Armed officers out.

Book numbered/drive numbered. Book photographed/drive photographed.

The drive fed to a forensic imager; the book pressed beneath the platen of a scanner. Platen shut. The pages bloomed as data on a monitor, lines of White's prose stacked with digital tags, chapter to page, paragraph to line, word to letter.

FK/TH/2012-12-26/INT-01
Intake completed under two-person rule, CCTV recorded.
EVID-2012-TH-001: Thumb drive (~8pp. cipher images) —
imaged, hash created.
EVID-2012-TH-002: The Once and Future King (Collins, London 1958, 1st UK ed.) — imaged, corpus indexed.
Physical items sealed post-process.
Digital deliverables packaged for secure transfer to GCHQ
Benhall, Cheltenham — node (legacy supercluster) — EXECUTIVE DECRYPTION TASK [FELL KING]".

♔ ♔ ♔

HITS OAKLEY instantaneous. Corpus ID blinked green; the cipher hash lined up on screen. The operator—in place; waiting the last two hours—moved her cold tea from her workspace. Made her log entry.

FK/GCHQ/2012-12-26/BC-INIT-01
Corpus: EVID-2012-TH-002_CORPUS (T.H. White, Collins 1958).
Input: EVID-2012-TH-001_HASH (cipher images).
Task queued 1607Z — EXEC decryption, runtime 72h.

Took a breath and did a strange trick with her hands—no one watching, only herself—she snapped every finger of both hands against her thumbs, perfectly and all at once: ten distinct snaps like a drum roll.

Hit *RUN*.

The fans spun up, and the room filled with a sound like rain made by machines. Screens rolled their greens along a far wall; rack lights stitched a slow seam of amber and blue. Air-conditioning pushed a clean, metallic cold across the racks; telemetry rose in thin commas on the big board. The corpus ID locked green, the cipher hash throbbed once and went flat. In the reflection of the glass you could count them—three rows of black boxes, a red ABORT bar under plexi. Beyond the glass two other pods glowed, operators small inside their hoods, and the clocks above—LON, ZULU, CHELT—kept three different versions of the same hour.

The decipher run began—Wart and Merlyn, Arthur and Guinevere and Lance, the Round Table and the long argument of justice and love—all converted to coordinates and indices. The operator excerpted a fragment and flagged the sheet as numeric-only cipher text in three- and four-number groups; she logged the example as a note to self, not a crib, and sent it on.

14 : 7 : 3 / 19 : 2 : 11 / 6 : 4 : 22
(Marked IND-UNDECIPHERABLE; forwarded to Oakley Supercluster — EXECUTIVE DECRYPTION TASK [FELL KING])
OAKLEY::TASK NEW --name=BC-KALEID-2012-12-26-INIT
--priority=EXEC
OAKLEY::SET CORPUS --id=TWHITE-UK-1958
--mode=BOOK_KEY
OAKLEY::LOAD
EVID-2012-TH-001_HASH,EVID-2012-TH-002_CORPUS
--channel=THAMES_INTAKE
OAKLEY::NOTE "Suspected book-cipher (numeric triplets).
No reliable crib confirmed."
OAKLEY::DETECT_FORMAT --modes=triplet,quad --index=(chap:page:para:word,chap:page:line:word)
OAKLEY::WINDOW SCAN --chapters=ALL --pages=ALL
--paragraphs=ALL --words=ALL --stride=1
OAKLEY::HEURISTICS
--enable=bigram,articleFREQ,punct-align
--boost=the,and,of
OAKLEY::KEYSPACE REDUCE --normalize=indexes --offset-sweep=±5
OAKLEY::RUN --max_runtime=72h --telemetry=BC-KALEID-INIT

And the cold rain of technology kept falling as it would now, without her or anyone, so long as the power held and the job stayed in the queue.

♛ ♛ ♛

THREE LEVELS down from the glass façade on the Thames, Vauxhall Cross shed its shine. The conference room was narrow, windowless. Furnished with cast-offs: a table scored by decades of staplers, chairs with upholstery gone slack, the faint reek of outlawed tobacco in the carpet. Light came from recessed panels, yellow and airless. No plaque on the door. In screw holes and faded squares, the wall showed ghosts of every unit's crest from every floor; so many fingerprints that none of the departments could ever be forced to claim it. A borrowed room. Used by whoever needed it. The kind of extra space where nothing had a header and nothing gathered minutes, and what was said belonged only to the men and women who carried it back out, planning to forget it as soon as its business was over.

Ned Trewyn, the Service's senior man on FELL KING, was a legacy bureaucrat. Not a field spook. Welsh—in all the right ways—he stood tall but stooped as if always listening for the punchline. Odd, because his wasn't a particularly funny business. In his late fifties, longish dark hair that didn't know the top of his head was shiny bald, big black glasses, he carried for the last fifteen of his years the title of Counsellor (Political) on paper and the weight of SIS Section Head in practice. With quiet pride, he represented institutional continuity balanced against the Queen's will through the service. By rights (according to him) and seniority (according to the ladder), he should by now have been comfortably ensconced in directorate leadership. He was not. He smiled, but it wasn't fair and he couldn't help it. The smile was a tic his mother had trained him into.

"Smile, Ned. Be a good boy: show teeth."

She was a camera bug from the days when cameras were a thing and film was a commitment. By the end of his life, Cary Grant had fewer photographs then Ned Trewyn had by the age of six—most of them taken (and developed—she was very good in a darkroom) by his mother.

"Ned: I am taking your photograph—smile, now! Show teeth like a good boy!"

Anything could trigger it—often nothing at all: the lips pulling back, the unctuous show of teeth for no reason. Like a compulsive nose-picker, he repulsed people and couldn't stop; trying only made it stranger. Years of that rehearsed grin had calcified into a streak of meanness in him, like a man who takes his biting dog to the children's park on purpose.

He was perfect for FELL KING. Out of cruelty he'd kept Fergus Lott after it for decades. And now his torture of that man had miraculously borne fruit, and he smiled at Silas Kingston in his Crown-faithed heart.

Captain Hollis, SAS Troop Commander, was younger. Extraordinarily competent in the field but fit as easily the administrative mufti he wore when reporting to Trewyn. It didn't disguise, not really; he had one of those heads they line up on bust plinths in museums—just the thick hair and the face—that you know without needing to see, below the neck there's a Roman Emperor or a proud war's general's kit with the medals and ribbons and the gun on the hip. His face had that same glossy sheen of polished stone and his eyes were just as dead as rock.

"We'll have this cipher unlocked," Trewyn said, the smile showing. "And the history to follow suit: Kingston with Moscow, formally and forever."

Hollis brought the update: Clive Lancer's drawn and dictated maps had been turned into plaster and ply-board. Foxtail Farm mocked to scale in a Hereford kill house. Hollis's SAS troop ran rehearsals every hour. Direct action. Clear-and-hold. Breaches blown, doors hammered, corners taken. All in pitch black. All NVGs and IR lasers on the rails. Drilled until the routes lived in muscle and the plywood held the paths flesh would soon be asked to take. And when the dust settled on the boards and the echo died in plywood rooms, the pattern lay there waiting, fixed already, only needing men to walk it through—FELL KING in motion before it ever reached the field.

There was a silence as the file closed. Trewyn's lips spread. Hollis shifted the folio against his knee, said, as if remarking the weather, "There are women. Children. We've worked in containment. But..."

Trewyn's expression didn't allow for the word "but."

"It will be clean. All of it."

"Foxtail will be taken as drawn. Anything left inside belongs to the drawing."

The rehearsal file was closed, stamped complete. The pattern held—Clive Lancer's drawn and dictated tour of the house rendered to plaster and plyboard, rehearsed until the routes lived in muscle and breath and firing pins. Yet the pattern was never whole. The very lack a kaleidoscope lives on. Were there one hundred mirrors inside the Foxtail Farm manor? Two hundred? Left off the map, absent from the kill house. Glass that would throw back light, split angles, mislead eyes. The plan was fixed. The pattern was drawn. And the flaw waited, quiet in reflection.

Hollis reached the door. Stopped. Glanced back. "And the one who did all the work on the map?"

"Orders already out to the other. Take-down confirmed. You'll take care of that one—Lott—upon arrival."

Hollis nodded. He would.

3.

T IME PRESSURE OF SELF-IMPOSED deadlines. That thing you need five minutes ago, wish you had yesterday, regret you didn't start hunting it two weeks back and were eating it now. Instead, you're chasing it with as much speed as you've got, hoping, but knowing it's bullshit that you'll ever catch up the time already lost. So maybe you seek that extra kick in the pants you can give yourself—might giddy-up some lost time. Might stop time itself. Give you some room between those echoing ticks and tocks. Manipulate your internal clock speed.

Some folks chain-smoke (not that smoking was allowed anywhere inside Headquarters anymore, but those who did smoke, track-starred back and forth outside to where the cloud still hovered); smarter smokers chewed their nicotine. Some charged coffee. Glugged syrupy caffeine soda pops. Some were gum snappers/mint crackers.

Morton Drexler ate.

Compulsively when on venery, the hunt not the lay, though both drove the same clock, and Lynn had blurred the dial.

Kept a bushel of cellophane wrapped "movie-style" popcorn bags inside the CIC Watch Floor Galley. A tiny SCIF-approved kitchenette tucked off the floor: beige laminate, a badge-locked pantry/snack room with a dorm fridge, TEMPEST-stickered microwave, drip pots, and a hand-lettered sign: "CLEAN YOUR MUG / NO DEVICES / NO POPCORN FOR YOU."

The parmesan cheese he rained over his popped corn he kept in his workstation drawer. The one that pushed against his fleshy right calf and constantly reminded him he needed to requisition a desk with a larger knee cubby. True, greasy/cheesy popcorn does not technologically cooperate with computer hardware. Drexler used a workaround. A plastic half-cup measuring spoon from home. Scooped popcorn, dumped it into his mouth. Washed down with beet juice. Blended/also brought from home.

Known fact: beet juice reduces blood pressure. (Secret truth: Drexler thought beets tasted remarkably good in tandem with powdered parmesan).

Popcorn spoonfuls shoveled like locomotive coal; oil-free keyboard clattering like freight cars over rails; little red dribbles, backhand-wiped from the corners of his mouth—cylinder condensation: Drexler ran down the Rock Creek Tennis Club Holiday Calendar. One copy, the "gift" from the Azerbaijan embassy; the other: independently acquired from the marketing and promotions office of the club itself. Pages strewn across his desk and credenza, so much skin discarded after the sweet meat—the photos—he'd fed into his workstation. Both identical. Same crop, same ink noise, same printer microdot. Meant the Azeris were an unwitting end-user. Recipient, not source.

Three hours just to get to that point.

Were he to have walked it into the Office of Technical Service they'd be done by now: metadata, compression and container analysis, ELA/splice/clone detection; instead of chowing parmesan popcorn, he'd already be reading the report that would tell him everything he needed to know about how the calendar was constructed, origin source for the photographs, how and with what capability the Lynn photo was composited. And those methods, the sequence of application—all the forensics added together—most likely would create a fingerprint from a finger pointing directly at a known adversary. Problem for Drexler: if that fingerprint belonged to Silas, it would mean the calendar came out of the office he'd tasked with the job. They'd know in a matter of minutes, a call would go to OTRAC, and life would go bad. Quick as a hog cut.

Drexler settled on the fact he didn't need to prove who inside OTS pressed the keys or the full chain of custody. Just that this composite wasn't civilian and didn't come out of Baku—or Moscow. He had that now. Amazing what open-source plug-ins can do with Adobe Photoshop. After four more hours and three popcorn bowls, and a run-out of beet juice/switch to water, this is what he knew: EXIF scrubbed. No camera, no lens, no maker notes. No ghost thumb. Compression seamless—no splice blocks where a paste-up should live. Noise floor leveled; PRNU uniform. Shadows right, highlights right. Too right.

And her face.

Just as he'd imagined her in his room.

Lynn Kingston young. Too young.

He burrowed the internet and worried out a set of Pancras Hall yearbooks. Found her. Same jaw, same chin, same wide eyes. The anomaly sat there, waiting. Her face, young again. Not the career officer in the file photos or snapped in surveillance. Not the woman the Azeris had in their cell. The girl at fourteen. A true smile, stitched into April like time could be rewound.

And the racquet. Just as he called it: badminton dressed as tennis. Wrong head, wrong grip, shuttle scuff still on the strings.

And these two elements combined did the rest. The Azeris burned her—yes—but the object they burned her with wasn't theirs, and it didn't read Russian. If Moscow made Layla as Lynn, they wouldn't need a boutique club calendar: they'd pass a quiet liaison tip for immediate detention or push raw surveillance stills—fast, ugly, attributable. This thing was too clean. Built to slip past off-the-shelf detectors. Read as in-house avoidance, not FSB flourish. Whoever built the forgery hadn't pulled from the open world. They'd gone home. Into the chain that held Lynn's past. Kingston-adjacent, if not Kingston-made.

It was enough for the trudge upstairs. And he didn't need to prove "why" not yet; he just needed to collapse the "who" to the only circle that fit. Silas and the kaleidoscope he turned.

※ ※ ※

FRAGMENTS of colored glass filled a crystal cylinder on the corner of an empty desk, battleship gray and ugly. Every other inch of Lynn Kingston's office—doorway-adjacent to DDO Gravin's suite—glowed with a shade of white Drexler knew he'd never encountered before. Neither warm nor cold. Neither soothing nor sterile; he found in its starkness an uncomfortable evocation of what he imagined was the light beyond life. The lighting—unnaturally bright; movie-set shadowless light—cast prismatic rainbows from inside the glass sleeve. He turned the vase. The colors moved around the room.

Ineluctable. Bright.

Two thoughts hit simultaneously: as much as he knew what he was looking at (his chest clenched, mind acutely aware of the manufactured warm air drawn through his nostrils, ballooning his lungs), Lynn had built it; these multi-colored shards were collected: they were not a decorator's device. And yet, with the same thunderous conviction he knew he stood inside a kaleidoscope, he understood Lynn lived fully blind to what her imagination screamed at her inside this institutional cell. Hidden from his active mind, though profound in its alteration to his psyche, Morton Drexler never could possibly know/have known Lynn Kingston because Lynn Kingston had only the most facile concept of herself.

Because the thought was buried in his subconscious, because that unsettled him, he focused on the bits of glass. There was every color Drexler could imagine; some shades he couldn't recall seeing anywhere other than in stained-glass windows of magnificent churches and wondered where she'd found it all.

He hesitated to sit. He was only in her office because, arriving precisely on time to Deputy Director Gravin's

suite at 8:15 pm for the thirty minutes Gravin had granted him, Gravin's Executive Assistant informed him Gary
would be delayed—"Syria, you know. No more than ten
minutes." He opened the connecting door. "He suggest-
ed you wait in Ms. Kingston's office. He'll be any minute,"
and could he get Drexler anything?

Each shard was sand-smoothed to pebble shapes
and muted/opaque as beach glass without the clarifying
wash of water.

After Iraq. After al Qaeda. The situation blowing up
in Syria, blowing up and down the Langley corridors,
blowing up international stability in every way shape
and form—he was glad to be in counterintelligence.
Glad his job looked inward.

He heard Gary's voice faintly through the door.
Turned expectantly. Heard him laugh. Speak and laugh
again.

Maybe it was the white light of the room, or the hyp-
notic spray of the beach glass, or his sensation of un-
accustomed/unusual feelings for Lynn that unbalanced
him so, but Gary's laugh struck a deep chord inside
Morton Drexler. A memory flashed, fully formed, filled
with time and timelessness from his core. Instantaneous
and gone.

*Earliest memories. Vague from first bed. In through
the corner window—"Fresh air, cowboy; best way to
sleep"—in through the never-new black screen. I'm
three, four; hear it, hide from it. Clearly known/antic-
ipated/frightened by five.*

*The cackling laughter. Always before the sun.
Always before Mama wakes. Sis'. A screeching
haw-haw/shrieking laughter from beyond the magnolia*

and its swing. Past the fence. From the hollow and the oil-still dark-pictured reedy pond where the palms rustle with rats and the ducks and geese never leave. Morning chatter like evil laughter and I'm convinced it's aimed at me.

"Morty, honey, they're birds. They don't know how to laugh. What's funny—? They just do that waking up."

"Can we close my window?"

"No. You need the fresh air. Get over it."

But I never do. Long after the age when I know Mama's right.

The sinking feeling the waterfowl know something about me I don't and never will.

But become.

"Sorry, Drexler. For the wait." Gravin pushed inside. Headset still pressing a crease across his crown. Shirt loose and wrinkled. Pressed jacket, hangered all day, thrown over it. Tie askew. The all-day Ops Center live event tightness around his eyes, sheen on his face. "Syria's shaping up. For once, a plan I don't have to apologize for."

Silas warned Drexler. Angleton before Silas. Truman before them both: the Agency diverted from its original assignment. Ops over intel. Spook remade as soldier. Soldier remade as policymaker. Each step another trespass, another wink and a nod, and dead drops become battlefield bodies dropping dead.

Yet he focused. Bore right in on Drexler with a half-knowing/half-expectant smile. Gary Gravin, genuine.

"I received your packet. I'm deep on the other, so I didn't get much of a look— Didn't want you waiting. The

Lynn calendar. Been suspect since the whole embassy mix-up started. Go: give me what you got."

Tone of command. Control.

Let him carry this.

Tone of a man he could trust to go the distance on this, and Drexler's relief came sudden and disorienting. Gravin gestured him into one of Lynn's white chairs. Took the other. Gripped the armrests and leaned in.

Drexler caught the smile, and the smile caught him. Something off. Something knowing. Like the DDO saw the Lynn he carried inside him. Pathetic longing. Angry lust and indecent guilt. He'd never known love; never met nobility. But Drexler staring into the hole inside him, walking its edges peering down: he knew their shape from their total absence. Gravin's grin carried neither quality.

All he said was, "Right." Because he knew something now was wrong. Red-faced. Forthright. Drexler laid it out. Calendar wasn't Baku. Wasn't Moscow. Calendar wasn't civilian paste-up and gave the "why" for that. Whole job too clean. PRNU too even, the face pulled from Lynn at fourteen, the "tennis" racquet a badminton head; whoever built that reached into Lynn's past. "And you know what that implies, sir."

A twitch that belonged to a second that Gravin hadn't given to his wife, given over to greater opportunity in the Ops Center, made him appear older. Made him look like he'd glanced at himself and didn't like what he saw. But Gary Gravin had a career. Had a wife and massive responsibility. And he had a style he could hide with a wry twinkle in his eye.

"Congratulations, Drexler. Truly. What you sent tracks with what we—and I mean the tight little circle of me and the Director—suspected. You've taken a stray wire we noticed sparking and you've grounded it. And your concern—admirable—goes to my officer. It's the Silas of it all. Not good. To prove anything, you'd tip it back to KALEIDOSCOPE and you of all people know how that ends up."

"Obviously, sir, KALEIDOSCOPE has all kinds of unchecked power, but to sacrifice one of our own—can't we agree that's too far?" Half-second. No response. Plunged on. "A move by us, me—I'd insist, on that—internally, might, in discovering and eliminating the leverage Silas Kingston created in burning his own daughter, could provide any number of new angles you can explore with the Azerbaijani's that could affect Lynn's release. In fact, I'm sure of it."

Gary Gravin leaned back. "What I will take away from this, tonight: is you, Morton. Nice to see this—" a hand to describe nothing in the air— "in you. I know you've never cared a bit for Lynn Kingston. And face it, she thinks you're less than dirt." He opened his palms, held them there between them, a birthday magician's show: nothing up his sleeves; nothing to give.

"Of course, it's not about 'release' anymore."

"What's that supposed to mean?" Drexler gruffed.

"Yes. Well. They brought in a tribunal. Couple days ago. Tried—convicted her. Past negotiation. Lynn's been sentenced."

"Espionage."

"That's right."

"That's death?"

Gravin sighed. Drexler felt the air weak on his face. His own blood pumped with heavier force.

Gravin: "How this played out. Right from the get-go—us/them face-to-face: it wasn't my call. And this is what's going to kill it for you: Harker gave Silas the lead."

Drexler knew the hedge was coming, the one Gravin was about to pass a buck through. "To protect the building, Lynn's situation has been accepted institutionally. It's—" Groped between the twigs and branches for counterfeit coins to offer back. Came up empty. "It wasn't unanticipated."

"Why didn't you stop it?"

You who loved her.

A hog in Sunday shoes.

"They did offer alternatives. I'd have taken them. Silas didn't bargain. He pressed. Pushed the execution forward. And Lynn..." A glance at the vase. Ineluctable. Bright. A roll of the eyes. "She accepted it."

No hand reached; no one to catch her.

Silence. Drexler noticed small flecks of color from the glass like fingertips of light upon his sleeve.

"You remember Russell Aiken, General Counsel's Office."

"We crossed paths. Why?"

Gravin reached into his jacket. A folded sheet of printer paper. "Different line of attack, but he tried the same thing you're trying. She had him advise her in the, you know, legal proceedings. I'm not speaking out of turn when I say, me, Harker, Silas, none of us liked that arrogant prick, but no one would ever argue he wasn't the best at what he did. Went to Baku with an appeal.

Couldn't get the job done. Best he could do—" Gravin handed over the document. "Yesterday's Post. We traced it back to him. He didn't deny it."

Drexler scanned the page.

Ex-CIA official alleges deadly incident and detention of U.S. operative...

"Last ditch. Court of public opinion. Didn't play. Not a peep." He stood. Reached for the outer door. Waited for Drexler to rise at the "time's up" signal. "Lynn doesn't deserve this. And it's out of my hands. But you got an angle. A good one. I'm Ops, but you're CI. There's always the Director." Door opened. Stepped aside the way you shoo a cat. "Maybe you'll get further with Harker than Aiken got with the media."

The door latched; electronic click. Drexler stood in the bland, unmarked hallway. From inside, faint, Gravin's laugh lifted one more time.

The hush again. The ducks, the geese, the pond.

Drexler carried his weight to the elevator bank. Still held the print-out of the article open in his hand like any moment he'd lift it, read it, find the secret. But it wasn't a secret: no one cared.

He had thrown rocks, once. Small boy rage. Wanted them dead. Faked stomachache to get out of church. Rocks collected; loose in overall pockets.

Arm cocked. Wrist grabbed. Neck grabbed. Daddy behind, wide as a horse. Expected the white leather belt, wide as a saddle cinch.

Rock shook free. Oats jammed into his palm. "Feed 'em."

Hissing bills. Pinched skin. Snatched groats. The boy stock still.

He always wished he'd turned.

Daddy: Angry? Grinning?

The next day was Monday. His daddy went back to work at the Spindletop sulfur mine. Drexler didn't remember any details of the day; didn't know he was supposed to; hoped they'd maybe feed the ducks again. The laughter-geese. Later. But that didn't happen. That was the day his daddy didn't come home from work.

No accident.

Not dead.

Nothing. Just never came home again.

And Drexler's reflection met him in the closing elevator door.

👑👑👑

FOUR HOURS LATER, Gravin closed the last secure VTC with CENTCOM and State. The Near East desk's final cable signed. Ops Center calls put to bed; Syria's fire and ash, blood and misery reduced for the night to talking points stacked on his desk for the morning deputies' meeting. Under the folio, a glossy "ISR augmentation" deck someone from Raytheon/SAIC had slipped in for a look-see; he'd stopped bothering to ask how the MIC got their sales pitch packets all the way up to the seventh floor where at that point his edict for the directorate—"My eyes see everything"—ensured they'd land on his desk. "They're a complex 'industrial complex,' Deputy Director, sir," Evan, his EA would grin.

From beneath the brochure, a loose red cover sheet glared at him. Gravin slid Drexler's CI write-up from beneath it.

*Operation: Borden Saint. Subject: Rock Creek Tennis Club (RCTC) – Calendar Image Composite; CI Foren-*sics. He pondered the whole of it without lifting the red cover sheet; the manila jacket showed a thin red stripe down the tab. He tapped the base of his pen on the red SECRET stamp.

Morton Drexler and his strange rhetorical puzzle. Lizzie Borden? A Saint? Sacrifice: only way one be-comes the other and we're left with both.

The sound of his pen matched the sound of the rain pattering the cold arrow-slit windows, dark at his back.

Breathe.

Lynn, long his bright star. Dimmed in recent time. By time and bad breaks and the chaos of that whole Kingston/KALEIDOSCOPE constellation she swirled within.

Think.

He let go an accumulation of air, every breath sucked into himself that whole long day—fifteen, twenty, across each minute—each charge of air held over each com-plexity unraveled; each rapid response thrown into each swelling breach; shadow insertions kept in shadows as the predator eyes allowed no shadow for their oppo-nents. A great suspiration. Damascus: dry and clear—ex-cept where they'd turned up the heat. Had forgotten, the wet and the cold outside.

Replaced the red cover. Pen dropped onto it.

Tapped the button. Summoned Evan.

Grabbed his overcoat.

True, what he'd told Drexler: Lynn was outside of his control now. She'd picked Aiken.

The ghost who stood between us. Close as we almost got—always looking past my shoulder just in case he was coming back.

Buttoned up as his EA came through. Grabbed his stack. Moved to his safe.

Key ring.

"Called your car a few minutes ago, sir."

Tumbler turn.

"It's waiting. It's warm."

If it hadn't been Aiken, they'd have assigned someone just-like—outside the Agency...after having been Agency. And Aiken—notorious oddball—had been the best.

Even that damn article leaked to the Post. Pension risk—especially the way Harker felt about him.

Right up there with Silas Kingston.

Grabbed his leather folio. One he carried every night.

Heroic—its own pathetic way.

About to snap the clasp—a flash of red, top of the stack, last chance for Lynn disappearing into the iron dark. Bolt heavy as judgment. Door about to take it and keep it in the black silence forever.

"Wait." Gravin stepped over. Widened the mouth of his document case. "I'll be taking BORDEN SAINT with me."

Drexler has legit CI position on this thing...

"Log it?" Evan.

"Already did." Hadn't. "Just forgot I wanted it." Ineluctable.

But I have the Chair of the Senate Select Committee waiting at home.

Thursday, December Twenty-seventh

1.

I N THE EARLIEST HOURS of the morning, on the day Clive Lancer was to die, there came a moment Paige Kingston would remember, when the blind darkness blanketing them—arms wrapped, legs entwined, naked beneath bedclothes—filled her with inward illumination.

Two lights.

Joined by a third.

Fused into fire.

She pressed her forehead against Clive's neck. Stroked his chest from behind. Felt it rise, felt it fall. Listened to the steady breath they shared in the small air around them.

Smiled at the day gone by.

Clive: awkward, nervous at the doctor's office; silly jokes to disguise his discomfort.

Warmed jelly, blue, onto my belly.

Baby's heartbeat.

Image twisting. The turn/slide/angling of the wand. The freeze frame.

"There's an arm. See? Those little buds, that kind of paddle: those will be its fingers."

Fingers into hands I'll hold.

All the mother's hands that held mine; Mom, Grandma Doris. Her mother before her—in her own way holding mine—and her mother, whoever she was, and hers before that. Hand to hand to touch to touch: all the way back.

A backwards chain of overlapping generations to the unremembered, unknowable first.

Clive seemed to shrug a shoulder. Breathed. Nestled into her warmth. And it came to Paige: there in that invisibly illuminated darkness: a strange ache; a delicate tenderness; a rush of feeling. Overwhelming and incredible love that diminished every conception of love she'd ever thought she knew she had felt. Not merely love for family—her sisters, parents, aunts-cousins-Papa—for him: Clive. For their own family nestled in the now of this togetherness; Paige's love-rush was not, it felt, even a whole-her love. More. It was more. This wave was the love of/from the universe, reserved for its purest expression—life-saying-no to death.

My promise.

Our promise.

This promise.

Chained to every birth that came before, by hands held, that universe-love: a charge running through us; a demand we carry to commit that love forward so that awesome simple-clutch chain does not end with me.

Or Clive.

Or you, child.

She pressed her tummy against the small of Clive's back.

That look on Melody's face when she knew I knew: the universe gives us more than blood to bind us.

The nurse's wand shifts.

Button nose.

Wrinkle of an almost smile.

Petals—not yet eyelids.

I look at Melody. See her as if I am Melody looking at myself. I say, "Time is sadness. Did you know that?"

And she holds me.

And she tells me: "If you care for it, give it the love it needs. I think sadness can be a seed."

For appreciation.

Compassion.

Paige listened to the house. Listened to the windows. The waves of night washed against the frosted glass.

The "love it needs," what sadness needs, what time must have that it might give...

That was the promise made to life for those distant generations moving in opposite directions. Unknown. Existent only in the promise each birth makes to every birth that came before it. Unremembered, unimaginable, incredible, impossible to remark. Vanished from Earth: their breath and what they breathed it for; vanished: their heartbeats, hearts, their bones, but not their blood: life: this "now" sparked to light inside of her.

Paige Kingston's gratitude flowed to that chain of hands clasped one after another behind her—hers reaching out to their child so it might reach forward in its turn and keep that promise, the promise of something that would be theirs alive in this world at the moment of first cry, first inspiration.

Echoed back to where time long ago turned bones to dust. Dust that once wished, no—not wished—

Wind rattled the windows. Wind moaned the chimneys. She lifted her head.

Not wished: vowed.

Doris's murmur encouraged her on the light-hot breath of the Yule log that rose on smoke and Christmas cinders into the black.

Clive's sleeping hand grasped hers.

Dust: vowed to live forward on the back of the beast of time bearing purpose, the eternal aspiration of the living to know/share love.

And suddenly Paige knew.

The sad thing about time is that the love you have—the love that carried you to you from primal human swamps, through vague aspirations of insufficient lives in deserts, forests, plains, towns, cities; stumbling histories, and the remembered voices: those who poured love into you—

If I don't carry love forward, that would be the sadness: collected sadness that happens when the chain of love, passed forward through the act of giving life and launching more love blows out like a birthday candle.

The universe was all that as love. The sadness was love's gentle and forgiving warning.

The Silvanus Bench.

The machete.

The warty jack-o'lantern.

Papa's hug; Papa, don't let go. Ever, ever, ever.

"There will be a time when he comes to you and he asks you—or worse, doesn't—but you'll know. He'll

want permission. At that time, you will do something for me."

"What?"

"Tell him this—"

She whispered. "Clive, wake up."

"Eenh, what?"

Rolled to face her. Touched her cheek. "You okay?"

"What Silas wanted me to tell you—?"

"What?"

"It's time. To talk about it."

He groped. Phone. Tap-clock. "Think we need to sleep more, luv."

Tried to snuggle back into her arms. She held him off.

"Okay. What?"

His eyes touched hers; she held them fast.

"He said to tell you. When the time came. And I know as I know anything, that time's now. 'The bravest people are the ones who don't mind looking like cowards.' We need to talk."

That look of his. Less than half a grin. More than half offense. "Now that's something to wake up to—old Silas taking the piss. That's what you've been holding onto all this time?" Offense dropped. "'The bravest people should look like—' what—'cowards?'" His grin completed itself.

Unmoved and unmovable, Paige's gaze was like a knife-point on his throat.

"Come on, Paige, everything's a bleedin' game with Silas."

She didn't blink. His Adam's apple bobbed.

"Even when I think he wants to help me. Us. All I get's the feeling he's pinched my head between his thumb and finger, you know, and just clunked me onto another square."

"Wouldn't you say—Silas has had a life of being really good at this game? I think he always wins."

"He's on the opposing team."

Her hands lifted his hands. Interlaced their fingers. One hand, the other, the dark/light stitch of their fingers gave the faint appearance of a fortress wall. She said: "Your trip to London. The stuff with the Hennessy Timeless. The treatment your *partner*, that Fergus, gives you? You feel like you're an integral part of that team?"

He retreated inward, wrestling with himself. And it pained Paige because—those eyes, that sad strength, that self-battery—in truth he'd been made his own opponent. Gently: "And...?"

"Hell. I'm bloody good at puzzles. Hit me with it again."

"'The bravest people are the ones...who don't mind: looking like cowards.'"

He thought on it in one direction. Considered it in another. Hoisted it up the brain-pole, and hauled it down. "Do you know what it means?" His eyes begged. Just a little.

Paige warmed. "You just said—literally-you-just-said *you* were good at puzzles."

An impish shrug; quick kiss on her lips.

"I dunno, Clive. You want to know what I thought?"

A slow nod, a steady nod.

"All this time, I've been convinced he was giving you permission—or, what's the word—? 'Absolution' to you, you know, to murder him."

"Well, I didn't want to say it."

"And is that you being brave or cowardly?"

"Hilariously helpful, luv."

I push through hanging cords of English ivy. Twisting vines like the coils of our lives, our once past, future come. Susceptible to one swift rip-it-down and done-gone-buh'bye. Only in their tangle/twists/strangulations do they become remarkable. Powerful. Overpowering, at times, lethal in the simple brutality of gathered mass.

Like family.

"Are you going to? Kill him?"

"Me?! Love-a-Christ you know I never would."

"Not *you*-you. Are *they*?"

Push through vines to Papa. To the Silvanus Bench. The machete.

"I think they will."

"I wasn't going to care about it. He told me not to, but he told me he did do it: what your people want to kill him for. But now—?" She thumped down on her pillow. Stared where faint light now faded onto the ceiling. "I can't be part of it."

"You won't. It's beyond us. And I'll protect you. You know I will."

"But it's not beyond us anymore. It *is* us. And it's alive now: his blood, my blood, your blood. And I don't know what to tell you—tell how to do what you have to do, but you can't, and 'you' means we—so I am involved now, deep as anything, deep as you—"

"Believe me, I won't be doing the doing. I won't be anywhere near— *We* won't—"

Overlapping: "—so I can't let you do it. Because it's doing it to our child. I can't let you do it to our child: because that's doing it to yourself."

Clive silent. Eyes narrowed. He thrust out of the bed.

"Where are you going?"

She watched him into the bathroom. The scrape of wood. Clink of tile.

He emerged, Silas's old Russian codebook in his open palm. An offering.

She took it.

Russian letters in boxes. Numbers. Printed. Some in red, some black. Some green and faded. Like a little book, but no paragraph, no starts, no stops.

She clapped it shut. He lifted the fuzzed leather book between their faces.

"He gave me this for Christmas. It's an old codebook. KGB era." Flipped the dogeared pages. "This finishes him unequivocally. Protects my government from yours. Saves me with my service. All I have to do is turn it in."

"Why'd he do that—give it to you?"

"Oh, I asked."

"And?"

"All I got was another bloody riddle."

The small leather book. Incriminating before her eyes.

Turkey's Swan Song. The warty goblin with the leery flickering face.

"You did kill them. What Clive said."

Papa. Mean. "I know. You looked foolish pretending I didn't."

"His answer? 'A wife. An unborn child. It started there for me.' Seems like he was asking me not to commit treason. For us."

Wind pressed the windows. Found the chimneys again. Found Doris but not in a moan. In a whisper that drew Paige back in time.

After the fireworks store. After we've met and I swirl with luxurious fall-in-love fantasy.

Doris's porch step. Before the barbeque. Before you become real. Football spinning in the air, into my hands, into the air, and it comes to me:

Sad and beautiful darkness come to Foxtail Farm. Grandma's voice over mine: "The glorious thing about him was his eye... This sad and beautiful darkness."

Doris's book.

White's unicorn.

A virgin.

The brothers.

Comets falling through her; Paige hadn't wanted to know.

Clive's eyes on her head, her heart.

"What?"

Paige touched the codebook. Her thumb grazed the cracked spine.

"Paige: what?"

When the brothers came to the unicorn, they slaughtered it without mercy.

Her stomach tightened. The virgin lure. Unicorn. Fergus and the slaughter.

"Clive: it's perfect. One riddle answers the other."

2.

M ORNING ARRIVED BITTER, SNAPPING on the frigid breath of the Khazri: the north Caspian Sea wind that blows across the Absheron Peninsula, one of the four winds that give Baku its name.

The City of Wind.

Four centuries, from ancient to medieval times, the Persian Empire ruled the Absheron Peninsula. Bād-kube, as Baku once was known—with its port, its petroleum, its caravan routes—was the dominant city of the region under Persian rule and its name meant "pounding winds."

Four prevailing winds that sleep—or rather, according to myth—*who* sleep in a black river underground, and manifest according to season, spirits of comfort or distress, to grant wishes, to tease, to torment. Of them, Khazri is the merciless one. Khazri, white-bearded and robed in blue, rushes among humankind freezing, stealing, destroying. City natives and familiar visitors are well aware that his sharp gusts and bluster can instantly blast gale-force; they know never to tempt Khazri and when he roams their city no matter the weather, they eschew loose garments, hats, scarves, umbrellas when it rains or snows; they avoid the Khazri entirely if they can.

These were the individuals this morning whose drivers stopped illegally—allowed/understood by Baku Expo Center security—for the conference delegates to rush the glass doors with singular focus and determination that straddled the border of rudeness.

Even the flags knew the ripping cost of toying with Khazri and at first breath coiled their poles viper-tight whiffling and hissing, their lines clanging to surrender.

Those individuals, however, who'd never met the Khazri, became the objects of mirth for those attendees safely inside behind the thrumming glass, waiting to be badged through security, and they grinned/laughed, mocked/whistled as coats billowed/tore/sailed, hats Frisbeed/bounced/ballooned into the sky, and dresses bo-peeped more than ankle and less of underwear than decency might have expected and certainly once required. Hairdos ruined. A toupee or two forever lost zipping away like scurrying rats.

Glassed and hard, the Expo's doors took the bodies shoved inside by the wind and spit them out; detectors ticked; badges pinged readers; metal cases popped through their x-ray exams and their clackety-clack of their wheels matched shadows thrown by suspended banners that chopped the air in pieces.

Two security men compared the same badge number on two different badges. Chose not to choose.

English collided with Russian.

Turkish with French.

Arabic with German.

Their rolling echoes made the mixture into a reverberant babel and what passed for certainty here moved slower than truth but faster than doubt.

Noise as light. Reflection. Refraction.

And, in HD, on the sponsor wall: the circular clarifi-er at the Heydar Aliyev Oil Refinery's wastewater unit rotated its bridge scraper; skimmer arm; scum trough; peripheral drive in perpetual motion.

(Oil.)

Light cut everything to its outline. Light climbed walls and fell again like an old idea trying to breathe again. The escalator carried men's suits, carried pant suits, skirt suits, sheath dress suits upward as if the building and its occupants ascended to grace only to have the last step collapse into itself and deliver only excited confusion.

The first panel, *Trans-Caspian Energy Corridor: Market Access and Regional Security*, started on sched-ule and meant less than the corridors that carried its echoes—the real negotiations ran in the margins, not on the stage. People drifted in pairs that wanted thirds, peeled away, rejoined elsewhere as if rearranged by magnet. A camera mounted above the press corral hunt-ed for balance and never found it; the lens opened, closed, opened—each correction a small annihilation before the picture returned.

A Kazakh minister practiced his speech outside a glass partition of the exhibitors' wing—a display case of drilling bit prototypes—speaking to his own reflection in the plexiglass until the reflection corrected him.

Reflection. Refraction. Repetition.

(Oil.)

A white room, lights off, dark but for the overhead cone/spot revealing an intimate round table of eight, intimately observed in the round by shadowed aides, fixers, translators, and the dull red eyes of recording devices tucked into the dark. A translator cleared her throat on loudspeaker. Did it again. Then did it again, then remembered the switch. The mic pop puppet-stringed the attendees to buck and chuckle (or chuckle and buck depending which side of the room was there to be startled—and which to take the other's money).

Liquefied Dreams: LNG Prospects Beyond 2020. Conference Room A3. The keynote's slides showed pipeline arcs like sutures. They held on screen just long enough for the press to catch them and lose them, the way a tide takes sharp glass in shards and returns it smooth and shapeless.

Motion.

Oil.

Pattern.

Oil.

Deals made. Deals broken. Gas and oil and global faith: all of it choreographed like a minuet performed in blindfolds—grace without sight, precision without mind. And the smoking section—moved indoors—clouded and ashed, and nicotine and coffee fueled the dancers, while the Delegates' Bar opened early "to cure the Khazri" and compete with the champagne and Caspian Sea cavier in the Bankers' Salon which had never closed since check-in.

A relay clicked—no louder than a nail jar settling on a shelf—but it wasn't inside the Expo circus.

✾ ✾ ✾

ACROSS THE RING ROAD. Behind glass: greasy, grimed, opaque. A dead firm's name along a lintel. A door shut on a stairwell. Cheap gloss paint in an embarrassing shade of green. Black sooty dust lined the molding cuts of the stiles and rails of its cheap pine construction. The place reeked with archival neglect—the scent of paper and old air—of places no one important used. The current lease had run long enough to be boring.

The door was locked, but when opened revealed its backside steel-reinforced. Top, middle, bottom: heavy sliding bolts. Upstairs, the rooms were small; municipal/second-hand auction desks, edges worn by wrists long-skeletal; carpets that refused to remember they once piled a nap. The small rooms all connected, interior doors removed, cable bundles like pythons, boas, anacondas writhed and twisted through throughout. The light took the intentionally greased window film and came in diffused. Dimmed daylight, leaving the rooms in a low false dusk where the LED monitors could breathe their own daylight back—echoes of the Expo floor rendered in pixel and static.

Audio channels played to solo headsets. Played aloud to KALEIDOSCOPE analyst clusters: the Azerbaijani Deputy Energy Minister in a corridor whispering with the Turkmen envoy about throughput guarantees and "winter dilution ratios"; the British commercial attaché calling London to press for "PSA exemptions under Article 23"; the European Commission directorate staffer texting—real-time grab-and-go—about "third-package carve-outs" she wasn't cleared to mention; the Iranian observer, unbadged, describing to a Georgian intermediary how easily TANAP's valve stations could be "re-pathed"; a Turkish procurement delegate caught in a hotel suite that wasn't a suite—her laughter scored under the sound of running water and a phone shutter.

They were all on tape. All plotted. Bathrooms, motorcades, elevators, brothels. Everything with a signal. Everything with a crack.

♔ ♔ ♔

MERYL HOFMYER, known in this city, to this Expo, as Irene Wren, concentrated on the Chinese trade group, sitting in the Four Seasons bar, explaining that settlement in yuan "would feel less colonial" if the glassware weren't German.

"Ha, ah-ah, ah-ahh. Tag potential Wànhuātŏng. I. Want. Identities, and—hmm—do nothing else until you take your last breath, or—" two tsks— "You put them on a—wont-this-be-nice?—small and neat piece of paper written out—plainly, glorious English and gloriously historied. Shall we, eh, chop-chop?"

An adjacent desk. Cardboard-placarded *Channel 9*. Replay of the night feed from a Russian limo. Two Russian voices. A voice-print analyzer. Two locks.

Analyst: "Confirmed: Subject A: Pavel Kravtsov, banker for Subject B: Saint Petersburg oligarch, Gennady Turov."

Wren, turned; Wren, focused.

Analyst, off headset, volume up to include her. "Logging them 'Private Discussion, leaving JW Marriott Absheron.' Flag Vostok Consolidated. Flag Nord Stream 2. Flag anti-Kalaydoskop alignment."

Analyst translated. Fast and clean.

Turov: "And Nikolaevich?"

Kravtsov: "Kolya's already trained off-leash. Picked him up solo at Sushi Room Baku on Nizami Street. Walked back to the Flame Towers and scratched at the door until Kolya let him in. On your word, our man from Stein am Rhein will make the approach."

Turov: "We'll wait for Kolya's play—when Mikhail's choke-chain has become unbearable."

A horn blast garbled the next exchange; the analyst picked it up on—

Turov: "...trouble laying the pipe. Friction issues."

Kravtsov: "Crude."

Turov: "Pressure in the line. Too high. Proposed solution: a lubricant. Viaxi."

Kravtsov: "As a mostly homebound banker, you have me at a disadvantage."

Turov: "Viaxi is a mess. It's foul. Awful."

Analyst: "We've not heard these issues regarding Nord Stream 2. Viaxi is not a known component..."

Rewind. Replay.

Wren blanked. Disbelief.

Analyst: "Could be a new crude pipeline they're here for. Logging possible designation: Viaxi. 'Friction—' I'm not so sure..."

Wren's skepticism fed slow and exact like a strychnine drip. "They're not talking crude. They're speaking crudely." She snapped his headphones over his ears. Hard. Raised her voice so he—and everyone else—could hear. "Viaxi is Turkish. It's a personal adult lubricant for another kind of pipe."

No one asked her how she knew.

As Meryl Hofmyer—she sent a compressed burst to OTRAC over the backchannel carrier—three kilobytes, layered in cipher, gone to Silas in the blink of a modem light.

Michael still with Kolya. Shadowed by the anti-Kalaydoskop bloc. Turov assigning surveillance to Stein am Rhein contact. Identity unknown/TBD. Will maintain passive hold on contact with MK until advisement post CINDER CROWN.

Transmission logged. Signal scrubbed.

As Ms. Wren—she moved through her domain, room by room. Past the analysts bent to their headsets; past the translation pods where Turkish, Russian, Mandarin, Azeri, and English overlapped in a continuous hiss; past the spectrum desk, where live feeds bloomed and died in green pulses; past the surveillance bank that mapped motorcades to microphones, hotel corridors to fiber taps, bedroom whispers to file names.

Everything heard.

Everything seen.

Everything breathing, accounted for, and nothing left to vanish in chance.

♛ ♛ ♛

IRENE WREN, trade-delegate observer, Department of Commerce liaison ignored the Khazri howling at her as one would ignore an old god one no longer believes in. Pushed into the Expo Center. Twittered at the security guard who ran her badge. Rose aloft to Conference Room A3, fourth floor of the Expo's west wing.

Trans-Caspian Pipeline negotiations already in session. The US team—two from State, one from Energy, one from Commerce—wired to her presence the moment she entered. A glance here, a half-turn there, each instinctively deferential. She took her place behind them, wordless, notebook open, pen uncapped. She scribbled. To all appearances a flurry of notes and, in a way, they were because they foretold the path Americans would use to turn negotiations to their advantage.

A crude map of Iran. Lots of comic explosions and little fires. A soft cluck in her throat passed as a personal conceit.

Her phone blinked once, then twice, then went black—the prearranged signal for an OTRAC burst-cipher. She shielded the screen with her notebook's spine and scrolled the plaintext as it unfolded like a telegram from the dead.

FROM: OTRAC / KINGSTON, S.

SUBJECT: CINDER CROWN — INITIATION

TEXT: Operational ignition imminent. Expect Tehran newsfeed within the hour.

Deliver "Proposal 7: Continuity and Resiliency Framework" to U.S. delegation concurrent with first reports.

Objective: exploit Russian withdrawal, stabilize TCP narrative under American custody.

She exhaled once through her nose. The faintest of self-instructing nods. Tore the corner of a previous page. Wrote across it in her minute block hand:

7 — Continuity / Resiliency = claim vacuum, rename collapse as leadership.

Folded it twice, tucked it beneath the pad's backing board. Still looking down, she switched pens. Drew a new box on her cartoon map—Caspian blue. Labeled it simply, "Advantage."

3.

T HE STRANGEST THING: NOT that Michael hadn't slept,
but the way he had slept. Sleep without sensation. Without perception. Sleep devoid of rest or rest-
lessness. Devoid of time. Devoid of life. He'd chosen
a random sushi bar for dinner where he watched his
food prepared from communal filets of raw fish; knew
he'd not been drugged. That Kolya willingly—unmoni-
tored/unrestricted—let him walk from the Flame Towers to the dinner of his choice, spoke to his keeper's
confidence that his sister's life was all the Russian needed to ensure Michael's cooperation. Control. Captivity. Chemical handcuffs were unnecessary. The odd-
est thing. Michael climbed into bed, shut his eyes, and
vanished from what he could only describe as his own
existence.

Not frightening. Not physically unpleasant. Only in
retrospect, unnerving.

Lights out. Repose. Eyes shut. Nothing. Total dis-
placement like a death without heaven, rest, reward.
A return to life/existence without spiritual transforma-
tion/enlightenment. By all things made absent, Michael
realized that all other sleep in his life came with intrin-

sic conscious or subconscious awareness. Acknowledgment. Reckoning. Peace or apprehension.

People suffering from extreme PTSD complain of "losing" time. Blackout periods that mentally jump them from one moment to another, leaping seconds, minutes, hours and, in the rarest cases, days entirely lost to them. But these psychic holes happen while the sufferer is fully awake, fully functional and behaving consciously.

Maybe this sleep blackout was something that happened to lots of people. Happened all the time. Maybe Michael just never heard of it. Never listened. And maybe, now, it could explain the bizarre dreamlike disconnect he felt—showered, shaved, dressed, breakfasted—standing by the glass-window walls inside Kolya Yurenev's Flame Tower suite while the old Kalaydoskop, his grandfather/his blood, gloated at the television.

BBC World News. IRIB's network held the shot: desert glare, heat, distance; a refinery perimeter; a column of smoke like the artistic pencil broadside strokes in Kolya's CINDER CROWN notebook. Sirens going one direction. Evacuees, another. Clipped Farsi from the on-site reporter while BBC's translation track followed.

"Overnight, coordinated insurgent attacks have struck Iran's Abadan terminal, the Ahvaz refinery, and South Pars production complex..."

A second feed stitched in from the south:

"Local sources in Sistan–Baluchestan report armed clashes along Route 95. Security forces have established checkpoints and diverted traffic."

Kolya made soft, pleasant, encouraging sounds. Said nothing. Michael let it play behind him. Wouldn't engage. Wouldn't do a thing until ordered. Watched a wild wind pound the glass and his reflection with sand and trash and the small pieces of random objects picked up from the beachfront far below, destroyed. The whirling windstorm added to his dreamlike state; within it he saw blackness and within the blackness he saw Lynn.

Unnourished. Unkempt.

Unfinished.

Huddled in a blanket.

Forced to look at me—knowing? Unknown? Unable to see; not showing she cared at all; eyes erasing: don't look, don't see, don't care.

"Lynn. I am going to get my agent. You are going to help me."

"Forget it! This isn't climbing over the neighbor's wall stealing oranges."

"You never climbed."

"Destroy anything you have linking you, our Agency, and our government to Cevik—"

"They'll execute him."

I dribble the pieces of my Picasso'd Kalaydoskop into the envelope I've prepared for Russell Aiken. The one-time drop I didn't know I'd ever need so many years ago.

"He's a priest. He's prepared."

Our rolls reversed—then, Turkey, Cevik—Lynn would have done the same as I. Had she wanted to stop me, she'd have moved—witting or unwitting as-sets, allies, authorities—to prevent me from going to the compromised drop at Vazelon. She hadn't approved of my choice, but had honored my reality. Had moved proverbial heaven and earth—betraying her oath and in that her country—to shield me and to attempt my rescue. Not once. Twice.

Michael's love for his sister was vast and deep. It was mighty. The kind of love from which irreproachable knowing told him Lynn was not a murderer. Lynn was incapable of taking a human life.

That didn't change her circumstances. After delivering his threat, Kolya showed him the judgment. Showed him the sentence. Although written in Azerbaijani, Michael didn't question their authenticity. He held no illusions; the result would be death for Lynn if he didn't cooperate.

(And I waited half-an-hour to find Mom and take her to Lynn in the black and secret room.)

He would betray his father. His true father. Silas Kingston.

He would betray KALEIDOSCOPE.

A beachball out of the swirl of sand thirty-three floors above the ground, bounces against the glass—

He would betray his oath.

—spins white, blue, red, green and away; I see it as a football—

He would betray county.

"For Pete's sake, boy! Turn on the juice!"

I fly over the emerald tournament field, riding the brand-new pigskin spiraling down to my fifteen-year-old self. Lynn, once more age ten and naïve as it should be—inside and out—dogs my pattern. Our bare feet churn in perfect sync. Lift us airborne as one for the ball.

Interception, Lynn.

"Pass interference!" Silas booms.

*Lynn jigs from his clutch and into an end zone marked
by miniature American flags.*

*"I said, 'Hold on.' Pass interference. No score here."
Silas tromps to Lynn. Holds out his hands for the pigskin.
Eyes slitted and demanding.*

Lynn. "Daddy?"

"Would I say so if it wasn't?"

Lynn looks past him. Lynn looks to me.

*I peer back. Stupidly. I cannot protect her, and I hate
that she sees this in me. Her face pleads I do better. I look
away.*

To save his sister—

*After the red balloon. After the Enchanted Forest kiss
that changes everything. Out of the car back home—*

The here—

"Michael! Let me hold it! I want to hold it, please!"

*Lynn, dancing foot-to-foot and four, begging for the
balloon. Dad looks over the top of the car. "God's sakes,
Michael: let her hold it!"*

The now—

*Mom crouches between me and Lynn. Her blue-blue
eyes (Kolya's eyes, I know it now) meet my eyes of smoke.
"Let me have it, Michael."*

*Her betrayal. I hand her the string. I fight my tears.
I stare at our hands— the string I give to her. And she
accidentally/purposely lets it go.*

Her eyes. My eyes. Our secret.

"Oh, look at silly me. Look what I've done."

*We lift our faces to the sky and watch the red balloon
rise and rise and float away.*

"Where do they go?" Lynn wonders.

To save his sister: Michael would betray the world.

"This CINDER CROWN goes rather nicely for Silas." Kolya came to his feet. "His last illusion of control, the operation meant to force my Russian hand, draw me into Iran under the banner of 'stabilization.' Leave Baku unguarded." He chuckled. It became a weary sigh. Content. Tired. Knowing.

Michael smirked. "The balloon's gone up, as they say."

Kolya studied Michael and Michael saw a physical mirror of how he would one day look if the years between now and death could ever stretch that far.

Kolya pointed him to the door.

👑 👑 👑

OIL AND GAS CONFERENCE. Inside the cafeteria. Late-lunchers hustling in and out. Food high-quality, practically gourmet, of little interest. Nervous men and women. A dozen languages murmured into phones. Finger-tapped texts. Tapped email.

Kolya chose a table against a service wall. Noisy. No one near enough to overhear. Privacy disguised as accessibility. Gave Michael a document. Three pages, double spaced.

"Your script, Mikhail. Familiarize yourself. You will read it exactly. Once the violence hits Tehran. But when you speak—" Kolya tapped his own chest— "you will engage your heart."

"My heart. You gotta be shitting me."

"The place where your blood flows—mine, and Lynn's. I will have it from your heart."

Michael studied the pages. Boilerplate betrayal. Specific. Revelatory. Banal in its damnation.

A shadow fell across the lines. Michael lifted his eyes.

Gray suit. Silky black beard. Hands folded at his belt. Soft, manicured. Gesture of a man used to waiting out decisions he didn't make. Badge read:

Dr. Arman Taghiyev
Deputy Director, Department of Pipeline Strategy
Ministry of Industry and Energy of the Republic of Azerbaijan
(AZE — Delegate)

Kolya rose slightly from his chair. "May I present my assistant. Mikhail Nikolaevich Morozov, with Vektor-Servis."

Taghiyev extended a perfumed hand. Michael stood, shook it. The man's skin was damp and cool. A wan smile. No words.

"Mikhail—if you would kindly excuse us a moment?"

Michael gave his chair, the script in hand, moved just far enough to seem invisible. Over the noise of plates and cutlery he heard Kolya begin, gentle, companionable: "Good news for your partners."

Taghiyev spoke low. Sharp at the edges. "Bad news for Russia. These attacks—"

Kolya interrupted in Azerbaijani. Michael couldn't follow, only watched the rhythm of it: Kolya's pitch, patient; Taghiyev's refusal, reflexive. The smiles too easy. Warmth rehearsed. Then the small, audible slap of Taghiyev's palm against the tabletop. Kolya took his hand. Fondly. Fatherly.

Pinned it.

With his free hand, Kolya lifted his phone. Angled the screen to the Azeri's view.

Whatever it displayed made Taghiyez recoil.

Kolya's warmth increased. He pocketed his phone. Leaned in. Nodded his head slowly, coaxingly until Dr. Arman Taghiyez nodded along with him.

Kolya gave the man's hand a playful pat as he released it and gestured: leave.

♔♔♔

TVs ABLAZE in Conference Room A3—images of Iranian rebellion in the regions; fire, smoke, wounded carried through the dust. Closed-caption in Azerbaijani, ticker in English.

Ms. Wren ignored the screens. Distributed folders to the US negotiating team.

Proposal 7: Continuity and Resiliency Framework — Strategic Stabilization of the Trans-Caspian.

Commerce nodded at the title. Energy steadied his copy. State skimmed forward, hunting for the sentence he could later repeat and claim his own.

Ms. Wren left them to it as the Azerbaijani delegates filed back inside. There were audience seats, and in them, various EU and Asian lookie-loos pretended Ms. Wren wasn't the focus of their attention as she joined them.

Her phone lit.

CROWN active. Deliver 7 concurrent with first confirmed report. Anticipate Russian withdrawal. Maintain advantage in finance lanes.

Concentrated thus, it caught her off guard when Kolya entered the aisle. Nodded at the seat beside her.

"Taken, Ms..." Pretended he needed to look at her badge. Smiled. "Wren, is it?"

"Hm. Um. Please, sir, do sir. Go right ahead."

Made a great effort not to notice Michael beside the man known to her by photograph and codename, Kalaydoskop. Michael returned the anonymity.

Dr. Taghiyev, last to enter, moved quickly to his seat with the Azerbaijan team. Michael knew whatever the Americans expected from him was already lost.

Energy presented charts.

Commerce presented numbers.

State presented infrastructure guarantees.

The Azeri team leaned together, about to confer when Taghiyev made a cutting motion with his elegant hand and rose.

"My most honored American guests, in light of circumstances far from our control but certainly involving our energy industries—" He opened his arms to the room. "All our energy industries and concerns—"

State's eyes. Energy's eyes. Commerce's eye. Swiveled like deck guns onto Ms. Wren.

She did the only thing she could.

"The United States," she said without affectation, tone piercing as an eagle's cry, "will guarantee stability of the TCP corridor under Proposal Seven."

Committed security. Forced might. Silas's anathema.

She crossed from the audience to the negotiation floor, straight for Taghiyev—so stunned he'd forgotten to lower his arms and looked for an instant to be awaiting a hug. When he realized it, his hands fell helplessly to his sides.

Ms. Wren laid her Proposal 7 folder flat before him, fixing him with her stare like a bird about to devour a worm.

"The deal we will conclude to both our satisfaction is inside this folder and complete." She leaned closer, voice for him alone. "KALEIDOSCOPE deals more harshly—and with longer reach—with those who forget longstanding friendships."

Michael watched Kolya's face. Implacable. Whatever he'd tried with Taghiyev, it appeared to Michael, Kolya had failed.

Kolya spoke behind his hand. Almost a whisper. "And that, Mikhail is how victory is made to appear defeat."

As they moved to leave, Kolya hesitated at the door. Something on the television had caught his eye.

Overhead footage: a long armored column carving the desert in convulsions of dust. The chyron: *"IRANIAN REVOLUTIONARY GUARD UNITS DEPLOY TO AH-WAZ — COUNTER-INSURGENCY OPERATION UN-DERWAY."*

Michael felt it first—the stillness in Kolya.

Not triumph.

Recognition.

Kolya's reflection in the glass flickered as the feed cut to close-ups—convoys, helmets, banners flapping green and white. The old man blinked once, almost smiled.

"That's not Silas." Quiet. Astonished. "Someone's turned his fire against him."

He pushed through the door, sudden, as though re-membering somewhere else he needed to be—leaving Michael as if forgotten.

4.

TODAY IT WAS CLUB soda. Christmas: she'd wrecked herself in vodka wallow, but who in her place—treated like *that*—wouldn't've? She'd disinherited her entire family at the Christmas Eve dinner table. Kid's and all, and didn't/wasn't-gonna feel bad about it. And so what if this disinheritance wasn't a money thing—at least on her side—what she did? She'd cut them all out of the will of inheriting any of the value of Gwen.

How're they gonna like that?

And I'm better for it. I'm centered now. First time in years. Not vindictive—

And: I'm going to prove it.

"I am—you are," she said to her mirrored reflection. She did her lipstick and took pause to judge her hair. For once it was perfect. Bounced the curls, just to test. "Perfect."

All I have to do is make the call. Make the call and I'm free.

Gwen had made her life decision yesterday. But she'd held off from the phone.

You don't act on a drunk decision on your hangover day. That's drunk behavior. Lynn behavior.

(Be nice.)

Why? She's not my sister anymore.

(Leigh.)

That's right—Leigh. And when the time's right, I'll go get her.

She's my daughter—Lynn doesn't want her; never did—and she's still untouched by the Kingston infection (somewhat/mostly).

I can make a life for her: for us.

But first things first: cut the cancer out. Completely. Now, Gwen.

This wasn't cruelty. This was self-care; she'd made her decision yesterday, but yesterday was more vodka than soda—

Sorry for the judgy abstainers, but you simply must work your way down. And today—

She lifted her crystal highball glass filled with cranberry infused Perrier—

To you, Gwendolyn. New life. New you.

You've earned this. Haven't you?

Gwen toasted herself, not believing it but liked the sound. In her head. Drank a quarter down. She got up from her make-up chair. Admired the black teddy she'd put on after her shower.

For herself.

Let herself feel every way the silk and lace, ribbon and elastic caressed her. Felt really, really good about herself.

Really good.

This is so right, what I'm doing— Just. Just right and justice. Silas will finally see (it'll be too late for that old loon, but he will see) that I am defined *by my grace.*

Corners of her eyes. Felt the sting. Stopped on her way to get her phone from the kitchen island. Topped off her mostly soda with Grey Goose. Swallowed enough to beat back the rising lump, and smacked her lips into a smile.

It's got to be done.

She dialed her lawyers. Closed. Until after New Year's.

Lazy fuckers.

But she put the smile tone in her voice. "Please do me the favor, because my case impacts world stage things, and it's important Senator Ossani knows—at least I *tried* to reach her about my decision. And that's all I think I need—fairly—to say to you."

Tapped off. Scowled.

Now what do I do? Get dressed? Maybe there are some sales...

Gwen liked the sound the bottle made against the rim of her glass.

My very own New Year's ring-a-ding.

She gave the lump another good dousing. Wondered how cold it would be outside and what she'd look best in when her telephone rang and the senator's name flashed upon her screen.

She smiled again, the way she'd learned to smile in mirrors, clicked the green button, and greeted the senator with her very-most professional, just a little extra-deep-for-mystery, hello. Lied about having a "nice Christmas" and heard something about the splendid choir at St. So-and-so-something-or-other Senator Ossani and her husband enjoyed Christmas morning.

I wonder if the girls like my presents this year the most?

But she said, "I should just get to the reason I've called."

"Certainly, Gwen."

Sip. "I didn't get anything on the recording." Sippier.

"Bring in the device. You might be surprised what we can recover from it."

"I didn't get anything because I didn't wear it."

"You didn't wear it. I see. May I ask why?"

The elevator dings. The Chinese with the briefcase replacing her reflection as the door splits her into pieces.

"I'm leaving, Senator."

"Leaving what?"

Gwen didn't answer.

"Washington? The country?"

Senator Ossani running her case files through the copier; the Chinese man putting them inside his briefcase.

Crazy. Bad. Wrong.

Gwen drank to prevent herself from revealing.

"Frankly, Gwen, you're making little sense. And if we're going to land this award at the best possible number—millions of dollars, Gwen. Money you deserve..."

She'd said 'eight or nine figures', that could be a hundred million dollars. Oh, God. Oh, God. What am I doing?

Finished her drink.

"I know, I know—"

Grabbed the bottle. Looked at it. The geese: strong, solid, flying with freedom and purpose. Everything vodka isn't.

"I'm dropping the case. No more Kingston—Silas, Michael—entanglements."

At the other end of the line, she heard the scratch of a lighter. Faintest of inhale-exhale. When Theresa Ossani spoke, Gwen could hear, almost smell the smoke.

Maybe I should go out tonight. A quiet dive-bar. I'll deserve it after this.

Gwen filled her glass as the senator filled the silence. "I completely understand how you feel."

"You do? You understand me."

"Completely. And you're very brave."

Gwen spun the ice in her empty glass. "I'm not. I just—I make people think—"

"A clean breast of it."

Gwen watched bits of light from the room catch and refract on the whirl.

"Yes. That's right."

"Gwen: have you thought about what you'll do for money? This gives Silas all the power over Michael's pay and benefits. We both know how vindictive that man is."

"I have my work. Once the holidays are over, home sales pick up." A laugh to perk herself up into believing it. "Buyers making New Year's resolutions. Historically, it's a very busy time for the real estate market." She heard how hopeful she sounded. Hated that sound.

"I'd like to return your retainer."

"Really?"

"Due to your circumstances, your bravery; and let's just say 'Holiday Spirit,' I'd like to cut you a check today for the full amount. I'd love it if I could get you in this afternoon. That way you can get to the bank before they close back up for New Year's."

👑👑👑

MARSH, GERTZ, and Ossani. Like last time: nobody home. But this time, the lights were *on* with nobody home. And the door was unlocked. And Gwen only stood in the bright, warm wood lobby thirty seconds before Theresa Ossani presented herself in a turquoise Chanel suit—raw wool, a dainty fringe, a secret weave of ribbons and sequins. Pure alchemy. A wearable jewel. Discipline in form; poetry in shimmer. Her feet were bare. And beautiful.

Gwen swallowed. Smiled. Felt the relaxation of her earlier beverages behind her eyes. The sour on the back of her tongue. Her Louis Vuitton sweats felt heavy. Saggy. "Santa was sure good to you."

Theresa made a stately turn, came out of it with a practiced laugh. "They were all here. I couldn't resist."

"They-what-were?"

Like a weird film cut, Theresa was beside her. Clutched her elbow. Led her deeper inside. All Gwen could think to say was, "Love the shoes."

Another laugh—made two for the entirety of their relationship. "My worst feature. Your size is smaller than my trotters, I'm ashamed to say."

Her breath smelled of champagne. The expensive kind that made Gwen's nose tingle.

"Come. I have your check right here. I'm sure you have plenty of pieces to start picking up. Out of the Christmas ashes."

They stepped into the conference room and the retort Gwen's tongue sharpened fell from her tongue.

Soft overhead lighting accented by garlands of crystal snowflake pin-spots.

A silver and gold champagne service: Roederer Cristal.

"Left over from our Christmas party."

"That's not."

A rack of designer dresses and suits.

"No, I had to pull that out where my team's been preparing. Some of it's terrible."

None of it was terrible.

Boxes of shoes.

"We were assembling an assortment for you. Your testimony before the Select Committee."

Gwen's fingers closed reflexively around the silver stem of a gold-rimmed flute—cold, like power—her eyes unable to leave the couture. She gulped champagne. Placed the flute on the table. Walked to the clothing rack. Touched.

"There's a right and a wrong way to do television. Believe me."

Chanel. Dior. Stella McCartney. Armani.

Math only came easily to Gwen when it involved a decimal point between whole currency and fraction. This rack was easily worth four times more than the retainer she'd come for. And she hadn't even looked at the shoes.

Smack. The leather board of a checkbook binder opened hard on mahogany.

Gwen turned. Watched money roll black and wet from the tip of Senator Ossani's pen. Point of her pen poised over the signature line: "Tell me. If you could identify one thing I, or my office, did to make you change your mind about our case—what might that be?"

In life, there was one other certainty beyond sex and taxes; it wasn't death—not in Gwen's book.

Because that's a stupid saying, because that's—by it's own word—not "life," is it?

It was: you don't get something for nothing.

This is a whole lotta something. And me—? I'm less than...

"What was your question?"

"Gwen, I won't have you get gushy-eyed. I think we're past theatrics."

Isn't that strange. I don't feel tears at all. I feel cheap.

Fine. You think I'm stupid? Fine-fine. You asked for it, bitch.

"I don't appreciate you photocopying all of my case-work and giving it to that Chinaman who visited you when you both thought I'd left."

"Racial slurs have no place in my offices. Or my presence. I'll thank you to respect that."

"Well? Want to explain or not?"

"I had hopes. I expected better of you, Gwen." Signed. *Rip.*

"No. You didn't. Not from me. You wouldn't. But you don't intimidate me."

Ossani stalked, slew footed, intimately close. "We're done." She bent the check. Gave it a knife-edge crease. Pushed it into Gwen's belly-pouch-pocket.

"You don't scare me, Senator."

"No. But you scare everyone."

Gwen stepped around her.

Lobby. Gwen let herself out. Marsh, Gertz, and Ossani: empty. Like last time. But with one wrinkle; in his security office, Mr. Pinchbeck, printed a selection of photo hardcopies from the camera he'd rigged above the dress rack. Excellent shots of Gwen—full front in approach, from behind in retreat, and enough close-ups of her face that even a stranger would recognize her on sight.

5.

WEEKLY SAVER ALERT! LAST Basket Deal @ Green Bounty — Earn 110 Bonus points in Frozen/Dairy. Limit one per customer. Not valid with other offers.

Sometimes when the walls are closing in and all remaining options to extricate yourself from their destructive certitude are distinguishable only by the degree of devastation, an escape hatch presents itself and you leap through it leaving the circumstances of your defeat to crush themselves without you. The email pinged Clive's phone at three p.m. while he and Paige, bundled like trappers, huddled close to the Christmas tree to avoid the wind gusting occasional sleet across the Old Town green where Charlotte and Leigh, dressed like ski bunnies, threw a soggy tennis ball for a great—not by increased size, but magnified enthusiasm—and grateful galumphing Beaumont, his first exhaustive exercise in days.

An off-the-shelf Android. A throwaway phone. A disposable SIM card replaced each Sunday after midnight. Clive's comms with Fergus while he pretended to be undercover at Foxtail Farm. Tucked into a *News* folder, hidden within a menu on a redundant weather app, a three-tap backdoor inside the seemingly non-function-al radar map, an MI6 messaging program—Palimpsest, they called it—that self-generates junk mail randomly four times each twenty-four-hour cycle. Signals from Fergus, rare as they'd become, appeared among them. This from Fergus:

"The header, 'Weekly Saver Alert,' tells me it's Fergus. 'Last Basket Deal at Green Bounty' means it's time for my final debrief at the listening post."

"Garde-Joyeuse."

"That's right."

"'Final debrief' as in before they send you home?"

"In theory." His face: skeptical. Hers: matched. Hope: nowhere. "One hundred bonus points gives me the hour. Midnight's ten, so one hundred."

Paige began on her woolled fingers. Clive chuckled. "It's the ten o'clock hour—I memorized the pattern."

She flipped the back of her hand into his chest. He smirked, and— "'Frozen/Dairy' is the thirty minute mark; it goes 'Fruits/Produce' for top of hour, 'Meats/Poultry' for the quarter—"

"What's the forty-five? I mean, just curious."

"Would be 'Bakery.' But it's not. He wants me there at ten-thirty, alone—that's the 'one per customer' and unencumbered: the 'not valid with other offers.'"

"What's 'unencumbered'?"

"No kit, no papers, no phones other than this burner which I'll turn in with the SIM cards. It's my final call."

"Shit. I can't believe it."

Bemused. About to re-explain, Clive realized he'd lost her attention to the girls. "Who's that?" They clustered around a teenage boy. A good-looking boy. And Charlotte's braces glinted exposed by her wide smile.

"Bobby-flippin'-Claypoole."

"Charlotte's going to start pulling in radio signals, she doesn't stop grinning."

"Would you shut up."

"How old's this kid?"

"Seventeen, I think. Morgan had her claws in him. He was a virgin till her and now look at him, rubbing up against my sister."

Clive gave Paige a moment to simmer. When it got to a moment too long, he cleared his throat. "If it leads to wedding bells, I'd like to be there, but we are trying to figure out...I don't know, my life? And *someone's* possible death?"

"I'm sorry. But we can—you can make this work somehow. I mean, after last night we knew you'd have to make some kind of move. The codebook—"

"The one that gets Silas definitely killed?"

"Clive, from headquarters or just bullshit from Fergus: this message is a trap any way you move. Real—they send you home: trap. You lose our family. Fake: you lose your life."

"Yeah. So I'm not sure what part of 'making it work' makes it work."

"The codebook." Like he's a dimwit.

"Am I a dimwit?"

"Are you?"

"I could be."

"The trap is set and now you see its shape."

Leigh stomped over. Good excuse for Beaumont to jump Clive. He grabbed the ball from the dog's wet mouth.

Paige. "What's going on with Bobby Claypoole?"

Leigh snapped her head back—a look—then back at her sister. "You don't see the obvious?"

"I don't think I want to..."

"He's drooling more than Beaumont."

"I got this." Clive hurled the ball. Right at them. It hit Bobby Claypoole and Beaumont was about to follow, but the boy gave a strange whistle. Beaumont stopped in his tracks and went down on his belly.

Paige. "Get your sister. We're out of here."

Leigh took the authority and ran it back.

Clive waited until she was out of earshot. "The codebook traps the trap."

"I'm no spy," Paige said. "But that's how I'd do it."

⚜ ⚜ ⚜

10:32 P.M. Fergus knew it for what it was the moment it came over Palimpsest—naked text where there should've been a mask. Typical Lancer: treason scribbled like crib notes on a shoe, the same bluff that carried him through school and into the Service.

Not walking into the post. Doesn't feel clean. I've got material that changes everything. We'll meet but not on your terms.

Typed: *What fucking material? Get your arse here.*

An attachment *pinged* through.

Fucking wanker. The Devil keeps his accounts—hold him off and the hangman oils the noose.

A pair of photos. Background dim. Caught in a flash. An old leather book on a table. Pocket-sized. Next: the book opened. Cyrillic letters, random numbers, boxed groups.

His blood thrummed hot.

The bloody fucking codebook. Kid'll get me a medal for this.

He'd planned to celebrate afterward, but this called for a pop. And a hard think; still had to funnel him into his sights. Fergus unscrewed the lid off his bottle of Dewar's 15-year. Took a pull.

Now where is he and how do I get him out?

The closed book stood on its edge. The flash illuminating the book hid the details of the darkened room around it. He clicked-up the magnification. Scrolled off the book. The shadows behind. Some of the light bled into the background. A shade of blue. Threw up a filter. Hit the exposure. Magnified. Magnified. Magnified. A ghostly patch revealed a bit of paneled wall. A seam where it came together at a soft angle. Realization slowly drew him in—

Demagnify, demagnify, demagnify—scrolled to the other side of the flash-haze—click-click-click, jammed in tight.

Same paneling.

Same seam.

Same angle.

The room was a decagon.

Realization hit all at once: the second-floor study. Here.

The bastard's in the house.

Fergus drank hard with cold ferocity. Switched bottle for pistol. Checked the magazine. The cartridge in the pipe. The seat of the suppressor.

He set down the bottle. Careful. Hefted the pistol. His orders were delightfully clear.

Slow. Cautious. He climbed the stairs along their side, flush to the wall. The aged timber didn't say a word.

♛ ♛ ♛

GARDE-JOYEUSE. Classic robber baron castle. Looming black and abandoned. Forbidding and forbidden.

Clive suspended halfway over the wall.

Elbow bent. Muscles gathered. Left arm extended, light for balance.

Claw hammer hooked behind his belt.

Time frozen.

Turn back the kaleidoscope.

Two hours before the photos.

Clive scales the mansion. Three stories in a chattering of ice pellets. Hammer claw to the termite-sponged sill of a cupola window. Not unlike university, only this time: here to leave behind rather than steal the test.

Five months to Paige's birthday.

"Men sometimes have to sacrifice to make hard decisions for a greater cause."

Paige's eyes convey more fire than the red sequins and glass beads of her startling dress.

"When you become a man—one without a pull-string—you'll understand exactly how true that statement is and how hardcore you failed it tonight."

Twist back the decades to Kingston children stealing oranges, because fragments of the past flash in vivid swirl with what will come, and time as color folds itself over the wall again.

Rough parapet coping under his palm.

Sleet attacking cheeks.

Sleet retreating until its sting subsides.

Sleet attacking again.

Paige, panting vapor, bundled in Melody's down robe, the shell pattering with sleet, shivered from more than cold, and watched him vanish.

The untended orchard. Lush fruit glowing orange beneath silver frost. Beautiful and strange.

Harsh whisper back: "How's it these oranges aren't dead?"

Harsh whisper over: "They're winter navels. Now's when they're first ripe. Bring me one when you come back?"

Clive freed the hammer. "That's a promise, luv." Clutched it. Sights on the high cupola, he ran toward the house.

♛ ♛ ♛

NO SIGN OF ENTRY. If Lancer had come through the front, the post's signal would have tripped. It hadn't. Nor had the sensors been tampered with. He'd come from above. Like a rat.

Fergus let his vision settle to the dark. Eyes ready. Weapon ready. He climbed the central staircase—each turn, each backward glance, each advance measured. He moved as he'd been trained thirty years to move: method before muscle, breath before bullet. There were back stairs. Both wings. A clever bastard could circle down and behind; Fergus's body turned reflexively to cover every angle.

10:45 p.m., he made the upper landing. The wrap-around corridor. Five closed doors. Two dark arches at either end leading to the wings. Instinct said clear the floor first. Training said take the bait-room and end it. The book waited in the decagonal study, and Clive Lancer—wherever he was—would be drawn to it, same as he.

The study had three entrances—hallway, bedroom, salon. The Kingston household had guns and Fergus had to assume Clive was armed. He didn't think Clive would be inside it, but if he was: even dead he could still get a round off. The open hall left him exposed to both wings; the salon offered cover and a flanking line.

He mapped the salon from memory: two tall windows with heavy draperies, shelves along the hall wall, the others bare. Card table, four chairs, low table, sofas swaddled in tarps like shrouds.

From the hall's shadow, Fergus quietly opened the salon door.

No reflex gunshots.

No sound of movement.

Back flat to the wall. Peered inside. The curtains made the air heavy with dust. Cigar smoke; the ghost of his own nights in this his kingdom.

A sidestep. A breath. He crossed the threshold in a rush, dropped left, crouched behind a sofa.

No gunshots.

No movement.

Only the intermittent scritching of sleet.

He rose. Advanced on the study door. Turned the glass knob. Slow.

Thump.

A footstep from the curtains. Eyes flashed. Velvet rippled. Fergus fired two silenced rounds. Glass shattered. A third round into the second drapery. More exploding glass as his shoulder, hammered from behind, exploded with pain. His hand splayed.

"You little bastard." *Didn't/couldn't kill me.* "Not in my fucking house." *And he doesn't have a gun.*

But now, neither did Fergus.

♔♔♔

FRACTION OF A SECOND. The thought to strike the skull, the blow that struck the shoulder—error inside instinct. The kind of fatal mistake supposed to have been trained out of him long ago. But killing's the only lesson they never teach for real. In lethal, zero-sum hand-to-hand combat, the man who's killed before will always prevail against the man who flinches from murder.

When Clive came in again, swinging to make it right, he was already at the disadvantage. Fergus didn't need the use of both hands to get inside of the blow that glanced his back; to get his strong, good hand around Clive's neck and use his momentum to hurl him into the study door; to drive his knee into Clive's belly, up beneath his ribcage; to drive his boot into the flesh above his groin; to push through the strike, crashing the younger man through the splintering door.

Clive backpedaled into the decagonal room, collapsing into the table where he'd set his trap—the codebook flying from the collapsing table.

Fergus lumbered in the darkness for his pistol.

Saw it. Rushed it. Hand seizing—

Clive tackled him and the pair collapsed but, so far, he'd had the sense to keep hold of the hammer. Fergus rolled, pounced for the pistol. Clive struck two vicious blows to the center of the older man's back. Both men screamed. Both cursed. Spit flew from both their mouths.

Fergus's fingers tangled with the gun.

Claw hammer dropped, Clive grabbed him from behind with—

"Want it that bad, you fuck: take it!"

—and plowed him headfirst into the far wall. Pulled him back and battered him headfirst again cracking the wall in a shower of weak lathe and plaster until his torso stuck into the innards of the house.

Panting. Breathless. Clive dropped him, eyes frantic for where Fergus dropped the gun.

Found it—still in the curl of Fergus's fingers.

The older man didn't lift it.

He didn't move.

But having fallen half through the hole face-up, his eye glistened. Blinked. A strange bleak, sardonic smile curled his lips. He snorted at what he saw. Muttered.

"You bloody broke my fucking back, you treasonous wee shite. Might as well grow a pair."

Fergus's pinkie quivered on the pistol butt.

Clive snatched the gun. Pulled the trigger. Spit a single round into the old man's heart.

He rocked onto his heels. A bitter, animal sound caught in his throat. He choked it back.

"Fuck you."

It was only after he retrieved the codebook, only after finding the orange he'd thrown from the corner of the room into the draperies, only after he widened the hole in the wall with his hammer, only after he dragged Fergus into the wall that he saw what caused Fergus to grin at his own demise. Filled with power and digital cables. The space wasn't a crawlway. It was a conduit. Silas's cruelest invention: the watcher watched.

Clive left Fergus's corpse and followed it.

♛ ♛ ♛

THEY SAT Paige's bed. Their bed—considering. She peeled the orange, and he told her about Fergus in as few words as possible. She peeled the orange as if it were medicine—slowly, carefully, the rind's tear louder than the words neither of them would ever say. There was blood somewhere in the night, she knew, and yet the fruit smelled clean, unblemished. She peeled the orange, and she didn't ask how it had happened, or what it felt like; she was afraid she already knew.

He told her the space between the walls was a passageway. Told her about the ladder and how it led to a separate structure, into a room apart from the house, beyond the property line, with its own concealed door. She split the orange into fragrant sections. She fed him first, and its sweet tang, its juicy pulp, quickened him more than he would have thought possible. She didn't ask where the hidden door had led and he didn't tell her about the antique books in English and Hebrew and other languages. Of strange trees and genealogies. He fed her, and they traded slices this way until all that remained were two broad, twisted curls of peel, softly gleaming with the patina of citrus oil.

They lay back. She held him, caressed his face, and before he drifted into sleep, two thoughts crossed his mind and curled together until they became one.

The bravest people are the ones who don't mind looking like cowards...and that the hidden door, opening into the Place of Blackness, is the same door the brave must one day surrender through.

Paige would understand why. Now he could sleep, and time—its fragments folding color over color—would turn the lock behind him.

6.

S ILAS'S 1992 CADILLAC BROUGHAM idled in the turnout. Waited on the shake and chain-rattle of the opening gate. A ship of sapphire black. Unnamed. Unflagged. Exhaust pumped into the freezing air, impatient to find safe harbor.

Headlights found the stone shield in the gatepost. The beam led Silas's tired eyes—whole-being weariness, thirty-four hours dragging CINDER CROWN through OTRAC.

What was Meryl thinking? Promising security commitments on the Trans-Caspian Pipeline? Panic dressed as strategy. All because the Ayatollah's Revolutionary Guards show up early.

Organized under blackout comms.

Massed in force. (How the hell'd they pull that off?) Not right/something off.

(Prior knowledge? Bad. Leak?)

Still: plays to the same Moscow pressure. Let the Guards thrash—Russia'll have to ride in to steady them. Kalaydoskop bleeds its leverage either way.

Jilly Bregado, old faithful Jilly, she'd pulled at the old Evander Lott thread, his/England's deadly flirtation with Kalaydoskop back in the seventies. Found the new suit of clothes they'd stitched together for Baku.

I let Kolya smoke me out with Michael back July Fourth; same trick, new tailor. British cloth. Russian stitch. Turning British energy equity against my TCP push.

...His eyes: dissatisfied: to words cut in stone.

Foxtail Farm – 1693 AD.

Poured in concrete. Left to weather into fact.

The book. The letter. The cipher. My confession—Cheltenham now, inside the Donut decrypting. The ax to fall as axes will. Onto the head most damned.

Gray as bone, three carved foxtails gleamed bright with frost. Three seed heads perched on lichen-scaled stalks. Deco hint of flame. Beneath them, four shallow waves, curved and stacked, the Patuxent rolling green-brown-gold with moss. A proud thing. Still. The story it told meant to be believed.

Below the stems, the stone turned pale. A half-moon scar. Michael's doing. Thirteen and wild with a Marks-a-Lot, he'd drawn a fox's tail slipping out from the reeds. Thought it'd be cute. Silas made him scrub an hour, then burned the ink caught in the pores with muriatic acid. Only thing that would bite concrete. The stone never healed. Nothing green would grow there. The patch glowed white in the beam. The ghost of a tail still twitched to get free.

He pulled inside. The porch-mounted exterior lights made the snow look new, though it wasn't. He parked in the gravel, slowing tires making the wet sound of seashore suck coming to rest. Headlights off, the night behind the North Vista Outhouse revealed itself. He witnessed Clive rise from the wine-cellar stairs, dash around the far corner. Silas craned his neck, a look behind, and observed the British spy come around the outhouse, dash the field, disappear onto the porch, into the manor. He felt his mouth stretch, his cheeks tighten, felt a rictus smile.

The bravest people...don't mind looking like cowards. I'll have to check on Fergus—if there's a Fergus left to check.

And, waiting for Clive to climb the stairway—return to Paige's arms, their growing family—other words came up unbidden. Courage and its afterbirths. Words Silas carried from starred eyes to dimmed age: Neither fear nor courage saves us.

Had Angleton said it first?

Or Doris, or their precious Eliot?

Maybe the line was waiting in him all along. *Unnatural vices, fathered by our heroism. Virtues, forced upon us by impudent crimes.*

By the time he reached the kitchen, the rest of the verse was there, the one that had always followed.

I have lost my passion... what is kept must be adulterated.

He shed his coat. He found the Timeless, reddish gold inside its crystal teardrop. Carried it by its platinum collar to the kitchen. Didn't bother with a snifter. A juice glass would do. Silas found one and found the wedding gift sorcerer's mirror Melody had used for the Bûche De Noël, washed and dried and waiting to be put away. Silas put the bottle and the glass on its center. Carried them to the island where he poured. A ring of Silases stared back at him.

"These reverse convex optics draw light and throw it around to magical effect."

His exhaustion, more than physical, a weariness of time itself, didn't allow him argument at the added sight of Doris's hand reflected above the glass. Silas drank and lowered his guard, and he invited it, hearing Angleton's voice—

"In a wilderness of mirrors, what will the spider do?" Silas turned the juice glass of cognac and broke the returning pattern, broke his face into shards; Doris's hand remained, but Silas saw it older—too young to be frail, too frail to be well—and a folder and the white and the colored "Your copy," "For the lab," "To submit to your insurance" pages ruffled until he shut his eyes and shut it down. Not tonight.

Oh, my Doris: Kolya has our boy. Truly has him now. And Michael knows. Must.

Michael at two, Doris teaches him to kiss. "Right here, Michael. On my lips."

He giggles. I cringe. "That's not what we do in this family."

Cerulean eyes flash ice. "In this family, from now on—" Flash warmth at our boy. "Like this." She kisses his lips. He kisses back. Michael giggles.

Silas opened his eyes.

I have lost my passion; what is kept must be adulterated...

He drank. Swallowed.

It rests on you, Doris.
You as Michael.
You as Lynn.

(What a fuck-up I've made of that. "To grab the lever that spins the globe." I've put it out of her reach.)

You as Kolya: the grip clenched in blood.

High-voltage current inside the yellow telephone on the wall hammered its twin bells, jarring Silas to attention. The family emergency phone. With almost disbelief, Silas watched it ring a second time before he stepped to the wall and lifted the receiver.

"Dad." Hal.

"Yep."

"It's China, Dad. Houton sold 'em your CINDER CROWN."

Silas licked his lips. Timeless: complex, burning. "Get home. ASAP."

"Yeah. Okay."

"Drexler'll have ghosted a manifest by now—CI air-clearance under a dead courier name. If you hit Erbil, they'll know what to do."

Hal paused. "Copy that."

The line died to brief static, then dial tone. Silas returned the receiver to its cradle. He returned to his stool at the island, to his drink and to his ghosts, but a look into the mirror told him—never Doris, never Angleton—the reflection he saw thrown around to magical effect was all of him. Softly, Silas told his ghosts: "After such knowledge, what forgiveness, eh?"

He'd used to think it meant the Agency; now he knew it meant himself.

Friday, December Twenty-eighth

1.

MORNING FOUND MELODY ALONE. Locked tight inside the manor. The temperature clung a tick or two above freezing. Thick, fast-moving clouds—a gray blanket pulled off the Chesapeake and over the river, over Foxtail Farm and the county—stayed dry; and though the wind turned, gusted across the treetops and fought back toward the river, at least the ice had backed off overnight. It made a morning the family could break away from, drive into Lexington Park. Breakfast out. Catch a Christmas matinee. Paige and Clive, unusually subdued, grew eager at the thought of spending the day huddled in the dark of a movie theater and Melody lent them her big red Billy Goats Gruff Dodge Ram to pile in with the four kids. "We'll cheat an extra seat in back; Jack and Little Silas can double-up with the middle seatbelt." Off they went. First stop Cracker Barrel, next stop Middle Earth and *The Hobbit* and, almost eleven now, Melody didn't expect them back until four o'clock. Plenty of time to finish what she began on Halloween. At the Patuxent Historical Society. The Kingston family horror story. Doris's last box. Of the last two, specifically earmarked for her.

Still—alone on the porch with her coffee and with Beaumont, with Hal's pistol in her sweatshirt pocket—Melody jumped at the gate-bell chime announcing Victoria's arrival. Melody opened the front door to meet her.

Victoria mounted the front steps carrying a banker's box, side bulging, its cardboard lid secured with packing tape. "Some place you got, Melody. Obvious why Colonel Vickery liked to ride out here and get bombed all those centuries back."

Melody smiled affection. "Did you have a nice Christmas?"

"Niiiice—but I swear: if I hear one more time how much nicer it would be with children, I may just make it my New Year's resolution to go online and find some Von Trapp widower with a whole crew of kids and marry him before next Christmas and then we'll see how much Mom likes it."

"Can you sing?"

Victoria gave her a funny look, then got it. "No. Even better." Melody led her inside. Bolted the door behind them. "Was yours nice here? It looked—driving in—you have your own church here. A whole one-stop shop."

"Without Christmas, I think I would have fallen to pieces." Melody took the box, set it on the floor, pulled Victoria in, hugged her.

"That rough, huh?"

Melody tried to stoop for the box, but Victoria hoisted it. "I got it, Mel. Need to explain it, anyway."

"Come on, then. Anyway, *I* need to explain to you."

"Your dark secrets." Melody worried her with a glance. Victoria: "I shouldn't've joked."

"Joke or not, it's the same. I need your help under-standing something, so I'm going to take you right up to the dark part. The edge of it."

Foot of the central staircase. Doris leaned toward them from her portrait on the landing above. Mischief in her vivid blue eyes. Victoria caught her breath. "Whoa. That's her: that's Doris Kingston."

"Yep."

"That portrait is incredible. It's absolutely—" searched... "magnificent." She faced Melody, her soft profile, her framing black curls, the faint scar from the owl attack. Innocent and bold rarely go together, but they did in the light from above and the imagined, yet visible despite that, beam that flooded from the paint-ing. "And you never met her."

"It's complicated. Not in person, I didn't." Melody flicked a finger, held it, her hand as if she might receive Doris's red river lilies. "My father painted it, so in a way, I've always known her. She's always known me. Since I was ten."

She backed into one of a pair of hall chairs. Sat. Indi-cated Victoria do likewise. Took the box onto her lap. The conversation would be here. With Doris to bless, to curse, to witness.

Victoria said, "Then her Post-it note—her wanting you to see this stuff—makes sense. But how did you not know her?"

"This was my father's last work. After that—maybe before, maybe always—he lost his sanity. He took me and we lived on the run. Undercover. False identities. My whole childhood. I did the bare minimum of school; mostly just learned from reading; I got my GED—which was an elementary school-level joke—when I was nineteen."

"Where was your mother?"

"Dead. I can't tell you about that."

"That's why you were living like spies."

"We were fugitives. Doris was the spy. She'd somehow kept in touch with my father; they had some secret way of communicating. She persuaded him to put me in Hal's path—fooled him, my father—"

Victoria's turn to point. To read the flourish. "Boone."

"Boone Kelso. Fooled Boone Kelso into thinking that marrying into the Kingston family would set up a blackmail revenge against Silas—out of the old Kingston horror he sent me to find." Melody's eyes went to Doris as if to check that she was getting it right. She couldn't help herself. "Victoria: I love my family. They're the air I breathe. I was terrified what I would find. What I did find."

Victoria touched her hand. "Your father now?"

"Out of prison. On his way." Melody interrupted herself with a deep/centering breath. The air between them, the air the house breathed. "I can see why she kept us moving—why she pulled me home. Maybe she thought she owed my mother. The Kingston way is tricks. Dodges. But this—" she clutched the edge of the box on Victoria's lap. "Why me? And why this way?" Her hands relaxed on the worn cardboard, fingers splayed as if the answer might rise into her palms. "She could have written it down. Instead she sent me wandering first—like she needed me lost before I could find her."

"He thought he was hunting you; he was delivering you."

Melody rocked in her seat, the motion of her body carried her nod of agreement. Her eyes slid between the two women: Doris—pure love—gone, but captured in spirit too-living above, and Victoria, alive, a true custodian of the past beside her. "Still. I came very close to misinterpreting the whole thing. Without you—I probably would have."

Victoria studied her. "You think she planned it like an operation. Maybe Doris just knew you'd only trust what you chased yourself."

"I wanted to quit."

Victoria grinned—just a bit—and Melody was reminded: Victoria liked mysteries. "I know you. You'd have come back to it. It's not about the way she did it, it's the way she made you do it: it means it's not just about the information, the story. Just facts she wanted you to have so you could regurgitate them into a multiple choice bubble like that test that was so easy, hm? She chose this way because she wanted you to live it. She wanted you to have the choice to quit and never come back to it, or quit and then come back. She wanted you to want it. Only that way—that true learning—does it become part of you."

"Maybe. Okay, I kind of see that, but why? What does she get by risking it all for me to abandon it, or get it wrong, or use it against her family or not even figure it out? She's dead. It's ancient history. If Boone Kelso stayed in prison, I probably wouldn't even have showed up at your archives."

Exasperated, she waited for Victoria to give her something else. But Victoria waited on Melody.

Melody shook her head. "Why not her own? Michael, Lynn, Hal—she has a whole dynasty for this." The Yule log popped, explosive and hollow, beyond the common room door. "Why hand it to me?"

"Doesn't that answer itself?" Victoria considered the portrait. Admired Doris. As if sitting beneath it she was beginning to know her living. "Maybe because they're the story?" Glanced back at Melody. "Blood can't read itself, Mel. It fills in what it wants to see."

"Doris and I are separate from it. From Kingston blood. We're the only two in the chain. And I'm the only one left." Victoria nodded. And Melody continued and it was almost to herself. "What good is any of it now? What in these pages keeps what's coming from getting here?"

The portrait seemed to turn its eyes back to the stairs.

Melody bounced a fist off the box top. "Two hundred, three hundred years ago and today don't connect in any kind of physical way."

Victoria traced a finger along the edge of the box. "It's interesting about this box. It came after she died... We get boxes like this, you know—antebellum apologia, Lost-Cause essays, blue-hair-auxiliary handwriting. It was shelved un-accessioned, waiting for someone to risk opening it." Victoria put the box where she'd been seated. "I'm worried about you, though. If your father is violent like you said and like you insinuate about your mother, and he's coming *here*—have you called the police? Informed the authorities?"

"The police have been here." It wasn't exactly a lie. "It's Silas his beef is with."

"But you're alone."

"Just right now. The place locks up tight. There are alarms. I'll be fine. And Silas isn't what you'd call a stranger to difficult, dangerous situations. I'll be okay."

She opened the front door for her guest.

Victoria briefly touched her wrist. "You'll call me?"

"I get to be a bridesmaid?"

It took the younger woman a moment. "Ah. 'How Do You Solve a Problem Like Victoria.' Haha. Very funny. Maybe." Friendly eyes. "I'll need to get that back into the collection before we're back after New Year's, 'kay?"

"I'll drop it by your house soon as I've had a good look." Walked her to her car. "I still don't understand."

Victoria's smile almost secret. "You will."

And for a moment Melody couldn't tell if that was promise or warning. Victoria got into her car, and Melody watched her through the gate until it clanged shut hard and final.

♛ ♛ ♛

Virtue veiled in sin becomes the veil it wears. The bridegroom can never lift it; the kiss of the Divine can never reach the bride. Until the veil burns. When the virtuous act is condemned, institutionalized as unlawful—when to serve freedom and life one must employ deception and dwell within the immoral—what sin, then, will you be called to pay for?

In the late summer of 1793, months after President Washington signs the first Fugitive Slave Act into law, a small-holding Maryland planter from the Patuxent Valley named Baker Drury (also chronicled as Druway) crosses the Mason–Dixon Line into Pennsylvania on a mission to retrieve two slaves who, accused of stealing a bushel of wheat, have escaped his farm. He believes if he can speak to them—reason, remind them of their debt—they will return of their own accord. But the fugitives have found shelter with a free man of color named Parker, and word of slave-hunters in the county draws armed neighbors to Parker's stone millhouse. Violence imminent, the planter steps forward to speak to the men he has owned and cared for since birth.

Gunfire erupts. Drury dead. His son wounded. His posse flees.

Word runs fast down the peninsula: slave riot and murder. Fiery talk ignites St. Mary's County hours before the body, cold and slung across the back of his mare, crosses back into Maryland.

The ensuing days bring political harangues from courthouse steps.

Broadsides cry: "Lawless Mobs!"

Circulars offer rewards for: "Abolition Conspirators!"

When local magistrates refuse to extradite the accused, calls to re-assert dominance ring out. Maryland newspapers, sheriffs, slaveholder committees clamor for stricter enforcement of the law. Patrols and informants grow bold. Local pro-slavery men enact stiffer penalties for slave infractions—real and imagined—while abolitionists feel a narrow window closing: act now, or the next rescue will be crushed before it can begin.

Most inflamed among the emancipators is Venct Claypoole. When he learns that Clair Kingston—the only son of Silvanas Kingston III—will transport two slaves, their wives, and five children for "rendering" at the

Foxtail Farm Place of Blackness, he melts lead. Pours it into a mould.

Some histories record the act and call it courage; others record the silence that followed and call it mercy. I write it as inheritance. Every moral fire begins long before its spark; the lead Venct Claypoole fluxes is only the latest alloy of older metals, of bargains struck in secrecy, loyalties traded for cover, debts concealed behind lawful papers and false confessions. These are Kingston forgeries alone: virtue veiled in operation, righteousness hidden beneath deception.

The Claypooles see only the veil and call it abhorrence.

Iniquity.

The Devil.

Our Kingstons, believing the mask can be worn without becoming the face, mistake concealment for control. Perceived as evil, they have lived a life of hidden virtue: deceit and deception, the Kingston legacy, practiced in the service of freedom and life. Because it is secret, it must purchase its disguise of sin, fund it, and even draw profit from its lies. Remember, Melody: as profit always bends toward corruption, it gives the world a false perception, one that Nika alone sees clearly.

A prisoner of the colony, later the state—restricted for life to Foxtail Farm, Nika keeps the ledgers in Turkey John Swann's hand: Rendered *for the condemned,* Rendered Unto God *for the saved. Whenever the mercy code appears—* "The Lord Giveth"—*she sings the countersign—* "The water show us forth"—*quiet, daily, disobedient to law. Obedient to God. The books stay hidden inside the old wharf house, the key pinned beneath* her apron. *In Nika, our family's secret conscience survives, a woman counted neither black nor white, neither Kingston nor Claypoole, yet bound to both with a name that means* Melody.

It is Nika who first understands that mercy, disguised too long, begins to resemble treachery. What she guards in silence becomes doctrine; concealment hardens into method. This is the first true code, the founding of every Kingston operation that will follow.

👑👑👑

*S*ILAS *K*INGSTON *III is old. Three times a widower. Father of two daughters—Mariah and Varinia—but without a male heir to take the name Silas and seat the Silvanus Bench; to assume the delicate work against the moral stain, that mortal wound America keeps living and bleeding through its trade in human flesh.*

When the chance to marry yet again presents itself, the prospect of sowing his seed—one final attempt to continue the Kingston chain—invigorates him to take Prudence Pratt as his bride. Had Silas III not been looking for a wife, he would never have looked that bright, ambitious girl's way.

But Silas knows her.

Some of his daughters' children schooled with young Pru. They praised her vigorous nature—fifty years his junior. More importantly, her mother was born a Claypoole. And genuine sins of his early manhood tug his sleeve for expiation.

Claypooles.

Kingston neighbors.

Landowners thirty years before the Kingstons' New World arrival, their fortunes turn with the Crown and, when the American colonists turn on the King, Claypooles run for Canada. Young, ambitious Silas Kingston III assumes their vacated plantation under Confiscation Act authority. Blankets it in tobacco. When, upon the Claypooles's sheepish return, patriarch Reaps Claypoole appeals for its restitution, Silas refuses. Insolvent, Reaps cannot buy back the land of his abandoned heritage, but a bargain is struck to Silas's advantage: the Claypooles may return to their former property on a long-term token lease.

Decades turn.

Harvests and funerals.

Tobacco as gold, chattel as oil.

Month by month, year after year, the lease renews, and while the rent remains trivial, stagnant, Claypoole humiliation increases in equal value to Kingston shame. Every renewal feels heavier. He tells himself it is justice, but knows it's dominion. Domination. The land pays him yet owns him. The conquest becomes its own confinement.

Old now, Silas III mistakes desire for atonement. Thinks a son might balance the scales. Pru Pratt—quick-eyed, willful, Claypoole to the bone—sees only leverage. And takes it.

She takes his name but not his code. To her, marriage is not covenant but contract, and every kindness Silas extends becomes another term to be exploited. He offers peace; she reads permission. He dreams of restoration; she hears restitution. In her veins the Claypoole griev-

ance quickens, ancient and bright as the bloodline she weds to bury.

There are rooms in Foxtail she will never see. Doors whose keys are kept in prayer books, ledgers written in two hands: one for the living, one for the disappeared. Silas does not let her close. The business of rendering is not for her knowing—who is punished and who is pardoned, who suffers and who is spared. To speak of it would expose our family's single virtue, and that virtue must live veiled if it is to survive at all.

Prudence reads his silence as guilt. She counts profit; he buries redemption beneath blood and calls it mercy. And the secrecy that spares others consumes them both; what he guards in faith she mistakes for deceit, and in that mistake their marriage rots.

In time, their union produces the Kingston heir. Prudence names him Clair Kingston. Masculine echo of her Claypoole mother's Claire.

The choice breaks old Silas's heart.

He will not quarrel; tells himself the boy can still be taught, shaped. But when he hears the name spoken back to him, it sounds like someone else's blood in answer.

In time, under Nika's quiet instruction, the boy learns what his father will never tell him. The work. The false ledgers. The hidden doors below the North Vista Outhouse where the cries rise through the floorboards, through the earth itself, at night. He has feared them all: his father first, Nika next, the darkness most, while his mother knows enough to guide him away from his Kingston blood at the elbow like a ghost, delivering him to the lazy laughter of his kin and their crumbling farm, good ol' days, good ol' boys, and good corn liquor.

It is Nika who turns the fear. Who turns the indolence.

She teaches Clair what the noise beneath the house means, what the boats at the wharf carry when the tide is high and the dogs are stilled. She shows him how to read a shoreline by feel. To count bends and creeks the way other men count coin. He sees that the Claypooles, who feed their stills with pig corn and shame, lower their eyes when Nika passes.

And he begins to understand—not black slave, not white master—why they look that way.

Through Nika, Clair learns the discipline that binds their secret: movement without trace, mercy without witness. But something else roots in him—not Nika's humility, but his father's mastery, the need to know each step, each risk, each life spared by his hand alone.

He feels the old darkness lean close, testing what kind of man he will become, and somewhere inside it, a word forms—a promise, a warding charm—to keep him from crossing that line.

(White wrote that Lancelot "made a Word to keep himself from the worst he might become," and broke it only when he loved too much. It draws me to that young man, Clair, when I read it.)

In time, Silas III lives long enough to rejoice a grand-son: the birth of Silas Kingston IV; hearing the wind sing across the common room chimney, he remarks, "Foxtail Farm breathes easy in its suspirations."

At dawn, the baby cries for suckling milk, Silas III lets go life, passes to his accounting—perhaps reward—and one mile away where the Claypoole acres that aren't corn patch, lie unworked tobacco furrows filled with ash from their stills, Venct's lead balls harden and are loaded

*into muskets. Muskets distributed to what remains of
the Claypoole blood, whiskey-stained, crop-poor men in
Sunday shirts with no Sabbaths left to honor, stock-still
and solemn in the moil and bay of their strange and
wolfish hounds.*

*By nightfall, Clair Kingston will follow his father. And
what cools in iron reignites in secrecy; the same fire,
passed hand to hand, outlives them all.*

♔♔♔

*FALLEN KNIGHTS. Broken kings. Queens who endure, who
remember, who forgive; it turns and it repeats and it
bleeds and cries and hungers; it never stops circling,
love and justice: where it and you are bound and bled.*

♔♔♔

*IN THE MIRRORS surrounding, peering over my shoulder:
the air holds their breath—the living and the dead—and
Doris speaks from within it, writing me as I read her
mind as she writes mine.*

*Whispers of Silas, the beginning of the holidays: "Who
do you see when you look into that canvas?"*

*"You won't like my answer, Papa, but I see Doris and
I see my father. And his lust for her."*

*"But this is also a portrait of you. I'm sure you see
that."*

Look into the common room fireplace.

*Look to the Yule log pushed that much farther
into—today—its pile of ash.*

The flicker that only pretends to live burns truer than life; that's where the souls dwell, the Holy Ghost per-haps—or only the hand of fate that took Doris and taught her there is no secret kept from truth.

⁂

"OF CLAIR KINGSTON," Doris Kingston writes, "little is known firsthand and only one autograph entry by the young man has passed down the generations. Pulled in one direction by the greed of his mother, who he rejected, and the secrecy of his father which he embraced in si-lence, only three sentences in his own hand exist. Written and initialed inside a Kingston bible:

'There are men of this state perceived as good but with hearts of evil intent.'

'There are men of this land perceived evil who live only to serve good.'

'Who must be Kingston?'

The ink is iron-gall blue-black, faded brown with time. Of the question mark, a strike-through in car-bon-black ink, unfaded, added sometime in the 19ᵗʰ cen-tury, along with a dash and a period affixed by Kingston hand unknown:

'There are men of this land perceived evil who live only to serve good—

who must be Kingstons.'

While the corrections belong only to a ghost, the hand-writing, those words themselves, match the handwriting of perfectly forged documents found on Clair's person after his killing."

Handheld lanterns light the carriage lot of the un-painted, broad beam and clapboard Ferguson mercan-tile and post store and aim through the ice-crystal dim up the Post Road (formerly King's Highway) that con-nects the St. Mary's peninsula to Annapolis. To anyone viewing the scene this mid-December night—one car-riage and a mule-drawn wagon, four men from Foxtail Farm on foot, two slave drivers—one of the lanterns would be remarked as unstable. Had he chosen, Clair Kingston could wait in the carriage. Often as a boy, a teen, and a younger man accompanying his father on these missions—he would. Did. But this chilled night, his emotions held the unbalanced/competing twins of unbounded joy for his newborn son, Silas IV, and the stifling grief at the passing of his father, Silas III. Clair paces vigorous circles only to quit.

To check his feet.

To peer at his boots as if they belong to a stranger.

Digs heels into the half-frozen mud as if driving fen-ceposts. He rocks once, twice, lantern swinging until burned by melted tallow splash, he stops, squares to the road and steadies his beam; a childish murmur of astonished rapture at his sudden family competes each turn with the grumble of pain inevitable and ancient that carries the irrevocable truth that all life must be reckoned finite, before he relaxes.

Breathes the chill.

Repeats the dance.

He waits to take custody of two slaves accused of barn burning—their conviction eliminating the ques-tion of proof—and of bodily assault in the striking of an overseer which neither man denied. Their master,

*eager to make a broader warning by their punishment,
but fearful of inflaming the county abolitionists, has
contracted Clair to "render" them to death at Foxtail
Farm. The Place of Blackness.*

*Clair takes the commission, but not the intent. Con-
vinces the owner to sell him the wives and children—five little ones between them—on the false pretext
that family wailing might stir revolt. He forges bills of
sale and death receipts to cover their future. Draws
the rendering fee to cover their purchase. Plans their
deliverance north. The men to be "Rendered Unto God,"
their families to follow under new identities.*

*The forged papers found and burned by Mariah
Kingston after his murder. For secrets, like mercy, draw
fire.*

*Colonel Vickery is the slave owner. He arrives first,
his condemned slaves, chained, hunched, and silent,
and their abject families, the smallest children shaking
more from fright than shiver of cold, all inside an un-
covered wagon pulled by a team of mudded and sullen
oxen. Vickery's overseer in knee boots, iced and flaking,
acts the drover. A switch and a quiet voice—probably
not needing words—that only animals and slave can
understand.*

*"Apologies for making you to wait, Mister Kingston.
Too many rivers outside their beds have made an atro-
ciousness of our journey."*

*"Let it be finished quickly then." Clair hands off his
lantern.*

*The same moment Clair steps forward, Venct and
his Claypoole men—bitter kin turned zealot avengers of
their ruined acres—scuttle from the woods in a scram-*

ble of snapping foliage. Stumbles. Oaths. A clacking of musket hammers.

"This finishes, Kingston, on my terms. The murders of your torture chamber slaughterhouse must end-and-will tonight!"

Two groups of men evenly matched in number. Weapons give advantage to Claypoole while the law stands clear/cold with Kingston and with Colonel Vickery.

"Cousin Venct: you swim out of your depth tonight. Go home."

"Soldiers in the Army of the Lord!" Venct raises his gun like a preacher raising the cross before battle, peering over his shoulder and making sure his confederates still back him. "Tonight, we light a fire inside the lamp of liberty and shine—with blackness if we shall—the truth that all men ARE created equally in the pursuit of...of..." Runs out of words. Neither minister nor Quaker, Venct Claypoole adorns himself this night in the long and formless olive drab coat, the low-brimmed black hat of a brethren minister; the only thing complicated is the confusion of syllables tripping over his teeth. "Of E liberty! E Pluribus!"

The colonel, more bemused than alarmed, orders his overseer to gather the slaves. Signals Clair to come forward with the paperwork.

Clair ignores Venct and his ruffians. Nods his wagoner to lower the gate. He says, "Excuse me, Venct. I appreciate your passion, but it is no substitute for Maryland law."

He moves around Venct, behind him, causing the Claypoole to draw down with his musket and utter: "Not one step more, sir!"

Clair ignores the command.

The musket belches fire. The lead ball passes through Clair's back, buries in his heart.

Venct runs.

His men run.

Clair's people circle his body.

Vickery orders his cart around, and the slave women scream; they understand what this means before any of the others.

Doris writes: "Venct wore the cloak of abolition but carried vengeance in his heart, the last Claypoole debt written in powder and lead. Clair bore true abolition bound in silence, his virtue sealed behind the family's mask. Both men sought deliverance and mistook the method for the end. Each acted in righteousness and met the other's shadow. Between them the veil tore, and the women saw through it."

(Good.

Evil.

One.)

"Their husbands are hanged without ceremony or witness the following morning at Colonel Vickery's farm. The wives and their children are separated. Sold separately. Gone by Christmas."

👑👑👑

Snow crusts the rooftops thin as breath, and the air of Foxtail Farm keeps two silences—one buried with the dead, one kept by the living who listen.

Prudence Kingston hosts Christmas in black silk trimmed with seed pearls. White triangles of lace at wrists, at throat. Her brothers arrive from the Claypoole tract with their wives, bright as porcelain, hearts fragile as bone ash.

Invited, Venct does not appear.

Clair's widow, Sarah Kingston, carries her child through the rooms like a lantern. Its small warmth keeps the dark from suffocating her. Clair's sister, Mariah—Silas III's eldest—watches from the doorway, her presence tolerated, her purpose unread, and after supper, Prudence presents her a gift.

A weathervane. Wrapped in canvas. Tied with crimson ribbon. When the rough cloth falls away, the room stills.

A crow wrought in black iron.

A bone clutched in its beak.

Prudence laughs once, sharp and uncertain. "For your widow's walk, sister."

"Say spinster's walk, sister, and I'll know you're generosities, same as day."

"Oh. Dear me. Well, it's only so the North Vista knows which way the wind now turns."

Mariah nods. Says nothing more.

Later, she gives it to Newton—Lavinia's husband—to fix atop the Outhouse gable. It will face east, toward the Claypoole ruin, and turns with the river wind and with the storms. As a gift to Sarah, Mariah invites the girl to move from the manor house into the North Vista where Lavinia will help rear the child, where Newton will continue the Kingston clandestine mission.

December moves to January. Prudence senses the conspiracy in their silence: Mariah, Sarah, Lavinia, and Newton—the new covenant formed in siege beneath that second roof.

Newton tends the hidden chambers. Newton keeps the ledgers, writes the coded entries for those Rendered Unto God. *The operation breathes again, and cries ring out from the chamber below; no one dares to hear the difference between pain and freedom.*

The last decade of the century begins with Prudence filing a petition for reclamation of the Claypoole planting acreage at the St. Mary's courthouse.

Doris writes: "Melody: read and learn. Understand: Law cannot teach goodness; it can only cage the wicked. Those who count themselves good by birth or right are already lost to pride."

When snow melts, the petition is heard. Mariah appears in the county seat with documents older than Prudence's claim—leases signed, lands neglected. The magistrate rules abandonment and reversion of title. The Claypoole agricultural acres return to Kingston in trust for the infant Silas IV.

Prudence's smile in the courtroom is thin as paper; her voice when she vows appeal, thinner still. Yet she feels something worse than judgment. The secret ledger moving against her, the widowed mother and the child she cannot touch. She files her appeal.

By Independence Day, she has shaped her revenge. If the court denies her claim, she will claim the county. Foxtail Farm will open its doors to every name that ever slighted her. She will drown the silence in music and gunpowder.

The house readies itself. The air thickens. The breath before the kaleidoscope turns.

Prudence Pratt Kingston nee Claypoole, traiteurs and confectioners, plucky musicians, taverners with beer wagons and cider barrels. Italian fireworks folders in flowered waistcoats and striped pantaloons. Invitations fly across the peninsula like startled doves at the lift of the hunter's gun.

His killing of Clair judged accident, his zeal recast as misunderstanding. The county nods and lets Venct pass. But guilt rides beside him, mule-paced, bottle-paced. He burrows into the ruin of the Claypoole tract where weeds outnumber crops, where the still burbles its sour hymn and the men who tend it reek of mash and failure. Each night Venct drinks until, in the bonfire devil dance, he sees his Kingston cousin standing in fire before him. The furrows stand flooded, black mirrors reflecting Foxtail Farm's chimneys in streaks of smoke and mud. The same blood runs both directions.

Mariah Kingston never attends the appeal. She returns to court for another petition: to terminate the Claypoole leases Silas III had granted decades before. The magistrate again rules abandonment. The curtilage—the hovels, the shell of the old plantation house its doors gaping, windows breathing wind—remains to

*that clan, but the entirety of the estate reverts in perpe-
tuity to Kingston ownership. Again, in trust for the sole
male heir.*

*America's Birthday arrives. Servants whisper that
Foxtail Farm breathes harder today. The windows
sweat. The walls exhale a fine mist of tallow. And for
the first time in long memory, decay.*

Prudence calls it festivity.

Mariah calls it fever.

*With the night, lanterns climb the drive like souls
refusing to rest. Horses sweat and shudder. Carriages
creak, wood swelling in the sunbaked yard. The guests
step down into the reek of perfume and pig tallow. Inside, the air trembles. Fiddlers scrape strings. A triangle
rings. A drum beats a heartbeat too fast. Wine spills, beer
swills, cider makes for sticky lips. Ice sculptures puddle
on the floors. Prudence Kingston glows moist in pale
satin, hunger bright.*

*Mariah won't cross the threshold. She watches from
the widow's walk beneath the black iron carrion crow
atop the North Vista Outhouse, where the hot river
breeze carries the manor-house noise. The sound is not
music. The sound is not conversation. The sound is not
laughter or joy or celebration. It is a great house choking
on its own breath.*

*Somewhere beneath the floorboards, deep inside the
soil, the blood of the farm moves slower. Thicker.*

At the tenth hour of night Prudence orders silence.

*Servants gather from cellar, the kitchen and the yard.
The fields and the barns, the sheds. Clutch hats. Aprons.
Wipe flour and sweat from their cheeks. Peer with
sparking eyes. Prudence raises her glass. Words spill—of*

generosity, of a gift: *"Yes, I have freed you. All of you, my dark-skinned children. Today, I give you independence and America!"*

The guests applaud politely. No one believes.

The servants do not move. The smallest child sets a candle on the floor. An older woman, born in bondage, named Bethany by Pru's dead husband, bent but unbroken, begins the old song. Nika's song:

"Our God, our help in ages past,
Our hope for years to come,
Our shelter from the stormy blast,
And our eternal home—"

It passes through the room like wind through foxtails. Heads turn. The fine folk retreat abashed to watch the fireworks display. The voices follow into the yard.

"Under the shadow of your throne
Your saints have dwelt secure;
Sufficient is your arm alone,
And our defense is sure."

The song rises. Folds back on itself. Breath in. Breath out. The house itself.

"Time, like an ever-rolling stream,
Bears all its sons away;
They fly, forgotten, as a dream
Dies at the op'ning day."

Prudence stands alone among her unfreed/free property.

"Thank'ee, ma'am. We's always lef' the water show us forth."

From the widow's walk, Mariah sees the shimmer of a candle bending toward the floor and thinks—not pity, not triumph—only the sentence her father once wrote *in a margin:* Mercy, if hidden too long, turns into its opposite.

In the fields, the Italians light their fuses.

Out by the Claypoole fence, men drink and spit and talk of justice. They pass a demijohn, fire a ten-gun salute that sounds like a gunfight. Muzzle blasts throw sparks. Straw takes them. Venct notices, finds he doesn't care. The wind decides.

Fields burn between the properties in two directions racing like a clash of bright and armored jousting horses.

By midnight a tobacco barn burns white-hot against the summer sky.

Foxtail Farm manor glows, flames behind glass, but will not burn. The brick refuses.

Mariah descends from the widow's walk to locate the lady of the manor.

Servants find Prudence at dawn near the edge of a field. Her dress charred. Her hands open as if offering the ash back to God.

No inquiry follows. The county calls it an accident.

The Claypooles vanish into the empty ruin. Only their dogs to watch them lick their wounds.

♛ ♛ ♛

MARIAH OPENS the shutters of the North Vista Outhouse and lets the ash settle where it will. She moves Varinia and Newton, Sarah and the child Silas IV back into the main house. Where they belong; it is not for her, the house she knows will not allow her mortal sin inside.

Foxtail Farm breathes again. The secret work continues through another generation, into a new century, into a Civil War. Mariah washes Prudence's blood from her dressmakers' shears. Returns them to their wicker sheath woven for her in the Indian fashion by her true flesh, Nikamon Swann Kingston.

"I won't be you, mother."

👑👑👑

THE PAGES RATTLED in Melody's shaking hand. Melody rattled.

White-faced owls. Strutting pop stars. Glam-gold glitter-eyes.

The Yule log crackled. The fire-end split. Dropped heavy. Disappeared into the ember mound.

A thrashing snake. Dead eyes staring. Spiderweb tangle on a holly bush.

Melody sat on the fat end of the cured red maple log the fire slowly ate. Thirteen days of Christmas. A low, heavy bench jutting into the common room.

I'll kill you! I lunge for my father. I'll kill you! My blood so hot, my rage so fat.

I hold his gun.

A heavy pistol in her pocket; a real thing against her thigh.

The only real thing.

Doris's last box between her knees, her legs bent and open around it. A position like birthing; an offspring unwanted.

Victoria. "Blood can't read itself, Mel. It fills in what it wants to see."

I still don't understand.

And now this dead woman she's come to love is projecting sainthood that asks for blood onto her, based on a coincidental and loose similarity in a translated name. Pages placed in their stack. Folder closed.

I won't understand.

Victoria. Secret. Knowing. Echoes: "You will."

Folder hover over box.

I can read your pages. I can hold what they hold: that good done in the dark changes shape. That the veil becomes the face if you wear it long enough. I can see that in you. In him. In all of them. I can even see it wanting me.

But I will not put on the mask to prove I understand the mask.

"These white gloves we'd like you to wear while handling the documents."

White cotton gloves over golden tobacco hands.

White cotton gloves burning my hands—

Melody felt the mirrors. Knew she had left the door open knew the image crept inside on canted glass and watched and canted about virtue; the ramblings of a haunted woman—blue-hair stuff—antiquarian, unmoored from the real world.

Crimson beaded gown. An offering of red river lilies throwing fire.

The top of her foot is the color of my eyes.

Except for the blood. Mama's blood. Until turpentine washes it clean. I cannot move. I stare as the turpentine evaporates on her black foot, momentarily coating it white. More spirits of turpentine splash over it. Over the floor from over the table and the chair she pulled down, and I know, it spills all over her body, torn dress revealed. Naked as the day she was born.

Naked as I was born, and she first held and first loved me.

The darkness closed in. Melody shoved the folder into the box. Grabbed the lid to slam it shut. Her mind spun; her soul peeled off like the wings of her private galaxy. All the atoms that made her, drove her, impossible to understand, not worth the effort.

Her eyes seized—hands hovered mid-air—a ledger sheet. Old. But not ancient. Financial. Not spiritual. Columns in Doris's neat hand. Numbers as long as railroad tracks. Dates that belonged to her lifetime. And Melody's. 1973. 1979. 1986. 1992. 1998. Transfers. Outflow. Inflow. A house of massive money on brittle paper.

A paperclipped card. A neat little title card. *Covenant 17.* Between the card and the ledger a folded yellow slip of carbon-less paper.

Melody pulled the yellow flimsy. *Bayfield Glass Company, Annapolis.*

Her atoms stopped. Her galaxy froze.

A snake's head: nothing more than dust and moth wing.

White-faced feathered killers: the whine and clack of beak, rake of claw, the sudden weight of pounding wings.

White gloves: only gloves. To protect, to preserve the secret and the sacred.

Fast through the doors, fast through the vestibule, no need to look at Doris hanging high, Melody *did* feel warmth from the portrait—uncanny as she'd felt it reading her second mother's words—it wasn't fire—

Fire in the kaleidoscope of stained glass.

Fire fingers running up the noose.

Boone Kelso face—leering behind it. Multi-colored flicker. His serpent tongue licking the panes. Licking Nika. Licking her dress/my dress—

It isn't Nika. It isn't me. We're the distraction. The deception.

It wasn't fire burning off Doris as Melody rushed past. No. It was love triumphant.

Scrapefoot: a toddler; love pours from his face gazing up at his mother, holy.

Melody pushed outside. Ran in her socks across the wet muddy tournament field, noticed Beaumont appear beside her prancing with playful high-strut front legs, bounding, knowing where she's headed. She seized the iron ring handles of the chapel's double doors. Everything turned on what she missed in the glass.

Wet footprints splashed across Doris's tomb in the chapel floor.

The blood across my mother's foot.

You can wipe, you cannot erase.

Melody staggered. Felt the rage of the Flint River rolling backward, spitting cars and houses, shingles like teeth.

A picnic table lifts upright and walks on its legs among the mad-eyed carcasses of cows and sheep and pigs and the sucking sound is a deep and horrible cackle.

Her hands hit the altar.

Water showeth forth.

"Water show us forth!"

I am a child. Terrified. I made a mistake.
It was an accident.
Turn back time.
("If I do not wash you, you have no share with me.")
Turn back time. Wash Mama's feet.

In her mind's eye, Melody did. And Beaumont sat beside, his eyes following her gaze to Doris's stained glass window.

The impossible boy. Scrapefoot never younger than Nika. By the time she was a girl who could walk upon a shoreline, Cupid Williams was already the victim of horrible misconduct and sexual abuse. Melody saw it now: Doris's choice, and her call to her became clear from what that choice said: collapse guilt; collapse prophecy; collapse hope into one tableau.

"What mercy would have looked like if the world hadn't broken it."

The glass threw color onto her hands. Green and blue and red.

I know that boy's face: Jack when he listens to Papa read from King Arthur. Little Silas when I kiss him goodnight. Hal's face peering at me from beneath the brim of a baseball cap, mixed with the face I've seen from every mirror I've ever glanced/looked/gazed inside of: mine.

"Not *be* Nika." Her fingers curled in Beaumont's funny topknot. "See what Nika could not keep." And Melody heard here—the meaning under the words, the thing Doris had been saying all along:

This hiding, this code, this way of saving by deceit—it must die. The mask that strives to save is made to smother. The light must hit it, Melody. The mercy that stays secret turns to rot.

Burn the veil. Tear open what they built.

Because what mercy buries will crawl back as judgment.

The pattern will repeat. That is why Boone comes.

2.

AT ABOUT THE TIME the Celtic Dobunni tribes opened their Iron Age forts to the Romans and, by capitulation and subservience to the emperor, got their Catuvellauni and Silures enemies off their backs with other men's fire and sword, the wild cattle of the region—too dimwitted to choose sides—fed all peoples equally. When Rome's armies wandered out of Britain as their empire collapsed back home (or if legend is believed, ran like hell after ignominious defeat by King Arthur), the Dobunni had already domesticated the wild herds. Cows flourished. Were slaughtered. Were eaten. Yet flourished. As years turned to decades, turned centuries, patient cross-breeding and hybridizing perfected the beef to bring such fame to the region that the cow was bestowed its name: Hereford.

A place of pastures chessboarded by hedgerowed lanes. Rolling countryside. From the steep hills of Credenhill and the Black Mountains, to deep/lush river valleys. Legendary, its cow. Renowned, its apple orchard cider. Venerable its cathedral, rising Gothically splendid like an organ symphony might if you froze a measure in a moment then cut that sound clean from stone. Quietly famous/hushedly infamous: the headquarters of the 22nd Special Air Service Regiment (SAS), hides in you-better-not-look-here plain sight in Stirling Lines, a British Army garrison in Credenhill where the men of the FELL KING detachment devoured the tender and juicy, rich and perfectly marbled beef between running reps of their Foxtail Farm construct. The wild herd perfected into muscle; obedience cooked rare.

Inside the hangar-style warehouse known affectionately as *The Cowshed*, England's myth met its machinery. Plywood worn/warped with drill; doors reborn/broken again; paint ghosted white by a hundred gloved hands. Night-vision rigs blinked dead green; an operator reset a breach charge with the quiet focus of prayer. Command voices curt as clicks. The choreography was faultless, and because it was faultless, it was empty—a religion of competence, faith stripped to drill. No one below could say who the enemy was, only that there would be one, and that knowing how to enter mattered more than knowing why; each detonation froze a measure of sound. Faith caught mid-note. Burned into percussion.

Observation deck above. Two men. Winter coats. Ned Trewyn, Captain Hollis. They watched the exercise below unfold: breach—clear—move—

Hollis's jaw tightened with each hammer of the ram; Trewyn's tic-smile, his mother's old camera-command, showed mule teeth every flash of red laser cutting smoke across the false corridors of Foxtail Farm.

Breach—clear—move— targets secured, sorted—nothing collateral (at least not this run)—Silas Kingston's stand-in acquired. Dispatched.

Troopers peeled off helmets. Steam rose off their shoulders. Cordite clung faintly to the recycled air.

Water. Instructors' briefs.

Reset.

Trewyn gave Hollis the nod. The nod that says, *Impressive.* Got a *what'd-ya-think-you'd-see?* grunt in response. Trewyn served the Crown. Not Cabinet. Not committee—the monarch's will a prism that bent all policy into private rightness. It steadied him now. Gave the moment its calm. Conviction itself proof against consequence. He handed Hollis a printout.

Didn't yet look. "Am I cleared?"

Trewyn made the sign of the cross. "Enough."

BC-KALEID-2012-12-28-SEG-A

Corpus: TWHITE-UK-1958

Confidence index: 0.78

Recovered plaintext:

"May it please Your Majesty,

Truth has a way of rising no matter how deeply you bury it, and the demons never remain invisible.

In order to avert what I fear will be a terrible loss of lives, I offer you my confession—

Recruitment in Tula, by Nikoláj Yurenev, the long-reach hand;

attempt, near enough, on Colonel Bogdon Ogievich;

and the irrevocable: Evander Lott—taken and entered by deed,

collateral acknowledged, not sought.

I accept the sum entire."

End fragment // awaiting key-roll B

Hollis's voice came low: "A confession?"

"You don't question it, I won't."

Too glib. He did. "From Kingston. What happened to this being his instructions from his Russian handler as your man in the field claimed?"

Trewyn shrugged. Like this sort of thing he'd never encountered before happened all the time. "Tula checks out with the Kingston timeline. The cousins shared Ogievich product for years—to hear SIS/REE say it, that stream was always suspect. At least since this morning. And now we know why."

"What about this Yurenev?"

"High enough up the SVR Mount Olympus for me not to see him through the clouds—who knows—? but I'm assured his name's the one that's made half of Vauxhall tighten their cheeks."

Hollis was a prig. Didn't appreciate the vulgar.

"Bottom line—" Trewyn pressed his pun, took back the sheet. "Kingston confirms topping Evander Lott. And like him I accept the sum entire. The bloody thing's genuine."

"What's 'key-roll B?'"

"Reason I want you moving now. Kingston splits the cipher two ways. *Confession* A, with B—*the Who-Knows* and *Better-To-Not*—to follow."

Hollis shook his head. Liked it less. "Because he's onto Lott. Has been—God knows how long. And you think this is enough to run it up?"

"Enough to run it *through*."

The captain looked out over the false house below: the men resetting, the splintered doors, the plywood dust like pollen in the floodlights. "Far as I care, Numpty Lott's my bonus now. Orders to clean him still stand?"

Trewyn nodded.

The word for Hollis's expression was *smile* but there was nothing kind on his face. "The Lancer fellow?"

"We'll have final verification from your favorite numpty any time now. You'll move the detachment. Tonight."

"Before Oakley finishes the decrypt."

"Before Silas Kingston finishes *us*."

A short silence. The hiss of radios below. Trewyn's head tilted, eyes on the rehearsal, the calculated motion of men who never looked up. "He's running the clock," he said softly. "He knows exactly what he's given us and what he's kept back. Still—we've enough. Moscow's hand. A dead Briton. A confession to the Queen."

They stood awhile longer, above the repetition. The men of the FELL KING detachment began again.

Breach—clear—move.

The fall of boots in clouds of plaster dust and splinters. Gun smoke.

All precision, no hesitation. The rhythm of certainty: cold, perfect, until even the false house believed itself real.

3.

THE PLAN HAD ALWAYS been for Clive to peel off and do what he had to do— "I'm not telling you where, when, or what. When the twins ask—when your sisters: tell them I had some work to catch up on."

"No one thinks you work."

"Say I took on a new job—but that I want a full report on the movie. Especially, if there's a dragon. That'll keep them off my scent."

A pit in Paige's stomach. After the orange. After they'd made love. She'd hardly slept. She knew the pit would hollow out further the more she found out. They'd agreed she would never find out. Not one bit more. She hoped, prayed, that time and the things time gave would fill it out and one day cover it over. Like the leaf pit in fall for compost that in decay and spading over, in decomposition and spreading, might lose its dead form, return to soil richer for the process and, spread, might fertilize something new to flower.

Time as sadness. Sadness as seed. "They know there's a dragon," she said. "It's in the commercial." Eyes glistening in theater dark. "Be careful?"

He winked. "If they know about the dragon, we'll have gobs to talk about when I pick you up later." Kissed the top of her head. Came back once with popcorn and Icees, Red Vines and the Toblerone chocolate Leigh liked and said she'd share, and then he was gone.

The previews ended. *The Hobbit* began. Charlotte left the row faster than Bilbo the Shire, leaning to Paige as she passed—"I'm going to sit back there with my friend."

Paige craned her neck, watched her file into the back row, picked out Bobby Claypoole before Charlotte reached him. He offered a popcorn tub in greeting.

Fuckwit bought her a whole 'nother drink. Wasting Clive's generosity. No wonder she was so squirrely at breakfast with her phone.

Chill. You were fourteen. Once.

Her hands went to her belly.

You'll be too, baby. With your mommy and your daddy. Please, God—the "and your daddy?"

She peered back one more time. Charlotte getting her first kiss. Their eyes meet. Paige/Charlotte.

She wants so much for me to be excited for her.

"Shit."

Jack: "Shit." Little Silas: "Shit." Leigh: rolled her eyes and shook her head. Pointed her older sister's eyes to the movie screen.

♕♕♕

TAKING A LIFE. Nothing like the movies. Absolute zero in common. The body doesn't go away with the set dressers and the scene change. The pacing off—neither hyper-jerky cause-and-effect kinetics nor slow-mo fluid, inevitable ballet. It's both: a blur of confusion, thoughts frantic, grasping hands, memories of decisions already made. In the split-second of it all, you live in the chaos of the split. The sound is wrong. It's all breath and throat, the cracks and crashes are only feelings. Noise-overflow you didn't hear and later can't escape. Hard muscle and bones are distinctive—when it floods back—with that horrible knowledge: every part of the human body, even the hardest, is covered with something soft and slightly giving. You don't get a new costume. No off-screen airline ticket. No clean gun with a glamorous boat-chase in Venice.

The body remains.

The remains stay where you left them.

And that's two places: physical and mental. One of them, you can drag, hide, bury. The other—you can't. It stays. It's never done. It never decays.

Clive pulled dusty shrouds from old furniture cluttered about Garde-Joyeuse. Bundled/dragged them into the inner-wall passageway. Night before—he'd lugged Fergus's corpse to the lowest point within the conduit of passages. Within/behind the listening post wall. Back down there now: a faint sweetness, vaguely metallic, vaguely shit, and ammonia and...wet leather—of all things. Throat clenched. Stomach bucked. Swallowed the breath he held. All involuntary recoil—he'd smelled things worse—but this was primal. Something ticking inside him like a Geiger counter gone wild. "Fight or flight" a cosmic joke. There's only one endpoint and it/you are already non-existent in its absolute embrace. That's what made his stomach buck: not the smell, the vertiginous worthlessness.

He held his breath, best he could. Shook out the canvases—bedspread, tablecloth, drapery—overlapped them like a kind of runway. Got down and rolled. Fergus was gray, blotchy, stiff but not rigid. Clive reached in, re-coiled—the man's clothing unexpectedly damp—rolled him/felt unnatural slosh. A tacky sound from within Fer-gus's chest as he completed the first rotation. Met his eyes. Mistake: not that Fergus was looking, but that they were clouded and collapsed. Clive turned away.

Condensation crept up the walls. The ground where Fergus had lain was wet. It wasn't blood. Clive shud-dered with the realization that decay and putrification enveloped everything around it. He gave a harsh, loud grunt because he needed to assert life. Then he asserted himself. Strong. Violent. Loud and hard until the corpse was thickly wrapped and, more exhausted than antic-ipated, he squatted on his heels and knew his effort wouldn't do a damn bit of good disguising what the earth would reclaim its slow and only way.

Impossible to catch his breath. He could taste the man. Pushed out of the small chamber, plunged the narrow shafts, scrambled the laddered chutes, back out the wall-hole he'd made with Fergus's head. Didn't stop moving until he'd dragged a sofa across the opening.

He collapsed onto it—feet on the floor, hands on his knees, head almost between them. Kept shaking his skull to rid himself of the smell. The sights.

No one here—America—would miss him. A foreign agent undercover, he'd lived like a ghost. Now a ghost in permanence. Bought his food in bulk. No rhyme or reason where—no local or retail or commercial con-tacts. Liquor store: only place that might recognize him, but they never asked questions, rarely answered, and existed on the inevitability that their best customers always disappeared. At some point.

Good enough at his job, Fergus had never brought a moment's attention to himself that would need to be answered by local authorities or anyone else—town, county, state.

No one came to the house; the bank that supposedly owned it—didn't, and with what was coming: possession would be abandoned, untraceable afterward.

A wall and a football pitch's worth of property on other side separated Garde-Joyeuse from the house at Foxtail Farm. No one would notice the smell. No matter how bad it got. He just needed time. Get himself and Paige out of there. Out of the country. If he could. The morality. The legal, political, treasonable reality/ramifications. He'd show his back because he didn't care how he looked or what he'd be called.

A wife. An unborn child. It started there for me.

Governments, their machinations, could go to hell: only one thing mattered and Silas had been perfectly clear and perfectly right. He got it now.

As Silas knew he would.

Somehow that made Clive proud.

The only people who'd care what happened to Fergus Lott were at Vauxhall Cross. This moment—? Only to the extent of making sure that Fergus was alive and Clive was dead.

Turned out the other way.

And that needed attention.

Clive needed a bodge to steal some time; made his way down to the listening post.

As Fergus left it. Bottle out, systems running. His personal terminal, hours ago defaulted to auto-off. That would have pinged back a heartbeat alert. If Clive tried to pass himself off as Fergus, attempt to confirm his own demise, he'd blow the protocol he didn't know and only succeed in confirming the truth that their careful op had gone arse-about-face.

They'd be anxious to fix that. Might try to wrap him up at the motel. He wouldn't go back. At that point, they'd know he was at Foxtail Farm; if they were coming in for Silas, they wouldn't come twice. They'd hit them both at once.

If he did nothing, they'd assume the same: Fergus failed. Clive prevailed. Same flipping result.

Same result if he logged in/checked in on his own terminal, pled his case. Except they'd probably mock him before they dropped him.

I have the codebook to offer.

Never cheat the same card twice. And who am I kidding? They'd just nick it off me once I was down, thank my dead ass kindly. Call it tidy work.

Bloody hell.

Everything boiled down to this: Clive Lancer had only two allies left. Silas Kingston was one, but Silas belonged to Paige; when they'd need him and what they'd need him for belonged to Paige.

The other—? I don't even know his name. What could he possibly do? Would he even care to try?

Jolly Jack/Ruddy Cheeks/Jim-Cracky Cricket.

Clive knew him by one other thing. One other name. It was the only thing real he'd taken with him from his fall visit to Legoland.

He wouldn't need to phone HQ. He could wake Fergus's field terminal with a cached session token, present the little hardware crypto-fob Fergus kept on his keyring, and impersonate the post long enough to push a signed ingest up the Service pipe. He pulled Silas's KGB codebook from his pocket, opened it at a random page—randomness as cover—and photographed the spread.

On the terminal he attached the image, invoked the emergency HMAC-signed upload routine, and dispatched the packet to MI6's secure ingest (Palimpsest/Vauxhall queue). He repeated the process across three different pages so the payload would look deliberate, and to each transmission he appended a deliberate anomaly-tag: B.309C—the odd marker by which his confessor, his hangman, would know.

Throw smoke and hope the first out of the cloud wasn't a killer but someone who still cared to see him.

4.

I n Tehran, KALEIDOSCOPE's infiltration of deni-
able agitators into the capital to stoke street protests,
enflame them to violence, never sparked. Never even
smoked. CINDER CROWN operators were lifted in silence. Summarily executed. The march they'd planned
to flash into insurrectionary martyrdom—fed on rumor,
inflated by their own conviction—folded in on itself
when news came of the Guards' bloody triumphs at
Abadan, Ahvaz, South Pars; the brave ones left only to
mouth slogans in shuttered courtyards, filming themselves for no one to watch.

On the one hand, this was good for Russia—no need
for an allied rescue of their Iranian partners, no need to
pull Kalaydoskop from Baku. On the other, Kolya saw
his leverage with Michael fast diminishing. A podium,
empty but inevitable, signal bright/broadcast-ready on
the main wall display, duplicated on the camera mount,
duplicated in the control room, Michael hunched in a
chair by the teleprompter. Kolya against the wall beside
the door. Watched his grandson—foe but blood—and
marveled in his own way at the reserve of calm, the
emotionless mask worn all day and easy on his face even
now. Michael compared his notes against the scroll,

going so far as to offer language fixes that, making him sound better, sealed his treason more tightly than Kolya had written it. But what use would parading him across international airwaves with a scathing indictment of CIA overreach when that reach had ignited nothing and implicated Russia nowhere?

Daria.

He saw it. The tilt of Michael's head. The perseverant glint in his eyes. The angle of shoulders—not pride, never that; not confidence haughty and domineering, but a perfect centering—body to time to place—centered and claiming the space he filled (she filled/they filled) no matter the circumstances, humiliation—

A cold, grubby sickroom above the Technical Glassworks Factory Number 3.

—betrayal; that space belonged to this grandson of his, this Mikhail/Michael; shoulders that carried the shape of personal honor—his honor/her honor—that would not be moved or marred by the unpreventable manipulations of others thrust upon them. Him. Her.

Daria. Michael.

The Enchanted Forest. A red balloon.

Doris: "Ask before you assume he'd take that from you."

"Would you like a balloon, Mikhail?"

Gave me a funny look at his name, but— *"It's red. My favorite color's red. I've never had a red one before."*

And one year later—

"Mister: if you kiss my mother again I'll kill you with a knife."

"Michael! I *kissed the balloon man. He didn't kiss me. He's my—"*

"Shh. Daria. The boy is right."

Kind. Instantly centered. She tells him: "Take Lynn and watch the water show. It's almost time for the Lady in the Lake."

The boy dutifully pushes his sister in her stroller to the fence around the water.

Silas takes his time at the drop.

"Michael's getting too old to come. I'll just bring Lynn next time. He'd probably bring that knife and make good with it."

"You'd like that?"

"For a million reasons I can think off the top of my head. Yes."

Doris didn't smile. She wasn't angry, she was tired. I laughed.

Doris was nowhere in the room and everywhere in her son. Something rose inside Kolya. Something old and made small by lifetime effort. Dangerous. A warmth Kolya felt—forgetting Tehran/CINDER CROWN/Silas—for the briefest moment. Was only the briefest lapse. The hand of habit closed. Squeezed warmth into scorn.

The heart is the most dangerous spy; learned that long ago. Better to live bloodless than beat at what could have been forgiven.

The podium burned white against the wall; the camera doubled it; the control room doubled that. What passed for truth was always a reflection repeated till it obeyed. He watched Michael—

Genetic mimickry. Nothing more.

Three televisions along the far wall carried the outside world. The same news services Kolya had watched without rest for over forty-eight hours. Zahedan, Chabahar, Tehran. All of them now uniform in official language: *"With the grace of God, our forces neutralized the terrorists..."*

Kolya's mouth flattened. He had anticipated chaos, not containment. He took a commanding step forward, waving Michael to his feet. "Now or never, Mikhail." Michael nodded but his mouth stayed shut. His face said nothing. His impatient gesture pressed Michael to the podium. "The world needs a face. Strip the mask and let them see Silas Kingston in all his manufacture."

Michael adjusted the microphone. Faced the teleprompter. Faced the camera lens through his "confession's" glass scroll. The stage light went red above the door. Michael waited for the green on the camera. Kolya stepped back. Glanced to the booth. Gave the nod.

The director wasn't looking. Kolya waited. Michael waited. The cameraman looked between them all. Through the glass, the director's face had gone empty, the kind of emptiness that follows faith when it fails. The director jabbed a finger at the fourth wall monitor. His assistant's hands danced across the board.

The fourth television monitor woke. An image flashed lived. Red caught his eye from the corner. Red field. Five stars. Tiananmen beneath. The State Council Information Office sigil.

A woman's voice. Mandarin. Formal. Kolya's mind raced translation: *"Captured militants confirm training at Karpov Range..."* Something too fast. Mind lingered: *Karpov Range—?*

What could she possibly be talking about?

"Russian advisors implicated in support for insurgent elements..."

He waited for hedges—*alleged, suspected*—the small softeners that keep states from naming the guilty outright. None came.

English followed, flat and official: *"The Ministry of State Security today released evidence linking Russian advisors to the insurgent group operating in southern Iran."*

Kolya felt a small fracture at the back of his skull—old rehearsals that had always ended with a lie now had no place to perform.

A lifetime of rehearsed denials came up empty.

The camera now—just the green bulb waiting to be lit, waiting for the truth that wouldn't be good enough. Not now.

He looked at Michael.

The man had not moved.

No triumph, no fear. Just gray calm—eyes smoke, unreadable. He couldn't possibly have known; more possible: he didn't care.

And then Russian itself. Heavy with state diction. Each consonant landed like a hammer blow. A sickle across his throat. Dry. Tight. Easy to slit. *"Kitay: zaderzhannyye podtverdili podgotovku v Krasnodare."* China: detained militants confirmed training in Krasnodar.

Onscreen: men cuffed against sandbags, an airfield hangar with a number he recognized. A Kalaydoskop training regiment—obviously fake. Obviously a set. Obvious only to him.

The voice kept speaking, but his ears had narrowed to one sentence.

"...*Russian state sponsored support to terrorist elements...* "

Kolya felt the room tilt. Fractional vertigo. Waved the director off. "Enough."

The stage light stayed white.

The air stayed bright.

The teleprompter shut down. The purpose was gone; Kolya caught Michael's eye. Head-jerked his order they leave.

At the door, Michael: "If it makes you feel any better, old man, this hurts Silas's feelings more than anything I'd've said." He opened the soundproofed door for Kolya. Into the corridor. "China just took all his work and threw a 'Made in China' stamp on his ass."

"This isn't personal."

Michael laughed without humor. "Now you sound like the oligarch-mafia stooge Kravtsov. For you. My father. Myself. And mostly Lynn: it may not have been personal. Once. But, Gramps, personal's all it is anymore. You've been watching me so carefully all these years—I'm surprised you didn't see the lightbulb when it popped on over my head."

"You want to keep chattering? Do it on the way to the elevator. We're moving." Kolya's stride took great territory. A satisfaction at recapturing something with each step, a pretense that what he left behind remained his own.

Michael kept up just fine without the act. "I'll tell you one more thing, but I know you know it already: for my mother—your Daria, Silas's Doris, Guenever or whatever character she imagined herself from her treasured book because—and you missed out on this, your family—she read it to us. Me. My sister. My brother. All three of his in her lap, at her feet, draped over her shoulder—Lynn liked to do that, all lazy, their hair tangling—she'd do all the voices and when she did she lived all their lives."

Kolya halted at an elevator bank. Its golden doors at right angle to a mirrored wall. Michael punched the button. Kolya noticed their reflection, shoulder almost touching shoulder, duplicated again in the mirror's refracted blur within the brass depth of the doors. Kolya released a breath he hadn't realized he'd held.

Michael wasn't finished; his voice went soft. "Personal. That's the only thing any of it ever was. Her and you. The rest of us are just reflections of her face stepped out of the mirrors to haunt you."

He took the photograph of Daria from his inner chest pocket. From over his heart. The student girl at the KGB school. Michael gazed at it. Kolya pretended not to.

"When you gave this to me, I thought—how hopeful she looks. So much hope exploding off that girl's face..."

Kolya didn't move. Watched Michael reach across his chest and tuck the old photograph behind the perfect handkerchief in Kolya's breast pocket.

"That kind of hope? Comes from only one place."

Kolya's cerulean eyes flicked to meet Michael's smoky look. Beat back his own hope inside him. Not far enough. Michael caught it and said the word that wasn't *love*.

"That *loneliness* belongs only to you."

The elevator dinged. The doors pulled apart.

"The rest of us, Kolya: we're reflections of that."

Their double reflection—caught again in the hall-way's last-look mirror—bent, and Kolya saw Michael for exactly who he was: an animal mimicking its prey. He wasn't Silas, he wasn't Daria—

Their images fused.

Michael was him.

♛♛♛♛

MERYL HOFMEYR preferred elastic-waist pantsuits. Or jumpsuits; she liked those. Irene Wren—as KALEIDO-SCOPE's fabricators built the alias and kit—was made to present best in belted-dress business suits. While Ms. Wren may have looked fabulous in belted-dress busi-ness suits, Meryl hated belts. And silk—which these suits all happened to be—silk stunk. Just one whiff curdled her stomach. Got her thinking too vividly where it came from; massive factories filled with worms chomping mulberry leaves and secreting sticky fluids into threads by the ton.

There was a reason *belts* and *silk* and *roads* kept circling through her mind. The words had been creeping for a year through Chinese chatter: first as metaphors, then as fragments SIGINT pulled from aides around the new General Secretary—talk of a *silk road, a belt of trade, roads binding markets west.* They weren't naming it here, not yet, but this was the lead-up.

This was Wànhuàtŏng.

Tehran's line had barely cleared when Beijing's fol-lowed—Russia named, insurgency branded. Now, magical minutes later, Chinese and Iranian delegations stepped to the lectern in Pavilion B2. Folders printed. Flags lifted from their morning crates. Chinese manufactured/China ready.

Aid framework.

Pipeline financing.

Agricultural cooperation.

Port concessions.

Phrases pre-cleared; contracts in everything but ink. And the Made in China pens lifted.

Wren adjusted the ear-seal of her in-ear translator. Agency-issue with a coiled transducer line that pressed against the skin just behind the jaw so no sound escaped. She turned her Hofmeyr forelock as she absorbed it all from the second-tier gallery. Her mind whirred. Her thoughts click-clacked in odd patterns that matched her usual/unusual herky-jerky way of speaking.

Two KALEIDOSCOPE cutouts in the press rows worked the Expo's open AV circuit; their feed folded, encrypted, moved across the Ring Road to their dead import office. The safehouse. She visualized her crew: every angle mirrored, Chinese badges tagged as they crossed readers, faces logged, posture, proxemics. Real-time traffic. No theatrics. Just work. Her throat made a clucking sound.

The pattern to repeat itself. Empire stitched to empire by the same brighty-bright thread; they only change the hands that spin it.

The ceiling speakers carried the Mandarin press officer clean and official. Over her earpiece: *"In response to the tragic events in Iran, the People's Republic of China affirms immediate cooperation in regional stabilization and resource support... "*

Wren drew a hard line on her pad: *Wàn ascendant / Russia named.* She keyed a short transmission through the link—routed across the Ring Road, bounced once through the safehouse, and out to the A3 negotiation cell:

Keep to finance and continuity clauses—escrow, throughput, resiliency. Nothing political.

The confirmation icon came up on her screen—*TCP secure / received.*

Only then did she look down at the Commerce and DOE observers in front of her. White-faced. Hands tight on their binders. Waiting for instruction.

"Stay calm." Flat. Almost kind.

They didn't answer; the sound of applause from the floor rose and fell around them, and she felt, not for the first time, that she was listening to the beginning of something that had already happened.

👑 👑 👑

LIKE A STATION terminal. A cathedral. Seven work areas. Desk clusters old-world wooden and heavy; periodical-style lectern easels; library desks with long top shelves stacked with maps and treaties and international energy diplomacy ephemera.

Nothing that happens here happens fast, and oil policy of today has a tail as long as a dinosaur.

"It's oval-shaped—the window—what you're asking I look at, right?"

A wry smile stretches James Jesus Angleton's thin lips.

Silas stood beneath it. Watched the quiet work of his silent workers who drilled at the "whys", the "hows" of arcane and secret, overlooked or invisible geopolitics of fossil fuel diplomacy.

"I want you to imagine something. Are you ready?"

"So very."

"Look up and imagine that false dome flooded with light. Breaking apart. Bouncing about. Tell me the first word that comes to mind."

"Kaleidoscope."

"Marvelous. That's where you are. This place."

The center-dome skylight above Silas's shaved bullet head danced with the golden light that lanced between solemn gray clouds that marched across the late-day sky. It broke into color. Not bright. Not warm. Just enough to give the floor its old sea-change shimmer, marble veined with blue and rust like tide-lines.

Silas Kingston sheltered in the silence of the Beaux-Arts hall, doored-off from the action-area where KALEIDOSCOPE raced the digital superhighway. Silas didn't like it/trust it/ride it; kept the door shut and let that noise die on the other side while here the old room still answered to hand and thought. Stone and paper, it held its line.

This room had always been the heart; the broken light the pieces of his.

CINDER CROWN, ruined. China lifted the shape of his ignition and made it theirs—same smoke in Tehran, same stain on Russia, but the credit and the leverage slid east; Wànhuàtŏng turned a Kingston strike meant to break Kalaydoskop into a ledger where both Moscow and Washington paid. Iran strengthened. The pattern shifting, beautiful for the second before it falls apart.

He had built KALEIDOSCOPE to hold. Not out of stubbornness, but out of charge: what he had taken from Angleton without the mercy of a promise of success; keep the pattern when the men go; keep the quiet machine from becoming an engine of destruction.

Four years old. Hurricane of 1947. Clutching my grandfather's hand—Silas V—as the last planks of the wharf are devoured by the Patuxent, as the wind devours the weathered, shrunken-wood shell of the wharf house where Turkey John reared his family, where Doris's favorite—that Nikamon girl—once walked barefoot in her simple handmade dress, guided by the light of a burning pine knot, to a secret wedding without a priest inside our chapel; Silas III, Papa's grandfather, waiting with only the servants as witness, as guests; the only woman that Silas ever truly loved, and Papa says to me in the hurl of rain, "Endurance isn't the same as survival, boy. You hold until you can't. Then you watch."

He let the light turn on his face and did not move.

Jilly Bregado crossed the room. Slow. The hush stayed around her as she came. She didn't need to speak to announce what she carried; the weight of the file was its own voice. She stopped close enough for him to take it if he wanted. He did not.

"Commerce Pavilion B2," she said. "China and Iran. Aid, pipelines, ports. Wànhuàtŏng in plain sight."

"And the one in charge?"

"We'll know him by New Year's. You have my promise."

She shifted the stack in her hands. Beneath the heavy briefing binder a second file showed. Slim. Brown-tabbed. The color of yesterday. Of Moscow. Silas had no idea how Jilly had them, where she recycled them from, but she would hand him one when she wanted to touch the part of him denied the rest of the world.

She read his glance. "An intercept. Commercial sat hop out of London, bounced through Vauxhall—flag reads Joint side—but it's not theirs for us. The tortoises caught it in transit."

"Go on."

"Within minutes of the China–Iran announcement the traffic shifted. The Joint line went dark—clean disconnect—and a new route spun up through a private Belgravia exchange. Same key signatures, different encryption. Someone wanted the handoff local and off-record."

"The address?"

"A former diplomatic quarter, now a shell company front. Russian capital, British management. Energy trust filings under Crown Petroleum Group."

He looked down at the marble, its faint reflection of the sky. A pause. "Londongrad."

"The enemy of our enemy...?"

"Don't even think it. Never's been a head on a hydra—wanted to make friends." Conversation over.

Jilly lingered. In some ways he'd always be her charge; he led but she still guided. "I read in the paper. Day after Christmas. And I read between lines."

"What lines?"

And overhead, the gray clouds massed. The color was gone.

"The Azerbaijan Embassy. It's your daughter."

Silas held her gaze, let it penetrate, gave nothing in return. For Jilly that was permission.

"Is there nothing that can be done? You—Silas Kingston—of all people: you?"

He touched his lower lip with the tip of his tongue, afraid of what he could taste.

He could say she wasn't his to save. That the work had swallowed the reach. That kings lose their kingdoms by inches. But the truth was smaller. Harder.

Every rescue begins as a betrayal.

Imagined he tasted blood and let the thought stand between them.

Gray to black and evening fell and at the end of the day, the room was just a room and a handful of regular people with regular thoughts and regular unspoken troubles.

♕♕♕

HANDFUL OF WORDS. Since their conversation leaving the media suite and returning to Kolya's Flame Towers redoubt: perfunctory exchanges on movement, food. The Khazri. On bullshit drive-over talk. No China. No Silas. No next steps. Unspoken but felt like water rolling heavy over a sinking, drowning man, Michael knew he could leave at any time. Both of them knew he wouldn't. More than mission, less than duty, heavy as blood. Unspoken.

Unspoken: Michael had kept his end of their bargain—as far as circumstance had allowed—and now, Kolya needed to remove the sword from Lynn's neck.

Less than mission, more than duty, thicker than water. Michael knew Kolya wasn't ready; his heart only now a field turned and breathing, waiting the first seed. He would move only when the old man's will to live outweighed his will to win. To water the past with tears. And Kolya, he suspected, had never wept—at least not in Michael's lifetime—and the Kingstons were built on that drought.

A remark to the air that now he would rest, Michael shut himself inside his bedroom. Fell into a false sleep to knocks and doorbells, the sparrow-chirrups of Kolya's mobile phones, the shuffle and flutter of comings and goings that lasted well into the night.

As dreams do when sleep patrols the edge of operational consciousness, images attached themselves to Michael's vague/tormented overhearing. Kolya: everything to everyone, depending on the temperature of the room and those who joined him—singly or in small groups—he embodied an entire cast of characters as if directing himself in an elaborate play.

Compassion/vision/charm.

Rage/power/peril.

Humiliation.

Patriotism/duty/money.

He was everything to every one of his tentative visitors—nothing of himself— drawing from them their fear, greed, weary pride, the last glint of loyalty that still mistook survival for faith.

Through both walls—the physical and half-sleep—Michael heard fragments of Kolya's voice. Flat at first. Rising in oratory cadence.

"...the CPC expansion is the spine; the Black Sea the lungs. We hold that course. Nord Stream is poison—German leash, oligarch leash, war leash. You sell to them, they hold your breath. You sell east, they burn you. Ours is south. Our sea. Our blood. The West will never tolerate a Russian pipeline they cannot pretend to control. So we keep the illusion; we keep the peace. We keep the route. We gain Europe—all of Central Europe—by invitation, the comfort of warm homes at winter. The last generation forgot how to lift a forest ax, this generation will stop digging coal, and the next won't even remember the feel of fire on their hands."

A voice swore loyalty to Putin and Kalaydoskop, and Kolya gently added, "and to the Rodina." Weak applause. Artificial laughter, The scrape of chairs.

Whole truth in half-dreams Michael saw Kolya more animal than man—chameleon-skinned, peacock-feathered, the poison viper that appears the harmless vine; he saw Kolya's own people simply as rats.

At Pancras Hall and just-turned-twelve, compelled by my fencing coach to compete up a class in tournament. Fighting boys sixteen, seventeen, eighteen with twice the reach and muscled thrust. Clutching my mask, my foil. Wanting to pee. Biting lip. Fighting tears.

And Silas kisses my forehead—in front of everyone—but he looks me straight in the eye and there's power there, it flashes between us, his smile is teeth and merciless and he says the thing he always says—never makes sense but always gives me courage:

"'I think we are in rats' alley. Where the dead men lost their bones.'"

Each had come to defect from Kalaydoskop. Each left swearing they would not. But rats can't deny their nature; they always find a gap, an open hatch, a broken seal in the hull to slip through if only to buy precious minutes to drown alone later.

Michael stomach awoke him, the aroma of food drifted beneath the door. The living room was dark. The televisions dark. The sky dark and clear and star-scattered; their brilliant light cold and contained and refused. Lulu's former bodyguard, leered at Michael. Finished setting the dining room table for two. Poured wine. Disappeared through an interior door.

"It's local. Can't vouch for it being any good."

They sat. They ate. Michael watched Kolya waiting for him to meet his gaze. He caught him reaching for the wine.

"Why me?"

"Why you what?"

"Why not Lynn? Why not Hal?"

Kolya poured. Kolya drank. "Hal—? That should be easy."

"Too honest."

Kolya shook his head. Wiped his mouth with the back of a hand.

"Too brave." Watched Michael to see how that blade cut.

"And Lynn?"

Lynn/Doris—he must know how that ended: the silk rope and the fire.

Kolya ate a bite of food. Chewed contemplatively, eyes softening, warming to Michael.

He wouldn't have needed to see to know it: that's what's in my eyes and this animal can see right to it. We've run out of family that I know and I see the shadow of the other half of me, Lynn, Hal, Doris that he fears.

Kolya wiped his lips with linen. He released Michael's gaze and stood. He seemed taller. As if the space around him had adjusted. "There is a telephone call I need to make."

"Enjoy."

He watched Kolya vanish briefly into the darkened living room before his face lit green from the screen of his sat-phone.

Michael's hand dropped to his hip. It closed around the only thing he carried with him.

Kolya punched in a number. Didn't lift it to his ear. Watched it pulse, and pulse, and pulse until it gave up on the call—as devices know better than men when to surrender. In the faint glow before the phone shut itself off, Kolya's face belonged to a man alone. Then shadow. Then gone.

Michael's hand inside his pocket. Crushed round the miniature icon. Lulu's *Znamenie*. Our Lady of the Sign.

Holy Mother.

Tornado.

Only she remains.

BELGRAVIA IN THE RAIN. Fat drops splattered the window-pane. Rain fell like sparks in streetlamp glow across

Eaton Square. Trewyn watched the drops gather, split, vanish in gold smears down the glass.

The call had come. After China's stunt—inevitable. Let the bell toll out. No answer. No denial. Just quiet satisfaction of a line resurrected from the past gone dead. Kolya Yurenev had been a partner of convenience; Beijing had overturned the board, and Kalaydoskop's value with it.

The stake was oil—always oil—and the right place on the pipe. Britain off the Continent, needed a place at the valve.

A touch of the key beside his keyboard—the manual interrupt—let the connection fold into a holding server. A second later the encrypted route to Vauxhall dropped from the screen.

Now he sat back. The raindrops ran. The conservatives had a name for it now. *Brexit*. So cute. So debilitating. So inevitable. This way, though, buy into the spigot—twice the everything of the first—you maintain ownership of the EU winter.

Too late to pull the Crown out of the well now. Only thing left is hold the rope.

He typed a single message.

To: Vostok Consolidated

Subject: Re-evaluation of Baltic capacity proposal (NS-2 Annex)

Pressed *Send.* The cursor blinked once. Turned gray.

Trewyn felt his uncontrollable smile spread his cheeks. But tonight, he felt like smiling. He always did when a thing irretrievable was done. His mind photo-snapped a memory.

We'll call it independence, and still sell the continent its own fire. The Empire breathes through the pipes now—quietly, profitably, unseen.

He switched off the light and went to make a sandwich.

♛ ♛ ♛

ROOFTOPS AND WINDOWS. Warehouse gantries. Sometimes monuments. Bridges (if they were over pavement), high stairway balustrades, balconies; for Lev Rahklin, all it took to make the transition from the Russian Federation's Ministry of Internal Affairs to Gennady Turov's inner-circle security cadre, was launching manganese oligarch Maxim Sidorov—an informant for Kolya Yurenev's Kalaydoskop—from the top of Disco Chapel Perilous. And, same for Rahklin as poor Maxim, there was no going back to the moment before you lost your footing. Turov owned Rahklin from the moment he gave Lulu's husband the shove.

Couple the Maxim flight with Rahklin's grounding—Lubyanka-bred, fluent in investigative instinct, counterintelligence reflex—he'd now be running things for Turov out of the Vostok Consolidated tower in St. Petersburg (Turov never missed a chance to remind him this), had he given Sidorov's wife and daughter the same treatment.

He'd gone to the Skhodnya dacha. Dug two graves. Balked. Not out of sympathy, compassion, but the less forgivable sin: thought for himself and got it right. Ludmila Sidorova was the daughter of Pavel Orlov aka

Pinwheel, aka right hand to Nikoláj "Kolya" Yurenev; Kalaydoskop—Kolya was her godfather. Those murders would have lit a war Turov would have lost. The woman, the girl, shown mercy, kept hostage, pinned Kolya down. Forced equal footing. The Kremlin liked the result and power did drift Turov's way. When that proved out, Turov grudgingly rewarded Rahklin operational oversight of all external security—from the post no one wanted: custodian of the woman he'd been sent to kill, babysitter to her daughter.

This, more than anything else, was most prominent on Rahklin's mind as he walked inside.

He preferred these Bayli houses that pretended to be empty—plaster peeling, paint gone to chalk. To an outsider they looked abandoned, but the old masonry kept sound where you wanted it. Shed eyes where you didn't. Glass towers collected witnesses; villas like this collected silence. Wired the way Turov liked it: landlines buried, no signal bleed, two clean exits to the coast road. If the night turned, you could walk straight into the Caspian fog and vanish.

Rakhlin stood in the corner that gave him everything. The interior hall. The open kitchen beyond the bar—a cast-off chromium thing plundered from some chichi restaurant. The bar addition ruined the walk-through with its barrier, but barriers bought moments and moments mattered to men like Turov. Men like Rahklin. He scanned the terrace through doors that faced the sea.

The clack of cutlery. The table where Turov ate was walnut. Dark as oil. Fogged with white rings from a hundred meetings just like this where the sweat of men matched the sweat of water sliding down a last-drink glass before Rahklin took them out in the small boat for a view of the bay from below.

Kravtsov sat opposite, coat still on, elbows planted, hands bridged at fingertips the way some gamblers wait for cards. The vibration in the banker's pocket broke the quiet. He drew the phone, checked the screen. Blue light on his glasses, caught again in the window. "London replies. 'Subject: Re-evaluation of Baltic capacity proposal—NS-2 Annex.'" A corny laugh. "China farts and all the poodles start sniffing asses."

Turov looked up from his plate. Frowned. Kravtsov corrected. "The Square Mile's in. Wants a taste. Just enough to say they're not outside when the gas starts moving."

Turov's fork hovered. "London doesn't take sides. It takes percentages." He stabbed a cube of lamb. Rolled it in rice.

The television behind Kravtsov ran its crawl. China and Iran. Signatures and smiles. The next century sold as freight. Beneath it: *Russian Federation Delegation Silent on Infrastructure Cooperation Pact. Caspian Pipeline Consortium Negotiations on Hold.*

So it was official then. Kalaydoskop—the great sanctioned myth of control—outflanked. Rakhlin could feel it in the air: the tremor of empire folding in on itself.

Turov leaned back. "This gives Moscow its alibi. Yurenev's day is over. Written in stick-figure letters painted with chopsticks. Our hour has come."

"If Moscow refuses our ask to wet his feet?" Kravtsov.

Turov: "Moscow would prefer we ask forgiveness, not permission."

"Not yet."

Rahklin.

Both men looked at him.

"I've found Lulu. Alina. Sarpi—last Georgian village before the Turkish line, a strip of docks and a fish market clinging to the rocks. They keep a covered stall by the landing. The Chechen's still with them. He's preparing another hop. Don't know where to yet, but another kilometer and they're ghosts."

Turov's eyebrows lifted.

Rahklin took the risk. "You want Yurenev—Kingston's your way in."

Turov's fork stopped mid-air. "Kill the girl. That should get his attention. His *Sleeping Tsarevna* is next if he doesn't cooperate."

Rakhlin didn't look away. "If you kill the girl, you lose him. If you promise him all their lives, he'll do Yurenev himself."

"He's his son." Kravtsov.

"Grandson. That's confirmed." Direct to Turov: "Probably won't even need to ask 'please.'"

Turov went back to his plate. Rahklin waited for him to finish, cube by little-lamb cube. The oligarch poured wine into his glass. Into Kravtsov's. Gestured to Rahklin with the bottle.

Rahklin never drank with Turov. Tonight, he found his nod and "yes'd" it. This once; seal it.

"Fine." Turov swirled his Madrasa red as blood. "Offer him peace. Give him the story he wants to believe." He raised the glass. Not a toast. A verdict. "And when Yurenev's gone, you close the book you've left open since Maxim learned to fly. All three. No arrests, no spectacle. No hand-off to *priduroks* on a Rhine bridge. Kingston, the woman, the girl."

"Understood."

Turov drank. "Good. You'll like this thing finished."

Rakhlin thought of the woman's pale face. The girl's hand in hers. When Alina was younger, her hand in his own walking into the Lyceum. He thought of the Chechen standing behind them like a shadow that didn't move. He drank his wine in one long swallow.

Michael Kingston, who'd beaten him at Stein am Rhein, Lulu, Alina: prominent on his mind all night. And two of them already with waiting graves.

♚♚♚

Mrs. Polovetz had said, "Have a seat wherever you'd like. The Director will be with you shortly, sir," and now Drexler stood. His back to the Director's Executive Administrative Assistant. Back to the security officer's desk—the man on his feet at Harker's inner door. Back to the secretarial assistant desk, Drexler faced the only seats in the anteroom. A pair of Chippendale tubs. Colonial knock-offs for a government outgrown its furniture. He wouldn't try. He didn't fit. He was not humiliated and raging but merely waiting, hollowed and lessening, annealing to a soft place inside himself he couldn't yet name because it reminded him of what might be admired in the death of something simply because you relinquished it, that hush at last when the work abandons the worker.

The folder pressed between his fingers. Duplicate of the folder he'd delivered to DDO Gravin. Insignificant in his thick and massive hands. Like an empty bird's nest in the crevice of a fallen monument. It weighed more than the grotesque body he'd spent his life dragging through this building.

It was the second "Sir?" from Harker's body man, after Mrs. Polovetz's "Director Harker will see you now," that stirred Drexler to movement. First the bellows of his lungs filling, releasing, then an astonishingly light-footed pirouette—that Harker the dancer would be envious of—and he lumbered through the door.

The chairs before Harker's desk were built for men of every shape and size—physically/morally—and Drexler took his place before a man who worked at a spot on his glasses; Harker held the lens to the light, squinted half-blind through it, and considered them clean without truly seeing them, before tucking the temple tips back behind his ears. "And? CINDER CROWN?"

"My man's out."

"How quaint. By your 'man' you mean the Kingston scion you sent to spy on the father."

"There's never been a thing 'quaint' about me, Director. My op was approved. Top to bottom."

Harker flicked a hand. Brush it away. As if Drexler's remark had reminded him of a door he hadn't meant to open. Since he had approved the op, he didn't know what to say next. The silence fell between them like a dead fly on the desk.

"Hal Kingston is twenty-four into the forty-hours I have for him at Bolling. CI debrief, psych, scrub for leaks. He'll hand-off to the Debrief and Exploitation Center or wherever you'd like."

"I'd like it if you weren't handing me a crap sandwich. Silas didn't get a whiff CINDER CROWN was compromised?"

"All evidence supports that. Finn Houton sold it east. Chinese."

"We'll tip Justice Counter-Intel or FBI WFO, let them run the contractor. Keep our name off it."

"Leave it. Sir." Drexler spoke. Knew the voice was his yet not his, some buried conscience using him for its mouth. "The remarkable thing? Chinese proxy action in Iran destabilized both Kalaydoskop and the Iranians—precisely the chaos Silas intended, but better; KALEIDOSCOPE emerges cleaner than Silas could have hoped."

"So Houton walks. *Again*—if I remember his CV correctly?"

"Silas won't let that happen. Let him clean his own barn. I don't care about that."

"You want to tell me that again?"

"I'm beyond it. You need to move beyond it too."

"To what." A challenge, almost a threat. Not one bit a question.

Drexler placed his folder on Harker's blotter. Gazed at it, passing a prayer before he lifted his hand. Lifted his look. Harker's glasses caught the light. The director's eyes measured the air for more insubordination. Found only purpose.

"Lynn." Drexler didn't say Kingston. "File."

Harker didn't touch it. Didn't glance down.

Drexler knew he wouldn't. He'd known walking in. The refusal was the ceremony. Spit in the dirt, palm to palm—the way boys back home sealed rival promises. Hate before. Hate after. But for the moment the vow stood clean between them.

He turned to go.

"I haven't dismissed you."

"Don't bother."

Harker watched his massive back. Still wore a white suit middle of winter. "There is nothing to be done to save her. I advise you get over it. Her."

Something inside Drexler had altered. What he felt for Lynn was no longer that fever of wanting to claim her, to be the man she should have chosen. That had always been envy disguised as love, grievance disguised as honor. Dignity he'd pitchforked over by a manure of lust.

Now it was different. Drexler was different.

He wanted only to stand where no one else would stand.

To honor Lynn where the building and its little men inside would not.

To prove, if not to her, then to himself, that a man could be remade not by possession but by endurance. That when all options ran out, faith would have its reckoning.

It shamed him. It steadied him. He left the office and the thought went with him. It burned away the smaller hungers, left only the one thing he could still choose: to face Silas Kingston not as supplicant, not as rival, but as one who had finally put his grievances down.

The door shut itself behind him on electric/automatic hinges.

Saturday, December Twenty-ninth

1.

S ILAS LEFT THE NORTH Vista Outhouse with the first light of dawn. Trudged to the beach stairs. A look over the edge. The family shore. Storm strew/beach wrack. Frost furred the length of the driftwood trunk. Sunlight appeared a burning fuse across the dark wet line of the horizon. He set his radio on the flat top rail.

Old Realistic portable. Six D batteries fresh last night. Black-gone-gray plastic, scored dull by salt and sand. A Lynn to Doris beach-music birthday gift from before it all, before everything went—well, from *before*.

Extended the two silver antennas. WETA 90.9 classical. Two measures were all it took to recognize Hanson's Symphony No. 2: *The Romantic.*

Seeing things and hearing things for the first time—time in youth is longer for it. Then, almost without knowing, it's not. You stop seeing, stop hearing new things. Memory creates pattern. Pattern: recognition. Recognition smooths/speeds time. And you don't notice at first. You're in gear, moving quickly toward success which itself becomes the newness. The first times start over—but insidious memory/cancerous patterning: you already know how they come, how they process, set, resolve, propel you forward. Time never slows. Memory patterns categorized and competence accelerates and you notice all new things are false. Only variations of the old. Time quickens; no surprise, no wonder, no fresh astonishment. Mastering time, you confiscate its length from your inner clock. Sameness might be dull, but it collapses time efficiently. You can't get lost in it. And moments can't linger because they offer nothing precious you haven't already survived. Music reminds this; celebrates as it eulogizes this.

Ten measures in, brass rises behind the strings. That quiet self-certainty of recollection. The melody climbs, glances backward, carries on.

The sound was thin, warped by morning cold, but it was enough. In its own way, the music had caught up to Silas. The first movement always felt like setting to work on memory. It spoke that life is a struggle but romance is sublime; worth the fight and makes all effort worthy; it pretends it's about grandeur when love is really about perseverance. Continuance.

He laid out his ropes. Crafted loops. Tied knots. Twice checked them. Silas's lines were fast and measured and as the musical lines stretched, as the melody changed hands by section, patterns rise/fade/return. Effort compounds glory.

Silas built his block and tackle. A swing seat bowed with canvas webbing where his hips will rest. Tool caddy: larch box of his father's hand; a white-oak handle, dovetail joinery, square compartments holding a small handsaw, a chisel wrapped in cloth, a file. Relics of his grandfather. Sandpaper and balsa shims. Smell of oil. Smell of cellar. Smell of time.

The music steadied Silas. Allowed his turmoil release in the charging of the brass. This morning required steady hands. Intense focus. He tested the line through the pulley. Leaned out—eyes on the grain of the rail, on the frost-shimmered edge where the palisade plunges vertical to the beach.

Light off the bay sharpened, the surface wrinkled by wind. Silas clipped his safety line to the block. Held no illusion that the whole thing wouldn't tumble if he lost his seat. He sat into the swing. Scooted to the edge. Lowered an inch at a time.

The squeak of the pulley. The creak of the rope.

Gulls burst from nests. Yelled at Silas. Wheeled. Spied.

He shifted his weight in the air, swung under the stairs.

The radio carried on behind him and above—horns widened, strings gathered them, reminding them to re-member—and he dangled himself, a spider to his work. Wind moved through the risers. The day began its slow, unremarkable climb.

The day opens, but time already shrinks.

And the rot had returned, inevitable.

👑👑👑

THE ROT shows up in the beach stairs.

Lynn discovers it. Drunk. Stumbles climbing from the "why-wait-till-Halloween" Doris birthday clam-bake; Doris already knows how sick she is. She's seen the hematologist/oncologist. I don't know. Haven't even guessed.

Lynn says not drunk—wood cracked beneath her step—but she's run out of gin before tonic. She's drunk.

But it's Lynn who first notices the rot between the risers.

The creeping black.

I let it go most of summer.

Then August. Lower myself over on the swing. Michael is home. Here—'stead of wherever Gwen might be. We argue about my safety in the swing. I ask what he knows about carpentry. About repairing anything. He helps from the stairs. Helps with the fresh lumber. Helping hands through the risers.

September—when it isn't so hot—I go down to paint and seal.

And then her voice. And then her face.

Doris: "You weren't supposed to do this without some-one here."

"It's done. Practically. What did the doctor say?"

She says it—me hanging between heaven and earth—just says it.

No memory of hauling the rope. One moment suspended midair. Then solid ground, Doris in my arms, the earth pulled out from under me.

"I'm in no pain. No unusual symptoms."

"How can they say with any certainty?"

"I spent the first two years of my life crawling on a bombed-out glass-factory floor covered with lead-oxide dust. It was already fatal by the time I was four. Let's not have that useless conversation. There'll be a time to comfort me in my suffering. There will be time to release me to it. Now is not that time."

Eyes, cerulean blue are fists plunging through my skull, gripping my soul with both their hands. More serious than death: "I want you to make love to me, Silas. Wait. That's not right. I want to make love to you. I want to show God how much I embrace and honor the miracle of pure creation returned to its source. In joy, and now, and not in fear."

Her hands grip my face. Warm. The pulse in her wrist flutters. I look and see what I haven't let myself see—the faint sheen along her temple, beginning under the skin.

"We can't have another child; even if we could, I'm not so sure—"

"Shh. Silly man. It's my honor to show Him that I would. *That even faced with what is certain to be an awful, painful, heartbreaking, mind-breaking death—faced with all this horror life chose for me—I honor life. I honor the gift of it I was given, the gift I've given our children, they to theirs now and when more come. In the face of what I have, what will crush me and snuff me out, life's value—its gift—is so much greater; its future so much more valuable."*

Breath catching, she collapses into the grass, pulls me with her and the wind moves through the open risers, salt and cedar and paint. Everywhere her skin has a new shine I don't remember—the opposite of health—how did I miss that? It cuts through me, sharp as light on broken glass.

We make love like the tide pressed to the shore.

Again and again.

Days.

Weeks.

As if the pattern of time by sheer acknowledgement, full embrace, might keep her pressed to it.

The December wind caught Silas as he pulled close to the rot-wood. He quick-wrapped ankles around a flared anchor post. Steadied. Oiled the teeth of his saw.

We make love September into the frost of December.

Moments can't linger; they break and fall through you, same as sand through the joints.

Every release, the breath of a season that must be lost, stolen before it is lost. New Year's came, and that was the last time for the rest of her life. The world kept turning; we did not.

♛ ♛ ♛

THE FIRST MOVEMENT ended on a wandering, luscious sigh. Silas cut at the rotted place. The wind clubbed him from behind. Woodwinds above. The slow movement begun with new melodic promise, but answered by the original motto, the brass that carries the glimmer of the strings. Horn of promise, strength, and protection.

♛ ♛ ♛

"WILL YOU tell him?"

"I'll write the letter."

"Don't ask me to deliver it."

"How many letters have I written him?"

"Fifty? One hundred? Ten—I don't go through your private thoughts."

"How many have I had you deliver?"

"I wish you'd sent him none."

"Three, Silas."

"They're our children. Kingston blood."

"His blood was never the point."

"You didn't tell him that."

"I didn't need to. He knew. He knows. I will write the letter, a last letter, a last time—this letter now when I am more her than he—and you will make the signal and you will leave it in the dead drop, in the castle, where those two children disappeared—"

"Doris: that never happened."

"—in the old abandoned park."

And we both knew that it had—evil comes/children disappear—and I say: "Kolya will come. When he receives it: he'll come. He'll try to intervene."

"Then you'll do to him what he did to me."

"Do you hate him that much?"

"No, Silas. I love him. I'm just not the woman he needs forgiveness from. He must look into Sofiya's face."

♛ ♛ ♛

SILAS STEADIED HIMSELF against the harness. Rope tight. Weight centered. The block groaned. The third movement leaped bright into the sun. Celebration of the beauty of love—the first movement opening repeated, daring the listener to call it out, taken bright with trumpets chased by horns strings slash beneath all the hours of time, your time—both of you, the lover and loved—made joyful its mad can't-get-enough-of-each-other passage: and why not?

Silas swung gently and allowed the music's false promise wash him as sunny fingers touched skin with faint, striving, hopeful warmth.

Silas shut his eyes. He released the grip of his legs. Swung. Not mourning—that middle section of wandering melody, that middle age of life's one great affair—building, climbing, mounting—he spun around almost childlike, caught the timber between knees. Almost lost his box. Tapped the chisel free of the caddy.

Tested its edge against his thumb.

Wood joints give. Widen. Sand dribbles.

The body remembers what the music already knows: beauty fails in time, but failure is part of its song.

Chisel for the file. File for the nails. Worked his way, three steps down.

The air beneath the stairs blossomed with the smell of iron from the filing dust, moldy wood exposed to bay air by chisel and saw. Balsa shims into open joints. Tiny taps with the flat of the file, hidden in the pounding of the timpani. The scrape of sandpaper hidden between bars.

Lowers three more stairs. Leans in. The harness bit his hips. Repeats his work; everything Hanson wrote was about return. That's the part Silas loves. The theme that bends and comes back.

Like work.

Like faith.

Like Doris.

Like collapse.

✿✿✿

THE HOSPITAL. The Cadillac. A parking lot slot. Alone, my seat tilted back. Catch a nap. And I must have, hard I think, as my eyes lift to the passenger window—her insistent rap on the window coming what seems mere minutes since she's gone inside.

"That was quick." Check my watch. Appointment too quick. Impossible quick.

"Drive, Silas. I want to go down past the marsh at Cuckold Creek."

I raise my seat. Drive. Anger with Doris— with her disease—

Dark trombones. Herald trumpets saying, *Forget about it.* Roll of drum, shimmer of cymbal. Now the trumpet: angry, furious.

—my anger builds. Hate myself. Useless flesh standing at the edge of the sea, punching waves in their face. So nothing.

"You still believe in it?" She says as I drive the old Cuckold Creek road along the inlet, pure spring light off the marsh, white herons startled, lifting through the reeds frantic into grace.

"In what?"

No dressing on her hand.

"KALEIDOSCOPE."

She's refused her treatment.

"We all did, didn't we?"

"You and James did."

The truth. (The waves crash over me.) Release it. No difficulty now reserving truth. No point. "I don't anymore. Thought I could make the lies hold still long enough to serve a cause. But lies don't hold. They learn you to outlive you..."

To place you like wax fruit in a Christmas window in an old Stone House.

"What I built, I thought to steady the world, steadies nothing. Just keeps moving without us. The pocket-watch men. Lockhart. Angleton. Me. All ticking toward a truth that never struck because human systems exist to move and, because truth is immobile, it is incompatible. Too easy for everyone to step around when it's in the way. In my business, truth is a tree growing in the middle of the road. For years as we drive around saying, 'How nice,' secretly waiting for nameless men to come and chop it down, cut it up, drag it out, so we can lament it in our rearview mirror and enjoy the road faster."

Calm words, thoughtful words, but how angry I am—because I know her, because I know what she's done. Because I know what she's told her doctors. Chosen to put speed to now.

"It turns now only to collapse, and I go into OTRAC knowing this as sure as I know what you've done today. To watch it—maybe even help it—turn to its expected/necessary downfall."

She clutches my hand. And I drop it—useless from the steering wheel. Dropped onto my thigh. She turns it over. The soothsayer's palette.

So it lays there.

So she inscribes a heart upon my palm.

So she inscribes that heart with a cross before lifting my palm to her mouth and kissing it.

Lips you only see once in your life and long to kiss forever but forever is a truth too, the one life itself steps around. Steps around and finds an escape. Cuts through its trunk.

Tears scroll our cheeks. Glimmer in the flicker of sunlight breaking through the interlacing loblolly pines along the bend like the flicker of the film projector in my nightmares.

Doris's smile is sympathy and pure.

"You know my book. Remember my reading to the children? The children's parts where Merlin transforms Wart. The hawk, the ant, the fish. The goose—remember?"

"I didn't listen."

"You listened."

"I'm sure I was working."

"You listened. Each of them taught him something—the hawk, the ant—"

Can't fight her. Mumble: "'Everything not forbidden is compulsory.'"

"You're 'compulsory,' my love. My lover, my life. You. Medicine isn't. But, yes: the fish, finally the badger. Your final lesson: White's animal syllabus."

"Silliest part of the book. I hate that kid's stuff."

She knows I don't. And she does that thing where she sucks the air; mimics drawing from a straw the breath of my harshest bluster.

"Wart learned the world could not be ruled by power and tyranny; by violence couched in honor; totalitarianism stealing individualism by conformity. Wart didn't

learn truth. You're right about truth. Wart learned that peace and wisdom are born of mercy."

"And after all that, the Round Table always fails because the idealism behind Might for Right fails because the promise we'll be decent—mankind, the human race—is false."

Doris softly laughed, enjoying herself immensely. "Nope. Only because Arthur tried to make it perfect. Our lesson was never perfection, Silas. It was understanding. That comes from love—I suppose—and poor Arthur couldn't make that jig-jug with justice."

"I don't see the difference anymore."

"You will. You'll read to the grandchildren on the porch. In your lap. You'll remember to eat at our table. You'll keep Foxtail Farm alive."

I want to tell her—ten short years later—there's no one left to sit her table. Our children scattered. Out of reach. Betrayer. Betraying. Betrayed.

(No kingdom left; only little ones to hide from the thing coming in the night.)

Doris closes her eyes. We wind past the dirt hollow—the wound in the forest beside the clean blacktop—the boards laid over clay to keep tires from sinking; the half-collapsed fence swallowed by vile kudzu. A plywood sign. Red spray paint. CLAYPOOLE FARMS.

Smell of woodsmoke. Of wet mash. Sharp and green hints of yeast, of rotted grain. A slightly sweet odor like vinegar seeps through the air vents.

Those who never left.

The ones who cook their old stills and sell to those who know to make the turn.

I glance. See her as I saw her before the coffin lid was shut.

Doris, eyes closed—she didn't want to see that place or smell that stink or think about those people. She whispers, and singularly rare to Doris, her whisper can be her loudest voice: "Arthur knew when it was time to lift his sword without his scabbard. Lynn knew/knows: even as a child."

The costumed swimmer rises from the man-made lake in her beaded hood and pure white-makeup skin. And I watch Lynn gazing at Michael gazing at the Lady in the Lake and wondering why he looks at her that way.

♛ ♛ ♛

THE STAIRS FIXED as he wanted them. Needed them. The symphony climaxes in apotheosis; Solo violins; the original theme; the memory of the first fall to love.

The sun gave up before it made the sky.

The third movement wants to end. It explodes to tell Silas: all things end; it's beauty that hurts, the kind that knows it cannot stay. The fall from the swing: forty-five feet. More than enough. Love can't make life stay.

That's why the symphony—the *Romantic*—has only three movements.

The fourth movement is silence.

♛ ♛ ♛

A LAST BOX she's left behind. The thing she glaringly didn't burn.

It's not for me.

On its lid, a loose photograph. The one long-ago print-ed in the Swiss papers. Silver hair, through smoke. Ab-batantuono mid-toast. Champagne raised. His grin like it knows the camera and dares it. Doris beside him. Pen like Audrey Hepburn's cigarette holder, her champagne coupe catching the camera's flash.

Pell & Glatisant Trading Conglomerate. Geneva. 1972.

The day she christened it.

That man—dead now, and good for Michael—looks noble. Isn't.

"That's the beauty," she tells me.

She never wanted noble.

Wanted small. Manageable. The man who steals in inches. Cautious, self-protecting, venal in the quiet way that keeps a thing alive.

"Honest men ruin things faster." The way she says it, it sounds like faith. "He'll steal, yes—but he'll never risk enough to collapse what feeds him. He needs the bank to breathe. That's the governor. Its protection," she says, and grins. "Not goodness—containment."

I open the box. Historical records. The Kingston se-cret; the Kingston curse. The photograph doesn't match what's inside, but even in mystery, Doris is specific and I find the bottom folder. The one she labeled For Melody.

She'd meant to take it herself to the Historical Society; I carry the box inside and the blue heron director at the counter thanks me.

They have no idea what they are really taking.

Driving home from the Colonel Vickery House, I keep hearing Doris's voice, that slow professorial calm that prophesizes.

"You Kingstons think the mask can be worn without becoming the face. Concealment isn't control. We mistake deceit for virtue because it hides what virtue can't afford."

All that fortune: blood money dressed in ethics.

Her mercy wasn't forgiveness. It was accounting.

👑👑👑

SNOW has stolen the day.

Silas broke down the block and tackle. He laid out his ropes and worked open each knot. He coiled them before carefully cleaning his tools to the sound of a dull white hiss. With the sudden change of weather, *Bach's Mass in B minor* crackled. The *Kyrie*—fractured but indestructible. Silas let it play. The notes fall through static. Broken, beautiful, unbroken still.

👑👑👑

I CARRY HER to the Silvanus Bench. Doris's thin arms around my neck, her skeleton wrapped in dying flesh, wrapped in an old car blanket from the mud room chest, is the only weight I feel in the basket of my arms. The Bench to overlook Turkey's Swan Song. A field of animal bones in human caskets. The Kingston false graveyard for rendered slaves, who, Rendered Unto God by my ancestors were secreted to freedom.

Only two humans ever buried here: Cupid Scrapefoot Williams, Turkey John Swann.

"Nika may be here, too," she tells me. "Silas III, never put it to record. I'd like to hope she is."

Doris wants to sit. I want her not to. Her body can't. She insists, and I help her down—the bones too brittle, the breath too short, the wool hat swallowing the last of her hair. Her hands are burnt paper in my palms.

"Hal will bring her home."

"Who?"

"The other Melody. The one you think you ruined."

"Doris. You know that isn't real. Please."

Her lips. Her smile. The blood still red in them. Vivid against the pallor of her glassy/sunken face.

"Roberta's child."

The woman I killed. Sure as I pulled the trigger.

Why does her failing mind choose to hurt me with that?

Here? This dirty/sacred place? Now?

"She'll find him—soon, very-soon, Silas—and I know our boy and I know Melody and I know he'll love her. Instantly. I've had him leading her back to us all these years."

"'Him' who? Doris you're confusing—"

"Boone Kelso, of course."

Words too calm. Too clear. Too certain. The way delirium sometimes makes perfect sense. I think it's the morphine; I want it to be the morphine.

"This is where you brought my Beaumont."

The first Beaumont. The throwing ball. My pistol.

"You wanted so badly to kill me. Thought you'd take it out on my dog—you wretched man."

"Let's not go back to that. Let's go back to the house. Let me make you some tea. Make you comfortable."

"You had every right—what I'd done to you with my father."

"Kolya did it. To both of us."

"What is it you told me? When you brought Beaumont back?"

And there I am: My gun away. Her Beaumont delivered to her arms. Tail-wags and tongue. All exhausted. All alive.

"'What if we never get what we deserve?'"

"Not that, Silas. You said, 'Our tornado balances inside a kaleidoscope.' I've always loved that you said that."

"Loopy words. They didn't mean... I didn't know what I was saying." I wait to see where she's going.

"You'll know when it's time. When she's ready. You won't let her suffer. You couldn't do it then—but you'll do it when it's her."

"Beaumont was male. He lived many, many years, honey." I pretend I don't know what she's telling me.

Doris drops her head against my shoulder. Even that is an effort for her. I hold her until her breath steadies.

"You need to love her. This daughter we've made."

"You know I love Lynn. It's her drinking—"

"I'm not talking about Lynn. You two will find your path back to each other."

I've failed Lynn more than you'll ever know.

"I'm talking about Melody. The tornado stills with Melody."

✦✦✦

Silas clicked off the Lynn-to-Doris birthday-present radio. Snow thickened, it spirals in fast columns. Tornados soft and white. Imagined, briefly, the fall from the stairs. It's not the endless fall that terrifies. It's the fall over rock. The slow ruin. And the wish—when you think God might be listening—why not the avalanche? Why not just the clean burying and be done?

But that's dead and Doris gone.

No echo left. Just the hush before falling. The sky holding its breath.

Silas didn't worry about Melody or the children going down to the shore. No one ever did, this time of year. But he reminded himself to keep Beaumont away; the weight of a dog would be enough now to collapse it.

2.

Lulu's former bodyguard—Crazy Leer—didn't say
a word. Fine with Michael. Must have always been
Kolya's plant with her from the get go; he'd proven faithful to Lulu, to Michael for all that, and once cut out of the
loop of her escape returned to his master. He stopped
Kolya's S-Class in traffic long enough for Michael to
climb out, make the curb. Kolya had chosen the café.
One of the few places in the city that looked outward
instead of up. The open-fronted kind on Istiglaliyyat
Street where morning traffic—vehicle/foot—bright with
purpose stitched through narrow trees. Baku, awake and
industrious. The city felt older here, nearer to the earth,
farther from the Expo's glass and the mill-race gleam
of oil and gas that turned beneath it like a water wheel
grinding its own future to silt, the promise of energy
and wealth revolving without end, drawing men with its
shine only to sink them with its sludge, and Michael, felt
the wheel take him too, his thoughts caught in its slow,
black spin.

Kolya sat beneath the awning's inner lip, in shadow,
and Michael joined him, naturally like family, their resemblance would indicate to any casual glance. A brass
samovar breathed faintly in the center of a table of

small plates: təndir bread torn in halves, motal cheese, a saucer of honey, quail eggs in a copper pan. A careful arrangement of heat and salt and sweetness, as if balance itself could disguise the ruin they faced across it.

Kolya poured tea; Michael sat. No greeting. No smiles.

Noise surrounded: restaurant chatter, road clamor, spoons on glass. A burst of shouts—children somewhere down the block. Human noise that meant everyday life was to be lived. That the two of them were unusual. And Kolya's eyes moved, as if buried in the innocent sound was an intelligence he might decipher to darker purpose.

"Some show you put on last night for your parade of the faithful."

Kolya opened his hands like one might release a pair of butterflies, then made a fist, covered it with his other hand, hard, as another might crush them.

Next to his napkin, Michael noticed a Lufthansa ticket envelope. Crisp. New.

"Your Mikhail Morozov passport will get you through to New York. You can find your way from there."

They held a glance that communicated nothing. Certainly not the affection both men feigned to their theater in the round. Michael bent a piece of bread. Dropped cheese into it.

"Dip it in honey." Kolya pushed the saucer his way.

The night before—the visitors, the speeches, the claptrap of loyalty oaths. Kalaydoskop's last performance. Michael read the aftermath in the old spymaster's face. The set mouth. The hollow beneath the cheekbones. The calcined blue of his tired eyes. The men would be gone now. Michael knew and Kolya knew he knew. Out of Baku. Out of Kalaydoskop. The ship lighter for the drowning of its leaping rats.

"Any meetings today, Gramps?"

It wouldn't be ministers. No. Or Duma members. It would be the handlers-of-handlers—energy-bloc liaisons and SVR liaison officers. Perhaps even an envoy from the Security Council Energy Commission. Senior bureaucrats in bespoke suits.

Kolya took an egg. "We adapt."

Michael almost smiled. Wanted to ask what adaptation meant when a lifetime's design burned through itself and out.

Kolya chewed. He swallowed. Tea followed, and this followed that: "There are those who wish for reassurance."

What Kolya wanted wasn't survival. Not power. Just to believe the wheel still turned because of him, not over him.

"You said something the other day."

"What was that, Mikhail?"

"You and Silas. Opponents. Your systems each in total opposition, but apart from both your services. That those alternatives were worse, and you said—but for that, the blood between us, you could see us—you and me—what-was-it—? 'Fond'-of-each-other. That's what it was."

"And here—with business and 'alternatives' behind us, we are having a fine breakfast."

"Oh, you know better than I, but I'd say your meeting today—ostensibly, they'll say, maybe they've told you, they're reviewing damage from your CINDER CROWN fuck-up, but in reality they're deciding whether Kalaydoskop is folded under direct Federation control, or if it's easier to scapegoat you for the entire Iran-to-China loss."

Kolya finished his tea. Turned the glass in his fingers. Watched the leaf-dregs swim in the puddle of backwash. "You need to go home."

The PistenBully faces Les Dikiy. Lulu's Chechen faces me: "Personal thought/emotion, moral imagination, love—these things are discarded in Kolya's system."

"You're forgetting something, old man."

Still staring at leaves that turned too fast to read—"Take the ticket. You're leaving today."

"You know I'm not. I did what you asked."

Kolya faced Michael and it wasn't just resemblance, it was a mirror. "Did you? You appeared willing. But men like us can appear whatever way we chose. You did nothing and I owe you nothing. Not even a fucking red balloon."

Michael shut his eyes. Pictured Doris. Opened them. Gave it to him: "Aren't you something—fat with promises that are just a bunch of worms on a dead skeleton empty of honor."

A twitch in Kolya's eyelids. "Bravo. You sound just like your mother."

Wait him out.

He clunked his glass on the table. "But you're not like her. Or your father. What people say about me—? It skipped a generation. You have it."

"What's that?"

"The mimic. The wraith. We'd have made a fine team."

"We wouldn't have. Not the politics, the ideologies, the service. See—I love people." Michael circled a finger in the air to include the restaurant, include Baku, include the world. "I love life."

"Michael-michael-michael. Mikhail. Don't bother what you're trying. The nature of your argument—your pitch—is a built-in backfire."

"Maybe you're right then. You lured me here on blood: answer one question and if you're honest—if we are the same, I'll be the one who rides the ticket."

"The 'one' who rides the ticket." He catches my phrasing. The option.

"Now you're just being cute with it, boy."

The Les Dikiy. The Forest Wild. Grins. Waves. Fluffy snow suits. AKs, spears, vodka air-toasted/guzzled/passed.

"Long before Doris entered the picture. He was very young, the mother died."

Shouts: "Mikhail Nikolaevich!" Toasts: "The Skvoznyak!" The Chechen cranked the brake and gave me everything I need.

"I'm glad you asked. About love. You reminded me that story and the answer to it, the end that never comes: Kolya needs to believe the wound of losing that child—however horrifically he did—was worth it."

Everything but the lie. The wound was never the child.

Michael poured tea for both of them. "Who was my grandmother? She obviously didn't die in a tornado. I think I'd like to meet her."

"She's dead." Nothing moved but the eyes. Blue sharpening to glass.

I have you, motherfucker.

Kolya pushed back his chair. "I have a meeting."

Michael stayed seated. And because cruelty ran deep in his bloodline. "Good luck with that."

A small nod. He was listening, but it was as though he'd risen into the midst of a battlefield and he couldn't quite hear through the hammer of gunfire, the crash of explosion.

Kolya shook as he turned. Michael's voice stopped him.

"Don't leave her to die."

Kolya snapped his eyes back to Michael. Michael held the man's frigid gaze. Listened to Doris's voice inside him:

"Careful. Broken glass cuts worst of all."

"Don't leave her in the dark."

The words hung. Kolya's throat tightened, the brief convulsion of someone remembering too suddenly. A tremor, barely visible, passed through the hand resting on the chair. Then he left—no farewell, no final word—stepping into the light and the moving air, swallowed by the city's noise.

3.

A VAUXHALL FLOOR HE'D never been on. A room he'd never seen. A man he'd never met in person, but who had certainly aggravated Anton Hector since summer. A cold day in London—sat at freezing with no indication it would get up and move—a day he'd signed himself out for, elective on paper but obligatory to sanity. Hector hadn't made it from the breakfast table when the summons came. Counsellor Ned Trewyn was the Service's senior man on FELL KING. As Hector had it, Trewyn reported directly to Whitehall—a non-operational, policy-class officer—but as "Counsellor" he reported sideways to the Crown; and that, Hector thought, explained the rest. FELL KING, a Director-of-Operations albatross for over a decade, only the Queen's unforgiving interest in the Lott clan and poor Evander's suspected fate at the hands of Silas Kingston—and, by extension, Kingston's rumored entanglement in the old Angleton affair that once cast Her Majesty's own Prime Minister, Harold Wilson, in Moscow's light—had kept the thing breathing, kept it on Crown remit, kept it producing nothing. Proof of treachery had never come, only rumor, and rumor had been enough. Over the years, Operations Directorate cut FELL KING link by link from

Section Head, to Controller, to the point that DOps shoved it all over to Trewyn to deal once the Cold War tottered into retirement. Then Clive Lancer struck a vein of gold in America, Fergus Lott shrieked "Eureka!" and the long-bearded/sleepy Father Time shuffled off and Trewyn was the proud father bouncing a Baby New Year—blowing horns and tossing confetti—in his lap.

Hector had heard about Trewyn's smile. Now he received it inside this narrow unclaimed conference room, yellow and airless, a wall that looked like it had undergone a siege of woodpeckers—the amount of screw holes from every unit's crest that had once claimed then swiftly abandoned the room to anonymity. Too much table for the two of them, but here they sat, Trewyn flehmening and stroking the file squared before him—which he wouldn't open once during their encounter—as though it were a silky cat.

"We've a narrow point, Mr. Brown. But I'm of great hope you'll sort it out for me."

"In my narrow legal capacity, sir, there is only one point I sort out and that sorting, I believe—as it stands with FELL KING—is completely sorted. As I'm sure you fully understand, I'm unable to review or advise or update on anything operational once my job—my panel's work—is complete."

At this point, the folder ought to have been purring.

"Purely administrative. I assure you."

"All our 'T's have been dotted and our I's crossed'—as the tykes like to say—I assure you right back, sir." He tried one of his chuckles even as his mind went back, and darkly, to Trewyn's order that he change their outcome-vote on poor misused Clive Lancer.

"Right. Well, an ingest moved up the pipe from Garde-Joyeuse last night."

So the bloody deed is done. R-I-P, and I'm sorry I failed you.

Hector pushed to his feet. "I can't be involved in this conversation."

"Sit down. Brown." The unctuous smile.

Trewyn waited, back bowed, his tall frame hunched and forward, his tufted nose competing with his chin for *Best Jut*.

Hector lowered back into his chair.

"Photographs," Trewyn said. "Pages of a certain codebook, I know you are aware was being looked for. The stream carries a tag. B-309C."

Hector waited.

"B-309-C is your interview room."

"It is."

"Where you interviewed Clive Lancer—is that not correct?"

"Which way?"

"I beg your pardon?"

"'Yes' it's 'not correct' or 'no' it's 'not correct.' Your question is built so I can't give you a positive response."

"I'll answer for you: B-309-C is where you interviewed Clive Lancer from July to October of this year. Could he have observed this number?"

The young island lad— You got out from under it. Must have laid that execrable Lott—to rot.

"It's on the wallplate. All doors, if I'm not mistaken, have them—meaningless numbers. Anyone entering sees it."

"I've come to the same conclusion. So why? Why your number? Why you?"

Hector needed to be sure. "Did you say you received the ingest from? Lancer?"

"That's the question. It came from an older data channel run by Lancer's supervising officer."

"But you question the veracity of that?"

"You weren't Lott's 'anonymous'. He wouldn't know your room. A different communication was expected entirely."

I'll bet.

Trewyn narrowed eyes. Didn't like the way "Mr. Brown" was suddenly directing the interview. "Did you have any, how to say it, extracurricular conversation with Mr. Lancer?"

"Everything was done in-room. You have my notes. My report. All of it digitally recorded."

They stared at each other, one man bred to serve power, the other to serve principle.

"You still haven't answered my question—why you, you're room number?"

"That's easy—"

Ouch—that school-photo grin, all teeth for mummy's mantelpiece.

"He wanted to make sure I translate for you."

"Now we're getting somewhere. The translation: quick with it."

"He's topped ol' Fergus and is saying 'Bollocks to you.' Sir. Will there be anything else?"

"No..." Trewyn gave the file he'd never opened one last pat. "What was it—dotting I's and slitting throats? You've satisfied the record."

✵✵✵

B-309C. Hector gone to his office rather than leaving, opened the locked drawer in his credenza. Removed the original determination of leniency he and his working group had filed for Clive Lancer back in October. Added a handwritten note. Slipped the paper into an internal-pouch envelope. Sealed it. Dropped it in the blue sack for Registry pickup. A gesture equal to Clive's in its futility—but as soon as he did, Anton Hector leaned back in his chair and understood exactly why Clive had bothered to call back.

All those years of being the anonymous, the invisible signature that let other men stay blameless, and now this one line was his own.

Clive Lancer is not a traitor. Termination is political. Not operational.

Certain *fuck-yous* needed official registration because procedure, in the end, was the only language left to tell the truth.

And that was why he'd signed it: *Anton Hector, B-309C.*

4.

THEY CALL IT *BLACK January.* Some, *Black Saturday.* January 20, 1990, when 26,000 Soviet Special Forces break through citizen barricades. Pour into Baku. The shooting lasts three days. 800 wounded—

Michael walked uphill from the Istiglaliyyat café back to the Flame Towers high on the hill above; the Şəhidlər Xiyabanı, The Alley of the Martyrs

—the 147 gunned down, commemorated here.

Gray lane. White marble sidewalk. Black marble tombs slick like oil, slabs raised, low but altar-like. The solemn faces of each of the fallen looked upon Michael from black marble portraits on the white marble memorial wall. Beneath each, a long gleaming rectangle carried their epitaph. Most too young to have anything to say other than they lived, they died.

The Khazri, frigid, strong, had resumed its blow but without its usual haphazard whirl; its passing reverential, its suspension carried the scent of the sea mixed with the qutab-sizzle from the saj-griddle vendor carts at the entrance to Highland Park, but it was the tangy aroma of carnations—red carnations abounded, vivid against the white, the black, the gloss of marble—that caught Michael by surprise. For a moment he was back among the Turkish pines of Trabzon. The Romuleas. Where he'd hiked last spring—pink and purple along the slopes, burgundy in the shadowed vales.

He stopped at a pair of photoceramic squares. Stone faces: Fariza Allahverdiyeva and her husband, Ilham. Ilham was shot by the Soviets. Twenty years old and a student, Fariza committed suicide in protest. To the people of Baku, of all Azerbaijan, they are national symbols of love and fidelity.

I'm sorry for you. For all of you. It should never have to be like that.

Twenty-two years later, the Russian were this nation's friends once more and the Azerbaijan nation held his sister under a sentence of death in the middle of his own nation's capital.

Our stupid games. It shouldn't be this way.

You don't outlive the game, you learn to trade rules.

Kolya softening.

"He's ready to trade his life for hers, if I phrase it as mutual survival."

The old man listening now, wanting safety as badly as redemption. One act could save them both.

The roundish woman with the Teletubby curl at the U.S. Commercial Service table. And again—Conference Room A3, Kolya sat next to her. "Ms. Wren, is it?"

Wren. KALEIDOSCOPE: maybe. Agency: dead certain. Michael would find her. Wren would handle the corridor—papers, channel, the new name. The shape of it clean. Exact. An equation finally balanced. He'd sell no one, only trade consequences.

And what for me?

A thought of home. A thought of his daughters.

Paige, Charlotte, Leigh.

Leigh. He'd work with Lynn. With Gwen. Russell Aiken? Maybe. Maybe not—Lynn's choice. But there had to be a way to make that right. And then?

A small and leafy town. You know it's out there.

Wish your whole life for its pleasant, dreamy, warm-misted streets.

A town no one has ever found.

I could find it again.

Find her.

Find Lulu.

👑 👑 👑

THE FAÇADE of the Russia Embassy in Baku still wore its oil-baron bones. Sandstone the color of rancid butter. Curled iron balconies made in St. Petersburg a century ago. A courtyard gate inset with green-tinted glass, cracked and looking like a stained glass no one bothered to color, nothing to depict. A fig tree twisted around a drainpipe, half-alive and reaching to a roofline jagged with antennas and satellite dishes. Beside the doors, the Russian shield: bright and bolted over the original merchant's crest. Double eagle devouring the flame-shaped emblem of Baku's old nobility.

Simple meeting room. The kind where the agenda is a lie put to decisions already made. Nikoláj Yurenev. Foot of the table. Fingers interlaced. Placid as a stone to the cascade of inflexible disapproval that washed around the table and over him like the babble of a brook.

SERGEI POCHINOK, PRESIDENTIAL ADMINISTRATION/FOR-EIGN POLICY DIRECTORATE: "The Council expected clo-sure on the southern corridor. Instead, you turned it into doctrine..."

MAJOR-GENERAL IVAN TERENTYEV, SVR CASPIAN DIREC-TORATE: "—CPC Expansion was a pilot, not a crusade. You made it ideological."

Sofiya's lips move. "Poobeshchay mne: ona nikogda ne budet odna v temnote."

My promise in response.

Her eyes shut, but I see their color mimicked in the morphine-vial glass.

NATALYA GROMOVA, MINISTRY OF ENERGY/PIPELINE OVERSIGHT SECTION: "...with that, the Turkish line is dead. Tankers idle at Novorossiysk. Our partners in Atyrau are livid."

POCHINOK: "—need to understand: the Consortium lost two billion in hedging because you promised throughput you could not deliver. It's not the year you've wasted. It's the billions you've lost."

TERENTYEV: "You spoke of sovereignty. They hear re-bellion."

Daria's feet in mismatched shoes. Lead oxide dust billows. Tiny explosions more deadly than an artillery ripple across the southern freight-spur of the Stalingrad rail yard off ulitsa Burdenko.

GROMOVA: "...Nord Stream Two proceeds without you. The oligarch bloc insists on a unified narrative."

POCHINOK: "You've become that narrative's inconve-nience."

Daria's fingers release dented aluminum: the mess kit saucepan: filled with colored glass fragments for the window she never made where I would ride in my red cape on a blue horse—

"It will be about you, Papa, but dressed as Dobrynya Nikitich. The clever knight who fought the dragons and protected the princess and the princes with his golden spear."

My daughter driven off.

I consider retrieving her little tin.

I get into the black ZIM that takes me to Moscow. Leave the ruins of Stalingrad and her tiny collection of broken glass behind me.

TERENTYEV: "Our President values discipline. You represent nostalgia."

My hands cover my face. On the deck of the single-mast skipjack oyster dredger, in the bay, the waters of the Patuxent River, Halloween night—

POCHINOK: "—Effective immediately, Kalaydoskop assets fold into the State Energy Consortium. You will advise, not lead, then you will enjoy an honored retirement."

And Lynn, met and sent and failed, and Doris-my-Daria following her mother; the glow of Foxtail Farm aflame: light over the beach stairs, the palisades above.

TERENTYEV: "—Travel restricted. All communications monitored."

A folder slides. Seal red, wax soft. Kolya doesn't open it.

TERENTYEV: "The Kremlin appreciates service rendered. Regrets deviation."

Sofiya's lips: "Poobeshchay mne: ona nikogda ne budet odna v temnote."

Promise me: she'll never be alone in the dark.

When he rose, thanked them, mumbled something about regret and age and energy, about a return to Moscow—when they could arrange it—he appeared smaller, truly insignificant, as if the space around him had adjusted, and his tribunal each saw him in their own individual guise.

Pity.

Sorrow.

Revulsion.

Lost of dreams and ambitions, desires and needs. A weak man. He was almost, it appeared, invisible. Pathetic, really. And just the way Kolya would have it. He would find Michael. He would introduce them both—formally and on terms—to Meryl Hofmeyr.

♔ ♔ ♔

MARTYR'S ALLEY. The Khazri bent the Eternal Flame. It fought. It righted—faithful, unfeeling—and he walked beneath it thinking maybe this was all any of them were good for: to burn steady while the world mistook their heat for purpose.

The Ferris wheel inside Highland Park blinked lights and turned. Faint music. A car nosed along the curb. Engine running. Windows up. Blocked his entry into the park. Between the car and Michael, the man fell into step beside him, speaking before Michael saw his face.

"You fooled Kravtsov in Skhodnya."

Michael turned enough to see the face. The stillness. Rugged. Russian. Quiet authority more than muscle.

Rahklin matched pace and Michael crossed around the follow-car into the park.

Michael grinned. "First-class banker, I guess. Bad jokes. Idiotic laugh. Not much of a watchdog. You're with him?"

"I'm not a banker."

"A watchdog, then."

"Perfectly satisfied with just watching. Things have moved beyond the watching point. For those I watch out for, they've gone beyond watching for Nikoláj Yurenev. Kalaydoskop. The man Lulu and Alina call Uncle Kolya. Now someone needs to be called dead. It could be him. Or it could be—"

He turned the cell phone in his black-gloved hand. Michael caught the screen. The lights of the revolving Ferris wheel made it difficult to see. He cupped his hand. A photo. Sea cliffs. A narrow beach. Alina in white surf. Lulu—her cover-up caught in the breeze, tangled around her snow-skinned calves.

"That choice, Michael Kingston, belongs to you. One requires your commitment. Your active participation. The other, only your cowardice."

Sunday, December Thirtieth

1.

A T THE OLD GCHQ Oakley site, the Vault wasn't where the work lived. That stayed one flight below, in the Pit: cipher processors, cooled server cages, analysts' consoles. Down there the machines chewed code until it confessed; up here the humans pretended to interpret what they'd already decided. You could look through the armored glass, see the process without touching it, which suited Ned Trewyn. He preferred not to get his brain dirty with too much input/output certified-dull fact. The floor was noise; the vault was consequence. Between them, policy ran like water they could tiptoe across.

The cipher that had this morning's assembly dark-driving through cow country into Priors Road had chosen odd scripture: *The Once and Future King*. Strange choice for a code key; Trewyn couldn't help but think Kingston would convey some kind of meaning—maybe a romantic's idea of nobility—as if he still believed there was honor in confession. Kingston had picked the one book every schoolboy of Trewyn's generation thought made a gentleman, and by doing so he'd wrapped treason in nostalgia. Director Eldred of SIS Counter-Intelligence had remarked as much when he took his seat, but Trewyn didn't think so. The best the Americans had ever done with that particular literature was turn it into a Disney cartoon and a Broadway song-and-dance. Kingston was just another gormless American stealing their myths—myths never truly understood—only to end up tripping on Excalibur and poking it through his eye.

There was Eldred, tucking his loafers in the caster arms of his chair and pivoting slowly, a back-and-forth of his upper body like a boxer at the bell. Ms. Chowdhury from Cabinet Defence in the opposite corner. There was a pale Home Office plonker sent to mind optics whose name Trewyn lost as soon as he'd released his limp handshake; and two nameless GCHQ technicians—men who knew the cipher's teeth, had done the extractions, and were there to explain the dental work if it came up. Silas's messages had already bitten through the enamel of deniability—Reel A the confession; Reel B the indictment.

Eldred stopped his swivel. Punched his words. "It's not just Lott. Stand down now and we tell the Service the other deaths don't matter. Seven of our Sov' agents rolled the night Lott went under, and two other of our own into the ground on their way out. That's the tally. Kingston has put his name to the shot—'collateral acknowledged, not sought'—and 'accepts the sum entire.' Fine. We accept it, too. We finish FELL KING. Not for Lott's rose-colored legend—Reel B has torn that to ribbons—but for our two officers who died when his network blew. We don't blink on a confession to an MI6 killing because the victim proves dirty after the fact. We act for our dead, and we close the book before silence makes a legend of him."

Pronouncement from a Director—Ms. Chowdhury waited. Let it sink without the pretended "-in". Eased onto the mat. "I do find it interesting, though, Reel A—a simpler cipher we've been told—"

"The man's straight confession," Eldred popped her.

"Yes. Straight, but simple. His language reads as a full confession only because we know what he's confessing to and it's easy for us to extrapolate. Reel A—*really*—is sort of the fat around Reel B: the meat."

"You're a vegetarian." Jab-jab Eldred.

"Indeed." She lifted pages of the decrypt. Played at giving consideration to something she wasn't. Let a page fall. Gave the same pretense to the page that came before, then the one before that, reading backwards, backing out. The last page—which was the first that started it all—dropped. Her eyes give each at man the table a little tap. "We need to agree. It's time we scrub FELL KING." Eldred opened his mouth, but Chowdhury took his teeth. "Scrub FELL KING. Reel B changes everything. Evander Lott is not the martyr we built the myth on—he's the rot. Child sex traffic, Soviet back-channel, the whole bloody ledger runs through him. You take Kingston now and we look like we're silencing the only man with the proof. Washington won't see cleanup, they'll see cover-up. You want to explain to Langley that our 'fallen hero' was peddling children while cutting energy deals with Moscow? Kill Kingston: that's the headline. We don't bury the scandal—we own the grave."

Trewyn didn't like the sound of that. "You're making an assumption that Captain Hollis and his team will somehow cock it up."

Chowdhury turned her chin to him. "And why isn't the captain with us?"

Because he and his men are securely ensconced at their Norfolk, Virginia, black site prepping the jump.

"Oh, I'm sorry. I don't have that close of tabs on Hollis and his fire-eaters. Wish I did, wish I did." Bit his lip to keep a Cheshire Cat grin off his face. "I would offer, his unit is perfectly capable to lift Kingston. Trained in recovery as well as the kill."

Eldred wasn't having it. "Reel A, Reel B: real blood. The plan's been an assassination from the start."

The GCHQ technicians shared glances, each daring the other to speak. It didn't matter who, but one of them finally did. "You're missing a crucial point. Splitting the cipher was deliberate. Reel A—the confession—makes you leap; Reel B—the damnation—stalls you out. He made the cipher with a built-in timer. Time he's buying for something."

"All the more reason to hit now. Hit hard." Eldred stared.

Chowdhury stared. "All the more reason to pull the plug."

Trewyn clicked his pen. Drew the focus. "Then we are divided. And division, gentlepersons, is not ours to settle. The Palace will want its brief before midday."

When Eldred said, "Christ!" he spoke for both the SIS and Ms. Chowdhury's Whitehall.

Trewyn smiled like the Disney cat disappearing into its tree. Only the smile left behind. "Charter's been clear on this for, God-what? Ten years now, is it? FELL KING opened under Palace equities; anything that crosses allied soil or touches Lott routes upstairs. That's the charter."

♛ ♛ ♛

IT CAME TO PASS that the Crown's council met not in pomp but in quiet—the way a fortress sounds after the trumpeters have cleared their spit valves, packed horns in cases, and departed. A small fire, the color of coins, bent in the grate. The room was neither old nor new, merely continuous: oak that had survived dynasties, air that carried the smell of polish and Meryl Hofmeyr's mulberry chomping worms. The decrypt lay open on the tea table.

Trewyn waited. Legs crossed. Ankle to knee. Observed the gray Private Secretary, adjust his gold spectacles before reading aloud: *"If there is still friendship between our nations, then let it be tested by law, not by the rifle. I will surrender myself to England. I will stand in Her Majesty's court. That, at least, is the justice of allies."*

The paper trembled once in his hand before he set it flat. "Blackmail, of course. This—appeal—to be tried here. He knows precisely what it sounds like: chivalry, decency. He's baiting Her Majesty with her own virtues."

Trewyn stretched his lips to hide his noxious smile.

The Queen's Secretary looked to the window. Back to the pages. Beat the execution roll with his pen before he turned back to the middle. Read. Recoiled. "This other part, you denote as Reel B—my God. If Her Majesty read this—" He broke off. "Children. Russians. I'm astonished. I can understand why Whitehall wants to walk away. I can, in fact."

"Yes. Presumed you would." Trewyn uncrossed his legs. Leaned in. "What he's written isn't for Her Majesty's conscience. It's for her advantage. Eldred sees it. You must see what Kingston's doing. He's holding the relationship hostage, not the Crown. But the timing, Sir. The timing is perfect."

The Secretary drew himself up. "You think to brief Her Majesty on timing when the content is filth?"

"Filth is context. It's also opportunity leverage. The value of our arrangement with Kalaydoskop is nil after CINDER CROWN. The Russians have changed course in Baku. Their Nord Stream 2 is ready to dominate the continent. Our great unwashed will soon have us leave Europe. Our leverage is energy or nothing. Moscow will shift to Turov's Gazprom bloc, and if we're inside that room, we'll be buying the Continent's quiet obedience through someone else's valve by spring."

The Secretary looked at him sharply. "You mean to tell me that in the face of this—child trafficking, murder, confession—you're talking about pipelines?"

"A morality play the Americans have watched from the wings—if we're reading Kingston right—for years and done nothing. I imagine they want the curtain down on the filth as much as we do."

"We don't repeat the follies of King George putting soldiers on their shores based on imagination."

"Mad King George didn't even have steam to worry about. I'm talking about continuity. The one word that's ever mattered in this building. The Queen's interest is not the purity of men; it's the stability of the realm. Reel B changes the morality; oil keeps the Continent's lights on."

Trewyn was pleased to see some red bringing life to the Secretary's cheeks. The man slipped his pen into his suit pocket. Stood.

"Her Majesty will have the brief before luncheon. The Crown authorized the conclusion months ago. It will go unchanged. We steady the corridor, find a bright side to Brexit, when we finish FELL KING."

Trewyn gathered the file, the light of the fire running up the pages like ignition, and left the Secretary staring into the grate. The order had come; the machinery would follow.

👑 👑 👑

"So. Mr. Hector. You have chosen to make your objection formal."

"Filed it through Legal Adviser's. Keeps the paperwork honest."

"That is not your remit."

"My oath was to service. Not silence."

The colorless room without windows. The octagonal table of too many sides. The recessed pinspots that cast narrow cones around each chair were on—dimmed, but on—and each beam isolated its occupant. His Section Manager, of course, leading the inquiry and, though the Legal Adviser (SIS) kept back from the light, Anton Hector recognized him by his Roman beak that tipped into the light and bobbed at his each annoyed and heavy breath. His grating voice came at Hector from the cavern of his nose.

"The Service cannot function if every clerk with a conscience thinks he's a court of law."

Hector said nothing. He'd sat on that side of the table often enough to know how useless answers are once they've decided what you were.

Fitting, he supposed: they'd hauled in five of his fellow "anonymi"—Ms. Wilson and Mr. Davies (the toff they'd called *Toff'y*) among them, while the other three he did not know—and they, and his Section Chief, and the Legal Adviser went at him six more times. The same questions in different tenses. The same answers dressed in different politeness. Procedural repetition, not dialogue, until even they seemed to hear what they'd become: a room rehearsing itself. Wilson and Toff'y didn't participate in the gantlet. Perhaps they were there to witness his shame. Draw warning from it. And when the final charges were read—gross misconduct, breach of internal security protocol, and conduct prejudicial to the interests of the Service—Hector found he couldn't quite keep his smile down. "You can't breach what's already broken."

His Section Chief leaned into his little spotlight. "We ask you a final time, Mr. Hector: will you withdraw your submission to Cabinet? Strike your personal comment from the Lancer recommendation and acknowledge the disciplinary authority of the Crown in this matter?"

He could have paused. Hector could have spared them the nuisance. But he thought of the word used—*authority*—and the one forgotten—*responsibility*.

"I'd rather not. No. We no longer understand what it is we are defending. We burn good men to keep shadows intact. That is not statecraft. That is cowardice."

The words sat there. Air whistled faintly through the Legal Adviser's nose—a kind of reverse Sphinx as it was all and only nose that stuck into his little cone of light. A set of documents was placed before Hector.

Official Secrets Act.

His resignation.

"You'd like to sock me? Punch ol' Ruddy Cheeks in the nose? Get on the next boat to your coconut tree lagoon?"

"You can ask me to resign. Fire me."

"We would, but Fergus told you something he shouldn't."

"Don't those papers cover that? My obligation to forgetting? C'mon," Clive smirks. "Everyone leaves with secrets."

He read them. He signed them. He added the date. He capped his pen, unclipped his security badge, removed his computer fob, and fished his commissary coffee club card from his wallet—gave it a look like a loved one—"Only one away from the freebie. Bother."

"I'll take it." Toff'y.

He reached out. His wristwatch glistened. Anton Hector realized he hadn't glanced at it once. Maybe it meant something. Maybe not. But it was enough for a cup of coffee. He gave him the card and was gone.

2.

MICHAEL PICKED UP THE FSB surveillance team at the lower terminus of the Highland Park funicular. The microvan slipped into the parking circle. A young woman and middle-aged man climbed out. Went different directions as if strangers—the woman, into the terminal, a rack of tourist brochures; the man outside the glass wall, back to the door. Lit a cigarette.

Michael left the building. Crossed the lot. Passed the microvan idling in the last slot by the exit. Kept moving.

Vendor's cart. Black tea. Bag of almonds.

He walked a short distance. Sat on a low wall. Sipped. Munched.

Minutes later the middle-aged man passed.

Kolya came thirty seconds after, and Michael almost missed him. It wasn't the wool flat cap or the shapeless raincoat—no disguise could disguise the man. It was what Kolya no longer was: the purpose, the vitality, the composed quiet power stripped away like a reptile's skin. What remained in the raincoat was someone Michael had never seen. Older. Smaller. The lines of age unhidden. The gait slower. The hands curled like the last gray leaves on a winter tree. A grandfather.

"Green Adidas, white stripes ahead. Beige microvan. Flat suede boots, brown, behind."

Kolya walked on.

Michael waited for boots. Waited for the microvan.

Pulled a dull yellow watch cap from the pocket of his neon-green puffer.

Pulled off the jacket. Black sweater beneath.

Left the jacket on the wall.

Jogged across the street.

Cut into an alley. Increased speed. Cut to a parallel street. Ran. Reached the end. Peered.

Clocked the Adidas—past him, stopping.

Clocked Kolya getting into a taxi.

Further back: the microvan collected bootsie.

A blue Volvo appeared behind them. Rolled past.

Kolya's cab accelerated. The Volvo accelerated. Two cars between.

Michael let one pass, lunged out.

Civilian brakes. Tire smoke. A glancing clip to Michael's thigh—barely a touch—but he took it, fell back, blocked the blue Volvo nosing around.

The woman from the civilian car out—horrified. Michael rose slowly, dusting off, yelling in Russian.

The blue Volvo lay on its horn and Michael backed onto the curb the moment it jumped the sidewalk. He spun. He pounded the hood and gave a middle finger double-dose, keeping his hands in front of his face.

Spun back into the alley. Watched the Volvo go. Ran back half the route, chucking the watch cap into a bin, shaking out his surfer hair; shook out of his sweater—bin-chucked that as well.

A dogleg onto a wider cross street. Fast-walked half the block.

A bright storefront. Rainbow colored sign. White letters/English (somewhat): *Parti Rainbow.az*.

Popped inside a balloon shop.

Helium tanks hissed.

Already moving toward the stockroom doors when his mind caught up with what he'd just seen:

Shopgirl. Muslim headscarf.

Black-handled scissors making a cut—

"Chinese scissors are exactly what I need. But did you know? The story of the first pair of scissors?"

Hardware cashier in Trabzon. Leans in. Blinks eyes.

Father Cevik would be at the simit vendor's cart. Rolled up.

"Household scissors like these: opposing blades, center fulcrum screw—?"

Same Made in China scissors. And the Muslim girl cutting ribbon tied to a red balloon.

Slammed into the stockroom. Chased by yells out the loading gate into an alley, into the air, the daylight. Baku.

♛♛♛

HE SAW KOLYA again by the long bend of Mikayil Useynov. The flat cap was off. Signal: surveillance shaken. Michael caught him. They walked in silence. A gray Mercedes waited, flashers soft.

A red cardboard palm tree dangled from the rearview mirror. The interior reeked of coconut and cologne. Dr. Arman Taghiyev perched behind the wheel. Gray suit. Silky black beard. Manicured hands on the wheel. Deputy Director, Pipeline Strategy, Ministry of Industry and Energy— Kolya's man in Baku. No greetings, only a nod, and he drove them down the seawall road. Cranes swung like compass needles above the port. Farther out, flames flashed from burn-off stacks beyond the breakwater.

They rolled into the Azerbaijan Caspian Shipping Company headquarters, number 2 Useynov Street—marble façade, brass doors, security glass thick. Taghiyev spoke to the guard in Azerbaijani. Two words. Signed the clipboard. Barrier light: green.

Taghiyev led them through the no-expense-spared marble foyer to the elevator. Up two floors, and left down the expense-spared corridor: faux-wood paneling bulged; vinyl grain peeled. Drooped. A door marked with a warning in Azerbaijani that didn't apply to them. Taghiyev opened it. Another nod. Gone.

The room inside had been built better. Three walls paneled in real 1960s wood, fluted and holding up to time. Large framed photographs of the ACSC fleet—faded blues, graying seas—hung crooked, they cheapened the effect. Stacks of banquet chairs leaned against one wall. Folding tables another. Heavy draperies smothered seaside windows; their bottoms showed a water-stain tide-line. One central sweep of curtain pulled open, let in a wide stripe of sunlight thick with dust.

In that mote-floating, sparkling light, Meryl Hofmeyr sat at a rectangular table of heavy teak. Three plastic banquet chairs pulled close.

Three white porcelain cups.

A silver pot.

One black folder.

Meryl poured tea. She wore a yellow pant suit and Michael had an absurd and uneasy thought: what Ms. Hofmeyr resembled most—forbidden to his children, when he'd been around to forbid anything—was a Teletubby.

Kolya ignored the cups. He opened the folder:

DA-12 Defector Agreement.

Transfer of Custody Memorandum.

Annex C Family/Dependent Release.

TI-24 Travel & Identity Package.

He read Annex C last, and an hour passed.

"When I am aboard your aircraft, wheels up, my granddaughter walks from the Azerbaijan Embassy in Washington. Not before."

"That's, uh, not the arrangement arranged, hm?"

Kolya let his eyebrows do the shrug.

"Wheels up is too deep into our side of the commitment, with—mmm—none of yours. Let us split the difference instead of hairs, yes? When you are under Agency protection you will have her released and the aircraft won't—no-no don't say anything—take off until our officer outside confirms her—" her strange bright/dead eyes swept Michael, lids batted—"*your* fair sister, Michael-and-it's-so-nice-of-you-to-arrange-this freedom. Yes?"

Michael went still. Willed the heat from his face. The drumbeat from his chest. Said: "That *is* my sister. Only reason I care about any of this—either of you—and here's how it's going to go. She moves first. Before anything else. Before you—gramps—get into their car. You have the authority. Use it."

"Blood is blood. Hers. Yours. Mine. The moment I am safe I will make the call. It will save her, Mikhail. Michael. I am giving myself not to her." A flick of his fingers toward Meryl. "I am giving myself to you."

Back off.

For Lulu.

For Alina.

Back off.

Michael softened his face. He nodded once and pretended to relax.

👑👑👑

BUSINESS LOCALS, leisure shoppers, tourist families lunched at Huseyn Ridge Grill, one of a cluster of restaurants, bars, and shops on the slope below the Flame Towers. One o'clock and middle of the rush, the transformer behind a parking kiosk popped.

White flare.

Shower of sparks.

Diners startled. Half-stood, napkins in hand, looking about. Interior lights flickered. Nervous laughs. Sighs and chairs scrapping back to meals; some phones belonging to the selfie-addicted came out. Positioned and peace-signed themselves framing their shots to catch the smoke rising up the hillside, making it appear the three Flame Towers—soaring blades of glass, and shimmering bay water—were on fire.

The real fire was much closer.

Slow smoke seeped from Huseyn Ridge Grill's kitchen doors until chefs and staff pushed through them coughing, choking in rolling clouds. Everyone scrambled for the street. Fire filled the kitchen and blew through the back doors.

Up the hill: construction crews on Tower 1 and Tower 3, landscapers in the grounds, interior finishers unloading carpeting, stone, furniture—all stared downhill at the flare-up while security horns blared overhead. Everyone looked around. No fire here.

Tower security inside the lobbies and those stepping out of the air-conditioned vestibules chattered, confused about protocol.

Inside Tower 2, the chief of the afternoon detail checked his tablet.

Evacuation order: all floors clear.

Security herded the small gathering away from the towers toward the crest. Contractor trucks and vans backed out from the drives and loading bay.

The few Tower 2 occupants trickled out, bewildered. Floor 27.

Kolya's bodyguard—Lulu's former crazy-eyes—stood outside Kolya's doors.

He grinned once, nervously. Swiveled his head. Tried to locate the alarm source. Didn't know what else to do. Noticed the red light in the elevator lobby; two cars accessed the private suite hallway. One dinged green. The doors parted. A Tower security officer approached.

"Evacuation code is live. You'll need to clear the floor until the fire department gives the all-clear. Is Mr. Yurenev within?"

"No one. Just me. I can't leave."

"You have to leave. Look—don't make this a problem."

Crazy-eyes thought about fighting.

A second.

Five.

Thought better and called the second elevator—the one the Tower guard hadn't used. When it arrived, he stepped inside, hit the red emergency stop.

"That'll hold it here?"

Tower security nodded.

"Can you lock the fire stair? No one else is on this floor. It's not on fire."

Tower security nodded. Did it. Locked.

They got into the elevator the guard had ridden. On the ride down: Crazy Leer's sideways grin.

"I'm security too, you know."

Tower security nodded.

"When we get down to the lobby, I got to stay where I can see these elevators."

"You can watch from right outside the doors. Anyone tries to use them—you'll see."

And that was exactly what he did.

♛ ♛ ♛

A CEILING PANEL shifted. A stepladder came through first. Then Rahklin. Then a nerdy tech with a backpack lowered into the empty elevator car—the one stalled open on floor 27.

Rahklin swiped a card. "Two minutes."

The lock light blinked green. Rahklin opened the door. The tech went straight to the television credenza.

Disconnected the router. Swapped in an identical unit from his pack.

Rahklin crossed the room and entered Michael's bedroom. Located a dark suit jacket draped over the back of a chair. He slid the room card into the breast pocket.

Back to the living room. A pause at the windows. Far below, fire trucks with toy-sized lights, white smoke blown sideways—the restaurant blaze already knocked down.

Rahklin checked the work: both routers matched. Down to the serial number.

Out. Doors shut/auto-locked.

The tech mounted a micro-camera beneath the corridor's smoke sensor, aimed at the suite door. Rahklin checked the feed on his phone. Frame steady on Kolya's entrance.

They vanished back into the elevator ceiling cavity.

Pulled the ladder up.

Panel shut.

Less than ten minutes later, Crazy Leer reached in, flipped the red switch, and sent the car down.

♕♕♕

Pinwheel holds the quartz-halogen light bar.

What was the name of that sickly lieutenant? One with the camera? Too long ago to matter. Evander Lott on his knees. Silas behind him. I give him the gun.

"This shouldn't take long. Mr. Kingston, you know what is required."

The camera rolls. Silas fires. The pedophile's head goes pop.

Silas Kingston's eyes—the man who's stolen my daughter

(brought me a grandson)

—brim with terror of the irredeemable.

"An irrevocable act for CIA/MI6 viewing pleasure the first occasion you displease me."

And now we join once more.

Kolya signed the defection paperwork while Meryl Hofmeyyr filmed. Got in close on the documents. No going back. He looked at Michael, but his grandson didn't meet his glance. Kolya thought he understood.

"They have chosen Lynn's hour," he said when he had finished and he was theirs. "Midnight, the thirty-first—tomorrow. When the old year dies. When the new is born. They won't warn her. They'll take her from the cell for her wash. Let her brush her teeth. Do it there. Quick. Routine."

Michael struggled to find his voice. "Now you'll prevent that."

Kolya nodded. Placed his open hand on Michael's forearm. "Don't worry."

He closed the folder. Handed it to Meryl. "Prepare your aircraft. When I am in American hands she walks. That is the trade."

Meryl took the folder. Stood. Nodded at both men. "Until tomorrow." She left.

"Never mistake cruelty for control, Mikhail."

Michael met his clear cerulean eyes. His mother's eyes. "Or the opposite."

"Perhaps so."

The old Russian spymaster motioned them for the door. Their footsteps merged on the cheap flooring. This was how legacies traveled: room to room, man to man, choosing no man for virtue, only for willingness, and the past walked with him—yes—but now it slipped ahead, a shadow rounding the next corner. And this time Kolya knew he would not betray Sofiya; this time Daria, according to the stubborn myths of her faith, might be as Doris offering that small, impossible smile—if her God allowed such mercy, if such things were ever true.

3.

P EACH FUZZ. CHARLOTTE GRINNED. Hadn't stopped since she'd got up that morning. Wished she'd dreamed about him. Bobby. Bobby Claypoole.

"Rob-bert Claypoole." Charlotte practiced his name in an important TV voice.

Charlotte Claypoole?

I'd keep my last name. (Stop it! You're not going to marry him!)

She made an amused noise. Clipped Beaumont's leash. There *was* peach fuzz on his upper lip.

Like kissing a man, kinda. Or almost a man—not a boy, that's for sure. He even smelled kind of man-y.

She'd noticed the cologne he'd put on. And not too much—like some boys do when they show up to Pancras dances. This wasn't that. This was bigger than life.

And who'd a'known?

God, he's good looking. Bobby Claypoole is hot. Like Josh Hutcherson hot.

She grabbed her ski bunny hat. Remembered she'd worn the green one when they first talked. Dug around the pegs. Perfect. The *Love, Actually*/Claudia Schiffer crochet one. With the red stripe. Fluffed her hair hanging out.

Why's my heart beating so fast?

"Let's go, Beaumont. Secret mission."

Her Snow Angels crunched on the gravel of the parking area. Wind gusted. Beaumont tested the air. She tugged his leash. Wanted to get far from the house quickly as possible. Beaumont jounced toward the fields, the palisade—their old walk—but that was the holly tree.

"Not that way. We're not going near there."

Opposite direction. East. Into the short woods out behind the North Vista Outhouse. Silas's car was gone so he wasn't going to see her; she liked having the old stone guest house behind her. Just in case Paige or Melody glanced out their windows.

She made the woods. Wind wasn't as bad, so she wasn't as cold. They moved fast and quietly over the pine straw, a trail of breath puffing behind them.

Beyond were the old fields that were meadows in the spring, the summer, wildflower-picking—back when she was a girl—but too mushy, and the grove of the trail between the frost-burned brown lumps of flower stubble was muddy and slippery, but she'd said seven-thirty and she didn't want to be late.

Well, a little late wouldn't hurt.

I wonder if he misses me like I do him?

She jogged anyway. Couldn't help it. Felt light. Felt magic.

Cotton candy—that's what it's like. A cotton candy machine. Like I'm in a swirl, just getting wrapped up in soft pinkest-pink-of-all softness-of-sweet.

Beaumont bounded out onto the dirt road. Firmer. A little gravelly. And puddles in the tire ruts.

"Girls, remember: we don't go down that road. Play all you want in the fields around it—both sides, it doesn't matter—that's all Kingston, but this road doesn't belong to us and you don't use it." Papa'd said it a thousand times.

That's why Charlotte didn't like the wildflowers—the Claypoole easement: she'd been grown up to be scared of it.

The wind kicked up. The cold cut through her jacket. Veins of ice, from truck-tire puddles freezing overnight, fragmented like glass beneath her tread. Beaumont kept tugging. She'd wanted him right next to her before, but that was the holly tree, the strange man carving ugly words.

He did stop you from stabbing yourself with those scissors.

And now, going the opposite direction, Charlotte found she wasn't frightened at all. She thumbed the catch on the leash and Beaumont bounded to its full thirty feet. Ranged ahead, came back, his circle never wide.

Every time they passed a clump of woods his head went up. Testing air. Tension down the leash. The wind blew. The sky lighted to the dull gray it would hold until whatever tomorrow brought.

She had not told anyone where she was going. She had told herself she didn't have to. She'd be fifteen in March—so she was almost that already.

Bilbo is sneaking up on Smaug and our hands are touching on the armrest and he leans in— "So what do you Kingston girls do for New Years?"

"Shh."

"You doing anything? Or do you stay with your little sister?"

"I don't. I get to do what I want."

"Wanna go to a party?"

"Is someone having a party?"

"I want to take you to one. If you can get out—I mean it's late..."

Those eyes.

"For New Year's Eve..."

Such a Josh Hutchenson nose.

"...you know."

And he's kissing me.

He kissed me.

I kissed him back. I took a breath. "I'm definitely going."

He told her it was at the Enchanted Forest and he'd seemed to know she'd never been. No one her age got to go. Her mom wasn't around since Christmas. She didn't know if Paige would like it or Melody would let her.

"What if you don't ask/don't tell?"

Something happened in the rest of the movie and there was fire and dwarves and Gandalf and the Ring and she didn't have any idea and no one would know and—

His hands on the other side of my knee—

It's across on the outside of my thigh—

Between kisses she said, "I can't wait."

After the movie—the twins loved it—

(such a kid's movie)

—she told him she didn't know what she was supposed to wear. And he told her they did it every year like a cool costume party, and she told him she *really* didn't have something like that to wear.

"Don't even worry about it. I'll get you something."

She had given him her last crumpled twenty in the theater parking lot.

Now, here he came.

And he's got a bag.

Beaumont stopped in the road. Head swung back and forth between them, tongue hanging like a pink rag in the gray of everything else.

The leash made a whir as it retracted and Charlotte moved to meet him, the dog now close. He wore work boots, but not like other guys—boots that made it known he actually did outside work, and his jeans were cool-faded (not stonewashed) and his jacket was red-and-black plaid with a kind of fake sheep's wool along the edges and the collar, and he had like two open layers beneath—a flannel that didn't match at all, a denim and a black tee—and that was hardly what she was thinking about at all and felt so romantic when his arm went around her waist and he gently pulled her in and kissed her.

And tongue. We've made it to tongue.

Beaumont pawed between them. Bobby laughed. Didn't give-a-shit about the muddy paws, laughed and twisted the dog's hound-floppy ears, bumped foreheads. Said: "How be you, ol' Vencky dog?"

"His name's Beaumont. Not that other stupid name."

"This dog, Charlotte, my gramps named as a pup. It was Vencky then. He told your grampa when he bought him."

"He didn't buy him. He couldn't. He caught Beaumont wild in the woods. Like everybody always does."

"Yeah. And brought him back—down this-here same road—and paid my gramps two hundred dollars." Cocked a thumb over his shoulder. "He's there. He's up starting the fires. You can come back down and ask'im yourself."

Charlotte stepped away from Bobby and the dog. After about five feet Beaumont tensed, ready to join her if she went any farther. "Stay, Beaumont!" And she kept going back, ten feet, fifteen. Turned, and—"Vencky: come."

Beaumont leaped toward her tail whisking the air. Charlotte groaned.

Bobby threw back his head. Laughed. And Charlotte was back and pressed her chest (just a quick second) against his biceps and laughed too.

"It doesn't mean anything. I could call him Yankee-Doodle and he'd come with me."

"Try it."

She did. Beaumont didn't.

Bobby put down the plastic grocery bag.

That's not a store bag. He sure thinks he's the shit making this dress a big surprise.

Bobby crouched, loving the dog with his hand—head and ears and scruffy neck. Went nose-to-nose/eye-to-eye. "You remember your trick, Venct?"

"'Venct?' I thought it was Vencky."

"Watch. Sit, Vencky."

Beaumont dropped his rump, raised his chin show-quality proud.

Bobby shaped his hand into a pistol. "Alright, Vencky: hands up!"

Beaumont's paws lifted to his ears.

"Bang!"

And the dog fell onto his back. Played dead.

Charlotte loved it. Clapped once. "Okay, Beaumont." Nothing. "*Venct!*"

That got him and she held him off from pawing her.

"I don't know why Papa would lie about just finding him."

"I guess he didn't—I mean, that is where people catch Claypoole hounds. It's where he first found him."

"Yeah. One thing I know: Silas Kingston is not a liar."

"I didn't say that. He's better—in a way. Most people don't come down the road and pay anything. Just take 'em from us like they always done."

Charlotte went to the fence. Propped her elbows. Looked out over a long-abandoned tobacco field. The old deep furrows were still there after who-knows-how-many years. Bobby took a chunk of mud-ice. Threw it. Beaumont couldn't help himself and galumphed in pursuit.

Charlotte: "Let's us-not lie to each other."

"What do we gotta lie about?" He touched her cheek where her hair hung down from her cap. "Your hair's pretty."

Charlotte blushed. She looked at the bag. "So what'd you get me?"

"You're not going to chicken out are you?"

"Whoever said I was even thinking about it?"

"I didn't. It's just the sneaking out thing—you prob'ly never sneaked out before, and, dunno."

He thinks you're a kid still. Even after kissing. And I let him touch my boobs.

"I have. Lots."

That didn't feel so weird; to lie.

"With who?"

"Friends. Guys, too, from my school. You wouldn't know 'em."

He touched her chin. Made Charlotte look him in the eye.

"But you never let any other dude take you to the Enchanted Forest?"

"No!" She held his hand holding her chin. "You're the first. Now come on, stop holding out on me. What'd you get?"

Her hand shot for the bag. He yanked it out of reach. Stepped back. Reached in.

"Ta-da!"

Bobby Claypoole pulled out a dress that even in the gray light, the red sequins sparkled.

His smile was a mile long; Charlotte was having trouble stretching hers an inch. "I'll freeze."

"Well, bring a jacket. You won't freeze—you'll look hot."

"What size is it?"

He checked the tag. "It's a small."

"I told you I'm a medium."

"You said, 'girl's medium.' This is adult-small."

He offered it, hanging between them. She held the hem and ran a finger up the sequins, turning them dark side up.

It's a lot. That's really bad-girl sexy. But he's so excited.

"I don't know. What's the costume?"

"It's a 1920s party. Like the um—" searched—"Great Gradsby."

"The *Great Gatsby*."

"You got it, girlfriend."

Girlfriend? Just-a-phrase, Charlotte.

"I can see you at this party. The way you'll look, the kind of over-the-shoulder way you look at me." He swaggered his shoulders. "Maybe with flowers. That'd be sick."

And that's when it hit her.

The portrait.

Grandma Doris's dress.

Like Papa gave Paige. But this'd be for me. All mine. And I'm the one that looks like her. And I'd look at him just like with her look and he'd fall in love with me.

She grabbed the bag. Stuffed the dress inside. Didn't want to change her mind.

"You're right. I just wear a jacket over it. And I got the perfect flowers—Papa, my gramps, he gets red ones—I can just picture it perfectly—they're in the chapel, perfect red river lilies he changes every week. I can get those easy."

Bobby held both her shoulders. "You come out when it gets dark. I'll be waiting. This same road. It'll be perfect. You're going to kill it."

She felt her head bobbing, felt her heart loving on him, and she kissed him once, hard, backing up, tugging Beaumont, nodding as they parted and calling—"I can't wait!"

And Bobby nodded back, his tongue rubbing his lower lip where her braces had drawn blood.

4.

H UNGERED AFTER FOR YEARS. The banquet denied.

An old oak door. A faded sign. Office of Treaty Regulation and Administrative Compliance.

"Drop by OTRAC. We'll talk." Silas. Like *"We're all ribbin' it at the Pig Pit after we get off the oil patch—drop in for some bones."*

No badge reader. No keypad. No camera bubble over the door jamb. Drexler gaped at the sign. Lopped off the first letter from each word to make sure they were what they were.

O-T-R-A-C

The sanctum sanctorum, secret of secrets, sumbitch's throne room and all he got's a flipping doorknob and an old-timey key lock.

Two, actually. Deadbolt and mortise. Brass ball knob polished by a century of working hands.

He felt his breath catch once. Low, behind the ribs. Raw. Pulled from some deep furnace he'd spent half a lifetime smothering. His own fault, all of it, the weight, the hiding, the way he'd pretended he didn't have a body at all. Yet here it was, forcing itself into him, insisting it had never quit on him even when he had and now it felt like the lungs were reminding him they were still there, bellows still willing, still capable of filling past the shame he'd packed around them. Filling and igniting a fire.

He jerked the knob, expecting it to be locked; the prep for getting to an impatient—

Wanna play old door games?

—rattle.

The old OTRAC door swung wide.

If it opens easy, you're already in play.

For an instant he wished he had the bright red shield of his Lynn file, but what good would it do, what difference would it make when the man within had orchestrated every indictment he'd written inside?

Old marble took his weight like it was nothing. This was not the high-gloss corridor limestone. These slabs were dull, hazed, rough from scrubbing, and Drexler entertained a vision of Dickensian washerwomen, black skirts bunched 'round red knees, arms pumping scouring brushes. But the business here—oil and pumpjacks—replaced plump women and KALEIDOSCOPE opened before him wider than it had any right to, off that narrow hall.

Ballroom grand.

He counted seven work islands. Pods of heavy wooden desks, six to a knot. Tall lectern stations with newspaper sticks and stacked periodicals and maps—modern charts mixed with who-knew-we-cared antique. Long library tables, topped with bookshelves, and every surface carrying weight: open folders, onionskin copies folded back on clips, graphs-ledgers-cost tables; typewriters were as prevalent as laptops, and there were more pens and pencils than printers; yellow pads of handwritten notes abounded among the ribboned, stapled, half-rolled pages of energy policy: agreements, contracts, alliances, and treaties foxing at the edges. Three score or more banker's swivel chairs: empty and swung half-away from the desks like whoever had been sitting there a heartbeat before he arrived had vanished.

Everyone but Silas.

Drexler let the door click behind him and noticed, equally amused as annoyed, the sound of hidden locks electronically engaged.

Silas waited. Hands loose. Face decided.

Drexler felt the anger back on line. Good. Barged forward. Silas didn't move as, words spewing, Drexler shouldered up into his face. "Knives buried in backs is between last-sip coffee and toast crumbs most days for you. But Lynn?!" They'd have been nose-to-nose if Drexler's girth hadn't prevented that. Strangely enough, Silas leaned in—a fraction forward—enough to take the words full gale force. "Lynn! She's your fucking flesh!"

His splayed hands quivered and for an instant both men expected Drexler to shove him. The huge man threw his hands in the air like great uprooted trees and danced lightly back like falling leaves.

Once—twice— three times Drexler prepared to speak gulped back words, to gather more with force only to choke them back and sputter, finally, with deflating passion, "I looked up to you."

"You did your job."

"You trained me to see the inside man. To spot the elegant burn. You ran me through dozens of them and then you ran the same play on your own daughter and expected me not to notice."

Silas's gaze didn't flick away. Didn't harden. "Did I?"

"You used her. Same way you used me. Way you use everyone: take whoever's in reach and put them where the blast will be worst and stand here and call it necessary."

"Yes. The successes were towering. Invisible, but towering." Voice quiet. Words flat. "But those necessary blasts, small in the scope of things, the scheme of my mission, have taught me too late that even invisible towers can be made of sand, and the real damages, surgical though they may have been—'necessary?' I won't defend what I can't—they were real and they were permanent and not worth the price paid by anyone. Call it regret if you want. I'm still learning what that feels like."

Not for the first time with Silas, Drexler felt like a fly who just had its wings pulled. Nonetheless, he rallied. "Don't dare tell me you're going to let Lynn get her heart stopped just so you can prove your hubris to yourself. Gravin, Harker—they've written her off and laid it at your feet."

"Yes. And it seems to me, your barging in here is doing the same thing. Yet, same time, humiliating yourself by coming back to *me*—with no ability to effect any result on this yourself—you're clutching a little bright hope, that I'm going to tell you 'there-there, Morty, I got it all handled.' In every last hope, hubris stands a better chance than self-loathing."

And the geese have never stopped laughing.

"Drexler—" He felt Silas's hand on his elbow. "Come."

Silas's other hand gestured to the great hollow room, and Drexler noticed what he hadn't before. Wall vaults fanned to the ceiling—a barrel run of worked plaster and carved stone. The oval of a skylight floated in the center. Stained glass framed in curves usually seen behind altars. The waning light of the year leaked through, dull and thin, though still enough alight to drop faint bands of color along the walls and the fan ribs. In full daylight, this place would blaze. Because Drexler always dressed in white it did that more with him than with Silas.

"Why do you think I never brought you into KALEI-DOSCOPE?"

"Because you don't trust me."

"Wrong."

"Because I'm not blood."

"Also wrong."

Drexler snapped. "Then what?"

"This isn't your work. Counterintelligence is your blood. Better. Thicker there than mine."

Drexler blinked. That was not the answer he'd hauled up his anger to meet.

"You're the cleanest set of eyes left in this town. You see where the line bends before anyone else knows there is a line. If I'd dragged you in here years ago, you'd have learned the wrong loyalties. The wrong reflexes. This place runs on compromise. You don't."

Drexler puffed his lips. Charged air. "You kept me out to preserve me. That's what you're saying."

"I am."

"That's bullshit."

"You find the lines and you follow them and—" Silas changed thoughts mid-sentence. "You noticed the maps in this room, so many of them from all sorts of times and conveniences. You know the map I've spent four decades looking for? The one the geese V over where the lines don't matter."

Geese again. Story of my life.

Drexler shifted uncomfortably.

Oats jammed into my palm.

"Feed 'em," he barks.

Hissing bills. Pinched skin. Snatched groats.

And I never see him again.

"Keep talking bullshit, Silas. You won't sway me from my purpose."

"Yes. The delightful Lynn Kingston."

Drexler clenched a fist. Raised it between them. "I'm built just right to make this hurt forever."

"She was bait. That's the truth of it. Because the man we need to move only moves for something that looks irreversible. He had to know I'd let it happen. I had to trust he wouldn't."

Drexler felt his heart bang once hard in his chest.

Silas: "You see the cruelty. Good. It's there. I'm not asking you to like it. I'm asking you to understand there are pieces in motion you can't be tangled in. Yet. If you tangle yourself now, you'll fail exactly where we can't afford it."

"Where is that?" It came out more honest than Drexler meant.

Silas didn't hesitate. "Man: if you want to stand for her, then stand for her."

"Where? I don't follow you at all."

"But that's exactly what you'll do. You will follow me, and you will do it right. KALEIDOSCOPE is yours."

The room widened.

Doris touches my hand. "There's always a plate for you at this table, Morton. Always enough to eat, so don't be a stranger."

Doris's table. The pond's edge where his father forced the oats into his hand.

Kindness and demand.

Invitation and fear.

Both lives he'd never finished living.

"You're telling me your job is now mine?"

Silas nodded once. "It's outgrown me. But with the man Lynn's bringing back with her, it's going to fit you just fine."

Drexler felt something give way inside. Not relief. A kind of exhaustion that came when some old picture he'd carried for years suddenly turned and collapsed, and there was no putting it back the way it had been.

The air between them changed. Not warmer. Just stripped of the useless pieces, and Drexler's breath changed. Not the strained pull he'd learned to hate, but a clean rush that widened his chest before he could brace against it. Air in a room big enough to take him, for once. Air that tasted like it had waited here for years, held still in the high vault until the moment he finally claimed it.

Drexler exhaled slowly. "Back home we used to say a man can outwalk his shadow, but not his name."

"That's about right," Silas said, withdrawing his electronic badge, moving to the interior door that led to his office and the flash-modern technological side of the exhausted old operation.

5.

A SASSICAIA. FERRARI IN a bottle. Theresa noticed the blackberries and plum all the snobs raved about, but the flavor that sparked her palette was more subtle, complex in that it carried memories, hidden, freeing, treasured memories: menthol like the Virginia Slims Blue she'd burned through law school.

Overhead linear LEDs burned straight through her crystal globe, splitting the liquid color, stripping it from substance, laying it sharp, angled, slashed across her white countertop. Light bent cleanly here, nothing softened, nothing diffused. The opposite of white meant to smother shadow, keep the mind still. This was white built from edges and planes, modernist angles meant to engage, meant to cut and expose whatever touched them. Theresa set the glass beside the folder on the island. The CIA cover sheet was the only color in the room not cast by light.

Theresa Ossani's Market Square tower. Shared it with DDO/husband Gary Gravin who brought home nice treats.

Glass on two sides.

The Capitol down Pennsylvania Avenue lit under the winter dark; DOJ and Hoover in their gridded blocks;

the Mall cutting its long, purposeful geometry through the city.

Everything she worked: ordered and spread below.

She slid the last page back under the red SECRET cover sheet. Slid the file into her Bottega Veneta document case. Over her notes. Handwritten notes always/only. Nothing remarked electronically. She would photocopy what she wanted tomorrow—not so much to share as to tantalize. One hand to wash the other, but she kept the basin.

Sweet Gary had come through and she let that settle. A small—tender-in-its-way—peace offering for his blatant, schoolboy obsession with the Kingston girl now renounced. People mistook them often enough. Older woman, younger man. It bothered Gary, but Theresa never corrected it. It stirred something within her that clung the way fog sweat and sweatered landscape.

Thought can't be forbidden.

The mistake tantalized her.

She had chased KALEIDOSCOPE for years. Nothing to subpoena, nothing to corner, nothing that wore a badge or left fingerprints. Just Silas Kingston rumors. Former Director of Counterintelligence—it didn't fit with the whispers of 'Hegemony Through Energy.' And then she'd found it: a dusty berth in the Department of Commerce out of her Intelligence Committee reach unless she could make the connection.

Drexler's report didn't name the operation.

It didn't need to.

Theresa knew what Silas was.

Lifted her wine. Her lips parted on its edge. Her mouth filled red.

She could have been in St. Bart's this week. Everyone else was. She should have been at the Eden Rock terrace for Christmas Eve, a villa open to the sea, sunchair and a Chili Chili Bang Bang with a straw. Smooth, strong black hands on her back in the spa. The island sorted, without speaking, who still mattered.

Instead, she stood in a white box in Washington, her holiday wasted on Gwen Kingston and that pathetic lawsuit. A cheap little lever, ultimately useless against the steel of Silas's vault.

This was different.

This was structural.

She finally had something that could make the Agency flinch. Lynn Kingston wasn't a rumor or a theory; she was a CIA officer, clandestine op/cover blown by her CIA father. The panic her execution would cause inside Langley would force them to distance themselves from Silas. And distancing themselves from Silas meant exposing whatever he'd built in the dark outside their charter. They would call it containment. She knew better: it was fracture.

Wànhuātǒng didn't need the blueprints of KALEIDOSCOPE. They just needed it finished.

And she'd give them that now.

Not treason, not even compromise: just the first honest tool she'd ever had to pry open an intelligence apparatus that had stopped answering to anyone a generation ago.

It isn't treason to break open an agency that's made itself ungovernable; it's my job.

If it took a foreign service to see the advantage in that, boost her a bit, it only proved how insulated—how dangerously unaccountable—the CIA had let itself become.

Lynn was the entry point.

Silas was the fulcrum.

KALEIDOSCOPE would collapse when pressure landed.

Her phone lit on the counter.

Subject mobile. U Street bar. Proceed?

Gwen Kingston out on U Street—of course she was.

Some women needed the performance more than the act. The tits. The long curly black hair. The hunt. Theresa Ossani found Gwen vulgar but had to admit: the sex appeal that dimwit had could still turn men to ash.

Sad little rituals for fleeting delight.

She would open the KALEIDOSCOPE inquiry when SSCI reconvened after the third. A first-week action. Clean, procedural, unassailable. Silas Kingston would not slip from this net.

Theresa tapped the screen.

Yes.

♔♔♔

TWO DAYS SINCE she'd ditched the lawsuit. Two days since telling Senator Ossani to go straight to hell, and not taking "no" until she walked out of there with her ten-grand retainer back in her purse. A fricking scam—all that. She'd played it right, no lump/no tears, just business.

Always bring your game.

And your glam.

Game and glam and Gwen.

Wrecked since Christmas, adrift these last two days since she got her money back—tired so tired, and not even booze could buy her rest; curled up on the sofa, furious at Michael for dying or not-dying—

Just being Michael and giving up on your family.

Furious at Silas for living, furious at Paige—

Ungrateful. "We'll still be Kingstons"/not going to get me started.

And the amounts of her time she put into Charlotte and Leigh for what in return?

To what—constantly tell her how great Melody is? And that limp dick Clive?

Gwen had let their problems swallow her whole. Drag her into insolvency. Not just money but mental and physical.

So f-ing tired.

And the money, though, too.

When was someone going to comfort Gwen?

Then Nelson Fair. Her handsy escrow agent pal.

"Gwen, honey, this is great news. I've been *waiting* for you to get free of that lawyer nonsense. You're too hot to let 'em drown you in paperwork."

"If you're looking for a play-date, I'm not interested... Right now."

"Ha! Gwen. 'Hot' in your work. I know how to wait turns. I meant you have no idea who called asking about you— they saw the Rainor loft on caravan and were blown away."

He told her the broker. Georgetown. Big league residential. Then he told her the offer: "A Logan Circle rowhouse flip. Renovation signed off just before the holidays. Empty as a mouth. Five thousand for the full staging, another grand bump if it sells in the first week, plus Nelson's usual wink: "Nail this one, babe, it won't be a one-off."

It hit like oxygen and Adderall.

Between that and the returned retainer, she could make January.

She could make February.

Could flip that old Volvo for the Mercedes.

And, if anyone, I deserved one before lush Lynn.

Maybe she didn't need Michael's benefits.

(Right now.)

Maybe she didn't need *any* Kingston bitch-charity. Maybe she could march back into St. Pancras, shove her boobs in their faces and flip the girls onto *her* dime without asking Silas's permission.

But all that was for the morning.

Tonight—tonight was for christening the Logan Row.

Button-cute Tony: "You can't have passion for a home until you've had passion in a home."

Gwen smiled to herself. Twizzled her gimlet.

Someone always gets fucked in a real estate deal. Might as well be you, girlfriend.

The new bar on U Street— "Clancie's" with the "e" like a Sophia Loren wink. (Gwen liked to think herself built like a Sophia Loren)—had caught her eye more than a few times in passing. She liked the look of the clientele she'd seen through the windows; up-scale crowd, not stuffed, knew how to dress it up, but let it slip; how to smile, laugh, let go of life. Gave her a kind-of-a *grrrr*. So, she'd dropped in after the walk-through: contract and key, and her fifty percent retainer, thank-you-very-much, tucked in her Gucci clutch.

Early enough for a seat at the bar, and quiet enough—some low-playing 90's and 2000's dance, pop, and a little country-why-not? A Kettle One gimlet. And an opportunity to make some mental notes. The weird double parlor and the skylit kitchen and that ridiculous third-floor boutique closet room the developer thought women would kill for.

Don't fix that into something—only thing killed's your sale, babe.

Key was gonna be stroking the buyer into a take-a-deep-breath entry alcove, then grab them with the one-two living rooms—hers wet first—then stir his loins through the pocket door with 'who's the man of the house?' leather, glass, steel on the hardwood.

She'd chatted with the bartenders while she ate a cheeseburger—butch Katy (kinda tat-hot if that's a girl's thing) and white reggae Samson (as if/well-maybe)—chatted with a couple of retail chicks (boring), and a pair of douchey Hill lizards trying to hit on her (as if/as if). She'd hit on a Silicon Valley East money-to-waste big-laugher, and that mighta been fun—until his silicone front fiancé arrived and stole him away.

It was after nine and the bar was pumping gently. Not yet full. Gwen noticed two stools down, she was being noticed by a guy she'd not noticed arriving.

Notice those cheekbones: exact kind GQ spent the eighties dying to photograph.

*Not such bad eyes either. Kinda gray—*but not Michael gray—

(get-that-outta-your-head)

—*imagine looking up from knee-level into those?*And he'd been watching her since she walked in.

Not handsome. Useful.

He lifted his beer. Sizzled her with a smile.

Gwen twizzle-swizzled her gimlet. Dropped her chin at the two empty seats between them. "Doesn't seem fair."

His eyebrows lifted, inquisitive.

"Just saying—if a party of three comes in..."

He smirked. "They get a lot of threesomes here?"

Gwen's face: like when hit by an icy blast.

He looked away. Sipped his beer. Looked back: "Sorry. Really—I beg your pardon."

Gwen frown-pouted. "Some guys get tired early. Need a stand-in."

Guy gaped.

Gwen grinned. Winked like "Clancie": "Don't beg me a second time. Scoot over. Tell me a story."

Li'l frog-prince hopping lily pads—couldn't have jumped quicker.

Warm, familiar, comforting.

He flagged Samson—hands sculpted hard, no stranger to work—

Mind if I take your hands?

—"I'll have what she's having." Teeth-flash her way. "And she'll have another."

Gwen unclipped her purse.

"No, I got this."

Best coy ever. "Thank you." She looked inside, past the papers—heart pumping like it hadn't in weeks—for the Logan Row keys.

♔ ♔ ♔

WHEN INDIAN CREEK overflowed, the Lady in the Lake Lagoon flooded with the rest of the bottom area of the Enchanted Forest, and although only the remains of the jousting field had joined the expanded creek bed, nature turning it into a thriving marsh, the water that had filled the empty gunite basin of the amusement park pool never receded and with rain and snowfall more successful than evaporation over three years, had made the former water show attraction an insect ripe home to ducks, heron, turtles, frogs and snakes. Dark. Miasmic. Haunted. Paige stood in front of Clive, bundled up and bundled together, his arms wrapping her, their hands interlaced over the place their child grew, in the winter silence of the abandoned park.

Paige leaned her head into the crook of his neck. "They had a swimmer. Like someone my age, I guess, or college, a real good swimmer like a lifeguard type, and she'd wear a glittery bathing suit—kinda like Bilbo's Mithral Coat."

"I missed that part."

"You know, to look like sparkly woven metal. It was a bathing suit—and Dad said a golden-chain head dress."

"Sequined bathing cap."

"Michael Kington didn't see it that way. And she was all white—body make-up—"

"Like an albino."

She swatted his hand. "Stop it. I'm trying to tell you something. So Aunt Linny—when Dad'd tell that story—she used to tease him about his *albino* girlfriend. Like their whole growing up. Dad says even at four she was jealous of his crush on the Lady of the Lake. After seeing her—Lynn says—he never paid attention to her again." Paige pointed. "See that broken platform?" Clive rubbed his cheek on the side of her head—an affectionate nod—and Paige slipped from his arms.

She crouched real low. She raised her arm, an imagined sword and acted out her words. "The Lady in the Lake would rise from the center holding high Excalibur and the fountains would dance, and all the colorful lights would spin and scatter in the water droplets."

She moved to the broken sandblasted plaster-made-as-wood railing and leaned toward the pond desperate to see what they once saw. But all the color left was the frigid white of moonlight on the ice-spackled black water.

"They would always come." Low, disquieted. "Twice a year. Papa and Grandma Doris, Aunt Lynn and Dad, Hal too—though he doesn't remember. It meant a lot because how busy Papa was. But it was a tradition."

Clive knew what the ache in her words meant. "We'll make our own traditions."

"All I've ever wanted to do was leave mine and now that we're going..."

She found his hand. She kissed the glove upon it. "We'll come back. This'll still be here. This can be a tradition."

"I thought the rule was sixteen."

"Fourteen for the parking lot parties."

"They doing something tomorrow night?" Clive.

"No. No one comes during winter. 'Cause you can't build fires. Look at us. We look like Eskimos."

He said, "If it was so popular, I wonder why it closed."

She said, "Times change. Things end."

Clive's eyes flashed spooky. "Maybe it was because of those two kids."

She pulled him by the hand. "C'mon. Let's say good-bye to the knights."

They set off on the broken asphalt away toward the swamp. Paige pulled, anxious to move quickly so that she had to turn and walk backwards. "There are so many stories about that. I don't know if any of them are real."

"Stories like that begin somewhere."

"I did hear, one of my teachers who came when it was still open, that it just closed all at once. Literally, people were turned away at the gate—but I told you that—like the owner couldn't take it anymore all-at-once."

"Or someone just wanted it shut down—they couldn't take the bleedin' sight of it."

"Thus, the stolen children."

"Thus?"

She pushed through ropes of vines shed of leaves. "Isn't 'thus' what you Shakespeare-talking King Arthur people say?"

"Hiya, I'm Clive from Tortola. Cracking beach you got here."

Paige laughed. "Hope you brought sunscreen and watch the ice on these boards or the only thing cracking around here'll be your head."

👑 👑 👑

GWEN PAID for the next round. One more, she'd be ready. Chuck already was and Gwen was looking forward to it. He was telling funny stories about the band he'd left college to start and how that somehow got him into Bitcoin when she leaned in, planted a wet one on his cheek and said, "Hold that thought, I gotta use the restroom."

"I'll keep our seats warm."

She got up, loose-limbed and relaxed. Not too bad. Steady. Had a sip "to go" and he matched. She took her purse and phone and left. Chuck picked up a coaster, his hand on Gwen's cocktail glass, but Katy swooped in for it.

"I know you were about to cover it, so you won't take this the wrong way." She removed Gwen's drink to the back of the bar. Covered it with a coaster there. Chuck gave a flat smile. Took his drink and turned to watch the lively/crowded room. Lowered his glass to his lap two-handed.

👑 👑 👑

GWEN FINISHED quickly. At the sink she checked herself out.

You still got it, babe.

Did her lipstick. Flounced her curls.

Soon ol' Chuckie'll have it too.

She kissed at her reflection. Checked the Logan Rowhouse keys inside her purse again. Moved them to the top. Went to put her phone inside, but what with the contract and the envelope with her retainer it wouldn't stay closed. She reached into her blouse and tucked the phone inside her bra. She adjusted her cleavage. Admired her stack with a mirror-wink and pushed back into the bar.

Chuck watched the crowd.

"Where's our drinks?"

Chuck lifted his from his lap and Katy brought hers from the back of the bar. Lifted the coaster.

"Oh. Thank you." Gwen leaned into Chuck's shoulder. "You weren't trying to get nasty with me?"

"Think tonight I won't need any extra help."

He put his glass against hers, took her face, and pressed his mouth over Gwen's.

♕ ♕ ♕

SNOW FROM BEFORE Christmas had piled in the plastic that covered the metal skeletons of the jousting knights, it hadn't melted and mantled upon them like broad shoulders, and the water, lower than when they'd last been here, had receded from the iron frames of their horse's head and drooping necks.

"They're actually starting to look like the real thing."

"Clive—I don't want to have to learn a new language."

"I told you, in Martinique I'll be speaking French, but they speak English. We'll get our shots there—you'll be in control of the situation. They won't give you anything that will hurt the baby. And in Gambia, English is the main language."

"But where we're going they speak Wolfish."

"Wolof and I speak it—even remember how to read it—and I have family there who'll take us in their village no questions asked."

"Well, first of all, you don't because she wasn't your real grandmother."

"I know how to find her daughter. When Grand-mère Amie got sick, she came and stayed with her. Paige: don't be scared."

"When I told Papa, is when it got weird. His eyes were wet. I saw tears—swear to God, tears, when I asked him to get us passports and *identity kits*." She enunciated the jargon still foreign to her. "When I explained why you thought we needed to hide out for a while, he was more into it than you. And he knew about the other, Fergus-thing—I could tell. He told me he was proud of you and I was lucky to have found you."

"I found *you*."

"Yeah, he said that too."

Clive bent over. Dug around in the crusty/muddy water and found a stone. "Think I can hit that one."

"Don't. You'll hurt him." He made a skeptical face. "Aunt Linny thought they were real. So when they'd hit each other with their lances, she believed the one that fell back was a real person dying."

"When they reset, didn't she figure it out?"

"She was four."

He threw the stone. Snow exploded from the skeleton knight's forehead.

♔♔♔

BARTENDER KATY collected their empty gimlet glasses and wiped the bar. Because her eyes were on Gwen's figure, loved the sway of her hips—could teach her a thing or two—she didn't notice that both glasses had her lipstick; the last one she'd poured for Chuck had it fresh.

♔♔♔

PASSING THE CASTLE. Crumbling plaster and broken beams. Paige veered off the main street. Grabbed a twisted jumble of chicken-wire, its hexagons rough with cement, flecked and faded like sea glass.

"Want to go in? I know the spot where they say those kids disappeared."

She pulled it back, and Clive ducked first inside.

♔♔♔

GWEN HIT a sidewalk tree trunk with her face. Chuck pulled her back.

"Easy there. This way."

Her glazed eyes shined. She sneered. "Silly me not watching the moving sidewalk."

He took her arm. Guided her close at his side. Kept walking. She didn't notice he was leading.

"It's right up here. Just a few more, I think." She gave him a lascivious/sloppy grin. "I jus' hope you're ready."

He guided Gwen up the steps to her new listing. She stood in front of the door. Opened her handbag. Hunted her for keys. "I'm thinking I'm ready to lie down." Couldn't find them. Didn't bother her. Her fingers moved automatically, still searched—no signal to stop. "But, y'know, there's no furniture so s'anding up's fun too."

She peered into her purse. No keys. Started looking for them all over again.

The surprise of being seized by two men didn't catch up to her until they wrenched her purse from her easy grip. Tossed it in the van. Tossed her right after it.

"Hey."

Asian and they're—

Where's Chuck?

Where are my keys?

Asian's taking me?

Why's Chuck just standing there?

The door slammed. Sound of the driver's and a passenger side doors after that. Gwen sat on the floor looking at her hands for her clutch. Telling herself she needed to scream but her brain wouldn't move. But she needed help and her purse and her phone.

The van took a corner, fast. Gwen rolled across the back, hitting the wall, not feeling it.

This is bad. This is bad. This is bad.

Where am I going?

Where's Chuck?

Asian is Chinese. The elevator guy. I should scream.

Another turn. Another slam.

Gwen's phone popped out of her cleavage. She fumbled for it. They weren't looking back.

Assholes.

She activated. Stared. Wondered what she was doing.

☙☙☙

CLIVE FOLLOWED Paige over some fallen framing timber. "Paige, this doesn't seem real safe."

"This doorway—This door—"

They stood on a scraped/dented/fallen fire door. The doorframe loomed but the passage was blocked by fallen debris. "They say a maintenance guy was behind that door, and the little kids—a brother and sister—in one of the cars that went through—he just—"

The ring of her phone made them both jump. Made them laugh.

"Well, that's something. It's my mom." Connected. "This oughta be good." Hit speaker. "Hi, Mom. Long time no talk..." She waited. "Merry Christmas..." Waited. "Happy New Year?"

"Paige? It's... "

"Mom: I can't hear you."

"Whisper."

"No don't whisper. If you're drunk call me—"

"I-love-you-I-love-you!"

"Jesus! Don't shout!"

"I'm not—I don' think—It's two—I'm—I'm—I'm sorry! You be mom now!"

Gwen made a weird/breathy grunt. A little growl—that was the only word for it.

"I will... Okay. Bye."

The line went dead.

The light went dark on Paige's device. Made the doorway blacker. If that was possible. She said, "Like if that was her way of trying to apologize, she fucked that up—what-a-surprise."

Teary eyes shine brighter in darkness. Somehow.

Clive tried to take her hand, but she pulled it to stuff her phone back in her pocket.

"I don't know. That was... When she said, 'I will,' I don't think she was alone."

"Yeah. Well, you know what she's like." Vicious.

"That sounded more than drunk, luv."

"So. Fine. What are we going to do about it?"

Tears gone. Never fell. She glared at Clive. Breath heavy. She tasted the dust. The time. And in her mind's eye she saw a man's hand beckon a little boy, a girl not much older to join him beyond the door. "We gotta get our baby out of here. Right now."

She shoved him and when he didn't move, she shoved right by. "It happened here, Clive." Her voice was shaking.

She bolted. He scrambled to keep up.

"Slow down. What happened. Your mom?"

Fast. Surprised by her own words and annoyed she said them, she hurried toward the night, Clive trailing on her voice. "Those two kids. Little. They were real. Followed him—went with him. Right through that door. Right inside. I don't want to think about it. I don't want to be here—Why the FUCK did she call me like that?"

When she reached the night, Paige ran for the parking lot.

👑 👑 👑

A CALIFORNIA KING on a low pedestal, teakwood on black granite without a frame. Without a footboard. For the headboard, only a long silk-brocade bolster. Subtle sheen. Pattern like something lifted from a medieval choir stall. Theresa Ossani lay beneath the down comforter, a Hästens Eala, light as air over her skin. The scented candle she always burned for Gary when he worked late flickered spiced clove and myrrh on his nightstand: her private liturgy, the closest she came to devotion.

He'd called before she'd gone to bed—Syria blowing up, so what else was new?—and now, approaching midnight, she was awake to hear the soft hiss of the elevator doors signaling his arrival to their floor. She feigned sleep as he came in.

He blew out the candle. Removed his shoes and then—turned inside his closet—the rest of his garments. She watched his back ripple in the faint light rising from the city. He reached for pajamas.

"No. Don't."

"I thought you were asleep."

She opened her covering. She was long and fit and nude. "I want you tonight."

He went to her two slow steps, then hungrily, and she took him.

And she imagined Gwen Kingston, a finer figure, every detail vivid.

Gwen hadn't earned this tonight. Gwen never would again.

♛♛♛

"HE WOULD PAINT her in movement, turning as though arriving at a grand and mysterious holiday affair, or maybe leaving to instigate one. He described her expression, the one he would capture, as a flash of knowledge, of recognition, enlightenment—no, that's not it; the word he used was 'divination.' Divination for the dance that transcends music."

Stone chilled through, smoke curling from candles on the altar, the only light; it was late—though not yet tomorrow—when Silas found Melody within the chapel. Perched, edge of her bench in the second row, leaning forward.

Elbows propped on the back of the pew in front.

Hands clasped in prayer.

Not supplication, but search, her eyes focused on the stained glass in the wall behind the altar, small, offset: not an afterthought but a witness beside the cross.

"Fine glass," he'd remarked as he slipped in beside her. "Special. Deeply meaningful to Doris."

She slid back, her words mingled in her sigh. "Mm-hmm. Me, too. Now."

Silas offered his arm. Melody wrapped into it. Into him. Lay her head on his shoulder. "You've learned all of it now," he said.

His heavy breath trailed blue in the still air.

"I've read it. I've learned everything leading up to what she wanted me to know."

"I think I know the question you might have."

"Covenant 17."

"My turn to say 'mm-hmm,' and I probably know less than you. That's how it was built. We have a more pressing situation."

As they spoke, her fog blended with his, the visible air of their words joining, mixing, blending their thoughts before dissolving and Silas told her about his first meetings with her father, the plan for Doris's portrait, the artistic vision.

"I never got the last part about the dance and the music, but he was an artist and I have spent a life in hidden secrets, and I knew Doris kept many—the one you've mentioned—brilliantly." He turned an unusually soft smile to Melody in the circle of his arm. She bathed in it. He said, "He came highly recommended. Really. Impeccably credentialed."

She made a scoffing sound. Irony more than sarcasm.

In the night and through the window, moving clouds made moonlight shift; both of them noticed how faint shifting colors skimmed gently across the altar and upon them.

He spoke. "When I recalled his use of the word 'holiday' it brought the events of Christmas Eve in sharp focus..." He looked into her eyes. He waited.

Melody's irony dwindled into bitterness, cynical without resentment. "Which means he'll come tomorrow night."

"New Year's is as radiant and ruinous as he could ask for."

He let the implication float, sink, and hit the bottom of his daughter-in-law's heart before he unwound his arm, before he turned and positioned them into the knee touching intimacy of interrogation and confession: truth in its cleanest form and, inside a church, the safest release of all.

"Melody. Tomorrow you have to—you must—leave with the girls and the twins."

"I need to face him down."

"Boone's coming is about Charlotte."

Either decided or ignored, doubtless both choices fluctuated within her, Melody clutched his worn hands. Her eyes fixed on him. Urgent. Earnest. Unabashed. "Silas. You know I never ask. I know the boundaries and I honor them, but where's Lynn? Is she with Michael?"

Gathering the family. Good. It was where he wanted her. His answer came measured, every word chosen.

"Closer to him than she realizes. She is in trouble, but trust me: she's going to be perfectly safe. Michael has seen to it."

"Does it have to do with Clive? Somehow—and I love him, Silas, I do; and I may only have not much of an education but I am 'perspicacious'—he's involved with all that. *Somehow* he's involved. Not in a way I can guess, but he is."

Silas softly chuckled. No vapor appeared; their bodies close, they'd thawed the air between them: a pocket of heat in a room built for raw truths. "He is. Not with them—any of that—but with what I need to divulge... It's bigger than that. It's everything, including why you must leave. He is, Paige is." And then he slipped and showed his devotion. "I've saved them. And I'm desperate now—for you and my lambs."

The one thing I do know, unequivocally about, perfectly, and with full knowledge, is secrets.

Making them.

Keeping them.

Forcing them and stealing them.

"I'm not leaving. I won't."

Buying them, trading them, fabricating, passing, treasuring, bleeding for and breaking and blowing them up.

"Do me a favor, Papa, and don't go telling me any of yours. I don't have room."

"My secrets are safe with me."

And then, they weren't.

"I'm not telling you to leave because of Boone Kelso. There are others most assuredly coming tomorrow night, the next at the latest. They've come a long way to kill me."

"Why would they?"

"I killed one of theirs. Murdered him."

"He was an enemy—"

"Only to me. And human decency. But legally he was an ally, and memories are long, and some grow into grotesque shapes."

"What did he do—? It was a he?"

A nod.

"The lens keeps turning. That's the thing people never understand about families. You think you've broken a pattern, but all you've done is shift the angle. Grand schemes. Small cruelties. It doesn't matter. The heart weighs everything the same. And every generation thinks they're correcting the last, but the correction only folds into the next turn, becomes another version of the same image none of us can see straight on. It's a kaleidoscope, Melody. No matter how many times you turn it, you never get a final picture—just fragments rearranged."

"Doris made a picture." Whispered. Awed. "Because you're right—she urges us to be wrong. To force the picture. But it only forms when we stop hiding from it. When we let the light hit what we'd rather keep covered. This man you killed—Silas: what did he do?"

"The same thing as at St. Ignatius you've read about by now."

"Who would defend that?"

"No one. That's the point. It's to keep it from ever needing to be defended. In the end, it's not the secrets, it's the lies secrets live and die in. And that's why you're taking the children and leaving. Tomorrow."

Her voice changed, sharpened, narrowed.

"If this terrible secret is so important that people have crossed an ocean to protect it, how could we ever be safer outside these walls than here? This is our home. Foxtail Farm is where we're safest. Even if it's only to hide until the danger passes—Silas, I know you. I know your heart. You want us here. You need us here."

"Need?"

"Because once the children are hidden, we will fight."

"That must explain this."

A voice from behind. Both of them knew it: any tone anywhere. Silas turned and Melody lunged.

Hal stood in the doorway beside Doris's memorial vases of fresh red river lilies. More brilliant for the dimness. An HK416D Recce carbine held one-handed like presenting an exhibit in court. His free arm caught his wife and kept them both balanced as she bound to him, hands pressing his cheeks, her lips pressing his mouth and face.

The lilies shivered faintly as her embrace carried them back against the wall.

The same impossible red Boone Kelso brought to life in Doris's portrait.

Red that shocks/mesmerizes the guilty.

Red that draws the eyes of children.

"Want to tell me, Dad, why Drexler gave me this? He sure didn't seem to know."

"Because Morton Drexler quit questioning me. Freed him up to start thinking for himself."

👑 👑 👑

UNINTERESTED IN HERSELF whom she didn't feel she was, right now, anyway; inarticulate not only of words to put to her thoughts, the things that felt like they should be fears but weren't this moment—maybe next/maybe the moment before, she couldn't recall—impartial and passive, Gwen/her/she unalive inside her.

Her feet—no shoes/lost shoes—crunched frost blades of grass she knew were cold but not to her.

And the wind blew hard and slightly damp upon her cheeks and she wished the Asian men, who'd assured her they were friends and urged her on beyond any capacity to resist—well, anyway.

Anyway. Of the voice she followed, or was led by—it came from inside her—she had a fogged and cottony idea it might be her soul and might have always been speaking to her, telling her—even whole-life denying it was there—but it wasn't there and the lump rose in her throat. And she expected that voice to tell her something/what-to-do.

Pushed to her knees.

The sandy frost cold/not cold, the wind stinging/not stinging, the pressure where she'd hit her face against the tree.

Not so funny anymore.

The rippling splash of a stream. Anyway.

Sleeping on the job—what her soul-voice was doing.

"Sleeping on the job. Sleeping on the job. Sleeping on—"

Her face broke the thin ice over the gliding water, her eyes open to all the tears she'd ever shed, registering this as though plunging through a mirror and she struggled but was also too weary to struggle much at all.

The word, *fight*, inside her: a word never so inexplicable to her as the moment her lungs gasped and flooded and her last sensation was release—

Those men, they've let me go. Anyway.

She gulped water-for-air once more, vomited into the Sugarland Run, and a foot on her back held her down until she died.

Monday, December Thirty-first – New Year's Eve

1.

LEV RAHKLIN straddled a bar stool at the cast-off chichi-restaurant bar—a short wall dropped between the old-world kitchen and the part of the Bayli villa where Turov took his meetings. One hand for his Turkish coffee, the other for his tablet. Watched Kolya's door. Around three a.m., the first of Kolya Yurenev's body men had come up, joined that crazy-eyed motherfucker that dog-watched the doors. Him/three others. Waiting. Pacing. Brief conversations. Turns to walk off frame for cigarettes and vapes. The angle was high. The quality from the micro-camera Rahklin's tech mounted under the smoke sensor—though steady and better than what you'd get in a liquor store—caught a bit too much glare from the corridor lights. Jerked a bit when motion became too quick. It was obvious the crew didn't know why they were there.

Suite doors opened. Michael first. Business casual under dark overcoat. Two pieces luggage. Yurenev behind. The flat cap and rumpled beige raincoat Rahklin observed him in yesterday. They moved to the elevators and out of sight, but—so far—everything moving as Michael Kingston had promised. Only thing left: Yurenev to come back alone.

♔ ♔ ♔

MICHAEL FELT the tension spike inside the elevator as it stopped at the fifteenth floor.

Kolya. "Relax. This stop is planned."

The door slid open. The barrels of three hand-guns equipped with suppressors met their faces. Before his bodyguards knew how to react, Michael led Kolya shouldering between them. Kolya faced his men from behind the backs of three black clad/black masked men.

"No one will be harmed. You've been faithful to me every minute of every day, and I know you would have given me your life if ever I had asked. I am now giving you yours. Where I am going, you cannot come. You cannot be involved any further for your safety and my own. Do not waste a minute of your future on anger or humiliation. Hate? Hate me as your patriotism must call you to, but I expect pride from you: with your lives, with your family and for our Rodina."

Michael watched fury sweep shock from their faces. Two more KALEIDOSCOPE operatives moved past the other three. Collected weapons. They got to Lulu's former bodyguard.

Michael said, "He comes with us."

A sixth and final KALEIDOSCOPE man, dressed in a Flame Tower hardhat and maintenance jumpsuit, stuffed his own handgun into his belt holster. Zipped.

Michael gripped Kolya's luggage. Led his grandfather after the false maintenance man into the second elevator.

The lights, control panel, the floor-movement indicator: off. Their escort snapped on a low-light helmet lamp as the door shut them in darkness. A spoofed security card unlocked the mall level. They rode in silence.

Unopened. Unfinished. Empty for the morning shift start. Michael, Kolya, and Crazy Leer moved quickly after their escort through the dim concourse—retail fronts papered over, kiosks shrink-wrapped, polished floor reflecting their passing like a half-lit runway. The hacked keycard got them through a security door. The maintenance corridors. Loading bays. They swiftly followed the man's dim light to a last door. Fire alarm cables hung disconnected.

6:01 a.m., they pushed into the Tower 1 underground garage. The lot was clustered with trucks and equipment of various construction/electrical/HVAC finishing crews, but the only people in sight were Meryl Hofmeyr and three of her team from the safehouse. Two of them stripped carpet-store decals from the sides of a delivery van; slapped on the emblem/logos matching the Flame Tower maintenance trucks lined against a far wall.

In her black pants, black parka, black ballcap, Meryl Hofmeyr looked like a bizzarro black Teletubby.

No greetings. No ceremony. KALEIDOSCOPE never wasted words at this stage.

Kolya came to a stop beside her. He kept touching his suit button as though checking he was himself. Michael stayed close enough to steady him without seeming to guide.

At this point—for what it's worth—Crazy Leer wasn't leering. Michael put Kolya face to face with Meryl Hofmeyr. Took Lulu's bodyguard aside. Indicated a motorcycle. Backpack/helmet on its seat.

"You're going back to Lulu."

"That's impossible."

"It's not impossible. The Chechen will know. If you reach out through enough broken channels, you'll see: one will fix itself and reach back for you."

"What do I tell him?"

"That Turov knows Sarpi."

"And?"

Open pilothouse of the single outboard, 7-meter Merry Fisher.

"You have what I need?" I ask him.

The Chechen watches the water. "I have Lulu. Waiting for you."

"He'll know better than I."

Hand in his pocket. Michael gave Lulu's *Znamenie* icon a squeeze. Rejoined Kolya.

Meryl read from a checklist.

"Documents."

Kolya nodded.

"Medication."

"I've been perfectly healthy my entire life."

"Hm. Splendid for you. Change of clothing."

The two bags Michael brought at his feet, waiting.

Michael added, softly, as though it belonged to the list: "And whatever personal things you want to carry forward. Only what matters most."

Stern eyes from Hofmeyr. Dead eyes back at her.

A small line. Nothing to it, old man. Except everything.

Kolya searched his pockets. Calm at first. Certain. Removed his rain coat. Checked his jacket. Outside breast. Inside breast. The lower pocket.

Cerulean blue to smoky gray—every time they hit him, Michael saw his mother's gaze.

"This is where you put it in my pocket. This suit. Correct, Mikhail?"

Brows knit. A suspicious eye dart Michael missed. Purposely.

Kolya dug again. Performative now. Nothing.

"I won't travel without my daughter's photograph."

Michael stilled.

If Meryl Hofmeyr was indeed a cartoon character, that stupid antenna would have popped the lid off the top of her head.

"We are, mmm, short on time." Meryl knew the exact time. Eyeballed her watch. Dramatic emphasis. "My team will, eh, collect it and I promise-swear-inform you: you will have it to kiss hello the minute you step off our plane in America."

He didn't hear her. Kolya lifted his face. Something old and wounded came through it. "I will not leave without it. I will not leave her in the dark."

The words struck Michael with his mother's cadence.

"Promise, Michael: I want your vow." Doris holds Lynn. The Place of Blackness.

Her vow Kolya's: older than Lynn, older than Michael.

Meryl Hofmeyr tap-tapped her wristwatch. Quacked half a dozen reasons that meant nothing to Kolya, who transformed into an unmovable power before their eyes, looking down upon all of them.

"Wait for me or don't. I am going back." Kolya turned for the fire door.

👑👑👑

RAHKLIN STOOD at the seaside windows. Beach, gray as the video window on his tablet. Waves lapped like a lake. Like the faint grainy lines the rolled from the top of the frame and down the empty hall before Kolya's door.

His tech, on his back on a sofa, flipped his detonator phone. Little spins above his face.

A shadow preceded a figure moving directly beneath the camera.

The rain coat. The flat cap. His gray hair around its edge. A flash of face.

Kolya Yurenev.

Key swiped.

Door opened.

"Get ready."

The tech caught his phone. Red to green. Screen winked. "Ready. You tell me."

Kolya left the doors open. Determined stride inside.

Rahklin counted a slow three.

"Now."

Tech's thumb. Signal out.

A massive blast through the doors. Static. The feed went black. Rahklin tapped a couple times just to make sure. No camera left to broadcast a signal.

Rahklin shut the feed window. Tapped his way into local news already interrupting their broadcast to announce the explosion.

👑 👑 👑

LYNN FLINCHED at hands shaking her from sleep. Her hands batted them away—"I'm awake! I'm awake! What?!"

Her female minder stepped back. A man not seen since interrogation stood at the door. Dent in his right cheek; gunshot scar tissue that offset long lady-lashed eyes. Mamma-something. Azerbaijani state security.

Chest tightened. Heart lurched.

"You'll come with me."

Pistol on his belt.

This was it.

Lynn hated that her hands shook as she tried—failed—to slip on her rubber clogs.

"You won't need them. Come now."

Lynn forced them over her socks. Pulled herself tall. Walked right up to him. To his face: "Good fucking morning to you too." Two proud steps past him into the corridor. Her minder stepped beside her. Placed a hand on Lynn's shoulder.

They weren't friends, but this woman and the two other female Azeris who shared her hygiene needs were the only personal contact she'd had since Thanksgiving. She'd never touched Lynn so softly. Lynn tried to catch her eye. The woman looked away.

"Don't worry, hun." Lynn, nothing if not encouraging. "We're all going to get over this. Me first."

Mr. Elxan Khalil oglu Mammadov, a colonel of the *Xarici Kəşfiyyat Xidməti*, stepped around them. Led the way.

They made the turn toward the bathroom. The door was open. A mop and bucket ready in the hall. Made sense: tile, drain.

Lynn prayed the Lord's Prayer to herself, but when she got to the "Forgive us our trespasses," she shifted to the Twenty-third Psalm; had no intention of forgiving those about to take her life.

Focused on Leigh. Imagined her daughter she'd never been allowed to love right—

Stop lying. You made the deal: you gave her up.

I'm sorry.

And her focus increased as they positioned her before the sink: she made herself see Leigh in the reflection in front of her.

"Wash your face. Would you like a toothbrush."

"You got to be shitting me."

She ran the taps. Filled her hands.

Water. Wet. Warm enough. That's an okay last feeling.

She felt Mammadov's hand moving low.

She clenched her eyes and covered her face with the water in her hands.

Lynn felt the brush of a towel against her shoulder.

"Dry off. Let's go."

Marched from the bathroom. Marched down a corridor she didn't remember from her arrest. A quick glance. Mammadov's pistol: right where he'd holstered it when he dressed.

A door unlocked. Her minder stepped aside. This time their eyes met.

Deference. The woman remained behind.

A working corridor. Embassy night staff in offices. Mammadov barked something. Along the corridor, rooms left open clicked shut.

A formal door. She recognized this one. Where the nightmare began.

Through the door: the half-floor mezzanine. Where the security guard she'd never seen again—not even at her trial—had murdered Roman at the embassy formal entrance.

The red carpet giving beneath her feet. Lynn quivered uncontrollably.

Get a grip. I was less a mess when I thought they were shooting me.

Mammadov stopped at the top of the short stairs. Lynn reached for the gold rail. Steadied herself. Halfway down she stopped. Shook her head in disbelief. "If I have to thank *you* for this..."

Her feet slapped marble in her rush to Morton Drexler—overbearing, impatient, slovenly in his dirty white suit. The force of her collision into him created the physics necessary to get her arms round his girth.

"Please, Ms. Kingston. We just need to leave. And quickly."

She stepped back. "You did this?"

He showed her all of his back and he opened the door. The morning still in blackness. Not a breath of wind or weather.

"This was all your brother. This was Michael."

2.

D AWN HADN'T YET TURNED the sky. Just thinned darkness enough that the promise of day lay flat on the
Sugarland Run Park trail like cast iron, heavy and gray. A
holiday Monday, the young algebra teacher who usually
jogged the river path with the running-friends she'd met
not long after arriving in Virginia—soon after her husband deserted her back to Manila—jogged alone. Faster
paced today, she pattered onto the second footbridge
and almost missed it.

A foot.

Snagged in the narrows beneath.

Algebra stopped. Bent over—just a sec—to catch her
breath. To prepare for the unpreparable. Leaned over
the bridge rail.

A foot with a leg.

She scrambled down the bank. Ducked the edge and
saw the woman. Whiter than white. White-dead. Felt a
sudden and gaping misery; the horrible surprise that no
matter who anyone is, everyone else shares with them
and each other the two most intimate parts of human
existence: birth and death. Nothing about them matters before—because there was nothing to matter—and

nothing about them matters afterwards because gone is gone is gone for all of us.

She reported the body to the police. Said she thought it might be a murder, because the woman wore a skirt. A fancy blouse. A fancier white leather coat. They said it was probably a slip and fall, and she held back from telling them the woman wore a corset because she didn't want to hear a crack about prostitution; she'd seen enough of that back in Manila to know this corset cost more than most prostitutes made in a year.

She refused to give her name, but said she would wait and look around. Hoped by saying that, it would hustle them up. She disconnected and, colder from that exchange than from the below-freezing temperature, she felt two little pinpricks in the corners of her eyes. She jogged in place and kept the lump down in her throat until the police rolled down the path and surrounded the Filipino and this dead woman she'd chosen briefly to love. She gave her statement, her contact info, was told she could go, but wouldn't. Didn't. Not until they took Gwen Kingston (Algebra wiped her eyes; made the sign of the cross) away.

♛♛♛

DREXLER DROVE a Mercury Grand Marquis LS. Bought new in 2009 with "all the extras"—when the salesman mentioned a suspension package; a man of his size perked up at that. Plus he liked the color. Or, more truthfully, the name: Pueblo Gold. The pueblo part. Western flair. Kicked some nostalgia every time he lumped into the seat.

Lynn hadn't said much. Plenty of time for questions after the holiday. He used the drive to relay what he knew—beginning with an admission she'd been right to go digging after KALEIDOSCOPE in her CLAVICLE clusterfuck.

"Your brother's been running it down all year. All across Europe. Ran circles around everyone. Right now, the Russian KALEIDOSCOPE is jetting back here. Full defection."

"The man Michael was chasing."

"Codename Kalaydoskop. That'd be him."

He noticed a secret smile curl the corner of her mouth. "*Kalaydoskop*? No kidding."

She enjoyed something about that. About the name. He let her have it. Nice to see her smile.

"You sure you don't want to just drive to the front gates? It's too damn cold."

"I need to breathe. Need the outside. I'll be fine. Just keep an eye out for a plywood sign says 'Claypoole' and something about trailers to rent."

"Oh. Kay."

He made a show of peering over his steering wheel.

"I'll tell you when we're close. What about Michael?"

"I'll know more when they land. But it was all him. Be a big step toward rehabilitating him."

"Michael's on the plane?"

Drexler saw the sign, saw the trench, same time Lynn pointed. Slowed. The boards over the drainage cut looked rotted.

"That sure won't hold you."

"Don't you recover quick."

"Your *car.*"

They both knew she didn't mean just the car. Gave him a wink.

"Soon as I know about Michael, I'll call Silas."

"You're speaking with Silas?"

"It's a long story."

She studied Drexler. Really studied him. First time in years. Something had changed in the man.

Aghast. "That smell is atrocious. Ms. Kingston: let me take you to the house."

"Old Claypoole cooks moonshine. His easement cuts our property. I've walked it a million times."

She got out. Shut the door. He was putting the sedan in gear when she rapped twice on the window. He lowered it.

"We're still not friends, Drexler."

She waited. Her face caught the thin morning light. Took it. Held it. Made it fiercer than the star that threw it.

When he didn't respond, she leaned in. "Don't you have some cornbread and biscuits comeback?"

He cocked his head. She'd pulled a grin out of him. But he didn't take the bait; his mouth remained shut.

"I'll give you mine, Morty. The man who got me out of that embassy—then gave all the credit to my brother?" Shook her head once. "You're out of Doris's book. I never saw that till now."

He made as if checking the road. She paused till he checked her again.

"I think she saw that when she met you; you are the only person I ever heard her invite back to our dinner table."

"You were a weird kid back then. Only gotten weird-er."

"Yeah." Her eyes touched his. "Too bad Pops didn't like you."

"Too bad for me. Like I said, I'll call him when Yurenev is wheels down. You: be ready for a rigorous debrief."

"Like a 'Texas turkey in a box of'— No, nothing?"

"Get lost, Ms. Kingston."

He cranked the shifter. Pueblo Gold rolled forward. He tooted the horn once.

♛♛♛

ACROSS THE OLD BOARDS, the easement road rose into a wedge of woods where old fields had long ago surrendered to pine and bramble. These in turn to kudzu. The morning light filtered through. Soft yellow. Color of mold. Lynn followed the track to where the Claypoole branch veered left toward trailers they rented to customers who needed a few days and easy access to supply.

What was left of the house—a highborn estate once of the firmest brick, the hardiest lumber—now leaned into itself on its eroded hill in profound desolation, a gray skeletal shipwreck, its vitality baked out of every joint and join by a hundred summers of deliberate neglect. Only the porch remained. Kept sittable by scavenged floorboards, patched clapboards, a handful of stubborn sills.

Voices carried from the shacks beyond the rotted hill—middle-aged men arguing over something—but it was the two men and a teenage boy reposed on that manor porch who arrested Lynn's attention.

She ought to have ducked her head and walked on.

This was the last bit of Claypoole property—such as it was. Silas saw only what they squandered, a plantation once larger than Foxtail Farm; Doris, what little sorrow was left of them: their last scrap of dignity. For Lynn it was a place where, one Halloween, she and Michael threw rocks at the windows (broken, but still jagged in their frames) until they were chased into the woods by loopy hounds and two loads of Gramps's birdshot.

Gramps Claypoole had been death's-old back then, but all they'd put in the ground so far were his teeth. He unscrewed a half-full Mason jar of white-whiskey corn liquor and sniffed at another man. Younger than Silas but aged beyond his time, the man's skin was leathered, his head compacted like a loose fencepost banged for years without complaint. He used the edge of a blade knife to crack a can of turpentine.

The teenage boy—had to be youngest, Robert—grinned as the turpentine man poured the stuff into the Mason jar. Gramps Claypoole screwed on the lid, shook it, unscrewed it.

A stopper popped. A sucking sound.

He let a green slosh of something darker fall inside.

Hands trembling, eyes dull with habitual ruin, Gramps gave the final mix a last long shake. He drank, passed it to the boy, who took it like a man practiced and resigned.

Boone drank last. His strange eyes glittered with the drug-bright sheen of a man who saw only the truth of his own delusion in all things.

Lynn shuddered. There weren't many rules growing up at Foxtail Farm. But the main rule was: leave the Claypooles alone.

"But their dogs are so nice. People love 'em and they love people."

"Those dogs don't know any better. They only do one thing good and that's keeping the Claypooles reminded they could always aspire to animals."

Two of the hounds huddled under the porch. Having caught wind of her, one thumped its tail in the dust while the other stretched, ready to say hello.

Lynn wasn't about to wait around for the barking.

She darted across the driveway and walked quick as she could up the easement until it widened into the old plantation road.

Held her ribs against the cold. Marched toward her family home. Unready for reunion or the bombardment of questions surely to follow, she made her choice: she would cut in from the back and, reaching the North Vista Outhouse first, would slip down and take some time for herself in the wine cellar. Where what she'd find was the thing she wanted most.

She needed to process—that's how she convinced herself. Not her captivity, but the strange future she'd allowed herself to see, honest and certain, but only after she'd believed she'd be dead and wouldn't have to account for any of it.

Now she would.

And, she knew—because premonitions are a kind of thought instantly confirmed—Michael would be down there.

Patient.

Smiling.

Waiting all this time—years of time—to see what his sister would do with the gift he'd given her.

♛ ♛ ♛

TURN BACK the kaleidoscope. Lumps of sea glass, blue and green, from a girl's beach collection; sharp-sharded ruby glass for signaling devices before the gold chloride ran out; peer through and watch stained glass fragments of a covenant church window that once told a story of two women whose names meant *melody* in their tumble into grace; without the mirrors they are fragments of time, time without pattern; patternless, they are water over a mill wheel or a flood running backwards. Without the mirror they are a jumble of historical trash.

Καλός (kalos) *beauty.*

Εἶδος (eidos), *form.*

Σκοπέω (skopeō), *look.*

Light is timeless, yet it measures time. With its mirrors, the kaleidoscope refracts light back upon itself, offering new shape to what has come and what will follow. They can't be changed—events, and to their pity—but they can be stilled by the turn of the lens to find in them a form unrefracted light outruns until the mirror catches it and defeats time's rush.

Kolya's defection.

The Tower 1 garage.

Kalaydoskop lifted his face. Old. Wounded. "I will not leave without it. I will not leave her in the dark."

Meryl tried again to stop him, but Kolya Yurenev would have none of that.

He towered. "Wait for me or don't. I am going back."

He turned for the fire door.

"Wait. Kolya. This is a mistake." Michael.

He caught up to his grandfather. His grip on the Russian's elbow was hard. Enough that Kolya gave it an angry look he lashed into Michael's face. Michael relaxed his grip. Relaxed it slowly enough to pass a message. *Listen. Hear me.*

"You've run these before. You know the clockwork."

"I won't leave without—"

"Stop. I'm going to get it."

Michael gave him the slow nod he knew Kolya would recognize; handlers do it with agents, it means—*Let's agree friendly because I run you and you're out of options.* But it also meant: *I've promised to keep you alive.*

Kolya had never allowed anyone control to him in this manner, dictate terms to him, since he clawed his way from the Stalingrad rubble. For the first time in his life, the chameleon in him didn't not know how to camouflage; the mimic, how to avoid or how to entrap.

"You're not coming on the aircraft."

"You know that's impossible. You made it impossible: I walked away from the Agency and have been disavowed. Getting on that plane's a risk I'm unwilling to take. But I am going to save Daria." He weighted his pause. "I'm giving her back to you, old man."

"How?"

Meryl shook her wristwatch: "We are out of minutes. I need you both in the van. Now."

Both men ignored her.

Michael locked eyes with his grandfather. "My mother once made me take a vow: 'Lynn: Ya kljanus', ya obeshchayu, ya davaiu klyatvu—vsyu moyu zhizn', za vsyu ee tsenu—ya nikogda ne ostavlyu tebya odnu k temnote.'" *Lynn: I swear, I pledge, I vow—my whole life, for all of it—I will never leave you alone to the dark.* " It meant everything. To both of them."

"Daria. Told you. Taught you."

"For Lynn. You bet."

Michael stepped away. Picked up Kolya's raincoat. Snatched the flat cap off his head. "I gotta keep it for them. You, old man, gotta keep it for me."

Michael jogged to the fire door. Stopped. Looked back a final time. "Make that call and get her out of there. Now."

He didn't wait for Kolya to take out his phone; they were blood and both of them knew.

Then Michael vanished.

3.

A CHERRY PICKER. A folding ladder. Two town workers fought a long white banner more interested in
the wind then allowing them to attach it to the Christmas tree on the Old Town green. Canvas slack, fast
hands, slung wires, canvas tightening—but not enough.
A billow, a slip of a glove, and the last of the December
wind whipping it like a war banner or a medieval pen-
nant in the air. At the back corner table, at the last corner
window, Silas observed the struggle as Jilly Bregado slid
into the opposite seat. Slid a padded envelope between
them.

Fat. Flat. U.S. Post Office Tyvek. Silas let it lie. Two
futures sealed by tape.

Peppermint steam rose from her latte. "Prima-
ry EU-compatible passports. Not flashy. Not exot-
ic. Belgian for Paige—smooth entry into French ter-
ritories; non-cultural/non-linguistic expectation. Soft
edged. Irish for Clive—passes lightly through French
Caribbean traffic."

A faint nod from Silas.

"State licenses—South Dakota. Minimal digital
cross-check and nobody in TSA audits them twice."

Another nod.

"Credit cards: low-limit, pre-aged, Kansas community bank. OFAC never glances that direction. Two grand euro, cash so they blend in Martinique. Dollars stay buried until the Gambia leg."

Silas's eyes flickered approval.

"And two SIMs, prepaid, African routing. Registered in Estonia. Oh—and Paige's cover leans medical. Lab tech/medical assistant."

Silas almost wistful. "She carried the hawthorn branch at her graduation. An award—"

"For college pre-med coursework." She was so fond of this man. "Do you think I *don't* listen to the small precious things you tell me?"

He saw pain hidden behind her smile. "Hawthorn branch: Piscataway Indians of these parts used it to protect young virgins' fertility. Lotta good that did us."

"Both the island and Gambia: once they see the medical-adjacent legend—always attractive—airport clerks will pass them right through."

Silas's eyes penetrated. "Thank you." A move of his hand. The postal pack disappeared from sight.

Outside the worker on the lift lost his end of the banner. Comical the way he cranked the basket high and low to make the catch, hands on the gears making it impossible to time. His partner on the ladder shook his head at how stupid they looked.

Jilly clutched her cup in black velvet gloves. Blew steam. Sipped. Licked froth off her upper lip and filled one cheek with half of a smirk. "Putting Drexler in the director's chair—be something of a surprise when Meryl returns."

"Hell. No different than with me in it. She runs the show. Director OTRAC's just there to take the bullets."

"But *Drexler*? You've been awful to him. For years."

"Never liked the way he looked at my daughter."

"Jesus, Silas." She lay a hand on his. Lanolin soft and he stared at it: she'd removed the glove to touch him.

He wasn't ready. Silas shot her a hard look as if hard seeing held any strength against hard truth.

"Michael's vanished."

Silence.

Doris's round table—July. Lynn's reflection in a hallway mirror.

"Didn' mean'ta be late." Hammered drunk. "Oh... Hal foun' Michael. And Hal's gon-be fine. Yep. He's comin' home. Mike's..."

"Some wine?" Give it to her. Now."

Melody gulps from her goblet. Hands it to Lynn who finishes it with a single quaff.

"What about Michael?" Gwen. "Lynn: tell me!"

"I'm sorry, Gwen. You guys. Kids. I din mean t'do it this way..."

"Give her another one." But Melody won't.

"A kaleidoscope turns on itself."

"What did you say?"

"I said, 'Michael's vanished.'"

But that wasn't what she said.

Past, present, and future come.

He would never be ready.

"Jilly, that's absurd. No one vanishes."

Jilly's fingers tightened. "It is when we honestly don't know."

A husk in his voice he couldn't quite hide: "It sounds like you do know."

"This is what we know. It comes from Meryl en route. Michael did it: what no one could. What *you* could never do. He turned Kalaydoskop. Got Kolya Yurenev to defect."

"Boy was always a pain in the ass—but he's never gone *half*-assed."

"He's his father's son."

Silas faced the window.

Wind slackened.

White banner caught.

Top wire looped. Racheted tight.

Silas knew what it said before they uncoiled it in its spiral. It always read the same. He returned Jilly his most placid face.

"Michael made the hand-off in the Tower 1 garage. Every move right to the minute. Meryl says they'd planned Michael would be with them. Then there was some business with one of Kolya's bodyguards; off-pattern—we don't know what that was, but we will. Kalaydoskop says Michael had *never* planned to proceed past that point."

"Every word out of that man's mouth is a lie..." How stupid he heard himself sound. "But it's not unexpected. Michael went off the reservation. Involved himself in some dirty business all across the Continent and we disavowed him."

Jilly nodded; get-it-all-out sympathy.

"And?"

"There was a question of a forgotten photograph. Meryl says: a deal-killer for Yurenev."

"What the hell photograph would be that important?"

Jilly's eye glistened as she spread her lips, closed and flat-line, corners tight but faintly raised: compassion, not a smile.

"Stop that. What was the photo?"

"His daughter."

Doris: red river lilies/Angleton's prized orchids engulf her fists; she smiles from behind her wedding veil.

Doris: spinning in fire on a burning silk rope.

My hand closes around her fingertips.

Her eyes are saying something.

Her lips move. Smoke obscures. The silk cord snaps.

"Michael volunteered to go back for it."

"Hmm. You do know why?"

Jilly nodded.

"And?"

"He was going to get it to them. That's was enough for Kolya to make the Lynn call."

"Michael *is* very good at his job. Better than I ever was. And?"

"He went through a door."

After Hal caught the football, before cake, before candle wishes: my beautiful—my lambs walk the beach.

I'm halfway down the steep and rickety stairs. Stop when I hear: "Lynn, I married Daddy because of the wonderful thing inside him missing in me; I knew with him I would be whole and happy. Silas married me—"

"Because of what was in you that's not in him?"

"Yes. Since you were born, both of us see perfectly within you: not ourselves alone, but the thing we wished ourselves to be together, complete. Your father—the work

he does, the world as he *knows it—in the face of your perfection..."*

"Later—but not much later—a bomb went off in Kolya Yurenev's suite."

Silas's fingers gripped Jilly's hand.

She gripped him back.

Her voice remained steady: "Was it FSB? The oligarchs—?"

"They've been coming at Kalaydoskop like wolves."

"They have. Maybe. Or maybe it was Cheng."

Silas's eyes were back on the window. The cherry picker lowered. The man off the ladder walking the banner a last turn around the tree. A strange calm descended on Silas. He knew the inevitable words the banner would reveal.

"Cheng?"

"Cheng Li-Qiang. Military Intelligence Bureau. Former rank of Captain of the PLA Liberation Army, Navy: runs Wànhuātŏng. Maybe it was them. We don't know. The entire suite was obliterated. No witnesses. No bodies. Everything blew out through the glass thirty-three stories over the city. Out to sea. Nothing to say it touched Michael."

Michael yells from where he's wandered ahead. "'If people reach perfection, they vanish, you know.' That's from your favorite book, Mom, huh?"

"In that story, King Arthur was talking about perfection as meeting God."

Jilly's eyes followed Silas to his feet. "You okay?" The town workers posed before the tree for a photograph. Thumbs up—

Welcome 2013!

"Nobody vanishes, Jilly. Not really."

He leaned. She tilted her cheek. He touched it with his lips. Whispered in her ear: "I'm counting on you to remember that for me."

When he opened the door, he wagged the envelope in the air and thanked her.

Not the cold through the door, but his words—*Remember for me*—froze her in a way that never thaws.

"I will," she said to herself, and Jilly Bregado sipped her drink and promised.

👑👑👑

THE NORTH VISTA Outhouse rose above her as it always had; the original manor—more like a blockhouse or a keep than a home. Lynn crossed from the woods, frost-burned grass beneath her clogs. She reached the wine cellar door. Stopped, almost gave up before trying; Silas never left doors unlocked.

She tried the knob and it turned.

She pushed inside. The smell hit first: old oak, dirt, the sweet decay of dust on bottles. She drew a breath. Felt it fill her. It was the first breath she'd taken that belonged to her; she'd been born at Foxtail Farm—Hal, and Papa (Michael had been born in Moscow)—and this air belonged to it, her, and had fed them all and in it, they would always linger.

Even those passed through the Place of Blackness.

Switched on the lights. Descended the stairs, one hand on the wooden banister, the other trailing fingers down the coarse and ice-cold stone. Same stones she'd touched as a teenage girl stealing wine.

Down the center aisle to the far wall rack: the one Silas had built to hide the infernal room.

The door hung open. Darkness breathed back at her. A lazy yawn. A relaxed dominance. Lynn ducked inside, and the Place of Blackness took her in without ceremony. She went to it. The platform with the stained wooden beams. The jawed iron collar. Black iron teeth. The faint, fetid smell of the clay walls holding the damp. The echo—if it was an echo—of her eleven-year-old pulse, the stutter in her throat, that moment Michael's abandonment became real.

The real hour that passed by.

The real belief she would die here and no one would come.

She walked around to the brace.

No tremor.

She opened the collar. Opened it as wide as it would go so that it would snap when she released it.

Snap. A final sound. As if a long argument had ended and the room had been waiting to hear which of them had won.

She put her hand on the wooden cross beam. Flat. Steady. Not the girl's hand. Not this time. Not the one that scraped and clawed for breath and freedom.

Not the child who waited for Michael.

Her hand.

Lynn's.

The woman grown.

She didn't know what would come now, only that it would; her prison had taught her that. She sunk down where her mother had held her. Shut her eyes. Shared the breath of all, black and white, who'd passed this way.

The echo of the Patuxent River. The Halloween sobering/not sobering. The decision to take the pillow to her mother's face. And the man in the boat: the man in Michael's Father Cevik photographs: Kalaydoskop.

Me forever clutching again the pillow Silas wants me to smother her with. She wants it as well.

"It would make a mockery of Kaleidoscope. My *kaleidoscope." She looks at me. The pain is gone. She savors her sorrow. "It would kill the only two men I love."*

"What are you talking about? You love *him?! All these years—some kind of affair—forever?"*

"I was faithful to your father. Always. And he knew everything."

Headlights from below wash the window. Wash the wall. Paint the ceiling.

"Is that Silas?"

I nod. Feel my bottom lip, fat. I might as well be four years old waiting for the mermaid to rise from the fountain with the sword.

"If they're both here— You cannot let either man inside. Go. Lock everything. Stop them."

"No. Tell me who he is."

Doris shudders. Focuses on the ceiling.

"Lynn... 'It is the doom of men that they forget.'"

"Forget what?!"

"Everything that matters. Like your glass. Now do as I tell you: lock everything. Stop them."

Whoever he was—Kalaydoskop, her mother's second love—it wasn't about him. It wasn't even *men* Doris was talking about in those last words she said.

She was warning about everything, about all of us: we forget what matters most right when we most need to remember it.

She was warning me against my father, against that other man.

She was warning me against myself.

That was the vow she made Michael take.

Because Danger is a shape.

It is not a name.

I spit in my hand. Moisten my first piece of glass and it glows a bright robin's egg blue.

I love Michael for it—did he see it in my smile?— "I'll save all the best ones from now on. You and Mom and Hal can help me find them."

"What makes the best ones best?" Mom.

"Magic. Magic memories."

I drop it into my shirt pocket. Hold out my arms and spin, and the sun in the sky and off the water, beams through the branches of the trees.

I am spellbound. I am dizzy.

I am whole.

♕ ♕ ♕

LYNN EMERGED from the wine cellar. All she wanted was a bed. Peace, safety, rest. She went around the front of the North Vista Outhouse. Through the open porch shutters she saw Hal and Silas standing over a table. It amused her—like two generals over their maps—and then it troubled her. A Hal-style military grade rifle was near his hand. Top of the steps, outside the door: the crate with the old Army mortar. More fireworks for New Year's Eve? She emptied her lungs. Silas noticed her.

Lynn raised a weak-hand hello. Silas nodded. A smile without teeth. For once. For a moment she had an urge to go inside. He must have read her mind, because Silas pointed three times at the North Vista door behind her.

Lynn went inside. Climbed the stairs. Found a bedroom. Slept.

♔♔♔

"WHAT AM I supposed to do? It's the fourth time they've called."

Escape kits—Silas explained. Packed. Ready to go.

Paige stared at the phone she was leaving behind. "It says the police. I think I should take it." Eyes pleading with Clive.

"We're off comms. It could be spoofed."

"If it's mom—"

"She probably got a Driving Under the Influence. Look: we just got to get going."

A door knock followed by Charlotte. Holding her phone. Spacy all day—now she looked concerned.

"They called you?" Paige.

"No one's called me. Who?"

Paige covered poorly. "What do you want? We're kinda busy."

"Have you heard from Mom?"

"Not since her Christmas Eve freak." Paige didn't give the lie a second thought.

"She usually's been calling me in the mornings. Her morning—like noon. I've text-bombed her like ten times."

Paige shot Clive a secret look. He purposely let her shot miss.

A knot twisted Paige's stomach. "Maybe she started partying a night early."

Charlotte tucked her phone. Checked out their two roller bags. "Maybe. You don't have to be so rude. I wish you wouldn't fight her so much."

"Me too."

"I don't even get why you want to go to Canada."

Clive: "Ski trip."

"She's pregnant."

"Doctor says I can ski up to the third trimester."

"You don't even know how."

Paige blanked at her sister. Charlotte was disappointed, but her brain was moving on. "Whatev's."

"You're good about tonight?"

"Melody's taking us all the way to Papa's North Vista for a surprise? Whoop-de-do. Fun times."

Soon as Charlotte was gone, Paige opened her phone. "I'm calling her landline."

Clive grabbed. Missed. Paige dialed. It rang once—connected. But this time, Clive got it. Shut it off. Shut it down. A step back. Bed between them.

"You heard it pick up. She's there. Now leave it alone. He stuffed her phone in his pocket.

His sudden/total aggressiveness froze Paige on the spot. "You are *not* fucking serious with that."

That: her phone, his pocket.

He fished it out. "Look. I'm sorry." Went to her.

"Don't touch me."

"This is deadly what we're dealing with."

Paige sat hard on the bed. Held her hand open over his shoulder. "I'm not going to use it."

Clive placed her old phone on Paige's palm. She opened a bedside drawer. Tossed it in. Kicked it shut. Looked back at Clive eyes brimming with feeling.

"I'm not leaving."

And they didn't.

4.

S ILAS WENT TO LYNN. They didn't speak about the embassy. They didn't speak about Michael. They spoke about tonight. He left her with clothing and Hal's shotgun. Told her where he wanted her and she thought that a good idea.

Hal came through the tunnels back from Garde-Joyeuse.

The Yule log smoked excessively; by sundown the house felt wrong.

Melody set out plates no one touched. She left the food out. Took Leigh and the twins with her to the North Vista Outhouse—Clive said he'd never mapped it. It wasn't a target. Hal was on the widow's walk. Melody and the children would be safest beneath him. Beaumont drifted in after them, pressing the twins along with that mute insistence of his, as though he'd felt some shift in the air the rest of them had not yet named.

Paige and Clive waited on Charlotte who'd made the ridiculous decision to shower and wouldn't come out.

👑👑👑

CAPTAIN HOLLIS and the Number Two rolled off a St. Mary's County rural road onto the private lane that ended half a mile further at the Foxtail Farm main gate and the Garde-Joyeuse listening post behind and an acre beyond. Number Two hadn't spoken since they'd crossed the Harry Nice Bridge. A little sulky the past two days since the assault team had reduced numbers by two and Hollis moved him to engineer/security.

Hollis wasn't happy with the change either but, as Trewyn put it, Ms. Chowdhury from Cabinet Defence kept beating the tribal drum to scrap the op entirely. "We are two-hundred years on the dot since the last time we ran warships up the Chesapeake and fought our way to a second inglorious defeat against the Americans," she'd said, dry as audit ink, meant to remind them the Crown still carried the bruise. Level heads, including the one with the crown, prevailed: six men won't leave a footprint; the target isn't fortified or heavily-armed—an old man, for God's own sake. The objective was not seizure, was not rescue, or hostage extraction, but air-tight surgical negation.

Bang-bang, Kingston dead, in-out/full-deniability.

Hollis aimed for a leafy area. Cut his lights soon as the utility truck was masked by trees. He gave Number Two some slack; the kid was part of the generation coming into the service off PlayStation rather than any of those other things that once forged soldiers.

Both men wore hi-viz utility vests over Carhartt work jackets. Over low-profile plate carriers—not as armored as the beach or overland assault teams, but they'd be running overwatch and needed to match the Dominion Power bucket-truck they would run up the transformer pole to cut power and comms. They would also run security and needed to look the part. At least long enough to get to the suppressed SIG P228 each of them carried.

Stolen US Army and serial-numbered. Moved it from deniability to blame, in case things went arse-up.

The truck had left the Norfolk black site at quarter past three after Hollis watched his four assault operators load the RIB (Rigid Inflatable Boat) craft, dry bags, suppressed carbines (also USA), their helmets, NVGs, climbing gear aboard the MV *Calvert Shoals*, flagged Panama, on a side-scan survey run. One more NOAA subcontract boat in a bay filled with them.

They idled. They watched last light fade.

At 5:20 p.m., right before civil-dark, Hollis received two-clicks on the radio. Meant the Garde-Joyeuse entry pair put ashore south of Foxtail Farm.

Ascend the palisade.

Work through the woods.

Hit the Listening Post: clear structure, secure material/sensitive gear.

Hollis keyed back once. Eased the truck forward. Passed a Subaru wagon—pretty shitty condition—half-in the roadside culvert. Hollis stopped, engine running, middle of the lane.

Number Two jumped. Scoped it out. Some painter's equipment in the back. Old fast-food bags. Walked round it—engine cold—up/down both sides of the lane:

no path fresh or otherwise into the woods. An abandoned job; nothing operational about it.

Number Two back in. Hollis rolled onward. Located the transformer pole at the bell of the last curve before the Kingston property. View of the gate. Its lights—darkness-activated—flashed on.

Number Two went up in the bucket. The pine break along the wall concealed the secondary living quarters from view, but their target (intel put him each night, kitchen/dining room/east porch six to seven/eight o'clock seven-out-of-seven) would be main-house occupied and from Number Two's vantage point he had sightlines to both the main house and Garde-Joyeuse, not to mention a clear line over the broad lawn to the beach stairs beyond.

He ran a fast thermal pass—no movement on the porch, east windows black.

Signaled Hollis they were set and covered.

Hollis opened the back where their folding carbines waited. Reached past. Tucked a work placard under his arm. Grabbed a stack of red cones.

Set the chokepoint.

Number Two prepared tools to pull the transformer and isolate comms.

👑👑👑

BASED ON SILAS's calculation of how long the decryption of his Christmas Eve confession—wrapped in a book cipher, hidden in a bombshell—and *Hear-ye, Hear-ye'd* to the Queen of England would take, he expected them to arrive tonight, New Year's, or the next. Hal enjoyed a chuckle each time he thought of that—*Dear Lizzie/Love Silas*—but didn't quite get the exercise.

"Just not sure I follow, Dad. You told me the second part of the code laid out every reason they should drop the whole case—like international-incident-quality minefield shit; maybe make a deal to let bygones and bury it. Protection for you, protection for them."

"Hal, that works when both side have somewhat equivalent power. Mine's only in my brain—they can shut that power off a little too easily for my comfort."

He'd split the cipher in two and had his reasons. Part one, the quickie *mea culpa*, would get the red-bloods frothing at the mouth and they'd go big and bellicose, and right out the gate the knee-jerk limp-wrists would already be fanning their handkerchiefs about imperial aggression. The complexity of the second part would necessarily be held up in translation: that was Silas's jack-in-box burst out with its sex trafficking and Kalaydoskop kissy-face, and would explode dissent within Whitehall, which would create a wedge. A compromise. A rush to in-action, and a change of plans. Didn't matter what they changed, just that they stuttered off the blocks and blew a stitch; in the art of counterintelligence you could never count on anything more than that, but how many good spooks throughout history, and over again, all of them presented the same, found if they pulled a single loose thread they could make the ruler/tyrant/dictator's, president/prime minster/king's—or in this case, queen's—trousers drop around their ankles long enough to help them trip themselves.

Hal had lost it at *mea culpa* but was glad: whatever Silas had done to deserve this, he didn't want to know about it. Happy to stick to the job he knew.

Tonight, tomorrow, or the next—up on the walkway around the North Vista Outhouse roof, family behind its stone fortress walls. One if by sea; two if by land—Hal knew: whenever they hit it would be both land and sea and he'd need all three proverbial lanterns because the British were coming and he would be damned if he didn't drop them dead in their tracks.

A survey craft on a bay that never stopped needing to be mapped, was no big deal. One that dropped anchor two miles out was another thing entirely. Hal passed down word it was on and the family got moving—he counted everyone but Paige and Clive, waiting up on Charlotte who didn't quite get, it seemed, the urgency of the message. Silas didn't want any of the kids to spook. Told Clive to give her a minute.

Short time after that, Hal's ear tuned to the sound of the night and the river, he heard the unmistakable muffled-putter of a fast-launch outboard—south beyond their bay. It was a guess, but Hal had been doing this his entire adult life, this would be a team—two or four—to secure Garde-Joyeuse and to take the western vector of the attack.

Next would be their own beach.

5:28, Hal watched the boat come in, a two-man team pulling it up behind them, out of view for their jumping off spot on the stairs. Hal checked his Drexler special: the HK416D Recce. Slid the charging handle just enough to feel brass, eased it home, breathed once, looked through the optic to settle the dot against the dark water, then the Garde-Joyeuse orchard wall: the two places the British would come from.

♛♛♛

BOONE REALLY needed to thank that Kirby fella at the bottom of the river for the jacket. A life saver this last week. Gave that secondhand rat pelt of an overcoat third-hand to old Claypoole who sucked gums and stuffed it somewhere and Boone Kelso never saw it again. But the jacket, in combo with a heavy goodnight dose of turp'sinthe, made that pop-up trailer the Claypooles were renting him for ten bucks a crash keep him bug-snug enough. That and the thought of new-Doris/blood-Doris/pure-love Doris in that perfect red dress spittable image for the one whore-Roberta made the lady-Doris-divine.

"A Polaroid camera might get the look you want in fewer tries."

"I don't want that look. That's your look. I want my instant memory of your look. That's my *look. That's what your dear Mr. Kingston is paying me for. Oh, by the way—one, two, three, go, go—do you give it to your husband, or do you just lie there?"*

Walk/turn/boo— "Is this the day the artist attempts to seduce his subject?"

"Puh-lease, Doris."

Doris pinches the hem of her sundress. Sudden flash. No panties.

That Bobby kid earned his eighty bucks.

Car stashed on the road, aimed out and away, all left for now: a walk down this old easement road, a hide and a crouch behind those fat windbreak pines and wait for my princess to come to daddy.

He swung the plastic bag from the Randy's Razzamatazz shop with the pair of long crimson gloves, the snazzy crown with the red feather, the pink plastic jewel. She'd like 'em, he could tell. The crown would be the last to come off.

♛♛♛

FULL-DARK NOW. Captain Hollis spoke into his comms—earpiece invisible/throat-mic in his collar: "G-J team, report."

"In position at the LP. Entry ready."

Hollis checked his chronograph.

"Clear to go on-time."

The sweep hit the top. 5:30 pm. He wagged a finger. Not so much a signal as a conductor's downbeat.

Number Two initiated a shadow outage—bleeding voltage just enough to trip the auto-reclosure without waking grid telemetry.

The gate lights flickered. Dimmed.

Ten seconds later, he cut the internet.

♛♛♛

THE ENTRY TEAM quietly breached the dead front door of Garde-Joyeuse. No alarms. No lights. Night vision on. The LP deemed low threat-level—operatives Lott believed DOA, Lancer off-premises, in the wind or a secondary target once they moved on Foxtail Farm. Operator One moved upstairs for a fast all-clear; he'd work his way down through the first floor. Operator Two went straight for the basement stairs, trading his weapon for a duffel backpack he shook out. Eyes taking in the equipment: he'd have just enough room to haul it out. MI6 fingerprints erased.

♔♔♔

CLIVE RECEIVED Hal's text they were live, two minutes before the internet and cell service dropped.

"Paige: get Charlotte out now."

Paige pounded on the bathroom door, shouting through it for her sister. Only sound returned: running water. Serious eyes between them, Clive braced.

"Move aside, luv."

Paige stepped with "Don't look—she'll never live it down."

Clive gave the door his shoulder twice and they were in. He grabbed her towel even as he noticed the open window. "Shit."

Threw the shower curtain. Empty.

Paige held a note. "*Sorry, Sis! Doing New Year's with friends—DON'T BE MAD!—but I got my first date! Be home by two. Don't tell Mom—if she calls make up with her. C.*" Wild eyes—"Fucking Bobby Claypoole, she's probably running down the easement right now. We can catch her!"

Paige lunged. Clive held her. "We let her go. Off-property, she's gonna be safer. But we've got to get you and the baby safe now, yeah?"

♛ ♛ ♛

SERGEANT NATHANSON and Deputy Ruiz had been 10-7 on the Old Town green when the call came in: "Nathanson, Ruiz—respond for welfare notification at Foxtail Farm. Herndon PD requests NOK notification. Victim: Gwendolyn Kingston." Tossed their Chick-Fil-A trash and got the details as they rolled. Herndon had been unable to reach the adult daughter all afternoon. A call from her cell that went to the deceased's townhouse line before being disconnected, traced back to Foxtail Farm.

Nathanson had been out there back on Thanksgiving. Escorted a Richmond DA with a threat-to-life warning to another Kingston living at the compound. That was a mixed-race woman, not this victim who'd come over on his MDT, but he'd gotten an eyeful of this one back Thanksgiving. This Gwendolyn: drunk and on a screaming tear, loading her kids into a car in the rain. He'd have waited around to hook her for a DUI if his VIP hadn't had a plane to catch. Now the woman was deceased under suspicious circumstances. Next of kin was the adult daughter. Just turned eighteen according to her DL; he had no desire to blindside the kid. He'd met the homeowner, Silas Kingston, and knew from their brief exchange: news like this would go through him.

Ruiz turned onto the private lane. Nathanson gave it a run-through in his head.

Mr. Kingston, I'm very sorry to inform you that your former daughter-in-law Gwendolyn Kingston has been found deceased in Fairfax County. Detectives there are conducting an active investigation.

Next moment, their headlights picked up the reflection of a Dominion Power worker sign. Cones. Ruiz took her foot from the gas and cruised in. A truck. Two workers. One on the ground flagging them down. The other on the pole.

♕ ♕ ♕

A CALL COULDN'T have come from the house; any cavalry would arrive in larger/harder force than two uniforms in a single car. Probably the shadow outage spooked someone else on the grid and this pair was in the vicinity. Hopefully they'd see the truck, the bucket, the open box and move along.

Number Two kept working above.

"Evening, officers. See you got the same call we did."

The female deputy gave a polite nod. The sergeant behind the wheel gave a whole lot less.

Hollis reached into the truck cab for the clipboard with the dummy work order. Loosened his jacket because the four of them out on this road knew two of them weren't here for the pole.

♛♛♛

CHARLOTTE NEVER WENT out the window. As if. Just waited in her the dark in her bedroom for Clive to crash
through from Paige's side. Window to stall them, and
miss her passing in the outer hall on her little covert
operation. Now, misinterpreting the deep embarrass-
ment that thrummed beneath her nervous stomach, her
outrageous excitement, for a certain adult feeling (but
she wouldn't go *any* farther with Bobby than kissing),
Charlotte threw some Lana Del Rey moves for Grandma
Doris, shining full-on *XED* (according to her and
Paige's kid's code for the portrait's moods) *Sexy Doris*
from her portrait. Charlotte grabbed a cashmere
pashmina her mother left behind from the mud
room—warm/snuggly, better than a jacket for
sure—and, happy Charlotte: the alarm was off.

Slow thumb on the front door latch.

Hardly a click.

It swung open, heavy without a sound, and the cold
slapped her right in the face. No biggie. She clamped
teeth. Trotted down the front steps.

♛♛♛

IF NUMBER TWO had not been watching the cops reacting
badly to Hollis's clipboard, if he'd not been surrepti-
tiously creeping his hand to his P228, he might have
seen Charlotte sneak from the house onto the gravel of

the parking circle. Might have seen the figure of a man lunge from the pine trees.

♕ ♕ ♕

THOUGH HE DIDN'T EXPECT to find anyone, the point man from the Garde-Joyeuse entry team entered the upstairs study—weapon first—through the salon. Visual sweep: the sofa pushed against the wall. The wall: the hole. The reek of human decay. He dragged back the sofa and found the battered hole. Drag marks through the dust. Death amounts of dried blood and a thorough interior surveillance system, the kind that read permanence. Into his mic: "LP House is hot. Multiple unknowns. Cameras online."

♕ ♕ ♕

NERVES/DEVIOUS hope swelled; Charlotte mistook the fast-moving figure for— "Bobby?"

The holly-tree man seized Charlotte with large hands. Hard-spun her into a violent, backwards embrace. His body pressed her from behind as he stuffed a noxious rag, foul with turpentine, absinthe's sweet rot, and raw corn-liquor sting, into her open lips. Squeezed the burning fluid into her mouth, clamping it inside, forcing her to gag and swallow and lose her footing. He dragged Charlotte as the chemicals dizzied, confused, overwhelmed her. Dragged against weak fight, clutch pressure obscene from his loins, wrenched/dragged/rag-doll shook her up to the pedestrian gate beside the black motorized roll-gate.

Boone Kelso twisted the handle and opened a space narrow enough to stick his head through.

👑👑👑

SERGEANT NATHANSON: "If you could step back from the vehicle, I'll need some credentials and your operator licenses." He unsnapped his holster as he shifted to exit his car.

Ruiz reached for the radio.

Hollis: "Absolutely." He stepped back, hand moving into his coat.

After the call from Garde-Joyeuse it was always going to end this way.

The Number Two fired two silent rounds through the windshield. Chest. Head. Ruiz.

👑👑👑

THE POINT MAN peered deeper into the passage behind the wall. Where the smell was strongest. Saw the corpse. Took another step onto some canvas to confirm.

Advanced state of decomposition, but a certainty.

"G-J One to Overwatch—confirmed body. Identification: Lott."

Awaited response and saw it: filament line running from the beneath the body up the wall. Tracked his night vision along the wire. A mortar round. Armed and ready to drop.

"Secondary device. Standby—this is a rig."

👑👑👑

THE WINDSHIELD shattered and the cop inside already dead. Boone Kelso was pulling back when the utility worker on the ground raised a pistol. One of those silencers on the end. The male cop went for his pistol. Fast. Cleared leather. The utility worker's gun spit twice into the male cop's forehead.

Fate's scythe was swinging for Silas Kingston.

There'd be plenty time to savor that with Doris later.

He pulled back. Squeezed the rag, filling her mouth again. Gripped her face to force the swallow.

"Look at you all dressed like a princess." Stared into her burning eyes. "Make a queen of you tonight."

He flung her around. Tightened his arm around her waist. Hauled her onto the lawn. He wouldn't have the tarps and paint from the crackhead's car, but he could make something work back at the Claypoole's. And if that old cracker and the kid put up a ruckus he'd take care of them and anyone else just as easy.

👑👑👑

ON THE POLE, Number Two pulled the secondary breaker, and dropped the feeder—street lamps along the lane winked out. The Kingston house went black. The whole spur of the grid died clean.

Hollis switched off cruiser lights. Checked radios. The MDT. No open lines. He keyed: "Overwatch: Red—"

Mission blown—
"Red—"
Eliminate all targets—
"Red."
All witnesses.

♛ ♛ ♛

CABLE AND SIGNAL-CAPTURE HEADS, tap-leads, packet-sniffer brick—Operator one in the Garde-Joyeuse basement zipped his pack. Threw it on. Threw himself up the stairs as two floors above—

The point man retreated from Fergus. From the boobytrap. From the hole. His foot, lifting off the canvas, released pressure on the drop-spoon: a tilt-plate cobbled from two rusted hinges and scavenged bracket wire that held the HE round suspended.

The Kingston's only used the illumination rounds with the mortar on holidays. They were gimmicks. Silas had saved the old HE round because, like he said, "Couldn't exactly leave 'em out for Goodwill," and the one in Garde-Joyeuse was special. It exploded into the room from behind the curtains, killing the SAS point man before he even turned—helmet lifted off, body punched flat against the far wall in a single concussive slap.

♛ ♛ ♛

THE EXPLOSION from Garde-Joyeuse echoed loud. Fire ballooned red from the roof and Charlotte tore from Boone Kelso's astonished grip. She spit the rag. Reeled onto the tournament field. Put everything she had into her legs to run. Into her voice to scream.

☙☙☙

RIFLE BRACED on the widow's walk railing—covering the three arcs he'd been counting down all evening: the black contour of the beach cove below; the orchard wall running south toward Garde-Joyeuse; the whole sweep of lawn between—Hal barely flinched at the explosion. His ears sorted it instantly: not the beach, not the house—Garde-Joyeuse going up. Picked up Charlotte off her scream.

Heart clench.

Forced relaxation.

A tremor of movement on the beach stair. Assault team coming.

Sighted in. Settled the dot.

☙☙☙

WITHIN THE NORTH VISTA Outhouse, Leigh screamed at the explosion; Melody's arms were already filled with Jack and Little Silas. Clive at the door, a tight/covered view through the front glass, Hal's handgun gripped two-handed, his eyes told Paige to grab her youngest sister—

And Charlotte screamed.

And Paige didn't think twice. Bolted outside, ignoring Clive's shout behind her.

⚜⚜⚜

NUMBER TWO breached the gate. Hollis took point through the opening. Both men brought up their compact carbines and advanced in a two-man stack. One high/one low. Bounding straight for the door.

⚜⚜⚜

BOONE KELSO caught Charlotte halfway to the beach stairs. She screamed and fought. Her red sequins caught moonlight and sparkled, and the only reason Boone Kelso didn't drop dead in that moment was Hal caught sight of the SAS from the beach: a first helmet rising from the assault up the stairs.

Half-an-exhale and 4.5 pounds of pressure and the round punched clean through the Kevlar lip before the man's brain could signal surprise.

Boone Kelso froze.

Charlotte went still.

The second man from the beach rose higher.

Hal's second shot was wasted; the beach stairs Silas rigged gave out in a wet, splintering collapse—boards shearing, the whole flight dropping in a single heaving groan.

OVER THE WALL, operator one framed Boone Kelso in his sights. Dropped him.

HAL SWEPT his weapon to the orchard wall. Acquired his target and fired. A split second after operator one's follow-up bullet flew.

PAIGE WOULD NEVER be fast enough. For the rest of her life she would tell everyone she loved that she'd dealt with her grief. That she knew it wasn't her fault. That she had tried harder, and braver, and with more purity and selflessness than anyone. She'd tell them that, and more, and make sure no one worried about her or her guilt. But Paige would tell herself she should have been faster.

She should have gone into the bathroom earlier.

She should not have gone to the North Vista Outhouse.

She should have found Charlotte first and alive.

Instead, she found her in blood, lying in a sad mockery of Doris's dress, dead in the brown frosted grass. And something in Paige's mind faltered there, caught, because her thoughts kept going, tumbling forward the

way they always had and would, while Charlotte's ended on a single unfinished beat. Life—supposed to roll
forward like the layered depths of the Patuxent—had
become nothing more than bright scattered objects left
on the sand when a final drought caused the river, its
teemingness of essence, to recede, to dry, to vanish. All
the bright small things a girl meant to keep, meant to
return to someday, lay cast and dull in the winter night,
left to a sister too late and clumsy with time to hold the
last might-have-been in place.

Her body quaked. She couldn't breathe, strangled by
her sobs. There was nothing she could do for Charlotte
and her bloody hands fluttered over her sister like panicked cardinals Charlotte always claimed but no one else
had ever seen. And beneath the panic, both darker and
quieter, was the knowledge that her own life would keep
moving, adding moments, collecting them, turning them
to patterns, while Charlotte's would never turn again;
that all her sister's brightness had been stopped here,
fixed and cold, waiting for Paige to bury it—not in the
Kingston earth but in her gentle fire alone.

Hal loomed over her. His eye behind his weapon. He
pumped two rounds into Boone Kelso's corpse. Went to
the palisade. Aimed down and fired two more into the
bodies broken below.

5.

I N THE TACTICS OF violence, Silas trusted Hal implicitly. The HE charge detonated in Garde-Joyeuse almost the exact minute Hal predicted; when the power into Foxtail Farm failed entirely, Silas knew the force that now would assault the house would be degraded significantly—not only by the loss of their Garde-Joyeuse unit in the explosion but by the precision of Hal's disruption itself: fewer men, more haste, a team suddenly blind on pattern and where it mattered—inside the house.

Pressed by a clock collapsing around them.

Compelled to strike stupidly fast before the ruin of their own operation caught up with them.

☙☙☙

THE KALEIDOSCOPE turns to final alignment.

Hollis keys: "G-J, status."

"Overwatch, G-J Two—over the wall, setting outer security."

He switches channels: "Beach?"

"Beach One—at base of stairs. Ascending."

Two clean reports. Hollis glances at Number Two. Nods once: hold position, wait for stack-ready.

꧁꧂ ꧁꧂ ꧁꧂

THE HOUSE had stilled. That way Foxtail Farm did when it made up its mind. Waited now to see how it would be met: in fall, in defiance, or in that still instant when old acts rise to meet you.

With night's approach, as the weak winter light faded but while electric current still provided illumination, Silas made the manor blaze. He walked the saturnine foreboding of its halls, room to room, each portentous: not of what was coming, but by what was past, what each wall contained, each floorboard had felt, its hanging air remembered of sounds, smells, and temperatures once held.

Births and deaths.

Souls and their residue.

Each door he opened, he left wide.

He adjusted each mirror as he had the year after Doris died—when he first let the looking-glasses fill the shuttered corridors—not to brighten but to multiply what the house refused to forget and what he refused to release.

The house's need was memory; his was reckoning.

Where the house held its past in stillness, Silas held it in motion, and between them—house and man—the mirrors made a third thing: a vigilance neither could manage alone.

✹✹✹

HOLLIS checks again.
   "G-J, report."
   Silence.
   He tries the beach team.
   Silence.

✹✹✹

SILAS TURNED each mirror by degrees. Not for vanity. Not for tactics alone. To let the old angles that had faltered in the chaos of the year return: Doris's portrait catching from the landing and flinging itself mirror-to-mirror into the closed rooms; the recursion of her face breaking and reforming across the glass; her presence traveling the dark as light does, not walking yet never still.

✹✹✹

SOMETHING gone wrong.
   Number Two cranks shoulders. Tight. Uneasy.
   Hollis attempts contact once more—hard clicks, rising edge of command. Nothing. Not even static. The kind of silence that meant bodies cooling. He raises two fingers: prepare entry.

�✲✲✲

AND STANDING in the converging sightlines, Silas felt—not protection, not omen—but the same solemn judgment the mirrors had always held: the knowledge that anything entering this house would be seen twice, and then again, and then again, until it was stripped of its disguise and shown for what it was.

The house settled into the shape of what was coming. Silas turned toward the front parlor.

✲✲✲✲

HOLLIS GIVES a decisive twist of the knob. Pushes inward. Number Two low beside him.

Both men cross the threshold and the mirrors take them instantly. Scatter their shapes in a dozen fractured angles before they clear the vestibule.

✲✲✲✲

MICHAEL'S VANISHED.

Lynn gripped Hal's shotgun. Stuffed it with 00 buckshot shells.

Her own words that July night Michael had spun the globe and the patterns of their known world, undependable but always balanced, broke and shifted irrevocably; Silas who had mocked her, returned her two words to her not with anger or anguish or impotent rage, but with a frightening acceptance—frightful because the tragic potential those two words held, words that begged resistance, he'd offered forgiveness within them—to her, to Michael, to himself—and she saw in Silas the essence of the man her mother had loved stubbornly, achingly, and against herself. They shook her, not for Michael, but for herself: her father loved her and asked for nothing in return.

Lynn realized, as Silas moved the Yule log out of its ember bed and to the side, as he tilted it so that the fire and its heat would bleed upward rather than down the length of the log, as she ducked beneath the mantel as she'd done often as a child to hide in children's games, that Hal had been bred and bred himself not to question mission orders but to execute; when Silas told the two of them what was coming, the violence intended, her instinct—coming out of years in ops planning—wanted to kick in, force a full briefing to better understand his/their enemy, but opposite to instinct, speaking to her in a voice newer and much louder in the new silences she'd discovered inside her mind when she'd given her life to death inside her embassy tomb where she had faced the truth of her life and her identity—abandoned selfishness and stupidity and the hardest thing she'd ever had to release: self-destruction—she knew she didn't have to know. She knew when her father put Hal's shotgun in her hands that afternoon, she would fight for all their lives and that tonight, whatever happened to her, she would do what she never could before.

She would kill.

Silas dragged the Christmas tree from the door side of the front parlor closer to the fireplace.

"Not so close, Dad. I fire this: that whole thing might go up."

Silas looked at Lynn. Looked at the tree. Grinned full teeth. "Try not to."

The doors left open, he went to the walls and the mirrors where Doris hovered and made adjustments to angles almost as if he didn't want Doris to see everything that soon would transpire.

"Why do I get the feeling I'm the Kevin McAllister in all this?"

"Who the hell's that?"

"*Home Alone* kid."

"Does he win?"

"Yeah."

"Then hold to it, girl. Hold to it."

With the last mirror adjustment, the Christmas tree lights extinguished with the power completely cut. She squeezed her eyes shut to bleed off the flicker of the Yule log, the glow of the ember bed. When the brightness dimmed she lifted her eyes and looked up the flue.

♔♔♔

"Low-low. On me." Barely spoken. A breath more than a voice.

Hollis's left hand ghosting the muzzle forward, right shoulder turned to eat recoil if it came, his partner sweeping the opposite seam.

The foyer swallowed them whole.

And immediately, the mirrors. Not reflections. Explosions of angles. Shards of hall and stair and doorway doubling back on themselves, glass-lit ghosts of a woman neither man had ever seen but who, here, multiplied like a queen in a deck of cards scattered, instantly reshuffled, scattered again.

Doris in the gilt frame at the landing—but not only there. She floated in the glass to their left. Again in the vestibule door. Again low in a bevel near the wainscot where she should never have been. Number Two glanced left; Hollis saw her right. Each saw a different Doris, and both saw too many.

NVGs tried to compensate. Failed. Flared blooming-white along every reflective surface. Auto-gain hiccupped. A half-second blindness. Enough. Both men killed their lasers at once, twin red threads snuffed before they betrayed more than they revealed.

They cleared the vestibule, weapons up, the parlor a dark box through open doors ahead—except for the pulse of the Yule log, its smoke drawn hard up the flue, ember-bed trembling with that witchy red-orange that made shadows leap long and then flatten.

Hollis cut a slice of vision through the room.

A man—? No. Mirror. Another—? Wrong depth. A third— Empty frame. Move.

He signaled Number Two to shift right. But the light jumped. Not the ember-bed. Not the mirrors. The woman: a blur beneath the mantel—not silhouette, motion—Lynn Kingston rising into the narrow hell-red light.

The blast came ferocious. 00 buckshot ripping out of the dark, slamming the room full-white, blowing past them in a storm of splinters and glass.

The mirrors went nova; their optics flared blind.

Number Two fired on reflex. Three fast suppressed rounds at the image of Silas, not knowing it was a reflection caught and carried in a staggered cascade across the parlor. His rounds exploded a mirror, shattered a second, killed no one but his own visibility as he aimed in the wrong direction entirely.

Hollis did not see Silas step from behind the tree. Duelist stance. As Foxtail Farm first christened, brother unto brother. His tiny .22LR already aligned. Not seeking armor, seeking the split between plates, the inch of living man behind all their ballistic faith.

Silas fired once. A sound as insignificant as a fork dropped in another room.

Hollis jerked, staggered—the round finding the gap of his plate at the underarm. The flaw no training could save. Breath gone, knees weak, heart penetrated, he folded with a surprised grunt, body hitting the hardwood.

Number Two wheeled, saw Silas—

Lost him—

Found him again—

Lost him once more in the mirror's recast, Doris's face sliding through the reflection just enough to steal the angle.

Lynn's second blast came blind but perfectly placed. Half-sound, half-force, full fury: a concussive bloom of fire and nine large pellets, three burying in Number Two's plate armor, throwing him back, sending him stumbling into the dark vestibule, NVGs whited out again as Lynn chased him with another blast and mirrors flared and died around him.

He breathed hard. Saw Hollis on the ground. Saw no target/saw every target. Saw Doris and he broke. Disengaged. Quick back-step toward the dining room doors, weapon high, breath ragged. Mirrors shone what came behind. An infinity reflection into a round convex glass that revealed a high-skill enemy operative, weapon ready, hunting him.

Number Two scrambled onto the stairs. Onto the landing beneath the towering portrait—the woman posed as if handing him lilies to honor his death. He plunged higher.

※ ※ ※

LYNN, out from the stone hearth, out through the parlor doors, the shotgun smoking faintly in her hands, angled toward the stairs, barrel rising, tracking.

Silas stepped into the vestibule's charged air, the house drawing him forward as though it recognized its moment.

Number Two stumbled across the upper risers. Saw the nearest threat.

Lynn.

Silas saw the moment forming. Not in a flash, not as the quick calculus of a fight, but as the manor itself saw: layered, recursive, remembering. The mirrors gave him the whole of it. He saw his daughter—this new Lynn, the one death had stripped of her self-punishment—stepping forward not in fear but in command. He saw the years she'd spent choosing collapse over action, choosing oblivion when the world asked her to stand. He saw the woman who had crawled out of her embassy coffin with nothing left except a decision: never again.

She shouted: "STOP! DROP IT!"

The sound struck the mirrors and carried through the house like a bell's toll.

Silas saw the operator. The split-second where youth and terror and training fought inside him. He was so young. God, he was a boy. He had heard the silence of his team destroyed; watched his commander die. He had run because instinct told him to run. And now the shout hit him and for an instant—just an instant—Silas saw him consider surrender.

Silas saw all that in the flinch of possibility in the operator's shoulders.

Saw Lynn understand it too.

But Hal came through the dining room door. Swept in from Silas's left, each motion disciplined, exact, the Drexler weapon raised, the muzzle already finding center mass.

Silas saw it all at once in the kaleidoscope of mirrors: Lynn shouting; the operator swinging his weapon toward her; Hal drawing breath—and in that single inhalation Silas understood everything about his children that he had feared and loved in equal measure.

Lynn wanted to spare a life because she had finally learned her own was not beyond saving; she spoke to halt the killing, seeing the muzzle lifting toward her and refusing to step aside.

Hal wanted to end a life because he had felt the millisecond slip—the single lost instant in which Charlotte's life was taken before he could take the man who took her.

Michael had vanished from their reach knowing at last what his blood required of him; had gone to the unseen margin where love is kept only by stepping aside, where loyalty outlives memory, and where the ideal survives precisely because he is no longer there.

Silas opened his mouth, but no sound could cross the vestibule fast enough. It didn't matter. Even if he had shouted, the moment had already chosen its owner.

The operator's barrel found Lynn.

Hal's shot struck first.

A single, merciless round. Clean. Decisive. Taking the boy before his finger pulsed: before he could surrender: before the possibility of life could bloom.

The mirrors caught the death and broke it into a dozen vanishing reflections. None of them touched Doris. Lynn's breath hitched; her hands tightened on the shotgun; her body absorbed the truth she had tried to prevent.

"Clear." Hal.

Silas reached Lynn first. Father. Witness. Keeper of the house that had watched Kingstons born and die across generations, and he understood the terrible symmetry: one child trying to end the cycle, one child shaped entirely by it, one child who had sacrificed himself to meet perfection.

Foxtail Farm held the moment in its kaleidoscope, and Silas saw her.

Doris seeing him.

Mid-turn, crimson gown alive in its strange sequin shimmer of sunlight emergent. The lilies lifted, sparked fireworks in her hand. Her gaze arrested him with its secret invitation to hold, cling to, possess the girl who stepped from a tornado into his life.

His first instinct: distrust; the old reflex warned: what is clear must be deception. But his mirrors, the wilderness he had created that had pushed life from his home to capture her a hundred ways in a forest of angles, lay broken at his feet.

Fragments could no longer feed that habit.

Doris remained whole.

Silas forced himself to let her meet him with the steadiness he had never allowed himself to accept. And in her gaze he understood: this was their wedding divination cast back. The only reflection that had ever shown him truth. The true mirror of a man, of any life, is the gaze of love.

Still.

Whole.

Upon you.

Her love had seen him fully when he could not bear the sight of himself. The stillness in Doris had never been illusion. It had been the rare, perilous eye at the center of a life that never stopped turning. The one point where his shape held steady, the place where the globe's wheel paused long enough for his soul to recognize its own outline, not by any lever he had seized or force he had claimed, but by the stillness she offered him to see himself.

Where she saw him as he was, as he had been, as he would ever be. Doris had stood for him from the beginning. Silas allowed himself to stand there now.

And with a kiss of the wind across the chimneys, that was the last the night would give. The rest would belong to New Year's Day.

Epilogue

THERE ARE NATIONS, NEITHER happy nor mindfully sad; sanctioned to deception, these nations kindle their purpose with the flint of authorized deceit. Their pyre is "stability," and it is "national security." Its flame is "duty." "Credibility." And above all it is "survival." Thus fueled, these nations allow this fire to consume their every honest emotion.

Relentlessly.

Equally.

And to completion.

Without protest (which could only arise from remorse they never will allow), they slough the cinders of charred commitments and incinerated commissions, sifting them through iron-toothed grates to conceal their treacheries, hide their betrayals, and bury their secrets beneath a shroud of ash: fluffed gray, velvety, and altogether dead. With the whole of what they should repent girded and unobservable, they are unrepentant.

Unredeemed.

The Kingstons of Foxtail Farm are the residue these nations burn through when the deed must be done in darkness; they are the necessary ash of a republic that long ago learned to sanctify its own obscurity.

It was agreed at Foxtail Farm on New Year's Day, in the Year of Our Lord 2013—by the appropriate authorities of the Central Intelligence Agency, by the British Ambassador acting in the name of government and Crown, and by the attending representative of the Secret Intelligence Service—that for the good of both nations, the events of the previous night would be recorded as an American matter alone: a tragic home-invasion at the Kingston property by a fugitive convict, Boone Kelso, during which two St. Mary's County sheriff's deputies were killed in the line of duty and Charlotte Kingston, granddaughter of retired CIA officer Silas Kingston, lost her life.

The story broke mid-holiday; by the evening of January second, the press—encouraged, then compelled—allowed it to slip quietly beneath the news cycle, another ember sifted into a silence both nations understood as part of the cost.

In the quiet aftermath, when the final statements had been signed and the bodies removed from Foxtail Farm, a second understanding—never written, only spoken—passed between the American service chiefs and their British counterparts. London, already reeling from the political schisms that would soon culminate in Brexit, and unable to withstand a scandal implicating the Crown's intelligence service in a lethal operation on American soil, agreed to lend its full diplomatic weight to the coming shift in Syria: support for expanded American intervention, operational latitude along the northern corridor, and the political cover necessary for the allied coalition to claim a stabilizing purpose. In return, the United States would accept that the United

Kingdom—strained beneath the swell of arrivals from failing states—would bear a disproportionate share of the displaced who would follow.

Neither concession appeared in any communiqué.

Yet both were understood to be necessary: two nations tightening the bandage over a wound they could not afford to expose, each wagering a measure of its conscience for the appearance of order.

For the Kingstons, the suspicious death of Gwen Kingston arrived as one more numbing blow following the loss of Charlotte and the unresolved disappearance of Michael. Melody had stood over Boone's body beside Charlotte's, the pain rising in her with a force so stark it emptied her of breath, and felt with a clarity that cut straight through her that the death meant for her had taken an innocent child instead. She retreated to her room, locked herself away from husband, children, family. Hal worried for her safety, but Silas refused to let anyone near her door. Beaumont sat at its foot and whimpered for four days.

Snow fell from the fat belly of a charcoal sky the morning of the fifth. Melody emerged. Not in black but in yellow; walked as sunlight across the snow: the light she'd sworn her life on, the light she'd promised her mother's soul she would always choose to be. The private funeral was held for mother and daughter in the chapel at Foxtail Farm, the Right Reverend Vivianne Tremelin presiding, and afterwards their coffins were lowered beneath the chapel floor to join Doris and the earliest Kingstons whose graves, cut from tide-stone and laid in the century of founding, generation beside generation, anchor the family to the land more surely than any living hand ever could. The old Kingston dead—the ones who felled the first timbers and raised the first beams—received them with the same silence that had greeted every Kingston lowered into that earth: the silence of work done, secrets kept, debts unsettled.

Paige and Clive departed before sunrise along the route already secured for them, a movement without fanfare or farewell, a slipping of names and documents into the stream of other identities where pursuit loses meaning. Leigh, last of her immediate household, might have folded inward upon her grief had it not been for Lynn. Lynn held the girl close with a steadiness that conveyed not only comfort but a grave, almost consecrating fidelity, weighted not by the sorrow of a truth she could not yet confess but by the bountiful love of a depthless connection Leigh could not yet name.

To the nation, Gwen's death amounted to little more than a mislaid headline in a season of worsening violence. What captured attention that same day was stranger: the thwarting of an attempted abduction in the Georgian coastal town of Sardi, where a woman and her young daughter escaped their captors through the intervention of a Chechen and his son who were passing through the resort from Moscow. Seven men linked to a Russian trafficking network were found dead in the dunes beyond the seawall. The woman and child vanished thereafter, leaving behind only the faint impression of a story whose truer shape would never reach the public record—a story that, like so many in those cold weeks, flickered briefly before being carried off by the wind.

♛♛♛

THE SAFEHOUSE stood at the far end of an abandoned officers' quarter on the old Patuxent naval annex. A low brick duplex sunk into leaf-packed woods where no one walked anymore.

Windows blacked.

Chimney bricked.

Wiring fed through a Cold War era breaker box.

Observation room inside. A two-way mirror bolted into poured concrete.

"You're certain you won't meet him?"

"Just here to look, Drexler."

"Then you already know: it ends the old way."

Drexler had lifted the method straight from Angleton's treatment of Nosenko. The same catechism Silas watched take root forty-odd years earlier. A sitting room with a sagging sofa, two chairs that didn't match, a coffee table. A TV on a too-low stand played the Weather Channel; a map of temperatures, of winds, barometric fronts, of the dull crawl of storm advisories a man without windows can only accept or deny.

A pressed-glass souvenir bowl with a loud *Welcome To Las Vegas* logo painted inside contained three polished stones. Black. White. Gray.

As if someone meant something by it.

Over the bricked fireplace: a cheap reproduction of Caillebotte's *The Floor Scrapers*; three working class men planing a Parisian floor. Light casts upon the men's backs, highlights their lean torsos, their bent shoulders caught forever in muscle-burning work forever unfinished; the shiny varnish coat, cut away in brutal curls to expose the raw and unprotected wood beneath.

As if someone meant something by it.

A worn paperback balanced on the threadbare end of the sofa arm. Spine creased past legibility; the cover carried the outline of an anvil fixed in a stone, a sword fixed through both.

Kolya perched in a third chair in the center of the room. Metal. Too high.

Silas watched his eyes move over the clutter. Micro-expressions. Little calibrations. Disconnected mimicries with no one to land them on, the old repertoire hunting a pattern the room refused to provide him.

And always returning to the book. Returning and shifting away.

Because someone meant something by it.

The book he never gave her. The code he broke in every shape a life can break it.

The book she made her philosophy, the architecture of her family. The Kingston family. His family denied him.

He looked. He looked away. Ache without reach.

"Sixty years running operations and this is where he lands. Supervised by Drexler. History lesson in that."

Silas stepped closer to the glass and spoke one of the dozens of lines of Eliot Angleton was fond of recalling. A line Silas now understood in a way he never had before.

"The only hope, or else despair,
Lies in the choice of pyre or pyre—
To be redeemed from fire by fire."

And the glass between them held. And it reflected no one.

✦✦✦

WITH THE ARRIVAL of spring, Melody and Hal traveled with the twins to Switzerland where the boys discovered the fountain.

Not the great plume in the lake, but the little one—a cracked stone basin set in a corner of Parc La Grange, the kind too shallow for coins, too old for signage. Still, the children believed in it. Their coins sparkled as they flew and splashed. Hal watched from the bench, his coat in his lap. His smile was a private thing. A dad thing.

Melody crossed the street alone. Let the smoked-glass doors of Pell & Glatisant draw her in on its air-conditioned breath. She had been warned she would need what Doris had fashioned decades earlier—the challenge code, and the parole; standing before the discreet vestibule, she gave them both without hesitation: "The Lord Giveth." And: "The Water Show Us Forth."

✦✦✦

A DISCREET ATTENDANT guided her down a narrow stair and through a chamber lined in limestone the color of dried bone. At the end of the corridor waited a single door. Plain-grained and nearly without feature, its edges softened by years of use and the long discipline of secrecy. He turned a key in the old brass lock and stepped back, offering the clearance Doris had prepared and the bank had guarded with monastic indifference.

The lock released with a hushed inward draw.

The door opened with the slow gravity of something long sealed.

Melody stepped inside.

There was no brightness. There was no gleam. There was only a stillness that reached outward as if the room itself were listening. Something waited inside, not a thing but a presence, a coherence of purpose gathered in the air like a memory returning fully to itself. Melody felt it before she saw anything at all. Felt it rise through her the way certainty rises, quietly and without argument, as if the world had aligned for one brief instant into the shape it was always meant to take.

She opened the top drawer of a dozen wooden file cabinets where what lay within revealed itself to her alone: the shape Doris had kept hidden; the inheritance not of wealth but of design, the deception of something meant to outlive them all. She felt, in that stillness, the loosening at last of Boone Kelso's hold, the Ziploc pistol he had pressed upon her life like a second spine gone with him when they lifted his body from the frozen earth at Foxtail Farm. The test had passed her by as quietly as breath leaving a room. The violence her father had shaped her for had never been the task Doris intended. Boone's winter had ended; hers had turned toward water and light.

👑 👑 👑

"I'M READY MOM!" Leigh called from the living room of Lynn's Rock Creek Terrace condominium.

Although the court date for the adoption judgment was still a month away, Leigh had insisted on it since Lynn's birthday when she'd offered the idea as the best possible present she knew how to give.

"There's tennis on—watch that for a minute! I gotta look at this."

Lynn sat on the edge of her bed. In her hands was the mailer pack that had come from the Azerbaijani private detective she had hired after no one in any government—Azerbaijan, American, Russian—had done anything to prove or disprove Michael had died in the Flame Towers explosion. This was his final report. From Russia where he'd tracked Michael's last movements before his departure to Baku.

The report was brief. There was nothing to report. Michael's fate would never be known. He had found something though, a photograph from a fancy candlemaker in a Russian village called Skhodnya.

The photograph. Michael dancing on a forest floor in winter moonlight.

Around him were Russians, old and strangely costumed. Playing the old instruments, mouths wide with song. There were chandeliers impossibly hung from mighty pine boughs, there were sleighs and there were divans covered with wild and elegant furs. And there was a banquet table; boar's head and hunters raising toasts:

the kind of fanciful, mystical scene romantic artists paint when painting fairytales.

She felt Michael's pure joy, his happiness, and a love that burned from the image straight into her heart. Her soul. Her being.

The object of Michael's unbounded feeling and faith: a woman embracing him embracing her. Lynn recognized her at once.

With clarity. With release.

The Enchanted Forest; his Lady in the Lake.

Michael had found her and Lynn knew her brother lived now in Avalon.

Not dead.

Not lost.

Taken beyond all reach in the only way Lynn's heart could bear to imagine.

Lynn took her mother's book from her bedside where she and Leigh would snuggle and read before bed. Tucked the photograph between the pages.

Dropped it on the bedspread.

When she emerged from the bedroom, Leigh noticed and asked if she had been crying. And Lynn, who would never lie again to Leigh, admitted that she had and would explain when they got home but—"I'm making us late and it's not nice to keep people waiting at a restaurant."

"And who are we meeting again?"

"His name is Rusty. And his wife Nina, and—I think I hope—their daughter Jessie."

"But why? You're making such a big, weird thing about it."

"It is a big, weird thing. And you're part of it and Rusty's the weirdest person I know, and he says he's going to explain. Which ought to be interesting."

"Do I call him 'Rusty?'"

"Honey—we'll all figure that out. But do it to start. He hates it."

"But why if he hates it—"

Lynn grinned. Hugged her. Tapped her nose with a fingertip.

Leigh's fingers touched her mother's throat. "Your scar's all gone. You can't even feel it."

"I hardly remember." She blew in Leigh's face. "Let's go get in the car?"

Leigh took Lynn's breath inside of her, and they left on that river of Kingston air.

About the Author

Award-winning novelist Michael Frost Beckner began a Hollywood career as writing assistant to Academy Award winner Barry Levinson on "Good Morning, Vietnam" and "Rain Man". In 1989, Beckner's script for "Sniper" launched a military-thriller franchise now in production on its eleventh sequel. Three consecutive record-breaking spec script sales and three films later, Tony Scott directed Beckner's original screenplay "Spy Game." An international hit that paired Robert Redford and Brad Pitt as CIA partners and rivals, it is now a classic in the espionage genre.

The pilot for Beckner's CIA-based television drama "The Agency" for CBS, predicted Osama bin Laden's terror attack and the War on Terror four months before 9/11. In that series alone, Beckner would go on to predict three more international terror events.

Having penned close to 100 original screenplays, adaptations, and teleplays in the employ of every major film studio, television network, and cable outlet, he is a Hollywood institution.

As a commentator on American espionage, Beckner has appeared on CNN, Fox News, CBS News, TF1 in France, and as a featured guest of Bill Maher on HBO.